FREAKY DEAKY

W9-BTM-088

FREAKS 'EM OUT!

◆

"STARTS WITH A BANG . . . races along like a cunning fox in front of the hounds. . . . Spectacular."
—*New York Times Book Review*

◆

"WONDERFUL . . . This is a real hustling-bustling—tough-and-breezy Detroit book, full of drugs and guns, grafters and millionaires, cops and hangers-on—and everyday plain-going people."
—*Detroit Free Press*

◆

"O.K. HERE'S WHAT YOU DO. Stand in the bookstore and read the first chapter of FREAKY DEAKY. Won't take long. Only ten pages. The store owner won't mind because he knows you will then buy the book."
—George Will

◆

"VINTAGE LEONARD CHARACTERS. . . . Elmore Leonard may be the best writer of dialogue alive."
—*USA Today*

◆

"ENORMOUSLY ENTERTAINING . . . The dialogue crackles with funny, dead-on street language. The characters jump off the pages with vitality, and the plot, which keeps going off in all kinds of crazy directions, is a treat. . . . Leonard is a national literary treasure."

—*New York Daily News*

◆

more . . .

"TERRIFIC . . . fast-paced with snappy dialogue and colorful characters . . . Leonard at his best."

—*Philadelphia News*

♦

"FUN . . . wonderfully entertaining."

—*Newsday*

♦

"LEONARD EXCELS HERE WITH HIS TRADEMARK MENACE AND DEADPAN THROWAWAY HUMOR. He starts and ends his latest page turner with a bang, and between explosions we meet a vivid group of characters."

—*Publishers Weekly*

♦

"EXPLOSIVE . . . a sure-fire blockbuster."

—*Detroit News*

♦

"THE MAN IS A MASTER AND A MARVEL . . . he trips from the 60s to the 80s with his most wonderful collection of rogues, kooks, and scalawags ever. . . . This is a fast-paced, uproariously funny, cleverly plotted romp. If you don't like this book, go back to watching TV."

—*Cincinnati Post*

♦

"VINTAGE ELMORE LEONARD . . . crackles with cool street-smart and dark-humored urban ironies. . . . Leonard's usual superb pacing, uncanny ear for patois, and menagerie of quirky characters are here in full force."

—*Kirkus Reviews*

♦

"AWFULLY GOOD, THE BEST IN THE BUSINESS AT THE TOP OF HIS FORM."

—*St. Louis Post-Dispatch*

♦

"WONDERFULLY WACKY . . . THE BOOK'S A BLAST."

—*Tulsa World*

♦

"IT'S TERRIFIC."

—*Toledo Blade*

♦

"CRISP DIALOGUE, SATIRIC WIT, AND CRAZY CHARACTERIZATION . . . with a wild finale that hoists the villains by their own petard."

—*Library Journal*

♦

"BEARS THE SPECIAL LEONARD BRAND: Attention to technical detail, the 'Voice' of the street, and architectural precision. . . . All of the seemingly unrelated episodes fit like stones in the Great Pyramid."

—*Arkansas Gazette*

♦

"COULD KEEP YOU UP LATE AT NIGHT. . . . Leonard's great strengths of dialogue and character construction are evident in this novel . . . a fast-moving story."

—*San Antonio Express-News*

♦

ALSO BY ELMORE LEONARD

*Published by WARNER BOOKS
**Published by THE MYSTERIOUS PRESS

ATTENTION: SCHOOLS AND CORPORATIONS

WARNER books are available at quantity discounts with bulk purchase for educational, business, or sales promotional use. For information, please write to: SPECIAL SALES DEPARTMENT, WARNER BOOKS, 666 FIFTH AVENUE, NEW YORK, N.Y. 10103.

ARE THERE WARNER BOOKS
YOU WANT BUT CANNOT FIND IN YOUR LOCAL STORES?

You can get any WARNER BOOKS title in print. Simply send title and retail price, plus 50¢ per order and 50¢ per copy to cover mailing and handling costs for each book desired. New York State and California residents add applicable sales tax. Enclose check or money order only, no cash please, to: WARNER BOOKS, P.O. BOX 690, NEW YORK, N.Y. 10019.

FREAKY DEAKY

ELMORE LEONARD

WARNER BOOKS

A Warner Communications Company

WARNER BOOKS EDITION

Copyright © 1988 by Elmore Leonard
All rights reserved. No part of this book may be reproduced or
utilized in any form or by any means, electronic or mechanical,
including photocopying, recording or by any information storage
and retrieval system, without permission in writing from the
Publisher.

Address all rights inquiries to: N.H. Swanson, Inc., 8523 Sunset
Boulevard, Los Angeles, CA 90069, (213) 652-5385.

Cover illustration by Dennis Ziemienski

This Warner Books Edition was published by arrangement with
Arbor House, 105 Madison Avenue, New York, N.Y. 10016

Warner Books, Inc.
666 Fifth Avenue
New York, N.Y. 10103

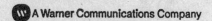 A Warner Communications Company

Printed in the United States of America

First Warner Books Printing: April, 1989

10 9 8 7 6 5 4 3 2 1

To my wife Joan
for giving me the title
and a certain look
when I write too many words.

1

Chris Mankowski's last day on the job, two in the afternoon, two hours to go, he got a call to dispose of a bomb.

What happened, a guy by the name of Booker, a twenty-five-year-old super-dude twice-convicted felon, was in his Jacuzzi when the phone rang. He yelled for his bodyguard Juicy Mouth to take it. "Hey, Juicy?" His bodyguard, his driver and his houseman were around somewhere. "Will somebody get the phone?" The phone kept ringing. The phone must have rung fifteen times before Booker got out of the Jacuzzi, put on his green satin robe that matched the emerald pinned to his left earlobe and picked up the phone. Booker said, "Who's this?" A woman's voice said, "You sitting down?" The phone was on a table next to a green leather wingback chair. Booker loved green. He said, "Baby, is that you?" It sounded like his woman, Moselle. Her voice said, "Are you sitting down? You have to be sitting down for when I tell you something." Booker said, "Baby, you sound different. What's wrong?" He sat down in the green leather chair, frowning, working his butt around to get comfortable. The woman's voice said, "Are you sitting down?" Booker said, "I *am*. I have sat the fuck down. Now you gonna talk to me, what?" Moselle's voice said, "I'm suppose to tell you that when you get up, honey, what's left of your ass is gonna go clear through the ceiling."

When Chris got there a uniform let him in. There were Thirteenth Precinct cars and a Tactical station wagon parked in front of the house. The uniform told Chris that Booker had called 911. They radioed him here and when he saw who it was he called Narcotics and they jumped at it, a chance to go through the man's house wide open with their dog.

A guy from Narcotics who looked like a young vagrant told Chris that Booker was a success story: had come up through the street-dealing organizations, Young Boys Incorporated and Pony Down, and was now on about the third level from the top. Look around, guy twenty-five living in a home on Boston Boulevard, a mansion, originally owned by one of Detroit's automotive pioneers. The guy from Narcotics didn't remember which one. Look how Booker had fucked up the house, painted all that fine old oak paneling puke green. He asked Chris how come he was alone.

Chris said most of the squad was out on a run, picking

up illegal fireworks, but there was another guy coming, Jerry Baker. Chris said, "You know what today is?" And waited for the guy from Narcotics to say no, what? "It's my last day on the Bomb Squad. Next week I get transferred out." He waited again.

The guy from Narcotics said, "Yeah, is that right?" He didn't get it.

"It's the last time I'll ever have to handle a bomb, if that's what we have, and hope to Christ I don't make a mistake."

The guy still didn't get it. He said, "Well, that's what Booker says it is. He gets up, it blows up. What kind of bomb is that?"

"I won't know till I look at it," Chris said.

"Booker says it's the fucking Italians," the guy from Narcotics said, "trying to tell him something. It makes sense, otherwise why not shoot the fucker? Like we know Booker's done guys we find out at Metro in long-term parking. Guy's in the trunk of his car, two in the back of the head. Booker's a bad fucking dude, man. If there was such a thing as justice in the world we'd leave his ass sitting there, let him work it out."

Chris said, "Get your people out of the house. When my partner gets here, don't stop and chat, okay? I'll let you know if we need Fire or EMS, or if we have to evacuate the houses next door. Now where's Booker?"

The guy from Narcotics took Chris down the hall toward the back of the house, saying, "Wait'll you see what the spook did to the library. Looks like a fucking tent."

It did. Green-and-white striped parachute cloth was draped on four sides from the center point of the high ceiling to the top of the walls. The Jacuzzi bubbled in the middle of the room, a border of green tile around it. Booker sat beyond the sunken bath in his green leather wingback. He was holding on to the round arms, clutching them, fingers spread open. Behind him, French doors opened onto a backyard patio.

"I been waiting," Booker said. "You know how long I been waiting on you? I don't know where anybody's at, I been calling—you see Juicy Mouth?"

"Who's Juicy Mouth?"

"Suppose to be guarding my body. Man, I got to go the toilet."

Chris walked up to him, looking at the base of the chair. "Tell me what the woman said on the phone."

"Was the bitch suppose to be in love with me."

"What'd she tell you?"

"Say I get up I'm *blown* up."

"That's all?"

"Is that *all*? Man, that's final, that's all there is all, nothing else."

Chris said, "Yeah, but do you believe it?"

"Asshole, you expect me to stand up and find out?"

Chris was wearing a beige tweed sportcoat, an old one with sagging pockets. He brought a Mini-Mag flashlight out of the left side pocket, went down flat on the floor and played the light beam into the four-inch clearance beneath the chair. The space was empty. He came to his knees, placed the Mini-Mag on the floor, brought a stainless Spyder-Co lockback pocketknife from the right side pocket and flicked open the short blade with one hand in a quick, practiced motion.

Booker said, "Hey," pushing back in the chair.

"Cover yourself," Chris said. "I don't want to cut anything off by mistake."

"Man, be careful there," Booker said, bringing his hands off the chair arms to bunch the skirts of the robe between his bare legs, up tight against his crotch.

"You feel anything under you?"

"When I sat down it felt . . . like, different."

Chris slit open the facing of the seat cushion, held the edges apart and looked in. He said, "Hmmmmm."

Booker said, "What you mean hmmmmm? Don't give me no hmmmmm shit. What's in there?"

Chris looked up at Booker and said, "Ten sticks of dynamite."

Booker was clutching the chair arms again, his body upright, stiff, telling Chris, "Get that shit out from under me, man. Get it out, get it out of there!"

Chris said, "Somebody doesn't like you, Booker. Two sticks would've been plenty."

Booker said, "Will you pull that shit *out*? Do it."

Chris sat back on his heels, looking up at Booker. "I'm afraid we have a problem."

"What problem? What you talking about?"

"See, most of the foam padding's been taken out. There's something in there that looks like an inflatable rubber cushion, fairly flat, laying on top of the dynamite."

"So pull the shit out, man. You see it, pull it out."

"Yeah, but what I don't see is what makes it go bang. It must be in the back part, where the cushion zips open."

"Then open the motherfucker."

"I can't, you're sitting on it. It's probably a two-way pressure switch of some kind. I can't tell for sure, but that'd be my guess."

Booker said, "Your *guess*? You telling me you don't know what you doing?"

"We get all kinds," Chris said. "I have to see it before I know what it is . . . or whether or not I can disarm it. You understand?"

"Wait a minute now. You saying *if* you can take it apart?"

"And the only way to get to it," Chris said, "is to cut through the back of the chair."

"Then cut it, cut it, I don't give a shit about the chair."

"You run into the frame, all that heavy wood and springs . . ." Chris paused. He said, "I don't know," shaking his head.

Booker said, "Look, motherfucker. You get this shit out from under me. You cut, you do what you have to do, you get it out."

"On the other hand," Chris said, "it might not be a bomb at all. Just the dynamite in there. You know, to scare you, keep you in line. I mean, is there a reason anybody'd want to take you out?"

Booker said, "You mean like just the shit, but no way to blow it?"

"Yeah."

"Like they telling me look what could happen?"

"Maybe."

"Say I could just get up, was all bullshit what they made her say to me? On the phone?"

"That's possible," Chris said, "but I don't think I'd take the chance."

"You wouldn't, huh?"

"Let's see what my partner says, when he gets here."

Booker said, "Man, I got to go the toilet, bad."

Chris watched Jerry Baker taking in the size of the house as he came up the walk, away from the uniforms and the blue Detroit Police radio cars blocking both sides of the boulevard. It was Jerry's day off. He wore a black poplin jacket and a Detroit Tigers baseball cap: a tall man, bigger and older than Chris, twenty-five years on the force, fifteen as a bomb tech. He remembered what day this was and said to Chris, "You shouldn't be here."

Standing inside the doorway, Chris told him about the green leather chair Booker was sitting in.

And Jerry said it again, looking at his watch. "No, you shouldn't be here. Forty minutes, you'll be through."

He looked outside at the guy from Narcotics waiting on the porch, waved him over and told him to call for Fire and EMS and get everybody away from the house. The guy from Narcotics said, "Can't you guys handle this one?"

Jerry said, "You'll hear it if we can't." Walking down the hall to the Jacuzzi room he said to Chris, "If we save this asshole's life, you think he'll appreciate it?"

Chris said, "You mean will he say thank you? Wait'll you meet him."

They entered the room, Jerry gazing up at the green-and-white tenting, and Booker said, "Finally, you mother-fuckers decide you gonna do something?"

Chris and Jerry took time to look at each other. They didn't say anything. Jerry got down to inspect the sliced-open seat cushion between Booker's muscular legs and said, "Hmmmmm."

Booker said, "Another one, goes hmmmmm. I'm sitting here on high explosives the motherfucker goes hmmmmm."

Jerry stood up, looking at Chris again. "Well, he's cool. That's a good thing."

Chris said, "Yeah, he's cool."

As Jerry walked around to the back of the green leather chair, Booker, sitting upright, raised his head.

"Hey, I got to go the toilet, man, bad."

Jerry reached over the backrest to put his hand on Booker's shoulder. "You better wait. I don't think you can make it."

"I'll tell you what I have to make. I mean it."

Jerry said, over Booker to Chris, "The boy looks fast."

"Used to run from the Narcs in his Pony joggers, one of those Pony Down delivery boys," Chris said. "Yeah, I imagine he's fast."

Booker was still upright with his head raised. "Wait now. What're we saying here if I'm fast? Bet to it, man, I'm fast."

Chris said, "We don't want you to get the idea you can dive out of your chair into your little swimming pool and make it."

Booker said, "In the Jacuze? I get in there I be safe?"

"I doubt it," Chris said. "If what you're sitting on there, if it's wired and it's not one of your friends being funny . . ."

Jerry said, "Or if it's not a dud."

Booker said, "Yeah, what?"

Chris said, "If it's a practical joke—you know, or some kind of warning—then there's nothing to worry about. But if it's wired, you raise up and it goes . . ."

"I couldn't get in the Jacuze quick enough, huh?"

"I doubt it."

"His feet might stay on the floor," Jerry said, "remain in the house."

Chris agreed, nodding. "Yeah, but his ass'd be sailing over Ohio."

Jerry moved from behind the chair to the French doors. "We better talk about it some more."

Booker's head turned to follow Chris. "Where you going? Hey, motherfucker, I'm talking to you!"

Chris stepped out and closed the door. He moved with Jerry to the far edge of the slate patio before looking back at the French doors in the afternoon sunlight. They could hear Booker in there, faintly. They crossed the yard, Jerry offering Chris a cigarette. He took one and Jerry gave him a light once they reached the driveway and were standing by the three-car garage, alone in the backyard. Jerry looked up at the elm trees. He said, "Well, they're finally starting to bud. I thought winter was gonna run through May."

Chris said, "That's my favorite kind of house. Sort of an English Tudor, before Booker got hold of it."

Jerry said, "Why don't you and Phyllis buy one?"

"She likes apartments. Goes with her career image."

"She must be jumping up and down, finally got her way."

Chris didn't say anything.

"I'm talking about your leaving the squad."

"I know what you meant. I haven't told her yet. I'm waiting till I get reassigned."

"Maybe Homicide, huh?"

"I wouldn't mind it."

"Yeah, but would Phyllis?"

Chris didn't answer. They smoked their cigarettes and could hear fire equipment arriving. Jerry said, "Hey, I was kidding. Don't be so serious."

"I know what you're saying," Chris said. "Phyllis is the kind of person that speaks out. Something bothers her, she tells you about it."

"I know," Jerry said.

"There's nothing wrong with that, is there?"

"I'm not saying anything against her."

"What it is, Phyllis says things even some guys would like to but don't have the nerve."

"Yeah, 'cause she's a woman," Jerry said, "she doesn't have to worry about getting hit in the mouth."

Chris shook his head. "I don't mean putting anybody down or being insulting. Like we're at a restaurant, one of those trendy places the waiter introduces himself? This twinkie comes up to the table, he goes, 'Hi, I'm Wally, I'm gonna be your waitperson this evening. Can I get you a cocktail?' Phyllis goes, 'Wally, when we've finished dinner, you gonna take us out and introduce us to the dishwasher?' She goes, 'We really don't care what your name is as long as you're here when we want something.' "

Jerry grinned, adjusting his Tiger baseball cap. "That's good, I can appreciate that. Those guys kill me."

They drew on their cigarettes. Chris looked at his, about to say something, working the butt between his thumb and second finger to flick it away, and the French doors and some of the windows on this side of the house exploded out in a billow of gray smoke tinged yellow. They stood looking at the shattered doorway, at the smoke and dust thinning, settling over glass and wood fragments, shreds of blackened green-and-white debris on the patio, silence ringing in their ears now. After a few moments they started down the drive, let the people waiting in front know they were okay.

Chris said, "Yeah, the twink comes up to the table, says he's gonna be our waitperson. But you have to understand, Phyllis wasn't trying to be funny, she was serious. That's the way she is."

2

Skip told Robin he had to blow up a car on the Belle Isle bridge either tomorrow or the next day if it didn't rain and then he'd be through. He said they called it the kush shot. The car would go flying off the bridge, explode in midair in this huge ball of fire, and when it hit the Detroit River it would go *kushhhh* and all this smoke would rise up.

Robin said, "Far out. You like your work, huh?"

Skip said, "Well, it's bullshit, you know, movies. But it's kinda fun. It sure beats working as an extra, standing out in the sun all day while the director and the star shoot the shit."

"There was a story in today's paper made me think of you," Robin said. "About the guy getting blown up?"

"Yeah, I saw it. Somebody slipped some dynamite

under him. But it wasn't me, I was working." Skip grinned, eating a breadstick. "I haven't shot off any dynamite in . . . well, it's been awhile."

"I bet you still know how."

Skip grinned at her again. "I bet I do too. But see, we hardly ever use that kind of high explosives."

They were at Mario's in midtown Detroit, waiting for their dinner order among white tablecloths and oil paintings of southern Italian villages: Skip drinking vodka, eating the breadsticks with a pat of butter stuck to each bite; Robin smoking, sipping red wine, watching Skip through tinted glasses.

"War scenes, like mortars and shells exploding? We use black powder, squib it off electrically. For the kush shot, or any time you see a car go over the cliff and explode? We put three or four gallons of gasoline inside in plastic bottles wrapped in primer cord and then fire it by remote control. Push a button, like you open your garage door."

"I park on the street," Robin said.

"Like you used to. I remember there was Daddy's garage door and Mommy's garage door and Miss Robin's garage door, side by side attached to a big house in Bloomfield Hills."

"Did you know Mother drove me to prison?"

"I didn't think you could do that."

"All the way to Huron Valley. She bought a gray pinstriped suit for the trip. She and the judge were hoping I'd be sent to Alderson—Christ—West Virginia, but Daddy talked to somebody in the Justice Department."

"That was nice," Skip said, "had you close to home."

"I was hoping for Pleasanton, in California. Get some sun."

"You see your folks?"

"Daddy's gone to heaven, he had a coronary. Mother,

I hardly ever see, which I'm sure you can understand. She's on a round-the-world cruise. That's what she does now. She takes trips."

"Your mom *was* a trip," Skip said, "had that sarcastic way of speaking. You do it better."

"Thanks a lot," Robin said. She blew her smoke at him and took a sip of wine.

"I rode a government bus down to Milan," Skip said. "I don't know where my mommy was. This bus had heavy wire over the windows in case we got loose of our hand-cuffs and leg irons. Me and a half a dozen Hispanic brothers with needle tracks up their arms. I thought, The fuck am I doing with these dudes? Man, I'm political. I should be going to one of those country-club joints like where they sent those Watergate assholes, but I guess they thought I was ba-a-ad."

"You were," Robin said. "I think it was blowing up the Federal Building that pissed them off."

"Yeah, but hell, the money they kept when we jumped bond, it would've paid to fix up the damage, wouldn't it? Some of it." Skip was chewing on a breadstick, crumbs in his beard. "Man, when they brought us up that second time, if they'd known even half the gigs I was into . . . I mean those years living underground."

Robin said, "Living out there with the great silent majority. I know why they're silent, they don't have a fucking thing to say. I got into shoplifting just for something to do. One time I even stole a bra."

Skip said, "I was living in a commune near Grants, New Mexico, with these leftover flower children bitching at each other, bored out of my skull. I went up to Farmington and got the job as a TV repairman 'cause, you know, I always had a knack for wiring up shit. This one day I said to myself, Man, if you're a wanted criminal then how come you aren't into crime? That's when I moved to L.A. the first time."

"You ever look for your picture in a post office?"

"Yeah, but I never saw it."

"I didn't see mine either," Robin said. She leaned in closer, resting her arms on the table. "When I finally got your number, and your service said you were in Detroit . . ."

"Couldn't believe it, could you?"

She said, "You know, you haven't changed much at all."

Skip said, "I may be a half a step slower, but I still have my hair. I lift weights when I'm home and I think of it."

"I like your beard."

"I've had it off and on. I first grew it when I was over in Spain. That's where I went soon as I got my release. Started as an extra in the picture business and worked my way into special effects and stunt work. This guy Sidney Aaronson was doing a big epic called *The Sack of Rome.* But what it was, it was a sack of shit. You know how many times I got killed in that fucking picture?"

Robin watched him reach out to stop their waiter going by with a tray of dinners. Skip ordered another drink and a bottle of Valpolicella. The little fifty-year-old waiter said with an accent, "Just a minute, just a minute, please," and hurried on.

Skip winked at her. "Time him. He gets one minute."

"You haven't changed at all," Robin said.

Skip Gibbs smiled, a thirty-eight-year-old kid: dull-blond streaked hair tied back with a rubber band in a short ponytail, bread crumbs in the beard that grew up into his cheeks; Skip the Wolfman wearing a black satiny athletic jacket that bore the word *Speedball* across the back in a racy red script: the title of a film he'd worked on handling special effects, blowing black-powder charges and squibbing gunshots. He said to Robin, "You still look like you can hit and run"—crinkling his light-blue eyes at her. "Man, there's something about a thin girl with big tits." Staring at her beige cotton sweater, three wooden buttons undone at the neck. "I notice they're still in the right place."

"You put on *Jane Fonda's Workout*," Robin said, "all you have to do is sit and watch it, you stay in shape."

Skip said, "I knew you'd be into something. Just don't tell me you've become a women's lib vegetarian lesbian, okay? I have beautiful memories of us in bed—and on floors and in sleeping bags, in back seats . . ."

Now Robin Abbott was smiling, sort of, agreeable without admitting anything: calm brown eyes gazing through the tinted glasses set against a pale fox face, her brown hair sleeked back into a single braid she would sometimes finger and stroke, a rope of hair, holding it against her breast in the cotton sweater.

"Your hair's different," Skip said, "otherwise . . ." He squinted at her and said, "The first time I ever saw you, Lincoln Park in Chicago, man, that was a long time ago. We were only—what, nineteen years old?"

"You were. I was still eighteen," Robin said. "It was the Saturday before the start of the Democratic National Convention, August twenty-fourth, 1968." She was nodding, seeing it again. "Lincoln Park . . ."

"Thousands of people," Skip said, "and I picked you out right away: Why, there's a little Wolverine from the University of Michigan. Though I hadn't seen you at school before. You had on a tank top and you were holding up a poster that said, real big, FUCK THE DRAFT, waving it at the cops. I kept looking at you, your little nips showing in that thin material, your hair real long down your back. I said to myself, I think I'll score me some of that."

"Your hair was longer too," Robin said. "Cops kept grabbing it, trying to hold you. We got away and I tied it up in a ponytail."

Skip said, "You think I don't remember that?" Touching his hair. "I don't ordinarily wear it like this, but I did this evening."

Robin said, "I'd know you anywhere. Remember the first night? In the guy's car?"

"The cops pounding on it"—Skip grinned—"whole bunch of them wearing those baby-blue riot helmets. I look up and see these pig faces staring at me. Cop bangs on the window. 'What're you doing in there?' I go, 'What's it look like I'm doing? I'm getting laid, man.' That's when they started beating on the car. The guy comes along that owned the car, remember? He couldn't believe it. 'Hey, what're you doing to my fucking car?' He tears into the cops and they club the shit out of him and throw him in the wagon. Oh, man." Skip rubbed his eyes with a knuckle. "I get tears thinking about it."

Robin said, "You remember the last time we were here?"

The waiter appeared with Skip's drink and the bottle of wine, opened it and poured a taste into Skip's glass. Robin watched Skip hold the wine in his mouth and wink at her, and for a moment she thought he was going to spit it out and do a scene with the waiter. Skip loved scenes. But this time he swallowed and gave her a sly grin.

"I wasn't gonna do nothing. Guy's a real waiter, wears a tux, probably been here all his life."

Robin tried again, patient. "You remember the last time we had dinner here?"

Skip had to stop and think. She watched him look around, maybe for something that might remind him. "We got picked up in 'seventy-eight. . . . It wasn't after they brought us back."

"Before that. Before we went underground."

"Man, that was a long time ago."

"We came here December fifteenth, 1971," Robin said, "about a week after we got back from New York." She waited again as Skip frowned, thinking hard. "We went to New York for that stop-the-war benefit."

He came alive. "Yeah, in that big cathedral."

"St. John the Divine," Robin said. "You sold tickets at the door and walked off with something like nine hundred dollars."

"I think it was more."

"You told me nine hundred."

"The People's Coalition for something or other."

"Peace and Justice."

"Yeah, they had a bunch of celebrities giving talks. It was so goddamn boring, that's why I ripped 'em off. I figured they weren't gonna cut it, so fuck 'em."

"But when we came here for dinner, you were broke."

"I'd bought a ton of acid and a few pounds of weed by then."

"You said, 'It looks like we're going to have to eat and run, fast,' and I said, 'Why don't you take up a collection?' Remember?"

He was looking around again. "Yeah, shit, I remember."

Robin watched his gaze stop and hold on a trio of strolling musicians across the room, short, heavyset guys in red vests, two with guitars, one with a stand-up bass. They were singing "The Shadow of Your Smile" to a table of diners trying to ignore the trio.

"I dumped the bread out of the basket and that's what

you used," Robin said, bringing Skip back. "You went from table to table."

Skip was grinning. "I went up to this couple, I go, 'Pardon me, but can you spare some bread?' The guy thought I meant *bread*. He goes, serious as can be, 'You ask your waiter, he'll get you some.' I like to died."

"You sound more Indiana farm boy," Robin said, "than even you did before."

"From hanging out with these two stunt guys from Texas. Couple of shitkickers, but good guys. I think before Mr. Mario told me to sit down I scored about fifty, sixty bucks."

"Thirty-seven," Robin said, "and the drinks and dinner came to thirty-two fifty. You might've left a tip, but I doubt it."

"Come on—you remember the exact amount?"

"After we talked on the phone I looked it up in my journal. It was thirty-two fifty."

"That's right, your notebooks. You filled up a bunch, huh, writing your column."

"I have everything we did," Robin said, "from the summer of 'sixty-eight in Chicago to June of 'seventy-two, when we were busted and jumped bail. I have the names of every single person we were involved with, too. Including the copouts."

"I always liked your stuff, had a mean sound. You kept writing, didn't you?"

"I did 'Notes from the Underground' the first couple of years. The Liberation News Service picked it up. Since Huron Valley I've written four historical romance-rape novels. Have you ever heard of Nicole Robinette? *Emerald Fire? Diamond Fire?*"

"I don't think so."

"I'm Nicole."

"Why'n't you write your own story? Be more exciting."

"I have a better idea," Robin said.

She waited for Skip's reaction, watched him pick up his vodka, drink most of it and rattle the ice in the glass. He was with her but not paying attention to every word—grinning in his beard now.

"Man, we let it rip, didn't we? Dope, sex, and rock and roll. Old Mao and Karl Marx tried to keep up but didn't stand a chance against Jimi Hendrix, man, the Doors, the Dead, Big Brother and Janis. Hey, and my all-time favorite outlaw band—you know the one it was? MC5. Jesus, those dudes, man. . . ."

Robin heard the strolling trio coming to the end of "Don't Cry for Me, Argentina." She said, "How about the dynamite runs? Stoned out of your mind."

"You had to be," Skip said, "car full of high explosives. That first time coming back from Yale, Michigan, M-19, two lanes, I kept seeing the road disappear, like a big hole would open up in front of us and I'd think, Oh, shit, we're gonna die. Except I knew I was tripping, so I'd hang onto the wheel like my knuckles were gonna pop. But I'll tell you something, I never had what you'd call a bad trip in my life. I mean dropping acid. The only bad trips I can remember is when I *wasn't* stoned. Wake up in some goddamn holding cell with these assholes giving each other peace signs."

Robin said, "I could tell you were a little ripped when you walked in."

"Not bad. All I had after work was some hash and beer. I'm still geeked on acid, but couldn't find none. I can get blotter in L.A. once in a while, it's okay. But old Owsley's preemo purple or even windowpane, that stuff could get you in touch with your ancestors. All they want to sell you on the street is crack and that's bad shit, messes you up.

Acid's good for you—I mean you don't overdo it, become a burnout. It's like a laxative for the brain, it mellows you while it cleans out your head."

Robin sipped her wine. She said, "I have some," and saw Skip's sly grin peeking through his beard, a sparkle coming into his pale eyes.

"You know I suffer from anti-acrophobia, fear of not being high."

"My apartment's right around the corner."

"Bitchin'. What kind is it?"

"Blotter. Has a little numeral *one* on it."

"Shit, I gotta go back to work. They're gonna shoot some night for night."

"It's there when you want it," Robin said.

Skip grinned at her. "You're setting me up, aren't you? You got a dirty trick in mind and you need the Skipper to help you pull it."

Robin gave him her sort-of smile.

When the trio in the red vests strolled up she decided to let Skip handle it, not say anything. She watched him look up as the leader asked with an Italian sound how they were this evening and would they like to make a request. Maybe their favorite song? She watched Skip's bland expression and saw it coming. "You guys remember a group used to be around here, the MC5?" The leader frowned. MC5? He wasn't sure. What was one of their tunes? She watched Skip, with his pale, innocent eyes, say, " 'Kick Out the Jams, Motherfuckers.' You guys know that one?" Robin watched, thinking, Oh, man, have I missed you.

3

Chris asked the St. Antoine Clinic doctor if he thought a psychiatric evaluation was really necessary. All he was doing was transferring to another section. He'd still be at 1300 Beaubien, up from the sixth to the seventh floor and down at the other end of the hall.

The St. Antoine Clinic doctor, a serious young guy with narrow shoulders and glasses, not much hair, was looking at the sheet Chris had filled out. He didn't seem to be listening. He said, "Tell me if anything I read is incorrect. You're Christopher Mankowski, no middle initial. Date of birth, October 7, 1949."

Chris told him so far it was correct.

The doctor cleared his throat. He cleared it a lot, faint little growls coming from deep in there. "You're presently a sergeant, bomb and explosives technician, assigned to the Crime Laboratory Section."

"I'm also a firearms examiner, you might want to put down. Or I was. Right now I'm not sure what I am."

"You like guns?"

"Do I *like* them? I *know* guns, I'm not a collector."

"How many do you own?"

"I carry a thirty-eight Special and I have a Glock my dad gave me I keep at work. I don't want to get burglarized and have some head running around with a seventeen-shot automatic."

"That's what a Glock is?"

"It's Austrian, nine millimeter. Very lightweight."

"Even with all those bullets in it?"

"That's correct."

There was a silence. Then the sound of a throat being cleared. "You've been with the Detroit Police since June 1975."

"That's correct," Chris said. "Another month will be twelve years."

The young doctor said, "You don't have to tell me when the information is correct. Only when it isn't correct." So when the doctor said, "You were in the military, honorably discharged, but you served less than a year," Chris didn't say anything. That was correct. He was stateside five months and the rest of the time with the Third Brigade, 25th Infantry, in Vietnam. Chris had a feeling the doctor didn't like to ask a question unless he already knew the answer. He was the type of person witnesses never remembered. The wedding ring didn't mean shit. He probably vacuumed and washed the dishes in his lab coat. It was like he wanted you to know he was a doctor, but wasn't that sure of it himself. Why did he wear a lab coat to sit at his desk asking questions? What did he think might get spilled on him?

Why was the chair, where Chris sat next to the desk, turned around instead of facing the doctor? So that they were both looking in the same direction, at framed diplomas on the otherwise bare wall. Two of them, from Wayne State. Chris would have to turn and look over his shoulder to see the doctor. But wouldn't see his face anyway, because of the afternoon glare on the windows and because the doctor almost always had his head down. Why was he hiding?

His voice said, "I gather, while in the army you suffered some type of disability?"

He gathered correctly, so Chris didn't say anything. There was a silence until the doctor cleared his throat a few times and said, "Is that correct?" Breaking his own rule. Chris told him yes, it was. Then had to wait some more.

"You attended the University of Michigan two years."

"I quit to go in the army."

"You enlisted?"

"That's right." There was no reason to tell the doctor he'd flunked out and would be drafted anyway.

"Why?"

"Why'd I enlist? I wanted to see what war was like."

There was a dead silence, not even the sound of the guy clearing his throat.

"When I came out I went back to school."

"And got your degree?"

"Well, actually I was about ten credits shy."

"So you're not a university graduate."

Jesus Christ. Chris waited again while the guy made corrections, got that record straight.

"You're single, have never been married."

That was correct, but required an explanation.

"You might want to know I almost got married a couple of times," Chris said. "What I mean to say is I'm not single by choice, I would've married either one. But once they start wringing their hands you know it's not gonna work. See, they were afraid, more than anything else."

There was a silence again, behind him and off his right shoulder, where the young doctor was making notes.

"Why were they afraid of you?"

"They weren't afraid of *me*. They were afraid, you know, something could happen to me, being a police officer. It's the same kind of situation I'm in right now, why I want to transfer. I've been going with a young lady—actually we're living together, in her apartment. It's right up the street, as a matter of fact, on East Lafayette. I can walk to 1300, or Phyllis drops me off if she goes in early. She's with Manufacturers Bank, in the Trust Department." Chris paused. What was he telling him all that for? But then felt he should explain why Phyllis drove him to work. "See, my car was stolen last month. Parked right across the street from 1300, if you can believe it. On Macomb. Eighty-four Mustang, they never found it."

The young doctor didn't seem to give a shit about his Mustang. Chris heard the pen tapping.

"Anyway Phyllis, we start out, was always a little nervous about what I do. The last couple months she's gotten more and more paranoid I'm gonna lose my hands. It's not what if I get blown up, it's just the idea of losing my hands that seems to worry her. How would I eat? How would I dress myself? I told her I'm not gonna lose my hands, I'm very careful in my work. But if I ever did, I told her she could help me out. See, at first I tried to kid about it, tell her different things she could do for me. Like when I go to the bathroom, things like that. But I realized it was the wrong way to handle it. She'd turn white. You could see her imagining different situations. But she brought it up so often I started looking at my hands. I'd be looking at them," Chris said, holding up his palms, looking at them now, "without even realizing I was doing it. I'd see things in my hands, lines, I never noticed before. I finally decided it wasn't worth it, talking about it all the time; I'd transfer to another section. Also, you have to understand, it isn't all that exciting. Most of the time you're just sitting around." Chris waited. Then glanced over his shoulder.

The doctor was busy making notes, shielding the pad with his left arm. "How long were you on the Bomb Squad?"

"Six years. I started out in radio cars, Twelfth Precinct. Sometimes I worked plainclothes. You know there's quite a gay community there, around Palmer Park, and when you have that, you have fairy hawks, muggers that specialize in gays. I'd dress up like a fruitcake and stroll through the park, you know, asking for it."

"That sounds like entrapment."

"It does, doesn't it. I transferred to Arson, I had some experience in that area from before. Three years I worked for an insurance company as a claims investigator. But I didn't care much for Arson. Walk around in water in burned-out buildings, your clothes smell all the time. I think that might've been the reason the second young lady walked out. I had to hang my clothes by an open window. So I transferred to the Bomb Squad."

"Why did you do that?"

"I just told you, to get out of Arson."

"I mean why did you choose the Bomb Squad?"

"I knew the guys there, I'd run into them."

"Was there another reason, a motivating factor?"

There might've been. Chris wasn't sure if it made sense or if he should bring it up.

"Something you wanted to prove to yourself?"

"Like what?"

"Say a test of your manhood."

"My *man*hood?" Chris looked over his shoulder at the doctor in the lab coat, head down, writing away. "Why would handling explosives be a test of your manhood? It can end your manhood in a hurry, blow your balls off."

He knew it was a mistake as soon as he said it.

"That's why I suggest you might have approached it as a test, a challenge."

Chris said, "You don't stay on a job six years to prove something. You have to like it. There's risk, sure. You accept that going in and you handle it, or you get out." Chris waited. The young doctor was hiding back there writing again, drawing conclusions, making judgments about him. Chris said, "I don't know what attracted me. . . . There was something I've wondered about that happened in Vietnam, if it hadanything to do with it. You know, like in my subconscious mind."

The voice said, "You were in Vietnam?"

"It doesn't seem to have a direct connection, though."

"What doesn't?"

"See, when I was over there I was assigned to a Recon-Intelligence platoon, working with mostly a bunch of ARVNs. You know what I mean? South Vietnamese, supposedly the good guys. One of my jobs was to interrogate prisoners they'd bring in and then recommend their disposition."

"Meaning how to dispose of them?"

"Meaning what to do with them. Let 'em go, send 'em

back to Brigade . . . but that's not what I'm talking about. Well, it is and it isn't."

There was a silence. Chris tried to think of the right words, ways to begin. *One sunny day I was sitting in the R and I hootch at Khiem Hanh. . . .*

"The day I'm talking about, I was sent out to question a guy the ARVNs believed was working for the Vietcong. An informer with a sack over his head had fingered the guy and they pulled him out of his village. I got there, they have this old man standing barefoot on a grenade with the pin pulled, his toes curled around to hold the lever in place and his hands tied behind his back. I never saw anybody so scared in my life. They have him behind a mud wall that used to be part of a house, in case his foot slipped off and the grenade blew. I had to talk to the guy across the wall with my interpreter hunched down behind it; he refused to stand up. The rest of them, the ARVNs, they're off about thirty meters or so having a smoke. Anyway, I ask the old guy a few questions. He doesn't know anything about the VC, he's a farmer. He's crying, he's shaking he's so scared, trying to keep his foot on the grenade. He can't even name his own kids. I tell the ARVNs the guy's clean, come on put the pin back in and let him go. By the time I cut him loose I look up, the fucking ARVNs are walking off, going home. I go after 'em partway, I'm yelling, 'Where's the goddamn *pin?*' They don't know. They point, it's over there somewhere, on the ground. I yell some more. 'Well, help me find the goddamn thing. We can't leave the guy like that.' One of them says, 'Tell him to pick it up and throw it away.' They didn't care. They walk off laughing, think it's funny. Some of those guys, they even knew the old man. They knew he wasn't VC, but they didn't care. They walked away." Chris paused. Man, just thinking about it . . .

"I crawled around looking for the pin, finally gave up.

The old man's crying—there was no way he could handle that grenade. The only thing I could think of, have him step off, I'd pick it up quick and throw it. But I couldn't tell him what I wanted to do, my *fucking* interpreter was gone. I did try, I went through the motions; but you could see he didn't understand. The poor guy couldn't think straight. The only thing I could do was walk up to him, push him aside and grab it. But I had to keep him calm. I walk up to him, I'm going, 'Don't worry, Papa. Nothing to get excited about.' I'm about as far as that door from him he can't do it anymore. He comes running at me, lunges and grabs hold, and in the five seconds we had I couldn't get the guy off me. I could *not* get him off. I tried to *drag* him out of there. . . ." Chris stared at the doctor's diploma hanging on the bare institutional wall.

"The grenade blew with the old man hanging onto me. It killed him and tore up both of my legs. I was in-country fifteen weeks and out of the army."

There was a long silence followed by faint sounds, the serious young doctor tapping his ballpoint pen on the desk, clearing his throat.

"As you approached the old man, Sergeant Mankowski, were you aware of being afraid?"

"Was I *afraid?* Of course I was afraid, I was scared to death."

"All right, but you also felt, I believe, a deep hostility toward the ARVN soldiers."

I have to get out of here, Chris thought.

"So that, in effect, it was your intense anger that enabled you to overcome your fear."

"That must've been it," Chris said, "my hostility."

"But now, in comparable high-risk situations, your fear is no longer dampened, let's say, by acute feelings of anger. It's out in the open and you have to deal with it. A fear which you equate, specifically, with the loss of your hands."

Chris turned in the chair, quick, and caught the sneak looking at him, saw his eyes there for a moment in round glasses.

"*I'm* not worried about my hands, Phyllis is."

The doctor had his head down again, checking his notes. "You said, quote, 'I started thinking about my hands. I'd be looking at them without even realizing I was doing it.'"

"Because of Phyllis."

"You're looking at them right now."

Chris put his hands in his lap, locked his fingers together and stared straight ahead at the asshole doctor's diploma. The thing to do was just answer yes or no, don't argue. Finish and get out.

There was a silence.

"I'm told a fatality occurred yesterday, a bomb exploded. What was the circumstance of the man's death?"

Chris said, "We believe the deceased attempted to outrun a substance that explodes at the rate of fifteen thousand feet per second and didn't make it."

There was another silence.

"You did everything you could?"

"I'll get you my Case Assigned report if you want to read it."

The silence this time was longer. Chris began to think maybe they were finished.

"Are you aware of other fears?"

"Like what?"

"Are you afraid of animals, insects?"

Chris hesitated, giving it some thought before saying, "I don't like spiders." That would be safe; nobody in the world liked spiders.

The doctor said, "Oh? That's interesting, a fear of spiders."

"I didn't say I was afraid of spiders, I said I didn't like them."

"Do you think you might be trying to minimize, substitute dislike for fear? I pose the question, Sergeant Mankowski, because a fear of spiders can indicate a dysfunction in the area of sexual identification. Or, more precisely, a fear of bisexuality."

Chris stood up. He turned his chair around and sat down again, facing the doctor.

"You trying to tell me if I don't like spiders it means I go both ways?"

The young doctor looked up. For the first time his gaze in the round glasses held.

"You seem to feel threatened."

"Look, they send me over here, it's supposed to be a routine exam. Has my job been getting to me? I feel any stress? No, I just want a transfer, on account of Phyllis. Now you're trying to tell me I have a problem."

"I haven't suggested you have a problem."

"Then what're you trying to do, with the spiders?"

The young doctor kept looking right at him now. "I'm suggesting the spider is a symbol—if you want a clinical explanation—that externalizes a more threatening impulse. One that quite possibly indicates a pregenital fear of bisexual genitalia, usually in the form of a phallic wicked mother."

Chris kept staring at the young doctor, who stared right back at him and said, "Does that answer your question?"

Chris said, "Yes, it does, thank you," and felt some relief; because all the guy was doing, he was playing doctor with him, showing off. Little asshole sitting there in his lab coat with all those words in his head to dump on the dumb cop, giving him that pregenital genitalia bullshit. There was no way to compete with the guy. The best thing to do was to nod, agree. So when the doctor asked him:

"What's your feeling about snakes?"

Chris said, "I like snakes, a lot. I've never had any trouble with snakes."

The doctor was still looking at him, hanging on, not wanting to let go. "You understand that your previous assignment could be psychosocially debilitating?"

Chris said, "Sure, I can understand that."

"Then there's the correlation between your fear of spiders and your desire to prove, through the handling of high explosives, your manhood. I believe you suggested the work could be emasculating. It can, quote, 'blow your balls off.' "

"That's an expression," Chris said. "You don't have to take it literally." He watched the sneaky doctor nod, thinking up something else.

"By the way, have you ever experienced impotence?"

Chris took his time. He didn't see a trap, so he said, "No, as a matter of fact, I haven't. Not once in my life."

"Really?"

"I've got witnesses."

"Well, it's not important."

Chris stared at the doctor's lowered head, the thin, carefully combed hair. "You don't believe me, do you?"

The doctor tapped his pen without looking up. "I suppose you could be one of the rare exceptions."

"To what?"

"Well, in a study made at the University of Munster— that's in West Germany," the doctor said, looking up—

"tests showed that assertive, self-confident, macho-type males, if you will, were found almost invariably to have a low sperm count."

"That's interesting," Chris said. "We finished here?" He got up, not waiting for an answer, said, "I have to get back, clean out my desk . . ." and saw the guy's innocent young-doctor face raise with a pleasant expression.

"Yes, you're leaving Bombs and Explosives. What we haven't yet discussed is where you're going. How did you put it, 'Up to the seventh floor and down at the other end of the hall'?"

The doctor waited as Chris sat down again.

"You seem somewhat agitated."

"I'm fine."

"You're sure?"

"I'm supposed to meet Phyllis at Galligan's." Chris looked at his watch: it was four twenty. "At five."

The young doctor said, "We shouldn't be too much longer," and smiled. He did, he smiled for the first time, looked right at Chris and said, "What I'm curious about, and perhaps you can explain, why you've requested a transfer to Sex Crimes."

4

Skip swallowed the tiny square of blotter acid, smaller than the nail of his little finger, dropped it with a sip of beer and got comfortable to wait for the cleansing head show to begin. The seams of the plastic chair were coming apart but it was fine, deep and cushy. The only thing that bothered him was the light, it was so bright in here facing that bare white wall and no shade on the lamp. It smelled like Robin had been painting, trying to make the dump presentable.

Here she was back in their old neighborhood, a low-rent apartment on Canfield near Wayne State, where they'd hung out years ago in their elephant bells, got stoned and laid and would slip off on dark nights to mess with the straight world. Back when this was the inner-city place to be.

That naked lamp was flashing now, pretending it was lightning, streaking across the bare white wall. Sometimes when he dropped acid everything would become suspended and float in space. Or things would come at him, like a person's nose, clear across a room. Robin came out of the kitchen with two cans of Stroh's and sure as hell her arm extended about ten feet to hand him one. It was pretty good blotter. She was speaking now.

"I've missed you. You know how long it's been?"

Only she finished before all the words got to him. This was something new. Skip raised his hand, waved it in front of him and felt water. That's why the sound of her voice was slowed up. She asked him what he was doing. He said, "Nothing." It was like being in a swimming pool lined with bookshelves full of books and a ton of old underground newspapers she'd saved; Robin now sitting against the desk piled with folders and notebooks and shit, the bare white wall behind her. Her lips moved. Now he heard:

"When was the last time we were together?"

Skip said, "You kidding?" Saw dates flash in his mind and had to pick the right one. "April of 'seventy-nine in federal court."

Robin shook her head and the water became sparkly, fizzed up like club soda.

"I don't count that. I mean the last time we were alone together."

"Well, that was in L.A.," Skip said. "Sure, that motel on La Cienega where Jim Morrison and the Doors used to stay."

"That's how you remember it?"

"Right off of Sunset. You walked in I didn't know if it was you or some light-skinned colored chick, your hair was all frizzed up in a natural. I go, Who is this, Angela Davis? Once I saw it was you underneath all that hair I couldn't get my clothes off fast enough." Skip grinned at the motel scenes popping in his head until he heard Robin say:

"You were Scott Wolf then and I was Betsy Bender. And five days later we were picked up."

"I'd gone to Venice," Skip said, "to get some dope. . . . I don't know how anybody could've recognized us, you especially, with that 'fro." And heard her say:

"I didn't either, at the time. I thought, Well, maybe it's just as well. You think it's going to be fun living underground, thrills and chills. I was never so bored in my life."

"I wasn't," Skip said. "I got into different gigs, some a little hairier'n others. I robbed a bank one time."

He heard Robin say something he believed was "Far out." Impressed, but calm about it. Not too surprised.

"Just the one, I didn't like those cameras they had looking at you. I held up some other places, grocery stores, Seven-Elevens. I liked Seven-Elevens except they don't pay much."

He watched her fooling with her braid. As she stroked it the end curled up and came toward him from across the room. Skip reached up to touch it.

"What're you doing?"

"Nothing."

He dropped his hand to the back of his head and felt his ponytail hanging there, behaving itself. He watched Robin take a sip of beer. Saw her eyes raise from the can; not wearing her glasses now. Saw her tongue touch her lips and waited for it to come at him, flick out like a snake's tongue. There was a little snake in her. She could hit you quick with a word or throw something when you least expected. She looked fine, not another one like her. The tongue slipped back in her mouth and Skip said, "You ever get laid underwater?"

"Not lately."

She looked like she was waiting to see if he remembered a time. The same as at the restaurant yesterday, it was like she was giving him a memory quiz, going back to things that happened during the past almost twenty years. She was asking him now:

"Were you zonked when you pulled the robberies?"

"You think I'm crazy? 'Course I was."

"Did you use a gun?"

"Not in the bank, it was spur of the moment. But after that one I did." He watched her take another sip of beer.

"Did you ever kill anyone?"

The sparkling water settled and he could see her waiting for him to answer, then smiling a little, holding the smile on him before she said:

"You have, haven't you?"

"I almost killed a guy with a sword one time. I had it in mind."

"Working in the movies?"

"Over in Spain. But the one you want to hear about—how I rigged a guy's car with a bomb, huh? Blew when he opened the door. I never met the guy or even saw him, outside of his picture in the L.A. papers, after. It was a dope business thing, this guy pissing on somebody else's territory."

Robin kept watching him. Interested but not the least bit excited.

"It was when I was using that safe house in Venice. I'd take a trip some place, come back, and there'd be a new bunch of freaks crashing there. I didn't think anybody knew me, except one time I'm there this geek keeps staring at me like for a couple of days. Finally he goes, 'You aren't Scott Wolf, are you? You're Skip Gibbs. You blew up the army recruiting office in the Detroit Federal Building, September whatever-the-date-was, 1971."

"September twenty-ninth," Robin said, "my birthday."

"The geek says he was in the Weathermen at Ann Arbor, but I didn't remember him. He'd fix me up with weed, all I wanted for nothing—see, he was dealing—and then he put me in touch with this Mexican dude that worked for the guy that paid me to do the job. Only I never saw the guy. Only the Weather geek and the Mexican dude."

"What'd you get for it?"

Skip watched her turn to the desk as she asked the question and pick up a can he thought at first was bug spray.

"I got five grand. That was my price, all hundred-dollar bills."

Not looking at him Robin said, "It can be worth a lot more than that." She was standing at the clean white wall looking at the can, reading the directions.

"Well, sure, it was about ten years ago."

Robin said, "I mean there's a way to do it now with a much higher price tag."

Skip was thinking, Has it been ten years? He said, "It was at least a couple years before we met in L.A."

Robin said, "We come back to that." Staring at him. "You know why? Because five days later we were picked up. You said, 'I don't know how anybody could've recognized us.' Have you thought maybe they didn't? They were told where to find us?"

Skip said, "I thought of that, sure."

"For how long?" Robin said. "I've been thinking about it for eight years. I made a list of names, anybody who had contact with us then or could've known or found out where we were. I've crossed out names until finally I'm left with two and they were at the top of the list all the time."

Skip watched her turn to the wall and begin to spray, her arm moving up and down and in half circles to form capital letters about a foot high, painting something on that pure white wall in bright red. She stepped aside and Skip was looking at:

MARK

"The hell's that suppose to mean?"

He heard Robin say, "Dark hair, brown eyes, nice body. On the staff of the *Michigan Daily*, sold ad space. How about Mark the mechanical mouth?"

"Mark Ricks," Skip said, "sure, with the bullhorn. He'd lather up the students, get 'em chanting, the cops'd come storming across the quad and Mark'd split for the Del Rio bar. Man, you're bringing it all back. 'Two four six eight, organize and smash the state.'"

Robin was spray-painting again, making waves, so Skip waited, thinking back. He could see a guy with dark hair and an Indian kind of headband on that corner by the Undergrad Library, the Ugli, yelling through his bullhorn, a guy with him beating on a tom-tom. Skip said, "'One two three four, Vietnam's the bosses' war.' With his mom paying his way through school, huh?"

Robin's voice said, "He carried Chairman Mao's red book in the glove box of his red Porsche."

She was looking this way now and Skip saw she had painted another name under Mark:

WOODY

"Shit, I remember him," Skip said. "Mark's big brother. Was always in the bag or stoned."

"Bigger but dumber." Robin stood there admiring her work. "Woodrow Ricks. We used to call him the Poor Soul."

Skip was nodding. "I can see him. Fat, sloppy dude with curly hair. He'd do this little wiggle and pull his pants out of his crack. Kind of sissified."

"Afraid of the dark," Robin said.

"That's right, we'd turn the lights out on him and he'd have a fit. Hey, but he always had dough, huh? Mark'd make him pay for everything."

"That's why Mark let him tag along. Mark would run out of money, he'd get Woody to call home and Mom would send a check. You remember their house? The indoor swimming pool?"

It gave Skip instant recall. *"That's* where we did it underwater. Yeah, we'd go there weekends to party." He grinned at the memory of that big glassed-in room, voices echoing. "Everybody'd get smashed, tear their clothes off and jump in the pool."

"Sometimes with our clothes *on,"* Robin said. "Their mother used to lurk. Remember that? Never said a word to anyone, but you'd see her lurking. She was a boozer. Mark said she drank at least two fifths a day."

Skip closed his eyes against the naked-light glare, to rest them, and listened to Robin tell him how Mark and his mom didn't get along, Mark being a little smartypants. How Woody was her favorite, her little prince, nursed him till he was about sixteen and they started drinking together. Skip grinned at that. Heard how the dad was gone by then, divorced, kicked out without a dime, the money being on Mom's side of the family. Her old man had invented hubcaps or some goddamn thing for the car business and made a fortune. Then when Mom finally drank herself under and they had the reading of the will, guess what?

Skip opened his eyes. "Mom's favorite made out."

"Woody scored something like fifty million," Robin said, "plus the house."

"And Mark got cut out for acting smart," Skip said, "picking on his brother."

"Well, not entirely. Mark got two million and blew it trying to put on outdoor rock concerts in Pontiac. Usuallyin the rain. He bought a theater and now he does plays and musicals. I think with Woody backing him," Robin said. "It's a second-rate operation, but it's show biz. You know what I mean? Mark's a celebrity. *People* magazine did a feature on him. 'Yippie turns Yuppie. Sixties radical cleans up his act and goes legit in regional theater.' I couldn't believe it. They mention Eldridge Cleaver, what he's doing now, Jerry Rubin, Rennie Davis, like Mark was in the same league with those guys."

"You're pissed off," Skip said, " 'cause you never got your picture in the paper. Or in the post office."

Wrong thing to say. Her eyes flashed at him.

"Sixties radical my ass. Mark was nothing but a media freak. He played to the TV cameras."

Skip said, being gentle with her now, "Sweetheart, that whole show back then was a put-on. You gonna tell me we were trying to change the world? We were kicking ass and having fun. All that screaming about Vietnam and burning draft cards? That was a little bitty part of it. Getting stoned and laid was the trip. Where's everybody now? We've come clear around to the other side, joined the establishment."

"Some have," Robin said.

Look at her telling him that with a straight face. Skip stared at the red names shimmering there on the wall, flashing at him.

MARK

WOODY

"Mellow me down with the acid," Skip said, "paint the names on big so they'll burn into my brain. You been taking me back to those days of rage and revolution, huh? I'm into a goof, but I can hear and think. What I don't see are Mark and Woody snitching on us. They weren't into anything heavier than a peace march. What'd they know about our business? Nothing."

Robin said, "They knew I was meeting you in L.A. Mark did. I saw him just before I left."

"Well, that doesn't mean he told where to find us."

"Skip, I have a feeling, okay? I know he did."

Man, she did not like to be argued with. Never did. It tightened up her face, put a killer look in her eyes.

"Okay, they informed on us and now they're sitting on fifty million bucks. You look around this dump you're living in and you feel they owe you something. Am I telling it right?"

"*We* feel they owe *us* something," Robin said.

"Fine. How much?"

"Pick a number," Robin said. "How about seven hundred thousand? Ten grand for every month we spent locked up. Three fifty apiece."

"I was in longer than you."

"A few months. I'm trying to keep it simple."

"Okay, how do we go about getting it?"

"I ask for it as a loan."

"Seven hundred big ones. I can imagine what they'll tell you."

"Maybe the first time I call."

"Then what?"

"Then late one night their theater blows up."

Skip said, "Hey, shit," grinning at her. "The subtle approach, blow up their fucking theater. I love it."

"The smoke clears, I try again."

"Pay up or else."

"*No.* This isn't extortion, I'm asking for a loan."

"That what you're gonna tell the cops?"

"I haven't threatened anyone."

"They're still gonna be all over us. Shit, me especially, I'm the powderman."

She was shaking her head at him in slow motion.

"They won't know anything about you, you'll be at Mother's. She's on a three-month cruise, you'll have the whole house to yourself."

Skip felt himself getting into it, wanting to move around. "I'd have to line up some explosives. Keep it at Mommy's. Man, I love dynamite, and I never get to use it. Dynamite and acid, man, that'll Star Trek you back to good times. The way it was."

Robin was smiling at him, raising her arms, and her arms reached him way before she did. Her hands came to rest on his shoulders. He had to tilt his head back to look up at her face, at her pale skin stretched over bone, her cheeks hollow, sunken in. He could see what her skull looked like in there. He could see hands holding her bare skull and a teacher voice in his mind saying this was a woman thirty-five to forty, a hunter. The voice saying, Look at the fucking teeth on her, this was a man-eater.

The jaw in the skull moved. Robin said:

"From that time we first met—oh, but we freaked them out, didn't we?"

Skip blinked, feeling his eyes wet. "You know it. Couple of the baddest motherfuckers ever to set foot inside of history."

Now the skull was grinning at him.

"You stole that line."

"Yeah, but I forgot from where."

Man, look at this fine girl.

Skip said, "You're working me over like you used to and I love it. Getting me to play your dirty tricks on those boys. . . . But just suppose for a minute, what if it wasn't Woody and Mark that got us busted?"

Robin's face came down close. He could feel her breath. In the moment before she put her mouth on his, Skip heard her say, "What difference does it make?"

5

Saturday noon in the kitchen of his dad's apartment in St. Clair Shores, Chris said, "This doctor, he not only won't look you in the eye, he doesn't listen to a thing you say. I tell him why I'm leaving the Bomb Squad. I don't see where it's any of his business, but it doesn't make any difference anyway, he's already made up his mind. I'm leaving 'cause I'm scared, I can't handle it." Chris was getting a couple of beers out of the refrigerator.

Chris's dad, Art Mankowski, was frying hamburgers in an iron skillet, working at arm's length so the grease wouldn't pop on him. His dad said, "Get an onion while you're in there, in the crisper. Listen, you'd be crazy if you weren't scared."

"Yeah, but this guy wants to read a hidden meaning into everything, like with the spiders."

"You want your onion fried or raw?"

"I'd rather have a slice of green pepper, if you have any, and the cheese melted over it."

"I think there's one in there, take a look. Get the cheese, too, the Muenster. Where'd you have it like that?"

"It's the way Phyllis makes 'em," Chris said. "You put A-1 on it instead of ketchup. See, if you don't like spiders there's something wrong with you, you're queer. So I *know*, after we get through the spiders and have I ever been impotent, if he brings up why am I going to Sex Crimes, there isn't a thing I can say the guy's gonna believe. I must be a pervert, some kind of sexual deviant."

Chris's dad said, "Well, I can understand him asking. Why not Homicide, Robbery, one of those? They seem more like what you'd want to get into."

"I *asked* for Homicide, I told the shrink that. There aren't any openings."

"Sex Crimes," Chris's dad said. "You know the kind of people you'd be dealing with?"

"Yeah, women that got raped and the guys that did it. Also different kinds of sex offenders. You sound like Phyllis. She can't understand why I'd want it. I told her I *didn't*. You go where there's an opening and they think you'll do a job."

Chris's dad said, "I can't imagine, with all the different departments you have in the Detroit Police . . ." He said, "You want to put your things away before we sit down?"

"I'll only be here a few days, a week at the most. I have to find a place in the city."

His dad said, "So you're gonna leave your things out in the middle of the floor?"

In the front hall three sportcoats, pants, a dark-blue

suit, poplin jacket and a lined raincoat lay folded over a mismatched pair of canvas suitcases and several cardboard boxes. Chris carried his possessions through the hall to a room with a hospital bed, where his mother had spent her last three years staring at framed photographs of her children and grandchildren. The pictures were taken at different ages so that Chris, his sister Michele and her three girls became a roomful of kids. Faces that gradually lost identity as they stared back at his mother from the walls, the dresser. . . . Chris had stood at the foot of the bed watching Michele comb their mother's hair, Michele saying, "Look who's here, Mom, it's Christopher." His mom said, "I know my boy." Then looked up at Michele and said, "Now which one are you?" He was hanging his clothes in the empty closet when he heard his dad's raised voice and answered, "What?"

"I said why don't you go back to Arson?"

Chris walked through the hall to the foyer. His dad was across the formal living room in the dining-L, the glass doors to the balcony behind him, filled with pale light. His dad was placing the cheeseburgers and a bag of potato chips on the table, ducking under the crystal chandelier, his dad in a plaid wool shirt, sweat socks, no shoes. Art Mankowski was sixty-eight, retired from the asphalt paving business. (Chris had grown up thinking of that black tarry substance as "ash-phalt" because that was the way his dad had pronounced it, and still did.) His dad went up north deer hunting in the fall, spent the winter in the Florida Keys bonefishing, and would stop off in Delray Beach to visit Michele and her family on the way back. After being with the three grandchildren Art would call his son the cop and ask him if he was married yet. In the spring he'd look out the window at Lake St. Clair, wanting it to hurry up and thaw so he could get out in his 41-foot Roamer.

They sat down to lunch. Chris said, "You remember the Huckleberry Hound cartoon where Huckleberry smells smoke, he goes looking for it and sees all this heavy smoke coming out of the birdhouse?"

His dad held his cheeseburger poised, picturing the scene. "Yeah?"

"Huckleberry Hound climbs up the pole and looks in. There's a crow sitting in there smoking a cigar, watching TV."

His dad, starting to smile, said, "Yeah, I remember."

"Huckleberry Hound says, 'Hey, are you burning garbage?' And the crow looks at him and says, 'No, I like garbage.'"

His dad said, "Yeah, you know what I remember? The way the crow was sitting there with his legs crossed. Talked out of the side of his mouth. 'No, I like garbage.' Your mother would look at us and shake her head, like we're a couple of nuts."

"The point I want to make," Chris said, "that crow would love the Arson Squad; you live with that smell, it clings to you. I can smell a burnt-out building just thinking about it." He took a bite of his cheeseburger with green pepper; it was good. "But what you said, Mom not understanding how we could sit there watching cartoons, that was exactly the way Phyllis looked at me."

"When you told her."

"Yeah, we're at Galligan's, it's Friday, so all the secretaries and young executives from the RenCen are in there looking for action. I get us a drink and tell her, Well, I'm no longer with the Bomb Squad. She just looks at me for a minute, sort of surprised. Maybe even a little disappointed, and I'm thinking, What *is* this?"

"Yeah?"

"I tell her I'm now with Sex Crimes and she gets a

funny look on her face and says, '*Sex* Crimes?' Real loud, everybody turns around and looks. She says, 'You're gonna associate with perverts, rapists, filth like that and then come home and tell me about your *day?*' I said, 'When'd I ever tell you about my day? When'd you ever want to hear about it?' She says, 'You don't tell me anything, you never talk to me at all.' She's crazy, we talk all the time."

His dad said, "You seem to have a lot of trouble with women. They keep throwing you out."

"I do what she wants, she comes up with something else, I don't talk to her."

"I don't know what it is," his dad said, "you're not a bad-looking guy. You could give a little more thought to your grooming. Get your hair trimmed, wear a white shirt now and then, see if that works. What kind of aftershave you use?"

"I'm serious."

"I know you are and I'm glad you came to me. When'd she throw you out, last night?"

"She didn't throw me out, I left. I phoned, you weren't home, so I stayed at Jerry's."

"When you needed me most," his dad said. "I'm sorry I wasn't here."

"Actually," Chris said, "you get right down to it, Phyllis's the one does all the talking. She gives me banking facts about different kinds of annuities, fiduciary trusts, institutional liquid asset funds . . . I'm sitting there trying to stay awake, she's telling me about the exciting world of trust funds."

"I had a feeling," his dad said, "you've given it some thought. You realize life goes on."

"I'm not even sure what attracted me to her in the first place."

His dad said, "You want me to tell you?"

"She looks like a bed doll—you know what I mean?"

"A big healthy one. I know exactly what you mean."

"But she's so serious all the time. She doesn't have much of a sense of humor."

"I'll say this for Phyllis," his dad said, "I like her idea, the green pepper with the cheese and the A-One. It's not bad."

"You can get tired of it," Chris said. He took a sip of beer. "I called you first thing this morning, you still weren't home."

"You were worried about me." His dad would study his sandwich before taking a bite. "I wasn't far, if it'll make you feel better. Two floors up. I was at Esther's."

"You spent the night with her?"

"Why, you think it's a mortal sin or what?"

"I'm surprised, that's all."

His dad said, "Esther's sixty-four, she weighs one eighteen on the nose. She's attractive, knows how to dress, was married forty years to a doctor and now she's having fun. I take her places—she never been to Hamtramck, if you can imagine that. Never listened to WMZK, the polka hour. You know what her favorite song is now? 'Who Stole the Kishka?' "

"No, I think it's nice you spend the night together now and then," Chris said. "Why not?"

"Couple times a week," his dad said. "Plus Saturday night if we're out late, which is usually the case. Esther likes to party."

"You mean you stay with her three nights a week?"

His dad looked up from his sandwich. "What's the matter, you surprised or what?"

"I never thought about it before, that's all."

"You remember when I told you the facts of life?"

"You took me to Little Harry's for lunch and after we

went to the show, *Our Man in Havana* with Alec Guinness. But I already knew all that. Ernie Kovacs was in it too."

"Maybe you thought you knew it. I told you the facts of life and your eyes open and you said, 'You do that to Mom?' And I said, 'That's it, there isn't any other way to do it.' I was just about the same age when I told you you are now. You see what I'm getting at? Your mother and I were married thirty-seven years. Counting before that when I was in the service, and then add on the five years since she passed away and I been seeing different ones, I'd say I've done it, conservatively, about five thousand times." Chris's dad raised his can of beer. "And not all of them done that conservatively, now that I think about it. You see my point?"

"I'm not sure," Chris said.

"What I'm saying is, going to bed with the opposite sex is part of life, it can even become routine. But at the same time, unlike the cheeseburger with the green pepper and the A-1, it isn't something you ever get tired of."

"I'm glad to know that," Chris said. "I was wondering about it."

"You know who Esther thinks you look like? Robert Redford."

"Come on."

"I'm not kidding you. She says that, it means she wants you to like her."

"I like her," Chris said, "and I'm glad you and Esther have fun together."

"We do, that's for sure."

"And I appreciate your taking the time to help me with my problem."

His dad said, "What problem?"

6

Saturday afternoon, when Skip called during his lunch break, Robin said, "I'm going after them tonight."

"All of a sudden?"

"Mark's picture was in the paper this morning, honorary chairman of a benefit to raise money for inner-city ballet programs. It's a buffet cruise on a yacht, from Lake St. Clair down the river and back, hundred bucks a head. Woody's going too, his name was mentioned."

"See beautiful downtown Detroit from a safe distance," Skip said. "I bet nobody gets off the boat."

"You sound like a tourist. Here's my plan. By the time the boat gets back to the marina I'll be waiting at Brownie's, sitting at the bar. They come in. . . . 'Well, hi, you guys! Gosh, I can't believe it, after all these years.' "

"What if they get off the boat and go home?"

"Brownie's is right *there* and Woody's never walked past a bar in his life. Listen, I've been getting ready for this, following Woody's limo around town. You know what he does? He eats and drinks, that's about it. He has lunch at one of his clubs, like the DAC, stops off at the theater some time in the afternoon and then goes down the street to Galligan's for the cocktail hour."

"I've been there, it's near my hotel."

"Or he goes around the corner to Pegasus. Remember Greektown? That one block on Monroe is the most popular street in Detroit, but I haven't been able to figure out why."

" 'Cause it's lit up," Skip said. "I know where it is. You go anywhere else downtown you're on a dark, lonely street. So who you gonna work on, Mark or Woody?"

"Woody," Robin said, "since he's got the checkbook. I'm not sure where Mark stands exactly. He isn't dumb. . . . I take that back, he wasn't too bright, either, now that I think of it. He's more of an actor, wants you to believe he's got it together. But Woody's our guy."

"Say you connect. Then what?"

"We're in business. You go to work."

"We're gonna be on the Belle Isle bridge later today, do the kush shot. Then tomorrow we ought to finish up."

Robin said, "You still like the idea?"

Skip said, "You're taking me back to the good old days. I'll call you tomorrow night if I can. Otherwise Monday, after I get to Yale and look over the dynamite situation. I hope the place's still there."

"I forgot to mention," Robin said. "Guess who Woody's driver is. Donnell Lewis."

There was a silence on the line. After a moment Skip said, "You didn't forget. You been saving him, haven't you? What's his name, Donald?"

"Nothing so common, it's Don*nell*. Remember the party to raise bail money for the Black Panthers? It was at Mark and Woody's."

"I remember you coming out of the toilet with a spade had a beard, wore a leather jacket—"

"And a beret, the Panther uniform."

"That was Donnell, huh?"

"It might've been, I'm not sure."

"It might've—you were in there fucking him, weren't you?"

"I don't remember. We could've been doing lines."

Skip said, "Hey, Robin? I got an ear for bullshit, having worked in the movie business. Don't give me this 'Oh, by the way, Woody's driver used to be a Black Panther' shit. If I'm gonna take part in this I don't want any surprises."

"That's why I told you."

"It's the *way* you told me I don't especially care for. Donnell wore black leather and had a house full of guns. I know, 'cause I tried to buy one off him. He gave me his big-time nigger look and told me to beat it."

"He wears a suit and tie now," Robin said, "and shines his shoes. He might even shine Woody's."

"Why do I find that hard to believe?"

"I don't know," Robin said. "You're the one told me everyone's sold out, joined the establishment."

Skip said, "Yeah, but I wasn't thinking of Don*nell.*"

That night she was tense for the first time in years, driving into the Jefferson Beach Marina past boat storage buildings and Brownies, the boat people's hangout, past light poles along the docks that showed rows of masts and cabin cruisers, and on down to the lakefront in darkness.

Robin nosed her five-year-old VW into a row of parked cars to wait and within moments felt relief.

Woody's limo stood off by itself, the light-gray stretch with bar, television and Donnell Lewis, tonight inside behind dark-tinted glass. Other times he'd wait outside the car, still sinister in a neat black suit, the shades, the mustache and little be-bop tuft curling around his mouth. He never said much to other drivers standing around, he kept apart. She had studied him for days, watching the way he moved, smoked cigarettes, one hand in his pocket, until finally she checked him out with the doorman at the Detroit Club, who told her, "Yeah, that's him, that's Donnell. You know him?" Good question. You can make it with a tall spade in the powder room during a Black Panther fundraising cocktail party and still not be able to say you know him. Or count on being remembered by him.

Robin smoked a cigarette watching the limo, the gray shape beneath a light pole, the windows black. She finished the cigarette, walked over to the car and tapped on the driver-side window with her key. Then stepped back as the window began to slide down and she saw his face in the dark interior, his eyes looking up at her.

"Are you waiting for that benefit cruise?"

"*Tranquility,*" Donnell said. "That's the name of it, the boat."

"This's the place then," Robin said.

"Went out from here, it has to come back. Pretty soon now."

Robin thanked him, watching his eyes. Not as close as she had watched them the afternoon in the powder room sixteen years ago, her jeans on the floor, hips raised against the rim of the washbasin, Donnell staring at himself past her in the mirror, eyelids heavy, a man watching himself making love, no strain, until he did look at her for a moment before his eyes squeezed closed. But didn't look at her again after that, as he collected the checks and left with his Panthers.

She turned with the hum of his window rising, went back to her car and sat there, not sure what she was feeling—if she wanted to believe he remembered her, if it mattered one way or the other—until she saw the lights of the yacht, *Tranquility,* a white shape, coming out of the night with the sound of dance music, society swing. A scene from an old movie. Robin circled back to Brownie's, went inside and took a place at the bar to wait.

She ordered a cognac and sat quietly in her raincoat in the nearly empty marina bar-restaurant, hearing faint voices, a woman's laughter, thinking, making judgments. Deciding that boat lovers were essentially smug, boring people. They came in here off their boats into another boat world with all the polished wood, the bar section that *was* part of a boat, and all the nautical shit, life preservers on the wall. Thinking, What is it about boats? Deciding boats were okay, it was the boat people who overdid the boat thing with their boat words, their boat outfits, the Topsiders and Sou'westers, and made a fucking ritual out of boats. That was the thing, they weren't real boats. They were phony boats for phony people who had to have a phony bar to come to after drinking on their boats and pissing in Lake St. Clair and the Detroit River all day.

She was tired of waiting for a time to come.

The cognac helped ease the knot in her tummy.

She was tired of remembering. . . .

Voices were coming from the front entrance hall, a mix of benefit cruisers arriving: traditional Grosse Pointe ladies with their scrubbed look, their out-of-style hairdos, their pearls and camel's-hair coats, followed by husbands out of Brooks Brothers; trendies now, younger women in real furs and fun furs, a couple of guys in form-fitting topcoats, styled dark hair glistening; more young ladies in layers of sweaters, scarves and coats, and a full-length coyote entering in a noise of voices. It was Woody, Woody's bulk filling the coat, Woody's hair down in his eyes. Robin watched, half turned from the bar. Woody didn't see her. Smiling faces at a table were raising their glasses to him. Woody lifted one arm with some effort, acknowledging.

Voices brought Robin's gaze back to the entrance hallway, to another group coming in, and now she saw Mark, a tan cashmere topcoat draped over his shoulders. Mark Ricks holding the arm of a girl who smiled at something he was saying. It wasn't much of a smile, there and gone. A girl with short red hair. She seemed tired, or tired of smiling. She came in and turned to Mark, as tall as Mark, then looked this way because Mark was, staring. Now he was walking away from the girl, coming this way.

Robin touched her braid, stroked it, waiting, and felt her plan begin to change.

Mark the producer, coat over his shoulders, said, "Come here," with no expression. He reached with both hands to bring Robin off the bar stool. He stared and said, "The last time we saw each other, was it yesterday or the day before?" Still solemn, deadpan. "I mean it's incredible. I see you, I get like a rush of instant recall, all the incredible things we did together. And yet I know it's been—what, eight years?"

Robin said, "Cut the shit, Mark. How are you?"

"Not bad. How about yourself? You haven't changed at all, you know it?" His eyes raised and he hesitated. "Outside of your hair's different."

Robin's hand stroked the braid and tossed it over her shoulder. The girl with short red hair was watching them. She wore a black double-breasted winter coat. She looked away and back again as Mark was saying, "I want to know what you've been doing and why you haven't called me."

Robin said, "Well, let's see. I did time, for one thing." Staring at his solemn brown eyes. "Thirty-three months and ten days in Huron Valley."

Mark said, "I was there, I was in court when they sentenced you. I couldn't believe it. Then I heard you went to New York after you got out."

"I wanted to start writing again, so I got next to some people in the publishing business, to find out what they're buying. Came back and went to work."

" 'Tales from the Underground,' uh?" He started to grin and touched his hair carefully, thinning hair combed forward now.

"I've written four historical romance novels."

"You're putting me on."

"With a lot of rape and adverbs."

"You know what I'm doing?"

"You kidding? I read about you all the time."

"You see the story *People* did?"

"I loved it. 'Yippie turns Yuppie.' "

"How come you haven't called me?"

"I've thought about it. I don't know. . . ."

Mark was getting a nice wistful look in his eyes, the cool deadpan expression gone. Beyond him, the girl with short red hair stood waiting, hands in the pockets of her black coat. Mark said, "This is totally amazing, we run into each other like this, eight years later."

Robin hesitated, looking down at her hands. "I didn't just happen to be here." She paused, raising her eyes very slowly. "I was hoping I'd see you."

"You're putting me on."

"Really."

"You read I was gonna be at this boat thing?"

"I took a chance."

"This is amazing."

"I couldn't phone you—I don't know why. I thought if we just happened to meet . . ."

"You sound different, you know it?"

Robin cocked her head to one side. "I do?"

"You're quieter. You used to be so ballsy. You know the first time I ever saw you on campus? You were breaking windows in North Hall, the ROTC building."

"The summer of 'seventy," Robin said. "We went to the Doors concert. . . . We went to the rock festival at Goose Lake. You remember that?"

Mark said, "Do I remember? I think about it all the time, constantly. I mean, after Goose Lake what is there? What's left you haven't done?"

Robin said, "You had a pretty good time, uh?"

"Not bad," Mark said, straight-faced, but couldn't hold it. He was grinning now. "You remember I got Woody to rent the limo?"

"If I'm not mistaken I put you up to it."

"You're right. It was an outstanding concept—we drove right in, no problem."

"I told you, like we were part of the show," Robin said.

"Two hundred thousand people," Mark said. "I think it was at that moment, driving in past everybody in that fucking stretch, I knew I would someday be in the entertainment business, produce shows of my own. I'll never forget it." The memory gave Mark a dreamy look.

Robin's gaze moved. She saw Woody coming away from the people at the table, several trendy girls following behind.

Mark was saying, "Listen, why don't you join us? We're going to my brother's for a little impromptu. Huh, what do you say?" There was an abrupt change in his tone, almost a plea, as he said, "Give us a chance to talk. Okay? Will you?"

She glanced at him and saw it in his eyes, Mark wanting to confide, tell her something. Then looked away again to see the full-length coyote coming toward them, weaving, veering off to one side a few steps, but not off balance. Robin watched Woody wrap a furry arm around the girl with short red hair and bring her along.

7

Chris was in the living room with the Sunday papers when his dad came in. His dad had a sportcoat and a parka over his arm and was wearing a dress shirt with the collar open, the tie hanging untied. Before closing the door he said, "You still here?"

"Where'm I gonna go? I don't have a car."

"I thought of it, you could've taken the Cadillac."

"I have to get a car, find an apartment, start a new job. . . . I have to get an apartment before they find out at work I'm living here."

His dad said, "I thought you were visiting."

"You know what I mean." Chris watched his dad drop the coats on a chair and come in stretching, yawning. "You stay at Esther's again?"

"We got in late."

"That's two nights in a row."

"We didn't do anything," his dad said, "if it'll ease your mind any. We got back, stopped at Brownie's for a couple and came home. We were bushed."

"How was the cruise?"

"It was nice. You want a beer?"

"Yeah, I guess so."

His dad was heading for the ·kitchen. "Take a look, you'll see the ship over at the marina."

Chris got up from the sofa and went to a front window where his dad kept a pair of binoculars handy on the sill. He raised the glasses, made adjustments and swept the gray expanse of Lake St. Clair, overcast, Canada way off somewhere, hidden. Then brought the glasses down to the Jefferson Beach Marina, just north of the high rise. He heard a beer can pop open and his dad close behind him saying, "Go all the way out from Brownie's to the end of the spit. You see it?"

"You can't miss it."

"It's a beauty, hundred-and-seven-foot motor yacht designed strictly for entertaining. You rent it for about seven hundred an hour, take your friends out, your customers, it holds about a hundred and fifty people. They set up a buffet in the lower deck, the salon. Topside there's a bar and a big open afterdeck."

"Wasn't it cold?"

"We wore coats, it wasn't bad. I told you, it was a benefit type of cruise, raise money for some foundation that has to do with promoting culture. Esther's into all that. Beautiful buffet, wine, any kind of booze you want—I only saw one guy smashed. Guy would finish a drink and throw his glass off the stern. The kind of thing you might see at a police outing, you and your buddies get together. No, this was a well-behaved crowd, so you noticed a jerk like this guy. Plus the fact when it got cold he put on a fur coat. Looked like some kind of wild animal standing up drinking martinis. Five hours, he must've had twenty silver bullets. I'm not kidding."

"Got his head bent pretty good."

"You'd think so, but he hardly showed it, outside of being obnoxious. I mean he didn't fall down or start a fight."

Chris turned from the window. His dad was on the sofa now, straightening the newspapers. "Where'd you go, south?"

"Yeah, down the river. They were making a movie on Belle Isle. We didn't know what was going on. Somebody said they were filming a car chase."

"Jerry Baker was assigned to it. He said they blew up some cars."

"Yeah, on the Detroit side, off the bridge. We heard about it but didn't see it. We had to go past on the Canadian side. This's a big boat, holds a hundred and fifty people."

"Jerry said it took all day to film the one shot. They built a ramp so the car would go flying off the bridge up in the air. They film guys shooting at the car with machine guns one day, then film the car exploding the next day. Jerry said most of the time all you do is stand around."

"We didn't see any of that," his dad said. "We cruised past the riverfront, checked to see if the Renaissance Center was still there, went down as far as Joe Louis Arena and came about. It was nice, they served the buffet, they had roast beef, chicken. . . . This guy, this jerk I mentioned'd drink his martini and throw the glass over the side? This guy, all by himself, sits *down* at the buffet table, people trying to get around him, and *eats* off the serving platters.

Pushes the salad around with his fork, finds a tomato, reaches over, spears a few shrimp, pulls the platter of smoked fish practically right in front of him. Unbelievable. You imagine? Who wants any salad after this guy's been eating out of the bowl? People have to walk around him— nobody says a word."

"I'm surprised you didn't."

"I almost did, I came close. Esther wouldn't let me. I'm telling you the truth, this guy must've had twenty martinis. One right after the other. Stopped to mess up the buffet table and went back at it. I don't know why he wasn't laid out on the deck."

"Fun on the river," Chris said.

"We had a nice time. . . . The guy was harmless, I shouldn't let it bother me."

"Who was he, you know?"

"No, and I see all these people coming up to him, shaking his hand, being very pleasant. This guy gives 'em a stupid grin, like he has no idea who they are. Acting goofy. I ask Esther, she can't believe I don't know who it is. So she tells me his name. . . . Now I can't think of it. Buddy? No, that's not it. I said to Esther, 'Where've I been? I must've been out blacktopping parking lots all my life, I never heard of this guy.' I said, 'What's he known for, outside of being a horse's ass?' Esther says you have as much dough as this guy you can do just about anything you want. Well, you can't argue with her there, you see the way these rich guys park in front of the Detroit Club. You or I, we double-park in front of a Coney, run in for a hot dog, it costs us forty bucks. And this guy also I find out never worked a day in his life. Anyway, what'd you do yesterday? You break down and call Phyllis?"

"That's over with."

"You feel okay about it?"

"I'm fine. I brought some case files home with me. Start reading up on sex crimes."

"How's it look?"

"There some weird people out there."

"Woody," his dad said, "that's the guy's name, Woody something."

Sunday afternoon Robin sprayed a circle around the Ricks brothers on the wall and began to fill it in, sweeping the surface with layers of red paint, gradually closing in on the names to take out WOODY first, then paused to look at

MARK

in the white center. Mark in the bull's-eye. The new Mark revealed last night at his brother's weird swimming party.

Mark doing lines at poolside in his wet silk undies. Mark getting high, talking about Goose Lake, playing tapes of groups they used to listen to in the sixties and early seventies. That was still the old Mark. The new one emerged as Mark came down from his high, sort of crash-landed and began to whine and roll his eyes, Mark trying to dramatize what it was like to have an idiot for a partner. (Interesting, Woody was an actual partner.) Robin, at ease in her black panties, began to frown and sympathize.

"But Mark, you're the one who makes it happen. You're the name, the star."

Of course he was, he admitted it, glancing at her breasts, telling her what it was like to feel his talent smothered. "What a waste," Robin said, noticing that as she continued to sympathize, Mark's gaze remained on her breasts. Before long he seemed to be speaking to them as Robin listened, telling her breasts he could be doing rock concerts at Cobo Hall and Joe Louis Arena. The money was there, all kinds of it. The problem was the immovable 250-pound moron sitting on it. Mark, before her eyes, presenting a new possibility, a different approach.

Monday afternoon Skip phoned from the bar in the Yale Hotel, Yale, Michigan.

"This town, I don't think it's changed a bit, except I couldn't find the goddamn dynamite place. I drove up and down M-19, I came back, went in the feed store and they said, Yeah, that's where it is, how come you couldn't find it? Shitkickers love to get smart with you, if you don't look like one of them. See, there isn't any sign on the place. I guess the house is the same, but there a lot more trees than I remember and they have a big new red barn with a white roof."

"Trees grow," Robin said.

"Is that right? Well, see, I didn't know that. So I got the guy's phone number and called, but nobody answered."

Robin said, "You're not going to buy it, are you?"

"No way. Michigan, I find out, you have to get permission from the State Police. No, I'm gonna wait till some farmer with ninety dollars and stumps to blow comes along and buys a case. He gets it home, then I'll lift it off him. Otherwise, if nobody comes along by tomorrow evening I'll have to bust into that barn. It's riskier, but then I know I'll get exactly what we need."

"Tomorrow," Robin said. "You're going to spend the night in Yale?"

"I don't have a choice. I don't want to drive all the way back to Detroit, I'm tired. We worked late to finish, then had to pack up. I'm suppose to go to the wrap party tonight but I'll be right here at the Sweet Dreams Motel. Honest, that's the name of it."

Robin said, "So I probably won't see you till tomorrow night."

"The latest. But it could be anytime, if the dynamite guy ever gets a customer."

"Whenever it is," Robin said, "call me here. Then I'll meet you at Mother's."

"You gonna stay with me?"

"You know I can't."

"Man, it's gonna be lonesome."

"Skip . . . ?"

He said, "Uh-oh. What?"

"Nothing's wrong. Listen, we may change our game plan. I ran into Woody."

"I was gonna ask you."

"I even got invited to his house. It looks exactly the same, all the heavy furniture, the life-size painting of Mom in the front hall, the only time she's ever appeared sober. . . . You know what we did?"

"I'm dying to hear."

"We went swimming. Woody makes you take your clothes off and go in the pool before you can have a drink or a line or whatever you want, he has everything. He cranks the stereo way up and everybody gets zonked. Donnell sort of lurks, the way their mom used to."

"Well, did you get Woody aside?"

"It wasn't the right time. The whole scene, it was too loud, confusing. Woody disappeared after a while, I don't know what happened to him." Robin paused. "I think we'll be taking a different approach anyway."

"Like what else you getting me into?"

"I have to work it out. But I will, don't worry."

"I'm not worried," Skip said. "I'm up here in Yale, Michigan, trying to rip off a case of dynamite in a rented Hertz car. What've I got to worry about?"

"I'm just about convinced we should go after Mark."

"He was there, huh?"

"Mark and Woody were together, but I don't think it was Mark's idea. Mark puts on his suave act, he still does that, wants you to think he's cool. And Woody still comes off as the lout, sort of an offensive Poor Soul. Only now Woody's got Mark by the ass for the rotten way Mark used to treat him. I have a hunch Mark even pimps for him."

"Well, you said Woody's got all the dough."

"Yeah, but I didn't think he had the brains to use Mark. That's what he seems to be doing."

"I guess you don't need brains if you're rich."

"Woody comes up with these shlock ideas—he loves those big Broadway musicals, *Oklahoma,* you know, *Fiddler on the Roof.* The next one they're doing is *Seesaw.*"

"Never heard of it."

"Full of hit tunes like 'Lovable Lunatic' and that showstopper 'It's Not Where You Start It's Where You Finish.' Meanwhile Mark's dying to put on rock concerts. Remember 'I Wanna Be Your Dog'?"

"Sure, old Iggy and the Stooges."

"Mark wants to sign Iggy Pop and make him a superstar."

"I'd go for that."

"Woody wants to get in touch with Gordon Macrae and see if he'll do *Carousel.*"

"Who's Gordon Macrae?"

"Remember Savage Grace? Ten Years After? The Fly-

ing Burritos? Mark dug out these old tapes Woody has—
Iggy doing 'I Wanna Be Your Dog'—all the groups we
heard at Goose Lake, the summer of 'seventy.''

Skip said, "That rock concert? I wasn't at Goose Lake.
They had me in the Washtenaw County jail for littering,
passing out all your pamphlets everybody threw away and
I got blamed for. I think ever since we met I been doing the
heavy work and you been having all the fun."

"I'm going to look it up," Robin said, "but I'm pretty
sure Mark's in my Goose Lake journal. Something I wrote
I think was like a prophecy."

"Goose Lake, sounds like a kiddie show."

"It wasn't bad. Woodstock without the rain and mud."

"Get laid by strangers. Was that your trip?"

"I knew everybody I slept with," Robin said. "You
should've been there."

"I should've been anywhere but in jail. Hey, I got one
for you. You remember Dick Manitoba and the Dictators?"

"Never heard of them."

"See, you don't know everything, do you?"

"I miss you," Robin said. "Anyway, if Mark's in my
Goose Lake journal I'm going to take it as a sign."

Skip said, "Does that make sense? If Woody's in
charge, what do we want to go after Mark for?"

"Because he needs a friend," Robin said. "Mark has a
major problem and could use some help. Trust me."

"Hey, Robin?"

"What?"

"I got another one. You remember Manfred Mann's
Earth Band?"

" 'Get Your Rocks Off,' " Robin said. " 'Bye."

She picked up the spray can from the desk, stepped to
the wall and swept the surface with paint until MARK

joined his brother, both of them now hidden beneath a brilliant socko design on the white wall, a sunburst, a bright red ball of fire, an explosion. . . .

Robin closed the red-covered notebook, her journal labeled MAY–AUGUST '70, and sat staring at the design on the white wall. Several minutes passed in silence before she picked up the phone and dialed Mark's office, murmured quietly to the young woman who answered, keeping her voice low, and then waited. Mark came on the line and Robin said, "Hi, you want to hear something funny?"

"Love to."

"You know the journal I kept?"

"Sure, I remember."

"I was looking through it, I came to something I wrote on August tenth, 1970." Robin paused. "If I tell you . . ."

"Wait, August 1970 . . ."

"We were at Goose Lake."

"Oh, right. Yeah, of course."

"You promise you won't laugh?"

"I thought you said it was funny."

"It is, but I don't want you to laugh."

"I promise."

"I wrote on that day, August tenth, 'I think I'm in love with Mark Ricks.' "

"Come on, really? Wow, listen, I don't think that's funny."

Robin said in her low voice, "You don't?"

8

On Tuesday, four twenty in the afternoon, the young woman with short red hair entered the lobby at 1300 Beaubien and stopped, uncertain. She expected to see police officers. What she saw was a bunch of black people with small children standing by the two elevators and in front of the glass-covered directory on the wall. It could be the lobby of an old office building, all tile and marble, and seemed small with the people waiting, the women holding on to the children trying to pull free. An elevator door opened and two young black guys came off grinning, playing with shoelaces in their hands, and were all at once gathered in by these people, who must be family. The young woman with short red hair edged her way around them and through a short hall that opened into another lobby, this one dismal with deep shadows, until she came to a long wooden counter beneath fluorescent lights. The uniformed police officer behind the near end of the counter, a black woman, looked up and said, "Can I help you?"

The young woman with short red hair said, "I want to report a rape."

The policewoman said, "This's Prisoner Detention," and glanced down the length of the empty counter. "You want to talk to somebody's with the precinct. They be right back. . . . I'll tell you what, or you can go up to Sex Crimes on seven, save you some time. Get off the elevator and turn right and it's all the way down the end of the hall. There be somebody up there will help you."

Chris was alone in the squad room, his desk piled with case folders he'd been going through for the past few days, learning about criminal sexual conduct in its varying degrees. At lunch he'd told Jerry Baker he didn't think he was going to like it. A guy throws a pipe bomb in somebody's house to settle a score, the guy could be wacko but at least his motive was clear. But why would any guy want to rape a defenseless woman? What was in his head? The interesting thing was that it didn't have that much to do with sex. Jerry Baker said, "Then what do you call it a sex crime for?" Chris told him the way he understood it, the rapist wanted to dominate or be destructive, or he gets off on somebody else's pain. So he picks on a woman he can handle. But the act didn't have that much to do with getting laid, per se. Chris said he wasn't sure he could interrogate a suspect they knew for a fact was guilty and not pound the shit out of the guy. It would require a certain amount of self-restraint. Or sit down and talk to the poor rape victim. That would be tough. He told Jerry the whole setup was different. Even the squad room. It was cleaner than other squad rooms, the desks were kept neater. There were even artificial flowers on some of the desks, if you could imagine, inside 1300. See, because it wasn't a twelve-man squad, it was a twelve-*person* squad, half the investigators were policewomen. Chris said he wasn't complainjng, not at all, it was just different.

Yesterday he'd walked down to six and stuck his head in at Firearms and Explosives to see what was going on. It reminded him of when he was in the eighth grade his family moved from the West Side to the East Side and all that summer he rode buses back to the old neighborhood to be with his friends. Chris was going to meet Jerry at Galligan's at five, have a couple before driving out to St. Clair Shores. Working Sex Crimes in his dad's Cadillac.

It was almost four thirty. Maureen Downey had the night duty. At the moment she was off somewhere. Maureen had spent a few years in Sex Crimes, then was in Homicide for a while and came back, she said because she didn't like all the blood you found at the scene or going to the morgue to look at bodies and get the Medical Examiner's report. Chris heard that sharp, clean sound of high heels on the tile floor and looked up expecting to see Maureen.

It was a young woman with short red hair, very attractive, maybe late twenties. She came in, Chris couldn't help notice the way her legs moved in her skirt: a short straight tan skirt that went from above her knees into a loose tan sweater. A soft leather handbag hung from her shoulder. She seemed calm, even as she said, "They told me downstairs to come here. . . . I want to report a rape."

As though she were telling him she wanted to report

an accident, something she had seen, but was not personally involved. Chris said, "Oh." He stood up, looked around and nodded toward a clean desk with blue flowers in a green ceramic bowl. He said, "I'm Sergeant Mankowski. If you'd like, we'll sit over there, have more room." Chris paused to watch the thigh movement in her skirt as she walked to the desk. He sat down again and opened and closed drawers till he found a yellow legal pad and a Preliminary Complaint Report form. Going over to the desk, where the young woman was seated now in a straight metal chair, Chris said, "This happen to someone in your family?"

She seemed surprised, the way her head raised. "It happened to *me*. I was forced against my will to have sex. If that isn't rape I don't know what is."

Chris noticed she had a slight southern accent, not much of one but it was there. She sat straight, looking up at him until he eased into the padded metal swivel chair behind the desk. Now they were looking at each other over the bowl of blue flowers. She had a long thin neck. Or it seemed long the way she was sitting upright or the way her hair ended just below her ears and stuck out on both sides, wavy red hair with a lot of body. Phyllis always had rollers in her pile of dark hair. Chris imagined this girl didn't have to fool with her hair much. He liked the way it ended and stuck straight out. She was holding herself rigid, showing him she was indignant, but didn't look as though she'd been beat up. Chris wondered if this was what they called in Sex Crimes a date rape.

"When did this assault take place?"

"Sunday morning, about two A.M."

Chris said, "Sunday? That was two days ago. Why're you just now reporting it?"

"What's the difference when it happened? I was raped."

Chris had been told eight out of ten rapes weren't even reported; they hadn't said anything about the ones that were reported late. "You know the suspect?"

She said, "*Sus*pect? I don't su*spect* he raped me, I know he did. I was there. Mr. Woodrow Ricks is his name."

There was that accent, soft, unaffected. It made her seem natural but also vulnerable. A guy rapes her, she calls him "Mister." Chris pictured the guy older. Looking at the PCR form he said, "I don't have your name and address."

She said, "I guess you want my real name. It's Greta Wyatt. My stage name I go by is Ginger Jones."

"You're an actress?"

"An actor; you don't say 'actress' anymore."

"I didn't know that." She did look more like a Ginger than a Greta. He liked Greta, though, better. "Let me have your address, too."

"I live for the time being at 1984 Junction."

Chris said, "No kidding. I used to live around there. Right by Holy Redeemer till I was in the eighth grade and we moved all the way over to the East Side, near Cadieux. I never wanted to leave that neighborhood."

"Well, you have a different feeling about it than I have," Greta said. "I can't wait to find a place and move out."

He liked her dry way of speaking, looking right at him. He asked for her phone number, wrote it down, and then her age. She told him she was twenty-nine.

"Married?"

"I was, I'm divorced."

"Children?"

"Not a one."

"You live alone?"

"I have been. It was my folks' house. They sold it when my dad retired from Ford's and they moved back home, to Lake Dick, Arkansas. I'm staying there just till the new people move in or they turn it into a Taco Bell, I don't know which."

"Is that where the assault took place?"

"Uh-unh, it was at Mr. Ricks'. I don't know the address, but he isn't there anyway, he's at the Playhouse. You know where I mean? That theater, it's just a few blocks from here. His big ugly limo was parked in front. I tried to see him. . . . I went there originally to see his brother. But they wouldn't let me in."

"What were you gonna say to him?"

"The rapist? Ask him if he'd like to come here with me, the son of a bitch. You want to meet him? Come on."

"We have to complete this report and have you sign a statement," Chris said. "Then what we do, advise him a complaint has been filed that could bring him up on a charge of criminal sexual conduct."

Greta said, "I love that police way you have of saying things. You're gonna advise him of a complaint—"

"I have to know his address," Chris said. "If it isn't in the City of Detroit it belongs in some other jurisdiction."

"It's in Palmer Woods off Seven Mile, great big mansion."

"That's the Twelfth." Good, it was a Detroit Police matter, he wouldn't have to give it to some cops out in a suburb. He wanted this one. "You were with this guy on a date and you went back to his house?"

"I was with his brother, Mark, the one owns the theater. He invited me on a cruise with him, this past Saturday, some kind of society thing to raise money, and after we got back we went to Woody's house for a party."

Chris took his time, looked up from the report form to Greta Wyatt. "Nice crowd of people, and here's this guy eating off the buffet table with both hands."

That opened her eyes.

"With a fur coat on," Chris said. "Is that the Woody we're talking about?"

"You *know* him?"

"You got off the boat and went out to Woody's. . . . Just you and Mark?"

"No, there were some other girls too. There were four of us from the boat, and then Mark picked up another one at Brownie's, but she was older. Somebody he used to know by the name of Robin. He spent practically the whole time with her."

"That make you mad?"

"Not a bit. I didn't know why he asked me, I just met him the day before. They were having auditions for *Seesaw* and I tried out because I played Gittel just a few years ago at the Dearborn Community Theater."

Chris said, "Gittel, huh?"

"Gittel Mosca. I thought I had the part, the way Mark was talking. Then I find out I have to go to bed with Woody."

"He told you that?"

"He practically did."

"Who, Mark or Woody?"

"It was when I went upstairs to change. Well, to dry off and put my dress back on." Greta stopped. "I forgot to mention, everybody had to go in swimming. If you didn't, Woody said his chauffeur would throw you in with your clothes on."

"Wasn't it cold?"

"The pool's inside the house, in a big room with a ceiling that goes up—like in a church."

"You have a bathing suit with you?"

Greta hesitated, but kept looking right at him. "I went in in my bra and panties."

Chris said, "Oh."

"The other girls didn't have bras. They looked at me like I was some kind of strange creature. It was like when we were little and we'd go swimming in the lake, this one girl's mama always made her wear a rubber inner tube. I felt like that little girl."

"The others didn't wear anything?"

"Couple of them didn't."

"So you were upstairs . . ."

"Uh-huh, and Woody came in the bedroom. I asked him to please leave, in a nice way, but he wouldn't."

"You have your clothes on?"

"I didn't have *any*thing on. He comes right in, goes 'Ooops,' but he knew I was there. He had two glasses of champagne with him."

"He make the moves on you earlier?"

"Uh-unh, not till then. He offered me a glass of champagne, I said no thanks, so he drank them both like in two gulps, dropped the glasses and came at me. That's when he said, 'Yes, you're Gittel.' See, what I mean? It was fairly obvious what the deal was. I told him no thank you, I didn't need the part that bad. But I could've been talking to the wall."

"What did Woody have on?"

"These tiny trunks you could barely see under his big stomach."

"Did he hit you?"

"Worse, he started kissing me, his mouth all wet and he had this awful breath from drinking so much."

"You scream?"

"For what? Who's gonna do anything? They're all

downstairs getting stoned. Woody just threw me down on the bed and got on top of me. You know what he kept saying? 'Boy-oh-boy.' "

"You tried to resist?"

"He turned me over so I couldn't, got my heinie up in the air and my face pressed down in the bedspread. I never felt so humiliated in my life."

Chris didn't want to ask her the next question, but had to. "He sodomized you?"

"No, he turned me over so I couldn't hit him. It wasn't long after that he got off me, rolled over on the bed and went to sleep."

Chris said, "Did he, you know, perform the act?"

"I guess as far as he was concerned. He's laying there, this big tub, he starts snoring with his mouth open. That's a sight's gonna stay with me, if you can picture it."

"What'd you do then?"

"I got up and looked for something to hit him with."

"You didn't, did you?"

"I left."

Chris wasn't sure if that was an answer to his question.

"You didn't tell anybody what happened?"

"I came downstairs, Mark and his friend Robin were gone."

"You know Robin's last name?"

"I wasn't introduced to any of them. The other girls had cute names like Suzie and Duzie. The chauffeur opened the front door for me, gives me a little smile and goes, 'You come back and see us, you hear?' If I had thought of it at the time I would've said, 'Yeah, with cops.' I walked all the way over to Seven Mile and Woodward, went in a place to call a taxi and you know what it was? A motorcycle gay bar. I'll tell you something—what's your name again?"

"Chris."

"Chris, you live half your life in a house the refrigerator's on the front porch and come up here a teenager, I'll tell you, it's a shock to your system."

Chris said, "You're really from a place called Lake Dick?"

"Don't ask me who Dick was," Greta said. "I left there innocent and grew up as fast as I could. I got into acting and have worked for scale or below all my life, waiting for the big break. I was in that movie they were shooting here. I read for a part, it was a scene in a bar where I've just met this cop and I try to guess what he does for a living. The director said, 'Do it again, just like that.' I took the part not knowing anything about the movie or how much I'd get paid. But I had a choice. They tell me I have to go to bed with a fat drunk if I want a part, that's a choice too. I'll do it or I won't, it's up to me. But when I get raped against my will, then I'm gonna make some noise and tell in a court of law what the son of a bitch did to me. I don't care who he is."

Chris said, "Well"—taking his time—"what's gonna make it difficult, you report a one-on-one type of situation two days later, there's no evidence, nothing to use against him outside of your testimony."

Greta was frowning. "What do you mean, evidence?"

"See, ordinarily, if the complainant calls us right away a radio car goes to the scene, the woman is brought to Detroit General for a physical exam and usually her panties are taken as evidence."

"Her *pan* ties?"

"They might be torn, they might have traces of semen. Or they find semen, you know, inside the complainant. It's checked for blood type to match against the suspect's. But we don't have any evidence like that, nothing."

"So you aren't gonna do anything."

"I'll call him, have him come in . . ."

"When, next week sometime? I just saw his limousine over at the theater, but you're gonna call him when you feel like it."

"I'll call him as soon as we finish," Chris said, willing to be patient with Greta Wyatt, have a reason to look at her, listen to her talk. "I'll have him come in, ask him if he wants to bring a lawyer. . . . You understand, we can know beyond a reasonable doubt the man's guilty, but if we violate his rights in any way he's gonna walk."

Greta said, "Well, thank you very much," getting up, pulling at her short skirt. "I already tried to see his brother, Mark. 'Greta who?' the girl in the office wants to know. 'What is this about?' I work up my nerve to come here, you're worried about Woody's rights being violated. Hell with mine. I wish you'd taped this so you could play it back and hear what a pathetic little weenie you sound like."

Chris said, "Wait, okay? If I type up your statement, will you sign it?"

It didn't seem likely. She was walking out.

"Greta, if you'll cooperate we can at least bring him in. See if we can get him to admit it."

That turned her around at the door.

"Woody put it a little different. He said if I'd cooperate we could fall in love."

9

Chris left his dad's Cadillac in the lot on Macomb, across from 1300, and walked down to Galligan's, thinking:

What kind of an impression was he making lately? There was the St. Antoine Clinic doctor accusing him of being a macho fraud if not bisexual. There was Phyllis practically calling him a pervert for going to Sex Crimes. His own dad looking at him funny, wondering why he was having so much trouble with women. Now a rape victim, a really good-looking one, had accused him of being a wee-nie. Walking along Beaubien in this old downtown section, past Greektown now, cars jammed into the narrow street, he couldn't get it out of his mind. Back when he was driving a radio car, a drunk, some guy being restrained from knock-ing the shit out of his wife, might look at Chris's nameplate on his uniform and call him a dumb fucking Polack. But no one had ever insinuated he was a pervert or called him a weenie. Jesus. He had never met a girl named Greta before, either.

He walked with his head down, serious, looking at the sidewalk, telling himself, Well, you go through shitty periods, things happen, you get your car stolen. . . . Things build up and you see everything at once instead of taking them one at a time. You start looking into the future and then you have doubts. The fuck are you doing? You should've gone into something else, computers, robotics. Right, get into something guaranteed to bore the shit out of you. Deal with *things.* Get a boat. He thought of times when he was a uniform, and kids, every once in a while, would do that number, "Your old man work? No, he's a cop." His dad had his own version of it. "You could've taken over the business, lease a new Cadillac every year." Estimating how many yards of "ashphalt" to do a shopping center parking lot. He'd say to his dad, "What I always wanted, a new car every year," and his dad wouldn't get it. Except he had to admit his dad's Cadillac Seville wasn't bad, sitting in there in all that quiet, effortless luxury. It beat the shit out of his Mustang that was now down south somewhere, repainted. Chris looked up and it was strange, in that moment, the way his mood suddenly changed and he came to life.

Parked at the curb next to Galligan's, on the Beaubien side of the two-story building, was a gray stretch limo.

He knew who the car belonged to even as he approached, walked past, and there it was confirmed on the rear end, the vanity plate that said WOODY. It was a nice day for a change, about 68 degrees, late-afternoon sun hot on the glass towers of the Renaissance Center, right there across Jefferson rising up seven hundred feet against a clear sky. A nice day to be out. Chris put his hands in his pants pockets and stood looking at the car with a feeling he liked. Being on the edge of something about to happen. At least the possibility. His dad had said one time, "You guys, you walk into a situation you get to quit thinking and act like cops." Maybe there was some truth in it.

See what happens and react. There was no way to make an arrest. But the guy who'd raped the girl who called him a weenie was close by. In Galligan's or in the car, hidden behind the black windows. Chris was standing there with his hands in his pockets when the driver appeared, rising from the street side of the limo, the driver saying, "The man should be back presently."

"Is that right?" Chris said. "What're you telling *me* for?"

"Say up there on the sign No Parking," the driver said, "and you the police, aren't you?" The guy politely offhand about it in his tailored black suit, his white shirt and black tie. Neat mustache, hair lacquered back. . . .

But also with a dull threat in his stare, a look Chris recognized, knew all about, though he said to the guy, "I don't know you. I remember times and places and you're not in any of them." Chris walked up to the limo to get a closer look across the pale gray top.

The driver shook his head back and forth, twice. "No, we never met."

"Then it must be my sporty attire caught your eye," Chris said. He was wearing his navy blazer with tan corduroy pants, a deep blue shirt and tie. "Is that it?"

"Must be," the driver said. "Or how you got something wrong with your hip, make your coat stick out funny."

Chris said, "Where'd you do your time, Jackson? Or they send you to Marquette?"

"Man, what're you coming down on me for?"

Chris said, "Because you're about an inch away from fucking with me, but now you know better. You're gonna watch that attitude your parole officer told you about."

The driver said, "Oh, man," shaking his head. "You right out of the book. Old-time dick like all of 'em, dumb as shit."

Chris laid his hands on the round edge of the car roof. "Where do you want to go with this?"

The driver said, "I don't want to take it no place. I don't want to take *nothing*. You understand what I'm saying to you?"

Chris said, "Why don't you get in the car and drive around the block. You'll feel better and I'll feel better." Chris already felt better. The driver was a stand-up guy and wanted him to know it, that's all. Okay, Chris knew the guy and now the guy knew him, the guy still giving him the look but with a little more life in his eyes. The look with the heavy lids would be a natural part of him, his style, to warn people he was bad and they better know it. That was okay, it was probably true. But it wasn't something between them that had to be settled. Chris said, "We're too old and ma- ture to get in a fist fight," and saw the guy's expression give a little more. The guy seemed about to say something, but then his gaze moved. Chris looked over his shoulder.

A beefy guy, his sportcoat open, trousers riding below his belly, was coming along the sidewalk from Galligan's corner entrance. And now the driver was at the back of the car, coming around to this side to open the door. Chris had to step away. Now he saw, beyond the guy, Greta Wyatt coming, trying to run in her heels, grabbing the strap of the handbag slipping from her shoulder. She was swinging it at the fat guy now as she caught up with him, yelling, "Chris, it's Woody!"

Look at her, hanging onto the guy, fighting him. But what amazed Chris more than anything—she remembered his name. Yelling it again, "Chris, help me!" He was moving toward them now, hurrying as he saw Woody grab hold of her wrist in both hands and slam her, hardly with an effort, against the side of the building. Chris saw her head hit the wall, got there and caught her bouncing off, stumbling into his arms, as Woody walked past them to his car.

Chris held her against the wall now, his hands gripping her shoulders. He said, "Look at me." Late sunlight in her face; he could see freckles beneath her makeup, her cheekbone scraped. "Can you see me?" Greta nodded, brown eyes staring at him. She seemed dazed. "Can you stand up by yourself?" She nodded again. "You better sit down." She shook her head. "Okay, but don't move." He took his hands away slowly, making sure. "I'll be right back."

Woody was inside the limo, the driver closing the door as Chris walked up.

"Open it."

"Nothing happened, man. Let it go."

"Open it."

"The lady was bothering him."

"Lean on the car," Chris said. "You know how, with your legs spread. You got two seconds. One . . ."

Woody's driver said, "Let me tell you something."

"Two . . ."

Woody's driver said, "All right. But don't touch me. You understand? Don't touch me." He turned to the car.

Chris opened the rear door. He had to stoop, lean in to see Woody in the dark against gray upholstery, the man's size filling half the seat. Chris said, "I'm a police officer. Will you step out of the car, please?"

Woody wasn't looking at him. He had a remote control

switch in his right hand and he was watching television, the set mounted next to decanter bottles on a corner shelf behind the facing seat. Woody said, "What?"

"I said I want you to step out of the car."

Woody frowned, his tongue moving around in his mouth. He said, "I just got in the car," still not looking at Chris. "Didn't I just get in? Yeah, I'm watching 'People's Court.' It's good. See, this woman says her boyfriend borrowed eighty bucks and won't pay her back."

Chris could smell salted peanuts. The guy was eating them from a can wedged between his fat thighs, raising his hand in a fist to his mouth, then wiping the palm of his hand on his pants.

"Sir, are you gonna step out of the car?"

Woody glanced at Chris now as he said, "I told you, I'm watching TV."

Chris said, "You don't get your ass out of there right now I'm gonna pull you out," and couldn't believe it when the guy put both of his hands over the can of peanuts, turned a shoulder to Chris and yelled, "Donnell! Who is this?"

Chris said, "I don't want your peanuts, I want *you.*" He stared at the guy another moment before coming out of the car to see the driver looking past his shoulder at him.

"Gonna pull the man out? I have to see this."

"He's resisting arrest. Explain it to him."

"You asking me to help you?"

"You'll feel better," Chris said. "Citizen cooperation being the key to a safer community. Tell him, he behaves I won't cuff him."

Donnell said, "Shit," and smiled, showing himself for the first time. "You never gonna bring him up. Print that man, his lawyer will sue your police ass."

"I've got assault on him, and that's just for openers."

Donnell said, "The man watches 'People's Court,' on the TV? Now and again I take him to Frank Murphy, see felony exams, see a guy standing on first degree cut up his woman, it's the same as TV to him, you dig? It's a show. That's the only time, the only reason the man will ever be in a court. You understand what I'm saying?"

"Where'd he get you, Donnell?"

"We go way back."

"Donnell what?"

"Hey, you want me or you want him?"

"I can't make up my mind," Chris said.

He looked over at Greta. She was watching him, holding a Kleenex to her face, her red hair on fire in the sunlight. He could see the way it winged out straight on both sides and made her slim neck look vulnerable. He could see it clearly against the tan-painted wall. Her hair, her legs in the short skirt. . . .

Chris turned, stooped and reached in for Woody, sitting in his limo eating peanuts, watching TV; said, "Come on, get outta there," and Woody raised one leg without looking and kicked at him until Chris came out of the doorway.

Donnell said over his shoulder, "You gonna need your SWAT team."

Chris went over to Greta holding the Kleenex to her face. She looked stoned. He brought her to the car, motioning Donnell out of the way, and opened the passenger-side front door. "You ride up here," Chris said. "Don't say anything to Woody, okay?"

"You're asking a lot."

She said it just above a whisper, looking at him. He held on to her arm, feeling a slender part of her in his hand beneath the sweater, until she was inside, closed off behind the black glass. Donnell was waiting for Chris to look at him.

"You expect me to drive you?"

"I think you're gonna give me some shit," Chris said, "but in the end, yeah, you will. So why don't you save us some time?"

"Man, I could see you coming," Donnell said. "I say to myself, There's one, look at him. See, even if I have any doubt, like you knew how to dress, you open your mouth you give it away."

Chris said, "Is that it? You through?"

"Play the hard-nose dick with me. Nothing ever changes, does it? Not if you like the way it is, you the *man*, huh? You call it. Well, you fuck with that man in there, you have something to learn."

Chris said, "Now are you through? You gonna get in?"

"I'm not driving you *no* place."

Chris said, "Okay, don't. When he asks me where you are, what do I tell him? You got tired and went home?"

Donnell kept looking at him but didn't answer.

"See? You really want to drive," Chris said. "You just didn't know it."

10

Twenty minutes from the time Robin arrived at Mark's apartment they were in bed. Robin's feeling was that if you ball a guy in a limo, in a tent and in the woods your first weekend together seventeen years ago, you could be taking off your clothes as you walked in, it was going to happen. But why hurry? They planned to spend the evening together. She wasn't surprised by Mark's serious look—the little guy was nervous—or the way he'd gone about setting the mood with cool bossa nova and chilled wine, lamps turned low, maroon silk sheet turned back. . . . This was the drill with successful guys his age, proud of their technique but, my God, so studied with the prolonged toying, the toe-sucking, all the moves they learned in magazines to bore the shit out of the poor bimbos they picked up in singles bars. Robin went along, writhed, moaned, finally asked him, "Mark, are we gonna fuck or not?" and was happy to see the old spunk still turned him on. Toward the end Robin gave him authentic gasps, came down gradually as Mark twitched and shuddered, opened her eyes as she heard him say, "Wow. That was dynamite."

Robin said, "It wasn't bad." She took her handbag from the bedside table into the bathroom, freshened herself and flipped the tape in the Panasonic recorder. She liked the way he referred to dynamite off the top of his head, but doubted that she had anything useful on the tape. Not yet, anyway.

Mark came out of his walk-in closet with two identical black silk robes, checked the size of one and gave it to Robin: phase two of the young executive drill, his-and-her shorty robes, playsuits worn over bare skin. They went into the living room and became part of it, Robin realized, blending with the silver and black decor, chrome and glossy black fabrics, black and white graphics on the wall she believed were nudes. Robin moved toward the big window, an evening sky outside, and Mark, pouring wine, said, "You've seen the river. It hasn't changed." He looked up and said, "You haven't either. Come here." Robin obeyed, joined him on the sofa, placed her handbag on the floor close between their bare legs, and let him study her profile as she stroked her braid and gazed out at the black and silver room.

He said, "You really haven't changed."

Robin remained silent.

He said, "You turn me on."

Robin said, "Maybe it's the robe."

"You like it, it's yours."

"Thanks, Mark, but it feels used. If I want a robe I'll get my own."

He liked that, shining his brown eyes at her. He liked her attitude, she began to realize, because he wanted some of it to rub off on him.

"I'm not kidding, you really turn me on."

She said, "That's what I'm here for."

"I don't mean just in bed."

She said, "I know what you mean."

He told her she made him feel different, got him worked up again the way she used to during the movement days when they were raising hell, running a campus revolution. He told her he felt the same way now, he could look at her and get high.

Aw, that was nice. It softened her mood. She said, "I missed you, Mark." She said it was weird, the feeling that she had to see him again. "Why now, after so many years?"

"I could feel it too," Mark said. He told her it was like some kind of extrasensory communication. Like they were thinking of each other at the same time and the energy of it, like some kind of force, drew them together. He told her that when he walked into Brownie's his mind had flashed instantly on everything they did together during that time. And now when he thought of her he'd feel a rush, like he could do anything he wanted.

"You can," Robin said. "What's the problem?" Making it sound as though there wasn't one.

"I told you: Woody."

Mark said that at this point in time she was the only person he could talk to, because she knew where he was coming from, the way it used to be with Woody, Woody always there but sort of tagging along, never part of the action. He told her this was the reason he'd brought it up the other night, his situation, Woody holding him down, smothering him.

"I felt you reaching out," Robin said.

"People don't understand. Guys I have lunch with at the DAC, they're into investments, venture capital, they don't know from rock concerts. That's what I want to do, produce concerts. But why should I have to bust my ass, go out and borrow money when it's right there, in the family? When it's as much mine as his?"

"It's a matter of principle," Robin said.

"Exactly. You know how long I've been carrying him?"

"Forever," Robin said. "But why doesn't Woody want to do rock concerts? Why *Seesaw?*"

"Yeah, or *The Sound of Music,* for Christ sake, *Oklahoma.* He's the one comes up with these dinosaurs, but I'm the producer, it's my name goes on the playbill."

"Not exactly hip," Robin said. "It looks to me like he's trying to get you to quit."

"You ask him for money, you know how he gives it to you? He hands you the check, only he holds onto it and it's like a tug-o'-war until he decides to let go." Mark was starting to whine.

"He resents you," Robin said, "your looks, your personality, everything about you."

"I know it, he's jealous, he's always been. Now he's getting back at me. It's all he cares about. But if I weren't there to run the show, you know what would happen? He'd fall flat on his ass."

Robin said, "But would it hurt him?"

Mark hesitated. He said, "No," sounding resigned, at low ebb. "Not with his hundred-million-dollar cushion."

Now Robin paused. "That much?"

"Close to it."

She watched him drink his wine and refill the glass. Poor little guy, he needed a mommy. She reached out and touched his arm. "Mark?" Felt his muscle tighten and took that as a good sign. "Let's get down to what this is all about. The reason you have a wealthy two-hundred-and-fifty-pound drunk sitting on you is because he happened to get the estate and you got screwed. But you stay close to Woody, you put up with him, because at least half that hundred million should be yours. Am I right?"

"That's right."

"Do you ever talk to him about it?"

"He thinks it's funny. I tell him it isn't fair and he grins at me."

"So there's no chance he'll ever cut you in."

"Not unless he dies."

"I was about to ask," Robin said. "If something happens to Woody, are you his heir?"

Mark nodded, sipping his wine.

"You assume that, or you know it for a fact?"

"That's the way it's set up, the trust succession. A couple of foundations get a piece of it and some aunt I don't even know, but I get most of it. At least two-thirds."

"Sixty million," Robin said.

"Something like that. The trust keeps making money."

"So now you're waiting . . . hoping maybe he'll drink himself to death?"

"You see how he was the other night? It could happen."

"Yeah, but Mark, who do you think should decide your future, you or Woody's liver?"

"That's good," Mark said, grinning at her. "That's very good."

Robin watched him look off, nodding, thinking about

it. She said, "Mark?" And waited for him to come back to her, eyes shining, hopeful. "You want to hear a better one than that?"

A woman detective named Maureen Downey asked if she just happened to run into Mr. Ricks at Galligan's. Greta said she went in when she saw his car parked there. The woman detective, Maureen, had nice teeth and appeared to be a healthy outdoor girl. Greta could see her teeth even in this dark end of the lobby that seemed like part of an empty building. The others were across the room at the counter, under the fluorescent lights: Chris Mankowski—who seemed to know what he was doing now, if he didn't before—Woody Ricks, his driver, Donnell, and three uniformed officers, not counting the ones behind the counter. Woody Ricks had not shut up since they brought him in, but Greta could not hear what he was saying. Maureen Downey asked if she felt all right. Greta said her head hurt a little and she kept swallowing, afraid she was going to throw up, but didn't feel too bad outside of that. Maureen said they were going to take her to the hospital. Greta said, Oh, no. Maureen said it was just across the street on St. Antoine; make sure she was okay. There was a commotion over at the counter. Greta saw two of the uniformed officers taking Woody by his arms, Woody trying to twist away from them. She saw Chris Mankowski pull a gun from under his coat, stuck in his pants, and hand it to the black policewoman behind the counter. He then took hold of Woody's necktie and led him to what looked like a freight elevator at the end of the counter, the two officers still holding on to Woody's arms. They went into the elevator and the door closed. Greta asked Maureen where they were taking him. Maureen said up to Prisoner Detention on nine. She said Mr. Ricks was not helping his case any: he'd be held overnight because of the way he was acting and be arraigned in the morning at Frank Murphy. Greta said, Oh, boy. Not too happy. She lowered her head to rest it on her hand. Maureen got up from the bench they were sitting on, saying she'd be right back, and walked over to the counter. Not a minute later Greta looked up to see Woody's driver, Donnell, standing in front of her. Donnell said, "You in trouble now, if you don't know it." Greta said, "Why don't you go to hell." He stood there looking down at her until she heard Maureen coming, Maureen calling Donnell by name, telling him to keep away from her. Donnell left and Maureen said, "Did he threaten you?" Greta shook her head, swallowing. She didn't feel like talking, not even to Maureen.

Skip remembered Robin's mom's house, big country place made of fieldstone and white trim with black shutters, off Lone Pine in Bloomfield Hills and worth a lot. The kind of house important executives lived in. He liked the idea of staying here but arrived bitchy; he'd been ready to come last night and Robin wasn't home.

"I was working," Robin said, bright-eyed, glad to see her old buddy, "and I have a tape to prove it."

"Full of grunts and groans," Skip said. "I know what you were doing. Me, I'm looking out the window of the Sweet Dreams Motel at car headlights. Did the farmer see me sneaking out of his barn? Shit, I don't know. Hey, but you know what else I got, sitting right there? A sack of ammonium nitrate fertilizer. On the way back I bought a couple alarm clocks. They're not the kind I wanted, but they'll do."

"When you're happy, I'm happy," Robin said. She showed him the way: in the side door from the attached garage and downstairs to the basement bar–recreation room, Skip with the case of Austin Powder, *Emulex 520* written on the side, *Used in 1833 and Ever Since.* Robin had his luggage, a hanging bag and a carryon. She told him he'd have to stay down here, not wander around or fool with any of the lamps that were on timers. The Bloomfield Hills cops could know which lights were supposed to be on. "Some fun," Skip said.

She had taken the shelves out of the refrigerator so he could slip the whole dynamite case in. Skip told her it wasn't necessary unless she wanted it out of the way in a safe place. Robin said it was how they'd stored it back in the golden age, shoved the sticks in there with the Baggies of grass and the leftover brown rice dishes. Remember? She said, "We'd sit at the kitchen table and you'd wire the sticks to the battery and the clock while I read the directions to you out of *The Anarchist Cookbook.*"

"Like a couple of newlyweds," Skip said. "I also picked up a lantern battery, I forgot to mention, hanging around Yale with my finger up my butt."

"You're ready to go," Robin said, "aren't you?"

"Depending what we're gonna blow up."

"Woody's limo."

"Not the theater, late at night?"

"The limo," Robin said. "With Woody in it. And Donnell too, his driver."

"What've we got against Donnell?"

"I don't like him."

Skip said, "I bet you said hi to him and he didn't remember who you were."

"If Woody's in the car, so is Donnell," Robin said. "How about when he turns the key?"

"Woody could still be in the house."

"You're right. . . . Maybe some kind of a timer then."

"We've used timers. We used 'em at the Federal Building, the Naval Armory, that bank downtown, but it was when nobody was in those places."

"Time it to go off while they're driving along."

"If we knew he went someplace every day."

"He does, he goes out all the time."

"But we'd have to know exactly when. I don't think it'd be good if it blew in traffic, take out some poor assholes going home to their dinner."

"You want to do it at his house."

"Yeah, keep it neat," Skip said. "Lemme think on it."

They went upstairs to the kitchen Skip said would make Betty Crocker come, one look at it, man, all the spotless conveniences, the copper pans he bet cost more than new tires. He told Robin Betty Crocker was the best-looking woman he ever saw and would like to meet her sometime, while Robin fooled with the tape recorder, stopping and starting, listening to voices, until she said, "Okay," and they heard Mark's voice say, "You really haven't changed. . . . You turn me on."

Skip said, "Jesus, he's serious, isn't he?"

Robin said, "Wait." She stopped the tape and ran it forward, stopped and listened to bits of conversation until she was ready for Skip again. "Here we are. You have to understand Mark wants help but is afraid to come right out and ask. He's just told me that if Woody dies he gets about two-thirds of the estate. Something like sixty million."

Skip said, "You mean it?"

"Listen." Robin punched the ON button and voices came out of the recorder.

ROBIN: So now you're waiting . . . hoping maybe he'll drink himself to death?

MARK: You see how he was the other night? It could happen.

ROBIN: Yeah, but Mark, who do you think should decide your future, you or Woody's liver?

Skip grinned, listening, fooling with his beard.

MARK: That's good. . . . That's very good.

Skip said, "You had that one ready."
Robin said, "Listen."

ROBIN: Mark? . . . You want to hear a better one than that?

There was a silence. Skip, running his hand over his chin, smoothing his beard now, looked at Robin.

ROBIN: What would you say if you didn't have to wait? If Woody were to suddenly disappear?

Skip said, "Shit," grinning.

MARK: How?

ROBIN: In a cloud of smoke.

Skip was still grinning, shaking his head.

MARK: Is this like a magic trick?

"Jesus Christ," Skip said.

ROBIN: Something like it, only better.

MARK: Yeah? Why?

ROBIN: Because once he disappears he never comes back. What would you say to that?

MARK: I think I'd say . . . yeah, I'd say how much is a trick like that worth?

ROBIN: You mean what does a trick like that cost, don't you? What it's worth to you is everything. Sixty million. Right?

MARK: It might not be that much.

ROBIN: Mark, if you're not interested . . .

MARK: I didn't say that.

ROBIN: Then don't fuck with me. Either you want Woody gone or you don't.

Skip made a face, pretending to be surprised.

MARK: I'm not sure I know what that means.

ROBIN: Yes, you do. Gone means gone.

MARK: Well, let's say like if I *were* to go along with it . . .

ROBIN: Cut the shit, Mark. You're a big boy. You say yes or no. If you say yes, your troubles are over. If you say no, you're on your own.

MARK: I don't know what you're gonna do.

ROBIN: Of course not. You don't want to know.

MARK: All right. How much?

ROBIN: You want it done?

Silence. Skip didn't move.

MARK: Yes.

ROBIN: Two million.

"Jesus Christ," Skip said.

ROBIN: We'll work out the payment, make it look like an investment.

Silence.

MARK: All right.

Skip raised his eyebrows at Robin, who stared back at him, holding up her hand.

ROBIN: There's one thing you have to do.

MARK: What?

ROBIN: Get me a key to Woody's limo.

MARK: How would I do that?

ROBIN: Mark . . . if that's all you have to do, don't you think you'll find a way?

MARK: I guess so.

ROBIN: Will you do it?

Silence.

MARK: Okay.

Robin pushed the OFF button. Skip sat at the kitchen counter nodding, thinking about it. He looked up at Robin. "What do you need the car key for?"

"So you can get in. I'm sure they keep it locked."

"Shit, that's no problem. I'd rather do it myself than wait for little Markie."

"I want him involved," Robin said.

"He's involved. He said yeah, he's gonna pay to see his brother disappear. What else you want?"

"How about a way to do it?"

Skip said, "How 'bout when Woody comes out to the car and the Black-ass Panther opens the door for him?"

"I like it," Robin said.

"Same as the one I did in L.A. many years ago. Put the charge in the trunk of the car. Dynamite, about five sticks is all, ammonium nitrate and a plastic bottle of fuel oil. Insert blasting cap in a stick and run two wires from it—one to the battery, the other to a clothespin that's got copper around each end where it snaps together—and run a third wire back to the battery. You got it?"

"You wedge the clothespin open," Robin said.

"You got it. Use a little hunk of wood and run a line from it through the trunk and around the side of the back seat and hook it to the door with a safety pin. The door opens, it pulls the wedge out of the clothespin, your circuit is closed, and the car goes up in a great big ball of fire."

Robin said, "How do you know which door he'll open?"

"If I have any doubts I'll wire 'em both."

"You're my hero," Robin said.

"What do I get for being it?"

"You get to trip," Robin said. "I brought you a present."

11

Chris was going to visit Greta on Wednesday, but before he was out of 1300, Wednesday had become one of the worst days of his life and he never made it to the hospital. He did call, late, and a nurse told him Greta was diagnosed as having a mild concussion and would probably be released in the morning, after the doctor looked at her. When he walked into Detroit General Thursday about 10 A.M. Greta had on her sweater and skirt, anxious to leave. She said, "This's the scariest hospital I've ever been in." Chris told her it was old. "I don't mean how it looks," Greta said. "There people in here handcuffed to their beds. I think half the patients have gunshot wounds." Chris said, Well, some of them. Outside in the sunlight he asked if he could drive her home or anywhere. Greta said she had a car.

After that, walking along St. Antoine toward the parking structure, she was quiet. He asked her if she felt okay. She said, Fine. Then she said, "How come this morning, Maureen stops by to talk? She tells me I have to come up to sign the complaint and all, acting like it's her case now. I asked where you were, she said you were busy."

"I was taken off," Chris said.

"Why?"

"It has to do with the way cases are assigned, according to the workload." He glanced at Greta and saw her eyes narrowed at him.

She said, "I can tell if you're lying."

"It's true."

"Yeah, but something happened you're not telling me about."

"Maureen's a pro," Chris said. "You have nothing to worry about."

He didn't have to dodge or add to that. They were in the parking structure now, Greta looking around. She said, "I left it right in this aisle, I *know* I did. It's a light-blue Ford Escort." After a while she said, "Shit. Somebody stole my car. Is that possible, a block from the police station?"

"They get stolen closer to it than that," Chris said.

They walked back to 1300, into the Clinton Street entrance and the dismal lobby that belonged to the First Precinct. At the counter Greta told the sergeant wearing a white uniform shirt her car had been stolen just two blocks from here, an '84 Ford Escort, light blue, license number 709-G something, like GTN. Or, wait, maybe it was 907. The sergeant asked to see her registration. Greta told him it was in the car, in the glove compartment. The sergeant said he would have to have proof of ownership before he could make out a report. Greta said, "You saw me here the other day, didn't you? You know who I am. You think I'm lying? It's got brand-new snow tires on it I bought at Sears instead of leaving this dumb town like I should've."

Chris, standing on one foot and then the other, said, "Sergeant, why don't you quit acting like a hard-on and just write the report. So we can get out of here."

The sergeant, in his starched white bodyshirt, looked at Chris and said, "From what I understand you're already out of here. I don't need any grief from you. I'll write the report when I know to my satisfaction a vehicle owned and operated by this lady's been stolen. I'd be a lieutenant right now if I hadn't filled out a PCR one time containing false information that could've been verified."

Chris said, "I'm surprised you're not a commander by now."

The desk sergeant said, "You ought to know better than that."

Chris said, "What I mean is, you're hard-assed enough to be one."

He drove Greta home in his dad's '87 Cadillac Seville, maroon with gold pinstriping. Greta didn't comment on the car or appear to wonder how he could afford to own it. On the way across West Fort Street, past warehouses and railroad freight yards, the Ambassador Bridge arching across to Canada in the car's windshield, she pinned him down.

"Are you gonna tell me what happened?"

"What do you want to know?"

"Before, you said you'd been taken off the case. And then that cop said something about your being out. Out of *here*. What'd he mean by that?"

"I've been suspended," Chris said.

"What does that mean?"

"I'm no longer a police officer. Until, if and when I'm reinstated."

"They kicked you out? Why?"

"You want the official reason or the real one?"

"Both."

"The real reason is because I put Woody in jail. His lawyer called the mayor's office and they dropped it on the department. Get the assault charge against Woody withdrawn on the grounds *he* was the one assaulted, not you, that he was defending himself and I overreacted and used force without due cause."

Greta said, "Wait a minute, he *raped* me."

"I'm not talking about the sexual assault, you can still press that one. I mean the one that put you in the hospital. The lawyer threatened to sue the police department and the city, this is on the grounds that Woody was falsely arrested, unless the charge against him is withdrawn and I'm suspended from the force subject to dismissal."

Greta said, "A rapist can do that?"

"I guess if you're from one of the right families or your lawyer is."

"Why take it out on you?"

"They got mad. You go after who you can get."

"That's the real reason. What's the official one?"

"They gave it to my commander, find some excuse to dump me, and he did. I've been suspended indefinitely and told to keep my mouth shut, pending a board hearing."

"For what?"

"Having a residence outside the city limits."

"You're kidding. You have to live in Detroit?"

"It's one of the rules."

"Then why don't you?"

"I did till last Saturday. It's a long story." There was

a silence. Chris said, "It's not that long a story, but if I told you about it you'd give me one of your funny looks. And I want you to have confidence in me. You'll have Maureen, but I'll be around too, in case you need me."

"Why?"

"Because I want to help you."

"Yeah, but why, if it's not your job?" She put her hand on his arm and said, "*I* got you fired. My God, I just realized that."

"No, you didn't, Woody did. Don't feel bad or give it another thought, okay? It's my problem and I'll handle it one way or another, depending on how chickenshit the department wants to be. But what it shows us, more than anything, is how much clout Woody's got. What'll happen, you'll probably hear from Woody's lawyer, thinking you've already signed the complaint, and he'll ask you to come in. You say no thanks. So then he'll give you a bunch of shit on the phone how it saddens him a nice girl like you is gonna get dragged through a lot of unnecessary mud. He'll probably tell you he has witnesses who'll swear you made the moves on Woody, took him to bed."

"Then I wouldn't have a chance, huh?"

"If you go to trial they'll do everything they can to make you look bad. You have to consider that. The lawyer could even give Woody a Bible to read in court, I've seen it. But he's gonna have months to work on you, the lawyer, before you ever go to trial, if you do, and I'm sure he'll try to scare the hell out of you."

Greta said, "I won't answer the phone if it rings."

She was afraid already. Chris could hear it in her voice.

"Maureen'll get the names of everybody who was at that swimming party, see what they have to say. One or two might have it in for Woody, for some reason love the idea of putting it to him. I told Maureen I might talk with Mark

Ricks after she got through with him. Maureen said okay, just don't tell me about it."

Greta said, "How can you, if you're suspended?"

"I'd talk to him man to man," Chris said. "Ask him what the deal is, if he pimps for his brother."

"He'd never admit it."

"He might, it's how you ask. He might even think being a pimp is cool. I remember Mark Ricks from way back, but I don't remember Woody, so I didn't associate the name right away."

"You *know* Mark?"

"I'd see him at school, when I was at U of M. You couldn't miss him, he loved to make speeches. Maureen'll talk to him first. Also find out who his friend is, Robin, if we need her. . . . You don't know anything about her, if she's an actress, maybe was in one of his plays?"

"That could be," Greta said. "She was kind of a showy type. Way older than the other girls, but had a nice figure."

"How old?"

"I'll bet close to forty."

"You said Mark picked her up at Brownie's. . . . How did Robin get to Woody's? She ride in the limo?"

"She had her own car there."

"What kind?"

"A VW. I remember, 'cause I was so surprised when Mark went with her. He drove."

"And you rode in the limo."

"Four of us, with Woody and his fur coat."

"He say anything to you on the way?"

"Not a word. The girls did all the talking. Woody drank and ate peanuts."

Chris could almost smell them as she said it. They turned off Fort Street to cross railroad tracks and a freeway.

"I might as well tell you right now, I don't see it coming to trial. I mean even if there was evidence, the guy's too well connected."

"So if you're rich enough," Greta said, "you can do whatever you want."

Familiar words. "You can even double-park in front of the Detroit Club," Chris said, "and not get a ticket."

They were driving north on Junction now, Chris's old neighborhood that was turning from Polish to Hispanic, the bell tower of Holy Redeemer in the near distance, Greta's gaze moving along the block of old-fashioned two-story frame houses with steps leading up to porches.

"There it is, the one with the real estate sign: *Sold.*" She said, "How about a grilled cheese sandwich and a cup of coffee? If I have any bread."

What she didn't have, Chris noticed, was furniture. She brought him into an empty living room saying everything had gone to Arkansas—well, except her bedroom set upstairs, the kitchen table and chairs, a TV and that telephone message recorder on the floor. A tiny red light on it was flashing. Greta said, "My mom's the only one ever calls me," went down to her knees and turned on the machine.

A male voice said, "Greta? You like Greta or you like Ginger? I like Ginger, myself. Anyway, about this situation happened between you and Mr. Woody Ricks? There appears to be some misunderstanding. All you have to do is call 876-5161. I believe we can settle this matter and everybody will be happy. Especially you, Ginger. Please call that number soon as you can."

Greta punched the OFF button and looked over her shoulder at Chris, frowning. "That was his *lawyer?*"

"It was his chauffeur," Chris said, "trying to sound like a lawyer. That was Donnell."

12

Thursday noon Donnell went out to the limo parked in the turnaround part of the drive back of the house.

The car had been standing here since bringing the man home from jail yesterday, the man saying all the way up Woodward Avenue, "They never clean that place." Couldn't believe it. "They never clean the floor, they never clean the toilet. The smell in there was terrible." The man should talk, with the messes he made, but that's what he'd said. The man had no idea of all the things he didn't know. Donnell had told him, "You think that's bad and that ain't even the real jail, that's the police jail. You have to be in the old Wayne County jail sometime you want to experience a jail." The man couldn't get over they didn't clean it.

Today the man was more his regular self, not knowing shit what was going on and not seeming to care.

This afternoon he was going to watch movies. "What ones?" Donnell asked him. "You want an Arnold Schwarzenegger festival or a Busby Berkeley?"

Lately the man liked Arnold Schwarzenegger being the barbarian with the big two-hand sword fighting the bad dudes. He liked to sit there with his martini and his popcorn and ask Donnell, if he was Arnold Schwartznigger— the way the man always said the name—which of the bitches in the movies he'd rather fuck. Like would he take that tall colored girl in the Conan picture or that Swedish broad in the other one? Wouldn't matter how many times the man asked it, the man's brain being mush, Donnell would say lemme think on it. Then he'd tell the man he'd take Grace Jones. Not 'cause he was racially inclined toward her, either, but 'cause she had a body on her went up and up and up and never stopped; though he would tell the bitch to get a wig if she couldn't grow hair.

Today the man wanted Busby Berkeley, which meant he would be smoking weed with his martini. He liked to be under weed when he watched those musical numbers, the chorus girls moving their arms and legs like designs changing in a kaleidoscope. But there wasn't any weed in the house. Donnell said he'd go out and get some.

He was standing by the limo, keys in his hand, about to open the door when he said to himself, Wait a minute, shit. He'd picked up most of a whole pound of weed must've been like two weeks ago. He turned, getting his head to remember where he'd put it, looking up at this pile of bricks where he lived, a house as big as hotels he'd known. It came to him the weed was still in the car. He hadn't taken it inside. No, it was still in the trunk. He walked back and opened it with the key, raised the lid. . . .

Donnell looked at the package, something wrapped in a brown plastic trash bag that wasn't weed, the weed was in the spare-tire well, and said, Uh-oh, his hand on the trunk lid, not wanting to move. He saw the wires coming out of the package to the clothespin. He saw the cord running from the clothespin to a hole cut in the wall behind the back seat and said it again, Uh-oh. He heard about clothespins with copper bent around the ends. He felt his body made of stone while his brain lit up to see the meaning of this, why it was happening to him. . . . Like the same thing with the dude that had sold him the weed, Booker. Exactly. One week ago this day it was, Booker raised up from his chair and got blown to pieces. Was there a connection? Donnell couldn't see one. Now it began to irritate him. He *bought* the shit, he didn't deal it. If he wasn't in the business, who wanted him to die? Nobody. Not lately anyway. Not even police. So the bomb was for the man. Open the door for the man toget in the car. . . . Yeah, it might be for the man, Donnell realized, but both their asses would get shot into the sky.

Who wanted the man dead? The man wasn't into nothing. Most of the time the man barely knew where he was at. There was only one person Donnell could think of would love it to see the man dead. That was the man's brother, Markie. Except little Markie didn't know shit, no way how to do a bomb. 'Less he got somebody who did.

Well, the man wasn't going nowhere today. If the man said he was, tell him wait till you get the scissors. Cut the string should do it. There wasn't a ticking sound, it wasn't that kind. Donnell paused on that. Uh-huh, cut the string, shit, and find out it's what they *want* you to do, it's a pressure re*lease* kind of bomb tricky motherfuckers rig up. The kind that did Booker.

Donnell kept thinking along that line now, wondering

should he talk to the dude was Booker's bodyguard, Juicy
Mouth. Where was Juicy when his boss sat down in the
chair? Ask him, yeaaah, did he know anybody was doing
bombs lately?

Donnell got the weed out of the tire well and brought
the trunk lid down, pushed on it gently till he heard the lock
click.

When he answered the front door he had on black
athletic shorts, a black sweatshirt and hundred-dollar running shoes. Donnell didn't run; it was one of his leisure
outfits. He looked at Mark Ricks standing outside on the
stoop and said, "Can I help you?"

Markie didn't like it when he played with him. The
little fella brushed past without a word, came in and, as
usual, looked sideways quick at his mama looking down at
him from the wall. Like he didn't trust even a picture of the
tiny bitch.

"How's my brother?"

"Beautiful," Donnell said. "The man remains above
earthly shit like jail. You know what I'm saying to you?
Man's all the way live and into his pleasures."

"I wish you wouldn't talk like that."

"I know you do."

Markie was trying to give him an icy-cold look now.

"Where is he?"

"At the movies," Donnell said, and walked past Mark
to lead the way into Woody's library, his hangout: a big
room full of books never opened, full of worn leather and
dark oak, figured damask draperies; but a bar and stereo,
too, and a pair of deep-cushioned recliners aimed at a 46-
inch Sony television screen. Woody sat in one holding a

straight-up martini in a wine goblet. Donnell said to him, "What can I get you while I'm up? You want something to nibble on? You brother's here. Turn your head this way, you see him."

Woody, smiling, paid no attention.

Mark said, "Woody, how are you?"

Donnell, looking at the screen, said, "Oh, I didn't realize." And said to Mark, "Don't bother him now, that's his favorite Busby Berkeley, the banana number. Fine young ladies dancing with bananas big as they are, huh? Look at that, making banana designs. Look at your brother now, starting to cry with the pleasure of it."

"He's laughing," Mark said.

"Little of each, crying and laughing," Donnell said. "Yeah, the banana number. Man eats it up. Now you gonna see Carmen Miranda come out with all the fruit and shit on top her head."

Woody, not looking at them, said, "Where my peanuts?"

"Got the munchies," Donnell said. "Huh, you got the munchies? Well, you done ate all the peanuts up. Have to wait till I get some."

Donnell was watching Carmen Miranda, her face all painted, the fruit and shit on her head. He heard Markie say, "Doesn't he keep peanuts in the car?" The little fella close beside him. Markie saying something now that was not like him at all. Saying, "I'll go look. Where're the keys?"

Donnell paused, his brain asking him, Did you hear that? Is that what he said? Donnell turned very slowly to Markie looking up at him with a big-eyed funny look, the little fella *wanting* to do it and like afraid he might be told no. Donnell stared into those big eyes looking for a tricky gleam of some kind. He said, "Yeah, the keys, they in the kitchen. On the hook by the door." The little fella started to leave. "Wait now. The peanuts have to be on the back seat. You understand?"

Markie nodded, anxious. "Yeah, in back. I know."

He left and Donnell eased into the recliner next to Woody, who was wiping his eyes, Woody saying, "I want to see this part again."

"We both do," Donnell said.

"But I want my peanuts."

"Your brother went to get 'em."

"My brother—what's he doing here?"

"We gonna find out," Donnell said. "Or, we might never." He started to grin. "Lookit, shit, how they holding their bananas."

Chris and his dad were in the kitchen, his dad frying hamburgers in the iron skillet at arm's length, saying, "You want the green pepper and A-1?"

"No, do 'em the regular way."

"Find out what she wants on hers."

"It's Greta," Chris said. He stepped into the doorway to the dining-L. Across the living room Greta stood at a front window looking out at Lake St. Clair.

"What do you want on yours?"

"Just Lee and Perrins, if you have it."

Chris came back to his dad at the range. "They're all different, aren't they?"

"I thought I told you that," his dad said. "How long she gonna be staying?"

"You mean Greta?"

"Greta—I want to know what kind of an arrangement we have here."

"You said it was okay."

"Well, you ask me right in front of her."

"What's the problem?"

"Esther and I're going to Toronto for a few days. I won't be here."

"You won't be here for what, to chaperone us?"

"I don't understand what's going on," his dad said. "Twelve years on the job and you get suspended, what's the first thing you do? You involve yourself with another girl."

"I'm not *involv*ing myself, I'm helping her out."

"You go from one to the next."

Chris said, "You want to know what *I* don't understand? You're going on a trip with Esther and you're worrying about me being alone here with Greta. Does that make sense? You're going for obvious reasons."

"To have a good time."

"That's what I mean. But we're here for one reason only. Greta needs a place to stay and she needs help. I'm not involving myself in any way other than that."

His dad said, "Who you kidding?"

They were eating when the phone rang. Chris said he'd get it and went out to the kitchen, leaving his dad alone with Greta in the dining-L.

Greta said, "I can see Chris takes after you. You sound so much alike, when you talk."

The dad said, "You think so?"

"You seem more like brothers. I'm not just saying that, either, it's true."

"He's got more hair," the dad said, "but I'm bigger than he is."

Greta smiled. "You see a father and son are good friends, I think that's neat. It says something about both of them. I like your son a lot. He has qualities, I swear, you don't see very often in guys these days."

"He turned out okay," the dad said. "I'll tell you something. He gives you his word, you can take it to the bank."

"That's what I mean," Greta said, "there's nothing phony about him. He looks you right in the eye."

The dad said, "So you went on that cruise, uh?"

Chris came back to the table not looking at either of them. He sat there thinking until his dad said, "You gonna tell us who it was, or we have to guess?"

Greta, smiling, looked from the dad to Chris.

"It was Jerry. Somebody blew up Woody's limo."

What was left of Greta's smile vanished. "He was in it?"

"His brother Mark was. They think he opened a door and the bomb went off. Killed him, like that." Chris took his time and said, "Homicide wants to talk to me."

Greta said, "Why?" sitting up straight in the dining room chair. " 'Cause it was meant for Woody?"

Chris nodded and his dad said, "Wait a minute. What've you got to do with it?"

"I guess they think if you can take a bomb apart," Chris said, "you can put one together."

13

The scene was back of the house, behind a police barricade across the drive, where the rear end of the limo was glued to the cement, gray metal scorched black, tires burned off, both doors and the trunk lid gone. The car had been blown in half, the front end driven thirty feet across the backyard where it lay nosed into a bed of shrubs. Fragments of glass, upholstery, torn bits of rusted metal were scattered about the drive in puddles of water. The evidence techs were packing up, getting ready to leave. The morgue wagon was pulling out as Chris arrived.

Jerry Baker had waited. He told Chris Homicide was still here, that's all, inside talking to Woody Ricks and his chauffeur. Jerry asked him if he'd stopped at 1300 on the way.

Chris said, "What for? To give myself up?"

He had parked in front and walked up the drive watching a TV newsman dramatizing to a camera, arm raised to the mansion, describing this scene of murder, foul play, a devastating act of destruction. . . .

Two of the garage doors, scorched black, were closed when the bomb exploded, protecting a gray Mercedes sedan parked inside. The third garage door was raised. Jerry told Chris that Mark Ricks had come out of the house from the kitchen and through the garage. He said that according to Donnell Lewis, the chauffeur, Mark was getting his brother's peanuts he'd left in the car. He must have unlocked the driver-side door and pressed the button to unlock the rear door. Then when he opened it, Jerry said, Mark was blown into the garage with the door in his hand, only the hand was no longer attached to Mark. They brought Woody out to look at the body, make a positive I.D., and he couldn't do it. He kept squinting his eyes, saying, What is that? The chauffeur, Donnell, very casual, wearing these sporty athletic shorts and jogging shoes, told him it was his brother. Jerry said the guy was burned but wasn't exactly what you'd call a crispy critter. He looked more like some giant hand had picked him up, squeezed him good and thrown him in the garage. Jerry raised his face to the overcast sky and sniffed.

"You smell it?"

"Ammonium nitrate and fuel oil," Chris said. "Somebody knew what he was doing. What else've you got?"

"A burnt-up battery, a spring off a clothespin. Let's see, I got safety pins from both the rear doors, stuck in bits of upholstery. We'll find out it was dynamite, I'm pretty sure. See if any's been stolen from around."

Chris looked up at the back of the house, taking in its size, all the chimneys rising out of the slate roof, more like a venerable ivy-covered institution than a home. He believed you'd have to be a millionaire just to heat the place. At the other end of the house French doors opened onto a terrace with an ornamental cement rail around it. The swimming pool was probably inside there. Chris said, "You know what it reminds me of in a way? Booker's, last week."

"It does me too," Jerry said. "It went through my mind there could be a nexus."

"Maybe it's the French doors. Or what you said about Donnell wearing jogging shoes made me think of it."

"I'm going more by my nose," Jerry said. "Walk in the house and take a whiff. They aren't smoking Kools in there. If this one's dynamite it'll give Homicide something to think about. They like to get into motives and all that shit," Jerry said. "I'm through here."

"Who's working it?"

"Half of Squad Seven's out doing a house-to-house. Wendell's inside. Wendell Robinson, dressed like he's going to a party."

"Wendell *is* a party," Chris said. "If I have to talk to anybody I'd just as soon it's Wendell."

After Jerry left, Chris waited by his dad's Seville, parked behind two identical medium-blue Plymouth sedans. It was a quiet street of old trees and homes built of old money. From the front, Woody's house seemed more like a residence, except for the two cement lions sitting on either side of the entrance, guarding the place for Woody and his chauffeur. Just the two of them, according to Jerry, living in this great big house.

The front door swung in. Now Wendell Robinson appeared with Donnell, two black guys against the dark of that

E L M O R E · L E O N A R D

arched opening: one with hands on his hips showing his
brown bare legs, the other in a beige three-piece suit, the
Homicide lieutenant. Chris watched Wendell come past the
stone lions now and down the slate walk adjusting his vest,
buttoning the beige suit coat, Wendell with his cool, pleasant expression, paisley tie in rust tones against a soft ivory
shirt. No way of telling a nickel-plated Smith auto was
wedged in tight to his right hip. Chris said, "You're looking
fine," and couldn't help smiling. There was something
about Wendell that made him feel good. "I understand you
want to talk to me."

"So you come here in your Cadillac and grin at me,"
Wendell said, "think it's funny. I like your style, Mankowski. You gonna confess or I have to beat it out of you?"

"I didn't do it, I swear."

"Okay, that's enough of that shit. But there other people, I'll tell you right now, probably gonna talk to you."

"Why?"

" 'Cause they upset. I'm talking about people on the
third floor. They want this one closed before it's barely
open. See, what happened, the inspector gets the call on
this while he's in the deputy chief's office. He calls me to
give it to Seven. I go down there, now your Major Crimes
commander is also present and some other brass happen
to stop in. You see the picture? They all in there theorizing
their ass off who could have done it. Nobody's even gone
to the scene yet. Your name comes up. Hey, what about
Mankowski? On account of the business you had with Mr.
Ricks. One of them goes, Mankowski, man, he's hotheaded.
Another one says you cold-blooded, tough cop who don't
take any shit."

"You serious?"

"A man was blown up. Okay, and you been around

people that have got killed and you know how to make a bomb."

"Jesus Christ."

"It doesn't have to make sense, it just has to sound like it does. You understand? Somebody mentions maybe Internal Control ought to look into Booker again."

"They think I did Booker?"

"They not thinking, man, they theorizing, trying to put little pieces together, see what fits, get it closed. They wonder, What about that girl the man was alleged to have raped?"

"Yeah, it was her," Chris said. "She sneaked out of the hospital and wired the car."

"Or does she know somebody could have wired it? Like they picking lint off their clothes. They nervous is what they are."

" 'Cause the guy's important," Chris said, "Woody. You have money, you have clout."

"That's what it might seem," Wendell said, "but that's bullshit. They nervous 'cause we had six hundred and forty-six homicides last year. We closed better than half, sixty-one percent. But the FBI, they tell everybody seventy-four percent is the average nationwide. So they nervous we don't look so good. Man, they don't give a shit about Woody Ricks or his brother, it's how *they* look. They think this one should be easy. Man gets a bomb put in his car, there must be somebody doesn't like him, right? Simple."

"Or somebody gains by it," Chris said.

"Yeah, except the only one would gain, according to Woody, is the one that got blown up. Least that's what I think Woody told me. The man's hard to understand. He has Donnell like interpret for him, say what he means."

"What about this," Chris said. "What if Mark was putting the bomb in the car, doing the finishing touches, and it blew?"

"I'm told he wasn't out there two minutes. How's a man like that know how to make a bomb? The man wasn't qualified. Look at it another way. If it was Mark hired it done, he wouldn't have gone near the car, would he?"

Chris looked at the house. "What about Donnell?" The front door was still open. "If he isn't on the computer it was erased."

"I don't have to look up Donnell," Wendell said. "The man's been arrested for assault, robbery, extortion, causing disturbances. . . . Did federal time back when he was a member of the Panthers, wore the little beret? They got him for possession of a machine gun and other contraband kinds of shit in his house, hand grenades and such."

"I think he's watching us," Chris said.

Wendell looked at the house. "Sure he is, thinking I'm gonna try to set him up. Which I might have to, 'less I find me a bomb maker someplace."

"How'd he get next to Woody?"

"Claims they known each other a long time. Says Mr. Woody took him in and it changed his life."

"That's what he calls him, Mr. Woody?"

"There is something peculiar," Wendell said, "how it is between those two. I said to him, 'You the man's chauffeur. Where's the rest of the help?' Donnell gives me his look, says, 'I'm all the help the man needs.' "

"Maybe the Panther lets Woody go down on him," Chris said, "and Woody lets the Panther do whatever he wants. He ever deal drugs?"

"Now you come to another theory," Wendell said, "tie it some way to Booker. I don't mean with you, I mean two bombs all of a sudden go off in a week. So we ask ourselves, who did Booker? Was it the people supply him?"

"He was leaning that way," Chris said.

"Okay, what if Woody was financing Booker, setting him up to go independent? How's that sound? The people up above find out and take them both out."

Chris said, "You want it to be dope-related, don't you?"

Wendell said, "I want it 'cause if it ain't, what the fuck is it? People kill each other in this city, if it ain't over pussy or fussing over who owes money or a parking place, then it's dope. Killing over turf or a busted deal. The vans they go around in? They call 'em gunships. Drive by a house and spray it with an Uzi. And you know what?"

"Half the time it's the wrong house."

"And when they do get the right one they shoot the wrong people. They shoot little kids happen to be in the room."

"This was a bomb."

"That don't bother me. They'll throw a pipe bomb in the house. You've seen it done. They can make a pipe bomb, they can make any kind. What's the difference?"

"What's Donnell say?"

"Somebody wired the wrong car."

"He tell you that with a straight face?"

"Why couldn't it happen?"

"Wendell, the guy'd have to come to the wrong house first. Look at it. With the fucking lions sitting out in front. A guy's gonna plant a bomb he scouts the place, knows exactly where he's going."

Wendell, hands in his pockets, stared at the house. The front door was closed now. He said, "Or, Donnell thinks it could've been wired when the car was someplace else. You know, parked with some other limos. They all look alike. Jerry say you have the package ready, you could hook it up in five minutes."

"Maybe Jerry could," Chris said. "I'd want to take a little more time myself. But where's Donnell go without Woody? I don't mean to the store, I mean where there'd be other limos. But if Woody's along—he gets out, the guy wires it and Woody gets back in, that's where it blows, right? Not in the backyard."

Wendell was nodding, resigned. "I suppose."

Chris looked at the house again, wondering what they were doing in there, right now. He said to Wendell, "How come Mark went to get the peanuts, not Donnell?"

"Donnell says Mark wanted to do it."

"What if Woody had his own car wired," Chris said, "and sent Mark out to get the peanuts?"

"He couldn't have, he didn't know Mark was there. The man doesn't seem to know much of anything. Eyes all watery like a skid-row burnout."

"Psychosocially debilitated," Chris said.

"I like that," Wendell said, "I'll put that down. I talk to him, here's his brother blown to shit just a while ago, the man hardly seems to realize it. I don't mean 'cause he's in shock, either. Man has a wet brain."

Chris was looking at the house again. "What if it was Donnell that set it up? Somehow he talked Mark in to getting the peanuts."

"I'm gonna collect my people and leave," Wendell said. "I'll tell them on the third floor I interrogated you and found you psychosocially debilitated, couldn't think of nothing but peanuts. How's that sound?"

Chris was still looking at the house. He nodded and said, "Planters Peanuts, in the blue can."

14

What the man liked to do for his nap time, couple of hours before dinner: turn on the stereo way up loud enough to break windows, slide into the pool on his rubber raft naked to Ezio Pinza doing "Some Enchanted Evening" and float around a few minutes before he'd yell, "Donnell?" And Donnell, his hand ready on the button, would shut off the stereo. Like that, Ezio Pinza telling the man to make somebody his own or all through his lifetime he would dream all alone, and then dead silence. No sound at all in the dim swimming pool house, steam hanging over the water, steam rising from the pile of white flesh on the raft, like it was cooking.

Donnell had changed from his black athletic outfit to a loose white cotton pullover shirt, loose white trousers with a drawstring, bare feet in broken-in Mexican huara-chis, dressed for an evening at home. Donnell stood at the edge of the pool watching the man float past, eyes closed, Donnell thinking, Stick an apple in his mouth. Thinking, I wish Cochise could see this.

Say to Cochise, "What's it remind you of?" Cochise would see it, sure, like the pig cartoons used to be in *The Black Panther.* Pigs squealing, a big black fist holding them up by the tail. Pigs hanging from a tree, lynch ropes around their necks. Pig in a cop uniform sweating bullets, going "Oink," a brother holding a pistol in the pig's face.

It was Cochise Patterson had brought him into the Panthers, Cochise telling him the basic tool of liberation was the gun. Cochise reading to him from the minister of defense, Huey P. Newton: "Army .45 will stop all jive. A .357 will win us heaven." It was all to do with the gun and it was cool. Justify packing. Have a reason. For only with the power of the gun could the black masses halt the bullshit terror and brutality perpetrated against them by the jive racist power structure. Cochise telling him they would never stop till they had destroyed and committed destruction on capitalism.

Except Cochise was back in the slam doing fifteen to twenty-five, saying fuck it and reading comic books. Some had learned, some had come around and joined the other side. Look at Eldridge Cleaver, the most famous Panther of all. After running as a fugitive, hiding out in Canada, Mexico, Cuba, North Africa, over in Asia and then France, he had found Jesus and was praising the American Way as the only way. Being called a "world-record-breaking belly crawler" didn't seem to bother him one little bit.

Donnell, too, keeping his eyes open to opportunity, had come around since those revolutionary times. He hadn't found Jesus as his redeemer, but somebody who might be even better.

"Mr. Woody," Donnell said to the white mound on the raft, "you haven't told me what you want for your supper."

The man floated in the steam mist with his eyes closed, hands trailing in the warm water. What would he be thinking, his head all fucked up from booze? What would he see in there? Sights maybe from a long time ago still clear, but the recent shit gone, not having made a good impression in his mind. What had the man done lately that was worth remembering?

"Mr. Woody?"

"What?" Eyes still closed.

"You thought about supper?"

The man worked his mouth like he was getting a bad taste out of it, but no words came from him.

Donnell put the tips of his fingers behind his ear and leaned out over the tiled edge. "Ain't that your tummy I hear growling?"

No answer.

"You upset about your brother, huh?"

No answer. The man was asleep or didn't know what he was talking about. What brother?

"You gonna be hungry you finish your swim. I'll fix you some chicken. How's that sound?"

No answer.

Call the Chinaman, pick up a load of chicken lo mein and pile the shit on a dinner plate for the man. Order some of that shrimp wrapped in bacon for himself. Sometimes they would eat together in the kitchen, the man calling him his buddy.

"You have a funeral parlor you want to use? . . . I'll look up see who did your mama. Don't you worry about it. I'll take care of everything."

Donnell had been doing most of the man's thinking for the past three years now, since one night at All That Jazz on Cadillac Square, never expecting to see somebody like Mr. Woody Ricks in a mostly black lounge. But there was the limo out front, a white boy with a chauffeur hat behind the wheel. Inside the piano bar drinking gin, dropping a ten in the tip bowl each time he spoke to Thelma Dinwiddy playing nonstop nine till two, Thelma playing under the name of Chris Lynn with her satin headband and her lovely smile, playing the ass off those show tunes the man requested. All That Jazz had once been a hotel coffee shop; now it was done-over dark to look like a nightclub: a place black entertainers came to sit in with Thelma's piano or to sing a number. Thelma would find the key and smile as she wrapped chords around a voice doing maybe "Green Dolphin Street" like they'd worked together forever.

Donnell went to the bar that time where he noticed Juicy Mouth was sitting and took the stool next to him, but didn't speak till an old man finished with "Tishamingo Blues," Thelma riding along, the old man saying he was going to Tishamingo to get his hambone boiled, on account of Atlanta women had let his hambone spoil.

Juicy was a Pony Down runner then, selling on street corners before getting promoted, because of his size and meanness, to Booker's bodyguard. Donnell finally said to Juicy, "See that fat man there? Lives in the biggest house you ever saw. His mama gave a party for the Panthers one time, not knowing what she was getting into. Thought it was to raise money for the zoo or some shit. Can you see her friends, these people trying to smile? Like they partied with brothers every weekend? Only you know they never been close to one less it was at the car wash or was a sister cleaned their house." Donnell said to Juicy, who was a kid and didn't know shit about Panthers or any of that, "I want you to do something for me. When the man goes to the men's room, I want you to follow him in and start to vamp on him. Tell him it's fifty bucks to take a piss or you gonna cut his dick off. See, then I come in just then and throw a punch at you like in the movies, dig? And save the man's ass. I don't hit you, I pretend to."

The men's room was out the door of the club and across the lobby, kept locked, so people wouldn't come in off the street and use it. You told the club doorman you were going to the men's and he buzzed the men's door open for you when you got to it. Mr. Woody finally went and Juicy followed.

Then Donnell walked over to the doorman, handed him a ten and said, "Let me have a few minutes' peace in there doing my business." He slipped on black leather gloves before going in and hit Juicy hard, the knife flying, blood flying, hit him in his surprised face again and got the man zipped up and out of there.

Sitting in the back of the man's car with him, Donnell pointed to the guy in the front seat with the chauffeur hat on and said, "What good is he? He drives you, yeah, but what *good* is he?" Sounding mad because someone wasn't looking out for the man.

The man said, "You saved my life," reaching for his wad of money.

Donnell stopped his hand and said, "I saved you better than that. Now I'll tell you who I am and what I'm willing to do for you out of respect for your mother, a woman I think of and admire to this day."

In the following months Donnell, wearing a tailored black suit now, white shirt, black tie but not the chauffeur hat, would sit down with Mr. Woody from time to time, look the man in the eye with sort of a puzzled frown and ask him:

"What do you need a cook for living here only cooks white Methodist food and acts superior, won't talk to nobody? I happen to learn food preparation in the slam. I cook good. . . .

"What do you need a fat maid for living here watches TV upstairs all day? I can get us a maid to come in, clean up and get out. A cute maid. . . .

"What do you need to write checks for, pay bills, be bothered with all that picky shit? Excuse me. I can do it for you. . . .

"What do you need to put up with your brother whining at you for? You the one has the musical ear. He don't like it, tell him go do his cock rock someplace else. . . .

"What do you need to call your mother's lawyer for, get charged two hundred dollars an hour? I learn food preparation, I also happen to learn about legal affairs. Most time you don't need to get in it, have to sign all those papers. I can talk. I can make deals. I can tell people how it is. . . .

"What do you need to go to court for, have that redhead bitch call a fine man like you a rapist in front of everybody in town? I can talk to her for you."

Coming up pretty soon he would have to look the man in the eye and ask him:

"Don't you need to change your will, now that your brother's gone?" Ask him: "Anybody else you want to put in it?"

Being subtle wouldn't pay, the man spaced on booze and now and then a 'lude slipped him to keep him mellow and manageable, the man always in low gear with his dims on.

It might have to be put to him: "Mr. Woody, I would consider it an honor to be in your will." Play with that idea. Say it in a way to make the man laugh and feel good.

There was a possibility with the redhead bitch to make some good money. If he could get her to go along. He could always write himself a nice check if he ever had to leave in a hurry. No, the deal was to get in the man's will for a big chunk and then work out the next step. Having Markie out of the way should make it easier to become the man's heir. Except, shit, what took Markie out was somebody doing a bomb, and that didn't make any sense however Donnell looked at it. Somebody wanted to kill the man and the man didn't even know it. Floating there this enchanted evening, dreaming all alone. . . .

The front doorbell rang.

Donnell left the swimming pool room, went through the sunroom and along a dark hallway to the foyer. The news people had stopped calling and knocking on the door. He'd watched them out front. He'd watched the dude cop talking to the hard-nose cop, Donnell wondering whose Cadillac that was, and couldn't believe it when the hard-nose cop, the now out-of-work cop, drove *off* in it. That had been about a half hour ago. Donnell was thinking about it again, wondering how it could be as he bent his head to peek through the peephole in the door, took a look and straightened quick.

The hard-nose cop was back. Standing there with a can of peanuts in his hand.

15

Chris said, "I hear you're out of these," offering the can of Planters Cocktail Peanuts.

Donnell didn't move to take it, Donnell in a loose white outfit doing his cool look with the heavy lids, the look saying he wasn't surprised, he wasn't entertained or impressed, either. Reserving judgment.

Chris said, "I hear if you hadn't run out of nuts the guy's brother would still be alive. Gives you something to think about, huh? If he hadn't gone out there—what's his name, Mark? Somebody else would've opened the car door."

Donnell stared, thumbs hooked in the drawstring on his pants. Or pajamas, or whatever they were.

Chris said, "I can't imagine Woody opening the door. That's what he's got you for, right? Open doors, drive him around. . . . What else you do for him? Call up a young lady, tell her there appears to be some kind of a misunderstanding?"

Donnell kept staring at him.

"That what you do? Ask her to call you? Tell her you have a way to settle the matter and make her happy?" Chris tossed the can of peanuts in the air, not high.

Donnell caught it in two hands at his waist, staring back, eyes never moving. "You believe I called some woman?"

"Hey, come on, I heard you. I know it was you. I'll get a court order for a voice print if you want and we'll nail it down."

Donnell, frowning, raised one hand in slow motion, holding the peanuts in the other, saying to Chris, "Wait now. What is this shit you giving me, what I did?"

"You phoned Greta Wyatt."

"Tell me who she is."

"The one you're gonna see in court, asshole, when your boss stands trial."

"Oh, that Greta. Yeah, see, I call her Ginger. Now what was it I said to her?"

"You're gonna make her happy," Chris said. "What we want to know is, how happy?"

"What you saying to me, you speaking for the lady."

"Like you seem to represent Woody," Chris said. "Who needs lawyers?"

Donnell said, "Yeaaah," and then paused, thoughtful. "I see you come to visit, policeman that use to be into high explosives, interested in such things—I thought you want to ask about this bomb business."

"I'll be honest with you," Chris said, "I don't give a shit about the bomb, that's your problem. You're gonna offer Miss Wyatt a payoff. I want to know what you have in mind."

"Let me look at it again," Donnell said, beginning to smile a little. "Drive up in a Cadillac you manage on about maybe six bills a week take-home. Yeah, I can see you interested in payoffs, rake-offs and such. Come on inside."

They walked through to the library, Chris reminded of Booker's house where the old woodwork and paneling had been painted an awful green. Here, there was the feeling nothing had been changed in the past fifty years or more. Chris chose a deep chair, watching Donnell reach beneath the shade of an ornate lamp close by. Low-watt lights came on to reveal the brass figure of a woman, dull, tarnished. Chris asked Donnell if those were pajamas he had on. Donnell gave him a dreamy look, patient, came over and sat on the fat cushioned arm of a chair facing Chris.

"Now then. What I get into first with the young lady, I let her know this kind of situation is not anything new to Mr. Woody. Being a wealthy man, getting his picture in the paper, the man has games run at him all the time. You understand? People looking to score off him. He knows it, he say to me, 'Donnell, it's a shame how people have to be so greedy. Even good people, they see the chance. What is somebody trying to stick me for this time?' I say to him, 'You recall this young lady name of Ginger?' Mr. Woody say, 'Ginger? Do I know a Ginger?' I say to him, 'Remember the party you had, this young lady took all her clothes off?' "

"You're telling her," Chris said, "what you're gonna say in court. Is that it?"

"I haven't even come to the good part."

"You're threatening her."

"I'm only saying what I *could* say."

"Instead of doing the whole skit, let's get to the payoff."

"Don't rush me, man. See, I could go on to tell how I happen to notice her fishing out Mr. Woody's dick, taking him upstairs by it, leading him along, you dig? That's the key word, *leading*. You understand what I'm saying? Means it was her idea, not his."

"So Mr. Woody's willing to pay," Chris said, "to stay out of court."

"Now you with it. Avoid the embarrassment, even though he's not to blame."

"How much?"

"We come to the part ain't none of your business. I tell *her* the numbers. She the only one."

"If you can find her."

"She don't call me, I call her. Mention the figure, see where her values lie."

"She's moved," Chris said.

Donnell took a little time. "She move in with you?"

Chris nodded and Donnell, watching him, took a little more time.

"I don't suppose you in the book. Being a cop, type of person could get shot through his window." Donnell said, "Hmmmm," thinking about it. "See, I understand where you coming from. You like the idea of the payoff. But see, look at it from my side, I don't need you fucking up the deal, getting the bitch to hold out when I'm willing to make a fair offer."

"What'd you call her?"

"Hey, shit, you her lawyer, what else? Gonna protect her good name? I tell you right now I saw her in bed with the man, doing a job on him, too."

Now Chris had to take a moment, settle down.

"Where is he?"

"Who, Mr. Woody? Having his swim."

Chris got out of the chair. "Let's go talk to him."

Donnell, sitting relaxed, round-shouldered on the arm of the chair, didn't move.

"Man, you love being a cop, don't you? I notice it the other day in the street. Come down on me like an old-time dick, being the *man,* huh? You play it a little different, more quiet about it, you don't get that mean red flush come over your face. But it's the same shit. Long as you have the big pistol you get anything you want. That's where it's at, the gun. I learned that many years ago, in my youth."

Chris said, "Is that it? You through?"

"Oh, man, you gonna work that hard-nose routine again?"

"Now're you through?"

Donnell said, "Shit," taking his time coming off the chair arm. "You want to see Mr. Woody? Come on, let's go see him."

They stood at the edge of the pool watching the naked man on the rubber raft.

"Is he all right?"

"All the way live as he wants to be."

"I don't see him breathing."

"Watch his tummy you see it move. . . . There. You see it?"

"That's what it's like to be rich, huh?"

"Have anything you desire."

"Why does somebody want to kill him?"

"The dude cop ask me that every way he could think of. Wants to know was it me. I ask him, what's my gain? Check it out."

"You know how to set explosives, don't you?"

"How would I?"

"You were in the Panthers."

"Never blowed up nothing in my life. I'll take a polygraph on it."

"What'd you do, in the Panthers?"

"Worked on our free breakfast program, for the kids."

"That what you got sent away for, making breakfast?"

"So they don't go to school hungry. You ask me a question, but you don't want to hear the answer."

"You did time."

"Got along fine. Left that behind and never look over my shoulder. I remember to speak politely. Not hit or swear at people. Not damage property or crops of the poor oppressed masses. Not take liberties with women."

"You learned that in the joint?"

"In the Panther Party, man. We had rules for clean living we had to learn verbatim by heart. Like no party member have a weapon in his possession while drunk or loaded off narcotics or weed."

"Okay, I believe you," Chris said.

"Like no party member will use, point or fire a weapon unnecessarily or accidentally at anyone."

"The key word being 'unnecessarily.' "

"And that would include a bomb. Even if I knew how to make one, what would be the necessity of it? You understand what I'm saying? What is my motive? What do I stand to gain?"

"It comes back to Mr. Woody."

"Every time. With the dude cop, too. Does he have enemies? Went all through all that, back and forth."

"How far back?"

"He does better going back than trying to remember what happened yesterday."

"He doesn't seem worried," Chris said, watching the man floating in a mist of steam, body glistening white.

"Mr. Woody can't think of anybody doesn't love him."

"He's sweating . . ."

"Want to say, like a pig, huh?" Donnell raised his voice. "Mr. Woody, you awake?"

Chris watched the man on the raft lift his head. He began to move his hands in a feeble paddling motion.

"I was thinking," Chris said. "Mark used to run with some freaks when he was in school. I didn't know him, I'd see him with his bullhorn trying to sound political. Only the guy didn't know Ho Chi Minh from sweet-and-sour shrimp."

"Can tell a fake, can't you?"

"I wondered, the Panthers ever get together with the freaks?"

"Social occasions. Bring a spade home and introduce him to your mama. Little Markie would demonstrate, get his picture in the paper? I do the same thing, get my ass thrown in jail."

"The way it goes," Chris said. "I understand he had a friend with him Saturday night, woman he used to know."

"Yeah, there was one come with Mark. I been trying to think—"

"Her name's Robin."

Donnell said, "Yeaaah, Robin Abbott," with a sound of relief. "That's who it was. *Damn*, I been trying to think if I knew her. She come up to me I was waiting for the boat. Yeah, shit, Robin Abbott. See, but she didn't say nothing to me, who she was."

"Didn't remember you, either."

Donnell gave him a look with the heavy lids. Then seemed to smile, just a little. "I don't know about that."

"How'd you meet her?"

"Look at Mr. Woody doing his famous aqua-ballet dog paddle. He has to go down the shallow end to get out."

"You meet Robin through Mark?"

"Right here in this house."

"What was she into?"

"What they were doing then, grooving on weed and shit. I'd see her on the street now and then, she was living by Wayne with this dude had a ponytail. I remember him good. They all had the hair. You know, that was the thing then, the hair. She had different hair, real long down her back. . . . I think she knew who I was at the boat but didn't say nothing. There was something happened to her I'm trying to remember. Like she got busted and took off. . . ." Donnell paused.

Chris waited, watching the fat naked man rise in the shallow end of the pool, the water at his belly, and blow his nose in his hand.

Donnell said, "Oh, you sneaky. We talking about the bomb, now you have us back on the other conversation.

You looking for somebody was here Saturday could be a witness, huh? Testify against Mr. Woody."

"Robin Abbott," Chris said.

"And that's all you get."

"What was she arrested for?"

"I never said she was."

"You know where she lives?"

"You have all I'm saying, for whatever good you think it's gonna do you." Donnell turned to the pool and raised his voice. "Mr. Woody, look who come to see you. It's the man had you busted."

Woody was out of the water on the other side of the pool, wiping his face with a towel.

Chris called out, "I brought you some peanuts," and heard his voice filling the room.

Now Donnell called to him, "See what he's doing, Mr. Woody? Wants to get on your good side."

Chris watched the fat man raise one arm, turn and enter a door with a frosted-glass window.

"Where's he going?"

"Have a cold shower, wake him up. He'll be out in a minute, start his cocktail hour."

Chris felt himself perspiring. "Why does he keep it so hot in here?"

"The way he likes it. The ladies get hot, take their clothes off and jump in the water. Like your friend I told you, Ginger."

"You go in with them?"

"Getting all wet's never been one of my pleasures."

Chris reached behind Donnell with one hand and gave him a shove. It didn't take much. Donnell yelled "Hey!" off balance, waved his arms in the air, hit the water and went under. Chris hunched over, hands on his knees. He watched Donnell's head come up, saw his eyes, his chin pointing, straining, the look of panic, arms fighting the water.

Chris said, "You don't know how to swim, do you? That can happen you grow up in the projects, never get a chance to learn. Some guys turn to crime."

Donnell reached the side of the pool and got his arms up over the edge to hang there gasping. Chris studied the man's glistening hair, the neat part, waiting until he calmed down and was quiet.

"How much you offering Miss Wyatt?"

Donnell wiped his hand across his face. He looked up, then tried to press against the tile as Chris placed his foot on Donnell's head.

"I didn't hear you."

"Five thousand."

Chris said, "Let me give you a hand."

He was thinking that seeing a guy naked could give you an entirely different impression than seeing him with clothes on. Woody was one of those fat guys who hardly had an ass on him. Why didn't any of the fat go there? He had milk-white legs and walked like his balls were sore, coming around from the other side of the pool now in a terrycloth robe, taking forever, his curly hair still wet, face tomatoed out. He had little fat feet, pink ones. Chris could see what Woody looked like when he was a kid. He could see other kids pushing him into swimming pools. He could see kids choosing up sides to play some game and picking Woody last. He could see little Woody sneaking off by himself to eat candy bars. That type. A kid who slept with the light on and wet the bed a lot. Though he probably wet it more now, with the booze, than he did then. Chris usually felt sorry for quiet boozers who didn't cause any trouble. He felt a little sorry for Woody, the type of guy he could see Woody really was. With a stupid grin now eyeing the bait, the can of peanuts sitting open on the poolside table. He didn't look at Chris, seated in the deck chair, hands folded, patient. He looked at the peanuts and then went over to the bar and poured a lot of scotch into a glass with one ice cube, Chris waiting for him to ask if he wanted anything. But he didn't. That was okay. Chris watched him fooling with the stereo now until the score from *My Fair Lady* came blasting out of the speakers and he turned the volume down. Good. Woody came over to the table and helped himself to peanuts before looking at Chris. Or he might've been looking past him, Chris wasn't sure. Woody's eyes didn't seem to focus.

He said, "Oh my. Oh my oh my. Yeah, I remember. You're the guy that put me in jail, aren't you? I remember you now, sure."

Woody seemed to be thinking as he spoke, hardly moving his mouth. It wasn't that he slurred the words, he sounded like a guy who'd been hit in the head and was in a daze. He moved like it, too, off balance as he pulled a chair out from the table and sat down.

"Oh my oh me," Woody said. "Life's too short, you know it? I'm not gonna be mad at you. Fuck it."

"Well, I'm mad at you," Chris said.

"For what?"

"I don't have a job. I got suspended."

"What're you mad at me for? I didn't do it."

"Who did, your lawyer? It's the same thing."

"Noooo, I didn't do it. Ask Donnell, he'll tell you." Woody looked up at the ceiling and called out, "Donnell! . . . Where are you, boy?"

"He fell in the pool."

Woody's gaze lowered to Chris, squinting now, thinking it over, then looked at the pool. "He's in the water? I don't think he knows how to swim."

"He's changing his clothes," Chris said. "He was telling me you don't want to go to court on the sexual assault complaint."

"The what?" Woody had a mouthful of peanuts now, chewing, working his tongue around in there.

"The rape charge you're gonna be tried for."

"I didn't rape anybody. I thought that was taken care of. Wait a minute. . . . Donnell!"

"Is he handling it for you?"

"Lemme think," Woody said. He picked up his glass and swallowed about an ounce of scotch. "I get confused sometimes, everything that's been happening. My brother passed away. . . ." Woody paused, squinting at Chris or past him. "Jesus, you know something? I think it was today. . . . Yeah, it was, my younger brother." He stopped again and seemed to be listening now and said, *My Fair Lady*. You know who that is?"

"Mr. Ricks," Chris said, "you made an offer to a young lady, or you plan to, so she won't sign a complaint against you. On the rape charge we're talking about."

Woody was nodding now. "Oh, yeah, that's right."

"I'm a friend of hers."

"Oh, I didn't know that. You're talking about Ginger. No, I didn't rape her. She was in my bedroom, didn't have a stitch of clothes on. She's standing there—what would you do? I mean if she wasn't a friend of yours. Wait a

F R E A K Y · D E A K Y

minute. No, I thought Mark sent her up, that was it."
Woody shoved peanuts into his mouth. The hand came
away and paused. "Listen. You know who that is? The only
guy in show business can get away with talking a song. You
know what I mean? Instead of singing it. Rex Harrison as
Doctor . . . you know, what's his name."

"Professor Higgins," Chris said. "You walk in the bedroom, Miss Wyatt's there . . ."

"Who is?"

"Ginger. You throw her on the bed . . ."

"I didn't know she was a friend of yours. I thought, the
way she was acting, you know, she was putting it on. Some
of them go for a little rough stuff, they love that. But I
didn't hurt her or anything, it was a mis—you know—understanding." Woody was nodding, convinced. "That's
why I don't know why she got mad. Let's forget it. I think
twenty-five thousand is fair, don't you? Yeah, I thought my
brother sent her upstairs."

"Twenty-five thousand," Chris said.

"Doesn't that sound about right? It's based on what
my time is worth. I think that's how we did it." Woody was
nodding again. "Yeah, that was it. So I don't have to spend
time in court, time being the . . . you know, what it's based
on. If it's worth it to me, it ought to be worth it to her. Don't
you think?"

"Twenty-five thousand dollars," Chris said.

"Donnell said she would probably like cash instead of
a check."

"You mention this to your lawyer?"

"My lawyer? No. We don't need him for this kind of
thing. He's with a law firm, they've been around forever,
they deal with city attorneys, with big development groups,
up on that level. Donnell says they can talk to *big* people,
they're the same. But if they tried to talk legal to this little

151

girl they'd take six months and charge me an arm and a leg for it."

"So Donnell's handling it?"

Woody paused, reaching for the peanuts, and gave Chris what might be his shrewd look, a squint with a grin in it.

"Donnell only went to the tenth grade, but he knows how to talk to people. He's smart. He'll surprise you."

Chris said, "Kind of fella you can rely on."

Woody nodded, eating peanuts. "You betcha."

Chris said, "Can I ask you a question?"

"Sure, go ahead."

"Does having a lot of money—does it worry you?"

"Why would it worry me?"

"I just wondered." Chris got up from the table. He said to Woody, "Rex Harrison isn't the only guy who talked a song. What about Richard Burton in *Camelot?* Richard Harris, in the movie."

Woody said, "Wait a minute," with his dazed look. "Jesus Christ, you're right. Listen, sit down, have a drink."

Chris shook his head. "I have to go."

Woody said, "Well, come back sometime you're in the neighborhood. Yeah, hey, and bring your friend. What's her name? Ginger."

Chris opened the front door and stepped outside. Donnell, in a suede jacket, hands in his pockets, stood against a stone lion.

"Been admiring your Cadillac."

"You like it?"

"I think you have taste. I think me and you, we both from the street, dig? We see what *is.* I'm not telling you nothing you don't know. You look at Mr. Woody, you don't see a man you give a shit about or what happens to him. What you see looking back at you is pickin's, is opportunity. Am I right?"

"You think I'm gonna shake him down?"

"I think it's in your head."

"How do you work it? He sends you out to buy a new limo, you keep the change?"

Donnell's brows raised, fun in his eyes. "Shit, it won't take you no time."

16

Here they were driving up Woodward Avenue, Robin still yelling at him about taking her mother's Lincoln. She didn't say "without permission," but that's what it sounded like. She told him she absolutely couldn't believe it and would like to know what he was thinking. She told him when he got back to the house he was to put the car in the garage and *leave* it there. All this while they're creeping along, getting stopped at just about every light. That was annoying too, the stopping and starting.

Skip said, "You know what I did at Milan three and a half years? I was a chaplain's assistant."

Robin asked him, now with a bored tone, what that had to do with his taking her mother's car.

"I'll tell you," Skip said. "It taught me patience. If I

wanted to stay in a nice clean job, out of trouble, it meant I had to listen to this mick priest and his pitch to win my soul morning, noon and night. There was nothing I could do about it, I was in a federal lockup doing five to ten. Hey, Robin? But I'm not in one now, am I? I can listen to bullshit, or I can stop the fucking car right here and get out. And you can do whatever you want with it."

Robin was silent.

"I did some stunt work, too. I tell you that? They pay you thirty-five hundred to roll a car over, smash it up," Skip said. "Less withholding and social security it comes to about twenty-six hundred. I have that check and another one for twelve something. But I can't cash either one. I can open a bank account, if I want to wait two weeks to write a check on my own money."

Skip paused to give Robin a turn. She smoked a cigarette, staring at the cars up ahead, shiny metal and brake lights popping on and off.

"What I'm saying is, if I keep paying forty a day for a rental, I may as well give the checks to Hertz. So I took your mom's car. But then what do I find out? I'm gonna have to spend my last eighteen bucks on gas."

Robin said, "Gee, at least she could have left you a full tank."

That was encouraging; even though she didn't look at him, she was lightening up, dropping that pissy tone.

"Look at it this way," Skip said. "If we get caught, what difference does it make whose car we're driving? We could even lay it on your mom, say the whole gig was her idea."

That got a reaction. Robin said, "Far out," squirming a little, flicking cigarette ash and missing the ashtray, not giving a shit. Good.

They drove along this wide avenue in the pinkish glow of streetlights, Skip trying to think of things to say that wouldn't rile her. They had already talked on the phone about the little asshole blowing himself up. Robin called as soon as she saw it on the TV news. *"Now* what do we do? Goddamn it." Spoke of time wasted and hinted around that it was Skip's fault: if he'd only waited for Mark to get the key to the limo. *That's* what she was upset about, the scheme was blown. Then had laid into him about taking her mom's car so she could at least hit him with *some* thing. Skip believed women were often fucked up like that in their thinking. Get you to believe they're irritated about one thing when it's another matter entirely.

"Woodward Avenue," Skip said. "This's the only town I've been to where the whores parade around on the main drag. Look at that one."

Robin said, "You don't know she's a whore."

Skip glanced at Robin puffing on her cigarette, still showing him some muscle. He said, "You're right. Ten o'clock at night this colored chick puts on a sunsuit to get a tan."

"It's a miniskirt and halter."

"I'm wrong again," Skip said. "How about, you hear the one about the guy that got bit by the rattlesnake right on the end of his pecker? The guy's up north deer-hunting with his buddy—"

"I heard it," Robin said, "years ago."

Skip thought awhile and said, "The way they got these lights timed, I don't understand it. They make you stop about every block and look at how depressing this town has become. Where *is* everybody? . . . I know. They're across the river at Jason's. They call it the Royal Canadian Ballet, these girls'll dance bare-ass right at your table. For ten bucks you can have your picture taken with Miss Nude Vancouver and her two breasts. There you are, the four of you smiling at the camera. Be nice to have framed. You know, as a memento, your visit to Canada. There's more going on over there than here. What I don't understand is why the car companies don't do something about it. They let the Japs eat the ass right out of their business. Just sat there and let it happen. Do you understand that?" No answer. She didn't know or she didn't care. "Well, I'm glad your mom buys American. I like a big roomy automobile. I don't know what all that shit is on the dashboard, but it looks good. You know?"

Robin said, "Why're you talking so much?"

"I'm trying to impress you."

"I don't get it."

Skip looked at her and said, "I don't either. I haven't gotten anything since I came here."

"We've been busy."

"No, we haven't. You bring me on and then slip me the blotter. Get me off with acid. Hand it out one at a time."

"I haven't felt in the mood."

"I know what it is," Skip said, "you're afraid I might give you something. Like the broad in that ad, huh? She says she likes to get laid, but she ain't ready to die for it."

"I don't know where you've been," Robin said.

"You mean who I've been *with*. I've never done it with guys. Jesus, you ought to know that."

"You can get it the regular old-fashioned way too," Robin said, watching the road as they approached Seven Mile. "You can't turn left, you have to go through and come back around."

Now she was telling him how to drive.

They would go by the house with the stone lions in front, circle around through Palmer Woods in this car that would seem to belong here, and return to make another pass.

"In there counting his money," Robin said. "You like that picture?"

Skip liked the way she was warming up, getting with it again. What they were up to now was something they'd discussed on the phone. He said, "I like the big yards too, all the trees you can hide in. I like not hearing any dogs. I hate dogs. Be working there in the dark and hear one? Jesus. You try and set high explosives worrying if some dog's gonna jump on you and tear your ass off. You know what I mean?"

"It might be too soon," Robin said.

"The sooner the better. While the first one's still ringing in his ears. You've delivered the message. The guy goes, 'Hey, shit, they're serious.' "

Robin was silent.

Skip eased around a corner, watched the headlights sweep past a house with darkened windows and settle again on the narrow blacktop, an aisle through old trees. He glanced at her.

"What would you rather do instead? I can think of something, but you're afraid I might be carrying the AIDS. What do you want me to do, get a blood test first? We're riding around with my wham bag in the trunk. It's got five sticks of dynamite, blasting caps and a loaded thirty-eight revolver in it and you're worrying about getting a social disease."

"I know why you're talking so much," Robin said, "you're nervous. Aren't you?"

"I'm up," Skip said. "I don't want to waste it, have to get back up again."

"What's the gun for?"

"Come on, what's any of it for? What're we doing?"

He saw her profile as she flicked her lighter, once, and held it to a cigarette, calm, showing him she had it together. She said, "I want to be sure I know what I'm going to say to him, that's all. I want to have it down."

"What you say, that's the easy part. You'll come up with the words. It's *when* you say it's gonna make the difference. The timing, that's what has to be on the button. I can set it for whenever you want up to twelve hours from now." Skip looked at the instrument panel. "It's now . . . which one's the clock? They got all that digital shit on there."

"It's ten forty," Robin said.

"They ever quit making clocks with hands on 'em I'm out of business."

"It's ten forty-one," Robin said.

He liked her tone. Drawing on her cigarette now and blowing it out slow.

"I can set it for ten tomorrow morning, any time around in there. Or how about this? I set it to go off like in eleven and a half hours from the time I place it down. See, then you figure to call ten or fifteen minutes before that."

Robin seemed to be thinking about it as she smoked. "If he stays up boozing all night. . . . You know what I mean? He probably sleeps late."

"I doubt he's gonna answer the phone anyway. That's what he's got the jig for, the Panther." Skip looked past Robin out the side window. They were going by the house again. "Guy likes animals, he's got the Panther, he's got lions out in front. . . . Listen, we can go buy gas, spend my last eighteen bucks and come back later. We have to stop by a gas station anyway, so I can use the men's room."

"You *are* nervous."

"My clock doesn't have a bell and hammer alarm on it,

I have to rig something up. You want me to wire it in the car? Or a place I can turn a light on, lock the door?"

"I want you to be happy," Robin said. She stubbed her cigarette in the ashtray, once, and closed it. "After, why don't I spend the night at Mother's?"

"You mean it?"

He looked over. She was stroking her braid now as she said, "On one condition. . . ."

Mr. Woody finished the pound can of peanuts during his cocktail hour, so he wasn't hungry till near ten. He was in a pretty good mood, seemed almost alert and was talkative. Donnell fixed him up in the kitchen, dished out his warmed-up chicken lo mein, whole quart of it on a platter, opened two cans of Mexican beer and sat down with him at the opposite end of the long wooden table. Donnell didn't like to get too close to the man when he was eating; the man made noises out his nose, head down close to his food like he was trying to hide in there.

"Mr. Woody, there something bothering me." It was a way to get his attention, the man thinking he was being asked his advice. "What the police will do is talk to the people were here. Try to find one will tell 'em Ginger went upstairs and then you went up there after her. I'm saying if Ginger doesn't accept your generous offer."

The man stopped eating to think about that, frowned with his mouth open, the overhead light shining on him, and Donnell had to look away.

"I doubt your friends notice you were gone, the condition they was in, flying high on the blow. But there was one lady there wasn't of your regular group. The older one, had her hair in a braid?"

"Robin," Woody said. "You remember her?"

See? He could do that. Pick somebody out from a long time ago. Like he had put certain things in his mind in a safe place the booze couldn't touch. Especially things and people had to do with his brother. Donnell settled in, leaning over his arms on the edge of the table.

"Robin Abbott, huh? I thought to myself, Now who is that? I didn't recognize her 'cause it had been so long. Was at the party your lovely mother had to raise bail money, huh?"

"Mom didn't want to have it," Woody said. "Mark begged her, she said no. I had to talk her into it."

"Had a way with your mama, didn't you?"

"We got along. Mark took after Dad, so she didn't trust him."

"Your daddy went out on her, huh?"

"I guess so."

They hadn't talked about the dad much; the dad had moved away and passed on. No problem there to come up unexpected. Donnell let the man eat in peace a minute before starting in again.

"Yeah, was at that bail party I met Robin. I was introduced to her and all those people and then after while I ran into her in the bathroom. The little one out by the front hall? I walk in, she's in there."

The man was listening, because he said, "She was in the bathroom, uh?"

"Yeah, she was in there, you know, combing her hair, prettyin' up, looking at herself in the mirror. She seem like a nice lady. Without knowing much about her."

The man said, "Who, Robin?" Digging into his pile of food. "She was something else. You never knew. . . . Like when she was hiding out she'd come to the house. Never call first, she'd come at night and stay here a few days. Mom didn't like her. She'd spy on her and Mark."

"Catch 'em in the toidy?"

"When they were talking. Then Mom'd get Mark to tell her to leave."

"Undesirable influence, huh?"

"After she was arrested, then we didn't see her till, you know, the other night."

"What'd the police get after her for, demonstrating? Marching without a license?"

The man raised his head from the dish. "Was the FBI. For the time she and her boyfriend blew up that office in the Federal Building. You don't remember that?"

"I must've been gone then," Donnell said, easing up in the kitchen chair, looking at the man grinning at him, lo mein gravy shining on his chin.

"When we were at school, you know what she'd do any time she wanted something, like if she needed money? She'd unbutton her shirt, hold it open and let me look at her goodies."

Donnell said, "Let you look at 'em, huh?" He said, "Mr. Woody, you telling me this lady knows how to set bombs?"

The man was eating and then he wasn't eating. He chewed and stopped chewing and stared at Donnell, swallowed and kept staring at him.

Donnell said, "Wipe your chin, Mr. Woody."

Skip told Robin when she dropped him off to give him ten minutes. Robin came around in the Lincoln, crept past the house looking for him, drove on and there he was up the street, the headlights finding him in the dark. It didn't take as long as he'd thought. Robin said he looked like a burglar going home from work. Skip said, home being Bloomfield Hills. Let's go.

Straight up Woodward out of Detroit without knowing it, except now there were four lanes of traffic both ways, people in a hurry, Skip looking at the miles of lit-up used car lots and motels and neon words announcing places to eat, Skip relieved, enjoying the ride, telling Robin he'd walked all the way around Woody's house, looked in windows at empty rooms and came back to his original idea: set it in the bushes up close to one of the concrete lions. See, then she could say to Woody on the phone, "When you hear the lion roar you'll know we mean business." Robin didn't comment on his idea. She was edging over with cars whizzing by to get into the inside lane.

"What're you looking for?"

"A drugstore," Robin said. "Did you forget?"

Skip said, "Would you believe I've never purchased any of those things in my life?"

Once they found a drugstore open and Robin was angle-parked in front, he asked her what he was supposed to do for money. Robin gave him a ten and he went inside.

Skip was wearing his black satiny athletic jacket that had *Speedball* written across the back in red. He unzipped it and put his hands in his pockets as he looked at displays along the cigar counter. When he didn't see what he wanted he moved toward the back of the store, taking time to look at the shelves, more things to beautify you than make you feel better. There were two people at the counter in the pharmacy area: a woman in a peach-colored smock who looked like she sold cosmetics and had most of them on her, and a young skinny guy with a store name tag that said *Kenny* and a half-dozen pens in his shirt pocket. The young clerk asked Skip if he could help him. Skip said yeah, like he was trying to think of what it was he'd come in for, glanced at the cosmetics lady and told the young clerk he wanted a pack of rubbers.

The young clerk said, "What is it you want?"

"I want some rubbers," Skip said.

The young clerk said, "Oh, condoms." The cosmetics lady, about ten feet away writing in a notebook, didn't look up. "They're right here," the young clerk said, raising his hand to a display on the wall behind him. "What kind you want?"

"I don't care, any kind."

"You like the regular or the ribbed?"

Skip hesitated. "The regular."

"Natural finish or lubricated?"

"Just plain'll be fine."

"Any particular color?"

Skip was about to ask the guy if he was putting him on, but the cosmetics lady was coming over saying, "The new golden shade is very popular. Kenny, why don't you show him those?"

The young clerk turned from the display holding a box that had a picture on it of a guy and a girl walking along a beach at sunset, holding hands. Skip wondered if you were supposed to think the guy had a rubber in his wallet and they were looking for a place to do it on the beach. They were crazy if they did. Even a car was better than the beach. Anybody's car that was open.

Skip said, "That's fine," getting the ten-dollar bill out of his jacket. "How much is it?"

"This one's the economy pack," the young clerk said, looking at the price tag. "Three dozen for sixteen ninety-five."

Skip had the ten-dollar bill in his hand. He put it back

in his pocket, took off his black satiny athletic jacket and said to the young clerk, "I'll tell you what," as he laid the jacket open on the counter. "Gimme about a dozen of those economy packs. Put 'em right here."

The young clerk and the cosmetics lady seemed to be trying to smile. Was he being funny or what?

No, he wasn't being funny. Skip reached behind him for the .38 stuck in his belt to show them he wasn't. He said to the cosmetics lady, "While he's doing that, you empty the cash drawer. Then you both lay down on the floor." He said to the young clerk, "Hey, Kenny? But none of those ribbed ones. Gimme all regular."

Robin pushed in the cigarette lighter, looked up and saw Skip coming out of the drugstore. He had his jacket off, bunched under his arm like he was carrying something in it. As soon as he was in the car he said, "Let's go." Robin held her hand on the lighter, waiting for it to pop.

"How many did you get?"

"Four hundred and something."

Robin said, "Well, we can always get more." She lit her cigarette. "You must've used a credit card."

"Let's go, okay?"

"My, but we're anxious."

"I can hardly wait," Skip said.

17

Greta lay in Chris's dad's king-size bed wondering, If somebody handed you twenty-five thousand dollars in cash, what would it be in? Would it be in like a briefcase all lined up in neat rows? Would you have to take the money out and put it in something and give them back the briefcase? Probably. She turned her head to look at the digital clock on the bedside table, green figures in the morning gloom: 7:49. She looked back at the ceiling and thought, Wait a minute. If ten one-hundred-dollar bills made a thousand, it wouldn't be much of a pile. Especially new ones. She held her thumb and one finger about an inch apart, closed one eye as she looked up and narrowed the space between them. Ten one-hundred-dollar bills wouldn't be any more than an eighth of an inch. Times twenty-five

. . . the whole amount'd be only three or four inches high. You wouldn't need a briefcase for that, you could stick it in an envelope. Twenty-five thousand didn't seem so much looking at it that way. She had to buy a car . . .

She had to get up and brush her teeth and take a couple of Extra-Strength Excedrin. She'd had four drinks last night at Brownie's. Bourbon over crushed ice with a touch of sugar sprinkled on top. Chris had never had one. She told him it was her dad's Sunday afternoon drink he called a God's Own—in the summertime with fresh mint her mom grew in the backyard. Two at the bar shaped like a boat, Chris smacking his lips with that first one, two more at the table, the God's Owns going down easy, and then a bottle of wine with the pickerel. Starting out quietly to discuss a serious matter and before she knew it they were having fun.

It was the way Chris told it, calling the guy Mr. Woody, describing this weird scene, Mr. Woody naked on a rubber raft, a mound of lard floating in the pool. Mr. Woody's colored chauffeur doing everything but kiss the man's hind end while he thought up ways to hustle him, hoping to skim twenty grand off the top of Mr. Woody's offer and give Ginger five. Chris calling her Ginger at first because they did.

She told him it was "Gingah" if he was going to say it, the way she heard it all her life from her family, and not "Gingurr" with his Detroit accent. Her dad gave her the name when she was little. Her sister Camille they called Lily, but they called her brother, Robert Taylor, always Robert Taylor. That was strange, wasn't it? Then she became Ginger Jones when she married Gary. She told Chris she'd planned to stay Greta Wyatt, but her mother had said, "You're not going to take your husband's name?" Like it was unheard of. (She didn't tell Chris Gary said it "Gingurr" too and after a while it grated on her nerves—along with everything else about Gary, who had a wonderful singing voice but would never leave Dearborn, Michigan, because he was a mama's boy and she kept a tight hold on him. Mothers could mess up lives without even trying.) So to please *her* mother she became Greta Jones till the divorce and she had it changed back. Except she got more audition calls as Ginger Jones, so she was stuck with it professionally. What she should have done before marrying Gary was made up a stage name that ended with a smile when you say it, like Sweeney. Say it, Sweeney. Your mouth forms a smile. And Chris said, "So does Mankowski. Say it: Ginger Mankowski." She did, exaggerating the smile for him, but it didn't sound right. Ginger Mankowski. (Without telling him, she tried Greta Mankowski in her mind, heard the sound of it and saw herself fifty pounds heavier, a night cleaning woman at Ford World Headquarters.)

Chris said to her, "If you're good, it doesn't matter what name you go by. Are you any good?"

She felt herself sag a little. "I'm good. But do you know how many Ginger Joneses there are just in Detroit? Before you even begin to count New York or Los Angeles?"

He said to her, "There's only one Greta Wyatt that I know of."

He called her Greta after that, saying he had never known a Greta and liked the name a lot, coming on to her in sort of a little-boy way, which some guys pulled in order to sneak up on you. Chris did it pretty well, with a nice grin, like he didn't know he was a hunk and women looked at him coming back from the men's room.

He said Mr. Woody, "that poor, pathetic asshole," reminded him of Bingo Bear, a toy he'd given one of his nieces for her birthday. You squeezed Bingo's nose and he spoke, he'd say things like "Give me a hug. . . . Scratch my ear. . . . Play with me." Bingo knew four hundred words. Mr. Woody might know a few more than that, but you didn't squeeze his nose to get him to talk, you fed him peanuts.

Chris said to her, "Have you ever looked at a dog or some animal and wondered what it thought and what it would be like to look out through its eyes?" Greta said, "All the time." And Chris said, "Mr. Woody's a person, and yet looking out through his eyes is unimaginable. Between the booze and all the smoke Donnell blows at him the man is just . . . there. I look at him, a guy with all his money, and think, What good is he? Do you know what I mean? He doesn't serve any purpose." Greta said, "How many people do?" but knew what he meant.

It was strange, when she thought of Woody Ricks now as Mr. Woody, this pathetic creature, it changed the way she remembered being sexually assaulted by him: being thrown on the bed and flipped over with her heinie in the air. Was that funny? Maybe it was from certain angles, or how you might look at it a long time from now. She could still act indignant, easy, and say he wasn't just sort of there, he was *there*, because she was there too, underneath the fat slob. What she couldn't say was that he had actually done it to her. When Sergeant Maureen Downey visited her in the hospital, Maureen asked if there had been penetration and she told Maureen, Sort of. Maureen said he'd either put his penis in her or he hadn't. And she told Maureen, truthfully, because of the state she was in at the time she wasn't sure. Maureen said it didn't matter, it was still criminal sexual conduct of one degree or another. "If we can prove it."

Greta said to Chris last night, "He must know what he did." Chris said, Well, the man had been told, if he didn't remember. She said, "Then maybe he's making the offer because his conscience bothers him." When Chris said the man didn't have one, Mr. Woody ceased being pathetic and turned cold and mean and Greta got mad. She said, "Then he's adding insult to injury, treating me like I'm some kind of dinky legalmatter he can settle out of court."

This morning, lying in Chris's dad's bed, looking at Woody's offer through a dull, semi-hangover headache, she began to think, Hell, even the amount was an insult. A stack of bills no more than three or four inches high.

Chris was on the phone when Greta came in the kitchen and walked past the table without looking at him, going to the range. She heard him say, "Just a second, Maureen." And then, "Oh, my goodness," before saying, "The coffee's right there."

Greta said, "I see it," standing with her back to him in a blue T-shirt that covered her rear end and stopped.

"There's coffee cake in the oven. There's juice. I'll fix you an egg, if you want."

"I'm fine," Greta said, pouring herself a mug of coffee.

"You sure are." Then heard him say, "Okay, Maureen, what's that address again?"

Greta bent from the waist to open the oven and gave Chris a shot of her plain white panties.

"Five-fifty? . . . I'm sorry. Yeah, I got it. Five-fif*teen* Canfield."

Greta came over to the table with her coffee and coffee cake.

"Maureen, I'm sorry. Hold it again, will you?"

They smiled at each other. Greta could feel hers and knew his was real. Look at his eyes.

"Will you sit down?"

"I don't want to bother you."

"You already have."

She said, "Okay," and sat down across from him and began listening to his conversation as she glanced at the front page of the morning *Free Press* on the table. They were talking about Robin. Her name was Robin Abbott.

Chris said, "Maybe she's at work." He said, "Well, you have to find out. Go there and talk to somebody." He said, "I'd be glad to. You're kidding, but I'm not. I'd go in a minute." He said, "Call Huron Valley, see if she had a job lined up." He said, "Oh, I thought she just got out. . . . Yeah, if somebody had been killed she could still be in. I remember Mark, but I don't remember a Robin Abbott. What was the guy's name, Emerson?" Greta watched him write *Emerson Gibbs* on the newspaper. "Give me the mother's name. . . . She's got dough, huh? Live out there." He underlined the names and then drew boxes around them. Greta watched him look up and smile and then look down at the names again as he said, "I'd sure like to go with you." He said, "I know, but you're gonna find that out. Have you talked to Wendell yet?" Greta watched him glance at the wall clock. It was eight thirty-five. He said, "You want to talk to Robin you're gonna have to hurry. Once Wendell gets on her . . ." He listened and said, "Yeah, but she's not gonna be in a very cooperative frame of mind if she's a suspect. Hey, you know what you could do? Wendell goes with you like he's with Sex Crimes and then sneaks up on her with Mark. What a tragedy, Jesus Christ, the guy steps out for a can of peanuts. . . . You know what I'm thinking? Since Wendell's gonna talk to her anyway. Take me with you . . . I mean it." He said, "That's beside the point. They're not gonna send a guy from the Bomb Squad, but that's who you need. I could look around there while you're talking to her. . . ." He said, "Yeah, I'll wait."

Greta smiled, watching him. He was performing, aware of her and maybe a little self-conscious. It reminded her of last night: still talking, high, walking back from Brownie's, but quiet riding up in the elevator, quiet coming into the apartment, neither of them saying a word as they turned out the lights in the living room. Then in the hall Chris telling her there were towels laid out for her in the bathroom. Greta asking if he was sure he didn't want his dad's room. No, all his stuff was in the other bedroom—where she'd looked at family photographs earlier and picked him out at different ages, recognizing Chris as the young boy with the blond crew cut squinting at the sun, trying to smile; the teenager with darker hair to his shoulders, not smiling. He stopped at the door to the room with the pictures. They were both so well-mannered in the hall saying good night after all the God's Owns and the bottle of Piesporter, after looking at each other in that warm boozy glow and knowing something was going to happen. So carefully polite closing their separate doors. Greta undressed, listening. In the bathroom she washed her face and hands, stared at herself in the mirror as she brushed her teeth, turned the water off and stood listening. She got in the king-size bed and lay there in the glow of the lamp, listening. Until that was enough of that and she shouted, "Mankowski!" Paused and yelled, "Are you coming or not?"

He came.

And now he was saying to Maureen, "Okay, will you let me know?" Listening and then saying, "Because I know more than any of you and if I can help, why not?" Saying, "Good. I'll see you. Maureen? Call me. . . . Right." He reached over to hang the phone on the wall and came back to Greta smiling. "Where were we?"

"They found Robin," Greta said.

"We know where she lives. It's a start. You know what else we know? She did time, thirty-three months, for destruction of government property. With a bomb."

Greta said, "Robin?" and saw the older woman with the braid at Woody's, perfectly at ease with her shirt off that night; saw Robin and was aware of Chris saying, *"We know,"* still a working cop in his mind. Greta said, "You only found out what her last name is yesterday."

Chris said, "Yeah, but also the kind of life she was into, going back to the seventies. If she associated with guys like Donnell, a Black Panther, that's a pretty good lead. Maureen didn't find Robin in the computer, so she checked with the Bureau, the FBI office here, and the agent Maureen happened to talk to knew all about her. Also this guy." Chris's gaze dropped to the newspaper. "Emerson Gibbs."

Greta looked at the two names he'd written on the front page. "Who's Marilyn Abbott?"

"Her mother. Maureen's gonna call her, see if she knows where Robin is. This guy, Emerson Gibbs, was convicted with Robin on the same bomb charge and did three and a half years. Both, it turns out, were heavy-duty political activists back at that time." Chris paused. "You know what I mean, back during the hippie days?"

"I was in grade school," Greta said. "But I was in *Hair* when I was going to Oakland University. I went two years." She sang then, in a soft murmur, " 'This is the dawning of the Age of Aquarius . . .' " stopped and said, "Were you a hippie?"

"I'm not sure what I was," Chris said. "I was sort of on the edge of it. I took part in a couple of peace marches, a big one in Washington, and I went to Woodstock . . ."

"Really?"

"And then I went to Vietnam."

"You did?"

"For a while. I came back they were still marching, but"—Chris shook his head—"I didn't."

Greta reached across the table for his hand, looking at his serious expression. She said, "Here we are playing house and I find out I barely know you." That got a little smile. "You have a lot to tell me about."

"I'll tell you where we are right now," Chris said. "Maureen looks for Robin as a possible witness in a sexual assault case. But all of a sudden Robin becomes a suspect in a homicide investigation. Which wouldn't have happened if you hadn't seen her there Saturday night. But now, you understand, Homicide will have a priority, first dibs."

"It's okay," Greta said.

"If Maureen talks to her at all, it could be in the Wayne County jail."

"Really, it doesn't matter," Greta said. "I don't see any reason to go to court if I'm gonna lose."

"Yeah, but at least you get to accuse him in public."

"I thought it over while I was taking a shower. I'm considering Mr. Woody's offer."

There was a silence. Chris stared at her across the table. Then shrugged. "It's up to you."

"You think I'm wrong?"

He took his time. "If you look at it as an out-of-court settlement for mental anguish, or for injuries received, something along those lines—"

"I like mental anguish," Greta said. "Remember the TV preacher who went to bed with a twenty-year-old girl? He did it once about seven years ago and lost his ministry and his theme park."

"I read something about it," Chris said.

"The preacher went to a religious psychologist on account of he was feeling so guilty. The psychologist said the preacher writhed on the floor for ten minutes kicking and screaming, making himself sick."

Chris said, " 'Cause he got laid, once, seven years ago?"

"His guilt was so enormous."

"I've heard of guys kicking and screaming when they *didn't* get laid—"

Greta said, "Listen to me, all right? The girl went to see a man who investigates preachers who fool around and get in trouble. The man put her in touch with a religious lawyer and they told the preacher they were gonna sue him for millions of dollars."

"You mean they blackmailed the poor asshole."

"No, they threatened to sue him, in court, on account of her mental anguish. See?"

"But if she went to bed with the preacher willingly . . ."

"She claims they put something in her wine—I don't know. But if you can make love to a guy and soak him two hundred and sixty-five thousand, which is what they settled on out of court, what is the mental anguish from a rape worth? I don't think there's any comparison."

"You want to get a lawyer?"

"No way. Out of the first payment received the lawyer, and I think the guy who investigates preachers who fool around, took ninety-five thousand and the poor girl got twenty. The hell with that. And now that everybody knows about it she probably won't get another cent. What I'm asking is, If that's legal, do you think I'd be wrong to accept Woody's offer?"

Chris said, "No, but you might be a little hasty. The way it was explained to me, the amount of the settlement is based on what Mr. Woody's valuable time is worth to *him*, without even considering *your* time, your mental anguish and so on."

Greta began to smile as Chris went on:

"No, I don't think twenty-five grand is fair to either of you."

Maureen Downey's voice said, "Where were you, in the bathroom?"

"I was resting."

"It's ten o'clock in the morning."

"I know what time it is."

"I'm at Five-fifteen Canfield, in the manager's office. He said Robin should be around somewhere, she doesn't work and hasn't left town. Her car's parked on the street."

"You call her mother?"

"I tried, no answer. Listen, Wendell likes your idea. Start talking to her about the rape and slide into the homicide. He's gonna meet me here."

"When?"

"In about an hour."

"Call me, soon as you talk to her."

"Why're you so anxious?"

Chris paused. "No—I'm coming too. I'll meet you there."

"Wendell won't like it."

"I'll talk to him." Chris said goodbye, placed the phone against his chest and turned his head on the pillow to look at Greta, her dark brown eyes looking back at him. "That was Maureen."

"I heard."

18

Skip had thought that today he'd pretend he was a wealthy suburbanite: drop his ration of acid, sit back with a few cold beers, his feet up, and watch movies on cable TV, cars bursting in flames, stunt men being shot off of high places—see if he could recognize the work, or how it was done if it was a new gag—and then Robin said they were leaving because the phone had rung.

He'd told her, "You don't think it was for you, do you? It's some old lady calling your mother."

She'd looked at that phone like it was wired to blow and told him to stop and think. What if someone called while she was on the phone talking to Woody? They'd get a busy signal, right? And that would mean someone's in the house, right? But her mother's friends would know she was on a cruise. So you know what they'd do? Skip asked Robin to tell him. *They'd call the cops—that's what they'd do!*

She wasn't thinking.

Skip said, If your mother's friends know she's on a cruise, why would they call?

Now Skip wasn't thinking.

Never use logic on an emotional woman. Or one in any state, for that matter. Robin gave him her killer look instead of an answer. So Skip tried another approach, trying to sound sincere. Robin? Even if the cops did come, what would they do? Ring the doorbell, look in some windows? They didn't have a key, did they?

Yes!

That was where she had him, got him out of the chair in front of the TV and into the car. She was probably lying; she still had him because he couldn't prove otherwise. But what pissed her off most was something he couldn't help but mention.

"If it could get us in trouble, why did you want to call from your mom's in the first place?"

She said, "Because you had to get laid. That's the only reason I stayed at Mother's house, for *you.*"

It hadn't even been that good. Not anywhere near as good as it used to be. As for her laying the blame on him, that was typical of a man-eater like Robin, who had never in her life admitted being wrong and would think quick to incriminate whatever poor asshole was nearest. In this instance Skip sitting next to her in the Lincoln, Robin driving, Robin hauling ass eighty miles an hour down the Chrysler freeway to get home in time to call Woody before eleven. Most other cars were doing about seventy. They drove as fast here as they did in L.A., except out in L.A. there were more places to drive fast *to*.

She was jumping lanes also, cutting in and out of traffic and getting horns blown at her.

If those other people were stunt drivers and he was being paid thirty-five hundred for this ride it might be different. It inspired Skip to ask, "How about if you call from a pay phone? We wouldn't have to rush so."

Robin didn't answer; she kept driving.

"Look over there, the Sign of the Big Boy. We could relax, have us a cup of coffee first."

Robin said, "You really think I'm going to stand at a pay phone in a Big Boy, with people coming in and out past me, and tell Woody, Now here's the deal? Somebody standing next to me, waiting to use the phone? 'Uh, we'd like a million dollars, Woody.' He goes, 'What'd you say?' He can't hear me 'cause I have to keep my voice down."

She seemed calmer doing that little skit and it made some sense. But she was thinking too much. Probably going over in her mind what she'd say to the guy. Skip thought of telling her if she didn't call him at eleven, call him later on, after the bomb went off. What was the difference?

But that made too much sense and could get her pissed off again. Or she'd say she didn't want to talk about it any more, so drop it. That was how some women miscalculated the guy's frustration level and got hit. The woman would still win. She'd keep showing him her black eye to make him feel like an asshole. It was best not to get worked up in the first place. What Skip did, flying down the Chrysler freeway, he went through his mind looking for harmless but interesting topics of conversation. . . . And thought of a good one.

"Remember that big Stroh's beer sign you used to see down a ways?"

He told her how a demolition company tore down the brewery, a sight he'd have come to watch if he'd known about it beforehand. He told her you didn't explode a building when you took it down, you *im*ploded it. He told her for the Stroh's job he read they'd set eight hundred and eighty separate charges and blew them at seven-and-a-half-second intervals, starting from the center of the structure and working out, blowing those support columns one at a time so that the building collapsed in on itself. He told Robin he was here in '84, right after he got out of Milan, when they tore down the old Hoffman building, Woodward at Sibley. They blew the charge and the building just stood there till four hours later it fell the wrong way, right on top of the bar next door. He told Robin that when you have space around you it's a different ball game. He began to tell her how you demolish a silo, how you notch one side and shoot light charges on the other—

And Robin said, "Jesus Christ, will you shut up?"

That did irritate Skip, but did not set him off. He had a return ticket to L.A. He had a hundred and forty-seven dollars from the drugstore, and he had four hundred and something rubbers he could blow up like balloons to celebrate getting the fuck out of this deal if she got any snottier.

Neither of them said another word till they pulled up in front of her rundown apartment building on Canfield and Robin turned her head toward him, hand on the door latch.

"You go right back to the house and stay in the basement. And I mean *stay* there. Don't even go *near* a window."

"What if the phone rings?"

"Don't answer it."

"What if it's you?" Skip said.

Got her.

Ten thirty Donnell brought Mr. Woody his eye-opener, vodka and pale dry ginger ale, half and half, two of them on a silver tray. He placed one of the drinks on the night table next to the flashlight the man kept there in case of a power failure. The man, being scared to death of the dark, had flashlights all over the house.

The way Donnell usually worked it, he'd touch the man then and say, "Rise and shine, Mr. Woody, the day is waiting on you," except if the man had wet the bed. Then Donnell would hold his breath and not say anything, just shake him, trying not to breathe in the smell coming off the man. Donnell would have to wait for the swollen face to show life mixed with pain, then for the man to get up on his elbow and take the drink. Donnell would then step out of the way. Soon as the man finished the drink he'd be sick right there if he didn't get to the bathroom in time. Starting this wake-up service, Donnell had brought the man Bloody Marys, till he found out being sick was part of waking up. Did it one week and said, Enough of this Bloody Mary shit, cleaning up a bathroom looked like somebody'd been killing chickens in it.

Today Mr. Woody got in there okay to gag, make all kinds of sick noises while Donnell slipped on his earphones and listened to Whodini doing the rap, doing "The Good Part," rappin' "When we gonna get to the good part?" Rap. Yeah. Donnell watching the man didn't slip and hit his head. "Mr. Woody?" Donnell said. "Get down to it, on your knees, you be safer." Man would be closer to the toilet too, wouldn't get his mess all over.

Mr. Woody came out catching his breath like he'd been crying, red face redder, and Donnell handed him his second drink, the one that would settle him, let his system know the alcohol was coming and everything would be fine.

There, the man said "Boy-oh-boy," showing signs he wasn't going to die just yet. Ordinarily about now Donnell would ask him what was on for today, play that game with him, like there was all this different shit the man could be doing. But not this morning.

This morning he said, "Soon as you have your breakfast we have to tend to some business." He watched the man stumble against the bed trying to put his pants on. "Mr. Woody, what you do, you put your underwear on first. Then you sit down on the floor to put your trousers on, so you don't kill yourself." Asshole. The man could barely dress himself, could never pick out clothes that matched.

"Mr. Woody, the funeral people called up. They getting your brother this afternoon, from the morgue. They gonna cremate him, but then what do they put the remains in? See, they have different-price urns they use. Then is he going out to a cemetery? You understand? The funeral people want to know what to do with him."

"Tell 'em—I don't know," Woody said from the floor. "Did you get the paper in?"

"Not yet."

"I want to know what my horoscope says."

"I'll get it for you," Donnell said. "Read it with your breakfast. We have to talk about getting the mess cleaned up in back, have it hauled away. You want me to take care of it?"

"Call somebody."

"I know some people do that kind of work."

"That's fine."

Donnell watched him reach under the bed for his shoes.

"We have to talk about getting you a new limousine. What kind you want, what you want in it, all that."

"I want a white one."

"That's cool. But what we have to do first, Mr. Woody, is see how you want to change your will, now your brother's gone. I thought me and you could rough it out. You understand? Put it all down on a piece of paper and you sign it, you know, just in case you don't talk to your lawyer for a while."

"I think I either want a white one or a black one."

Donnell bit on the inside of his mouth till he felt pain and said, "Mr. Woody, you want to look up here a minute? Never mind your shoes, I'll tie your shoes for you. Please look up here."

Multi-wealthy millionaire motherfucker sitting on the floor like a fat kid, not knowing shit.

"I believe you forget something you told me yourself last night," Donnell said. "This woman name of Robin Abbott? You remember her, was here Saturday?"

The man, looking up at him dumb-eyed, said, "Robin . . . ?"

"Use to show you her goodies."

"Yeah, Robin."

"You tell me she went to stir for doing bombs? Now your own brother got kill by one yesterday was put in your limo? Not his, *yours?*"

"Mark doesn't have a limo."

"Listen to me. You understand it could happen again?

Bam, you get taken out, you not even looking, don't even hear it. That's why I'm saying you have to get a new will, man, Mr. Woody, in case anything might happen you don't even know about."

Look at the man looking fish-eyed. What's he see?

"That's what we gonna do next," Donnell said, "while you having your breakfast. Write down things for your will." Shit. Quick.

Woody said, "Will you get the paper?"

Donnell went downstairs. He'd look at the horoscope box in the paper and pick out a good one, read it to the man while he at his Sugar Pops. *This is a special day for romance. Love is looking up.* The man liked that kind. Or, what Donnell was thinking of doing as he crossed the front hall, make one up. *Time to get your financial ass in order. . . . Don't put off making your will. . . . Put in it whoever has been most loyal to you. Whoever cleans up your messes.*

He opened the front door hoping to see the *Free Press* lying close by. It wasn't on the stoop, it wasn't out on the grass. . . . He'd told the fat-kid delivery boy, Man, if you don't have the arm then walk it up here on your young legs. But the fat kid's daddy waiting out in the car, most likely hating rich people, had told the kid throw it, that's how you deliver papers, throw the motherfucker. The fat kid would obey his daddy and the paper would end up half the time in the bushes.

The ones to the left of the door. Donnell went to the stone lion on that side and leaned over its back. There was the paper folded tight with a rubber band resting in the shrubs. There was the paper and there was something else looked like a bag underneath it. Donnell stepped around the lion and down off the slate front stoop. It looked like a new bag, not one had been out in the weather. The kind of black canvas bag a workman might have left? Or one of the police yesterday looking around. Donnell saw the bag in that moment as a *find*, something that could be worth something. He picked up the paper and the bag and went inside, closed the front door and locked it. Put the bag on the hall table with the paper, zipped the bag open, looked inside at the clock, the battery, the five sticks of dynamite and the wires going from here to there and said, "Shit. I'm dead."

It took a minute for Donnell standing there frozen to tell himself he wasn't dead *yet*. That the bomb must've been put there during the night and had sat there all this time. It took him that little while to adjust to the situation and tell himself, Be cool. Are you cool? He wasn't running off screaming, that was cool. He was looking right at the bag. He thought, Open the door, throw it outside. But couldn't turn his back to it. It was like if he kept looking at the motherfucker it wouldn't do nothing to him. Except there was a clock in there ticking toward a certain time or there wouldn't be no need for the clock. If he looked at the clock it might tell him what time the bomb was going off. Only the clock wasn't face up. To reach in, touch it, mess with the wires, that wouldn't be cool. Look at a clock the last thing he ever did on earth?

What did that leave for him to do?

Donnell wiggled his toes in his hundred-dollar jogging shoes.

He said, "You got to put it somewhere, man." Thought of outside, thought of down in the basement. He said, "You got to put it somewhere you don't stop and fool with doors." Thought another minute and picked up that bag again, the hardest thing he ever did in his life.

Donnell walked off with the bag down the hall, hurrying without running, the way those guys in a heel-and-toe walking race move their hips cute back and forth, holding the bag out to the side like it had a mess in it, went through the sunroom and out to the chlorine-smelling swimming pool, took some sidesteps turning, flung that bag *away* from him out over the water, ran back into the sunroom, hit the floor and covered his head.

There was no sound. Dead silence.

Then a ringing sound and Donnell felt his body jump. The sound came again and came again, Donnell hearing it through his shoulders tight against his ears. It came again and he took his arms away, gradually raised his head. It came again and he got to his knees and reached for the phone.

"Mr. Ricks's residence. . . ."

Robin sat at her desk in a swivel chair, close to the red explosion on the wall. She recognized Donnell's voice and said into the phone, "Let me speak to him, please."

Donnell's voice said, "Mr. Ricks can't be disturbed. You want to tell me who's calling?"

"Tell him it's quite important."

Robin was giving him her low, slow voice.

"You can leave a message," Donnell's voice said, "or you can call back later."

"I want to tell him I'm sorry about his brother."

"You can leave your name, your phone number."

Robin stroked her braid.

"I want to tell him it was an accident."

There was a silence on the line.

"What was?"

"His brother getting blown up. I want to tell him that. Why don't you ask him if he can be disturbed or not?"

"Don't have to ask him, he's the one told me."

Robin moved and the swivel chair squeaked.

"I want to tell him I hope the same thing doesn't happen to him."

There was a longer silence on the line.

"I can tell him that," Donnell's voice said.

"But I want to be sure he understands it. If you tell him, you're taking on quite a responsibility, don't you think?"

There was a pause and then Donnell's voice said, "How much you looking to get?"

Now Robin paused. The chair squeaked again.

"I'd like about a million. Yeah, let's make it an even million. Can you remember to tell him that?"

"I believe so," Donnell's voice said. "Would that be cash or you take a check?"

Robin hunched over the desk as she said, "You want to play, is that what you're doing? I'll play with you. In about two minutes, man, you'll *hear* the way I play. It's going to ring in your fucking ears so you won't forget."

There was a silence.

Then heard, "Hold it a minute."

Robin straightened in the chair. "Hey, what're you doing?" Silence. She looked at her watch. Twenty-five seconds passed.

Donnell's voice came on the line again. "All right. Tell me how you want this million dollars given to you."

"Oh, are you back? You ready to talk?"

His voice said, "Behave, girl. I can hang up, end this business right now."

Robin got her low, quiet voice back. "I'll let you know. How's that?"

"When's this gonna be you talking about?"

"As soon as he has it."

"If the man doesn't want to give it to you, what?"

"Bow your head and think of Mark."

"Say you gonna kill him, blow him up?"

Before Robin could answer Donnell's voice said:

"All right, it's cool. I'll tell the man."

The line went dead.

Robin eased back in the chair and didn't move. She wanted to believe she'd handled it okay—at least considering the way Donnell was all of a sudden into it, playing it back, and it threw her timing off. The idea had been to keep him on till she heard the explosion, tell him to have a nice day and hang up.

She might have to give Skip a different version. Otherwise he'd say she blew it, misjudged the guy. Try to explain that. Well, you see him in his chauffeur suit opening doors, Jesus Christ, you *assume* he's now a well-behaved brand-new house-nigger version of the old Donnell, right? And Skip would say, Hey, Robin? You decide this dude is born again and you haven't talked to him in like sixteen years?

Robin began to picture Donnell waiting by the limo, Donnell in his dark shades, the trim black suit. . . . She lit a cigarette, got more comfortable in the creaky chair and began to think, Yeah, but wait. What's wrong with the way it is? Dealing with the old Donnell. Jesus, and began to get excited about the idea. Seeing him as a Panther hiding in the chauffeur suit. Waiting for his chance to score, work some kind of game. The guy would have to be up to *some*thing.

She wondered why she hadn't realized it before. It seemed so obvious now. How could he resist? She thought about it another few moments and said, "Jesus, far out." Because if they were both looking to score and Donnell was inside, alone, and hadn't figured out a move yet . . .

Robin had an urge to call him back. "Hi, it's me. I was just wondering, you want to get in on it?"

But then looked at her watch. Shit, it was bomb time. Any moment now, *kaboom,* and the lion goes flying, disappears, the door blows in, windows shatter. . . .

And who sees it? Back when blowing up the establishment was popular, they'd set the charge on a timer, come back to park about a block away, smoke joints and at least *hear* it go off. She realized she was not working much of a fun factor into this deal. Thinking too much about money. Bad. Becoming way too serious. What she needed was a release, an upper that wasn't dope. A guy who could lighten her mood. Not Skip, he was basically a downer. Someone more spontaneous—as her mind flashed that scene in the powder room—like Donnell. Perfect. Assuming that in the last thirty seconds or so he hadn't opened the front door. It would be just her luck to lose him before they even got started. She began to wonder what Skip would think. She liked Skip, but he always had b.o. Which used to be okay, but not now. Having b.o. was no longer in. She kind of liked the idea of approaching Donnell first. That seemed like the way to go. . . .

The phone rang.

Robin waited for two more rings before answering. It was the building manager. He said, "Well, you're finally home. There's a couple police officers here want to talk to you."

"What about?"

The manager didn't answer. Robin heard him talking to someone away from the phone. She waited. And now a woman's voice came on.

"Miss Abbott, I'm sorry to bother you. I'm Sergeant Downey, with the Detroit Police? I wonder if we could come up and talk to you for a minute."

"It doesn't sound like a lot of fun," Robin said. "What's it about?"

"You may or may not have been a witness to a crime we're investigating. It'll only take about two minutes."

"It's not something I did?" Robin said.

The lady cop sort of laughed. "No, we're sure of that."

"How many are you? I only have three chairs."

"We won't even have to sit down," the lady cop's voice said. "Just myself and Sergeant Mankowski."

Donnell made himself stand at the side of the pool. The bag was floating still, as it was before, when he'd come off the phone to take a look. The stuff from inside the bag was at the bottom of the deep end by the diving board, in nine feet of water. Dark objects down there. The wires still seemed attached to the objects.

Donnell walked through the house to its other end and into the kitchen, where the man was watching "Leave It to Beaver" on the TV while he had his breakfast. It looked like Post Alpha-Bits this morning. The man liked a sweet cereal to start the day, then get all the sugar he needed in his booze. The horoscope page of the paper was folded open next to his bowl. The man glanced up, anxious.

"Listen to this. It says, 'You have a sense of inner and outer harmony. This would be a perfect day to start taking singing lessons; you may have talent.' What do you think?"

"Yeah, well, if we have time," Donnell said. "We got us a couple more pressing matters come up. First thing, we have to find somebody knows how to take a bomb out of the swimming pool."

That got the man's dumb eyes focused on him.

"How did a bomb get in the swimming pool?"

"Let's come back to it," Donnell said. "We also have

a matter, this lady called. Say she gonna blow you up if you don't give her some money."

Donnell waited for the man's mind to work and put this and that together. Like he fooled with the Alpha-Bits floating in his milk sometimes, trying to make a word out of the letters.

"The lady that called put the bomb in the swimming pool?"

"I 'magine she's the one."

"Is it gonna go off?"

"I don't know. That's why I say we have to get us a bomb man."

"Call the police, they'll take care of it."

"I'm afraid of what she'd do. You know, like she might be a crazy woman and it would set her off."

Right then Beaver's mama on the TV, a cute woman, began fussing at Mr. Beaver, giving him some shit. Doing it just at the right time.

The man shook his head, didn't know what to think. Had an idea then and said, "Was it Robin that called?"

"I suspect, but I don't know her voice."

"How much does she want?"

Here we go.

"Say she like two million, cash money, no checks. Get it from the bank and have it ready."

Look at the man blink his eyes.

"Yeah, she say to have it ready. You know, like in a box? See, then when she phones again, to tell us the time and place she wants it? You suppose to give it to me and I deliver it."

19

What happened: when Wendell didn't show up, Maureen called Homicide from the manager's ground-floor apartment. The manager, a sour old man, stood at a window watching for Robin, bifocals gleaming when he turned his head, more interested in Maureen. Chris was reading the Bureau report on Robin Abbott, times and places in it familiar. He heard Maureen say, irritated, "Thanks for telling me. You know how long I've been waiting here?" She hung up, saying to Chris, "Wendell's got a body in an alley: female, black." Chris said, "And you have me." Maureen said, "Oh, no. You're staying here." Chris said to the manager, "Try Miss Abbott again, okay?" The manager said, "She isn't back yet. I'd have seen her." Chris said, "But will you try?" And said to Maureen, the manager busy now, "You talk to her, I look around. You need me." Maureen said, "You don't have your badge or I.D. What do you show her?" As the manager was saying, "Well, you're finally home. . . ."

Going up the stairs behind Maureen's nice firm athletic calves he said, "Robin I see was at U of M the same time I was, before I went in the army. Right up from where I lived on State Street, by the Michigan Union, there was always something going on, some kind of demonstration. Nice little girls screaming at the cops, calling 'em pigs." He shut up as they reached the second floor.

Robin Abbott stood waiting for them, the door to her apartment open. She wore tinted glasses, her hair in a fat braid, shirt hanging out over jeans, barefoot, trying to look young and girlish and not doing a bad job. Chris checked her out over Maureen's shoulder, letting Maureen lead the way and introduce them. "Hi, I'm Sergeant Downey"—showing her I.D.—"and this is Sergeant Mankowski." Chris had his wallet out. He flipped it open and closed, staying pretty much behind Maureen.

Miss Abbott brought them in, saying, "Well, what can I do for you?" in a quiet, low voice, then lightened the tone as she said, "I don't recall witnessing any crimes lately."

Chris thought of saying he was glad she qualified that. Miss Abbott had been arrested in '78 after jumping a bond set years before, convicted and sent away in '79. Maureen had the Bureau printout in her bag; he'd get a copy of it to go over in detail. He wondered what the round red design was supposed to be, painted on the wall. The rest of the room was a mess. Miss Abbott sure had a lot of books and magazines, and what looked like old newspapers, piles of

them on a bookshelf. Chris wandered over there as Miss
Abbott asked if they'd like coffee or a soft drink, Miss Abbott showing what a nice person she was. Maureen said
thanks, but they didn't want to take up too much of her
time. Just a few questions, if Miss Abbott wouldn't mind.
Miss Abbott said, Of course; what would they like to know?
See? Cooperative as well as nice. Maureen became official
then, saying, "We understand you were at a party at the
home of Mr. Woodrow Ricks last Saturday evening?"
Chris, looking at books, heard Miss Abbott trying hard to
be of help, saying, "Was it Saturday? Yeah, I *think* so."

As Maureen said, "You think it was Saturday or you
think you were there?" and Miss Abbott laughed and said,
"Both," Chris let his gaze move to the desk close by, the
surface nearly covered with typed pages, file folders, mail,
magazines, notebooks. . . .

He saw a notebook with a red cover lying on top. It had
MAY–AUGUST '70 written on it big in black Magic Marker.

Miss Abbott came over to the desk for a cigarette and
Chris looked at the books again. She had an assortment of
paperback novels, several of each title—*Gold Fire, Diamond
Fire, Silver Fire, Emerald Fire*—all by the same author, Nicole
Robinette. Maureen was asking about the people who were
at the party. Miss Abbott said she didn't think she could be
of much help there; she wasn't introduced to anyone.

She had Bukowski on the shelf. She had Genet, Gins-
berg. She had Abbie Hoffman's *Woodstock Nation* and *Revolution for the Hell of It.* Maureen was asking Miss Abbott if
she went swimming with the others. She had *Soledad Brother.*
She had *Sisterhood Is Powerful, The Politics of Protest.*

Miss Abbott said she just sort of got her toes wet.

Did she recall Greta Wyatt going in the pool?

She had old copies of underground newspapers Chris
hadn't seen or heard of since he got out of school: *East*

Village Other, Rat Subterranean News, Fifth Estate, South End, the Wayne University paper. A copy of the *Berkeley Barb* dated May 16–22, 1969, with a headline that said PIGS SHOOT TO KILL. . . . Hearing Miss Abbott tell Maureen she wasn't sure who went in the pool and who didn't. He waited for her to mention Mark Ricks. He picked up a book called *Is the Library Burning?*, still waiting as he put the book back on the shelf.

He glanced at the desk as she tapped her cigarette toward the ashtray sitting there.

The notebook with the red cover was no longer in sight.

He heard Maureen asking Miss Abbott if she recalled Greta Wyatt going upstairs and Miss Abbott saying she wasn't sure which one Greta Wyatt was.

Chris picked up a book from the shelf with the dust-jacket flap folded into the pages and turned to Miss Abbott.

"You still reading William Burroughs?"

Miss Abbott looked over and seemed to notice him for the first time. She stared with no expression before gradually beginning to smile.

"You want to make something of it?"

"I was looking at your books," Chris said. "I've read some of them. Abbie Hoffman, I've probably read all of his."

"You like Abbie?"

"I don't know why he wasn't a stand-up comic. Yeah, I liked him," Chris said. "I felt sorry for him too. The poor guy hiding out all those years and nobody was even looking for him."

She didn't seem to care for that. Miss Abbott said, "He was wanted by the FBI, wasn't he?"

"Yeah, but how bad did they want him? It was like he

finally pops up: Here I am. And they go, 'Oh, shit. Now we have to arrest him.'" Chris saw her start to frown and said, "Yeah, all this takes me back," looking at the bookshelves again. "I went to Washington for the biggest peace march in history, the Vietnam Moratorium, one of a million protesters. I was at Woodstock . . . I think it was that summer, yeah, I was still going to U of M, I lived in a house on State Street right next to Pizza Bob's. It was that summer the ROTC building got trashed. I remember typewriters flying out the window." He was grinning.

It seemed to encourage Miss Abbott. "More than just typewriters, all the records. . . . Did you take part in that?"

"I watched," Chris said. "No, the only time I saw any action was when George Wallace was here. That time he was running for President and had a rally at Cobo Hall. He's trying to make his speech, we're in the balcony, we stand up and give him that Hitler salute and yell, 'Sieg Heil, you-all!' His fans didn't like it. There was a scuffle, pushing and throwing chairs." Chris grinned. "I remember Wallace yelling at us, 'Get a haircut and take a load off your mind.' I don't know why hair bothered people so much."

"Really," Miss Abbott said. "Or the way we dressed."

"And spoke rather freely," Chris said. "You were at U of M at that time?"

Miss Abbott drew on her cigarette. "I lived on Packard."

Chris said, "Packard, you could throw a rock from my front steps and hit Packard." He gave her another grin. "And some people did. You miss those days?"

"I have them." Miss Abbott said. "I can look at them any time I want."

That was a little weird. She seemed to want to get into it with him but was holding back.

Maureen, seated now in a plastic chair that looked like it was coming apart, was watching. She met Chris's gaze for a moment, not saying a word.

Miss Abbott said, "You were at Woodstock?"

"In the rain and the mud, all three days."

"I really wanted to go, but I had something on."

"You had to be there to believe it," Chris said. "Half a million people sitting there all wet and nobody cared. Saturday I got to see my all-time favorite, Grace Slick. I saw Janis, the Who, Santana. On Sunday, Joe Cocker. He had stars on his boots. You remember Ten Years After? Alvin Lee?"

"They were at Goose Lake, the next summer," Miss Abbott said. "You remind me of a guy, a friend of mine. He'll go, 'You remember Licorice? Who was she with?'"

"The Incredible String Band," Chris said.

They were grinning at each other.

"You aren't Nicole Robinette by any chance?"

"I'm afraid so."

"I haven't read any of your books, but I'd like to."

"No, you wouldn't."

Again, both grinned and Chris glanced at the bookshelves. "How'd you manage to hang onto all this? You've got *Rising Up Angry*. You've got the *Rat*, *Barb*, ones I've heard of but don't think I ever read."

"You never know," Miss Abbott said, "they could be collector's items someday. I stored everything at Mother's while I was in New York, working for a publishing house."

Chris said, "How about when you were at Huron Valley, working in the laundry?"

That took care of Miss Abbott's pleasant expression, left over from the grin.

She said, "I'm afraid I'm going to have to ask you to leave."

"You don't want to talk about old times?" Chris said. "Tell us how you got busted, any of that?"

"I don't care to talk to you about anything," Miss Abbott said. "Okay? So leave. That means don't say another word, just get the fuck out."

Going down the stairs Maureen paused on the landing to look back at Chris.

"I thought she might try to finesse around it, at least act dumb. No, *sir.*"

"She comes right at you," Chris said. "You notice she didn't say anything about Mark? Didn't want to go near that, get on the subject of bombs. Did you learn anything?"

Maureen said, "You mean outside of what she doesn't want to talk about? No. She won't be any help to us on the assault—yeah, I did learn that much."

"I wouldn't worry about that one," Chris said. In the front hall by the manager's apartment he said, "Can I make a suggestion?"

"Give it to Wendell."

"Yeah, but call him, from here. Tell him to get a judge to sign a warrant, so he can come right over and search her apartment. You could stick around, make sure she doesn't leave."

"What're we looking for, bombs?"

"Any kind of explosives, copper wire, blasting caps, timers, maybe some kind of remote control switch. Clothespins, the snap kind. Be sure to check the refrigerator."

"Clothespins?"

"Have Wendell put on the warrant you're looking for explosive materials and literature."

"What kind of literature?"

"A notebook with a red cover that's marked 'May to August 1970.' If you don't find anything else, at least get hold of the notebook. There's something in it, 'cause she hid it while you were talking to her. Covered it with some papers. Maybe she's got instructions in it, how to make a bomb. But even if it doesn't look like anything," Chris said, "hold on to it and let me see it, okay?"

Maureen didn't answer. She squinted, making a show of studying him. "I don't get it. You want to work so bad, why don't you straighten out your residence problem, get your shield back?"

"I don't think I like Sex Crimes."

"Okay, but why this? What're you trying to prove?"

"Nothing, I'm just going along."

"That's what I'm asking you. Why?"

He had to think of words to describe something he knew without words, something that came to him as he stood at Robin Abbott's bookshelf and looked at her past and realized her past was her present. "One thing leads to another," Chris said. "Greta takes us to Robin. You find out she was a hard-core revolutionary at U of M and I pick up on it because I was there, I saw what was going on. I was even into it, not much but enough that I could feel it again. She did too, when I was talking about it. You see her face? She was dying to tell stories, top anything I said easy, but she held back. She was afraid if she got started she might say too much, give away what she's into now."

"If she's into anything."

"Maureen, come on. Why'd she hold back? What's wrong with talking about old times?"

Maureen said, "It looked like she's living in those times."

Chris smiled at Maureen coming around. "Or she'd like to relive them, huh? But if she can't, then maybe she gets into it in a different way or for a different reason. You know what I mean?"

"Maybe she's mad at somebody," Maureen said.

It raised Chris's eyebrows.

"Maybe somebody, when she was busted," Maureen said, "turned her in."

Chris said, "That's not bad, Maureen." He thought about it and said, "Yeah, I like it. I might be able to look into that."

He remembered one night in the Athens Bar, a guy he'd see in there, an artist by the name of Dizsi, telling how they had planned to blow up a submarine, the one that used to be parked in the Detroit River behind the Naval Armory. It was for sightseeing, Dizsi said, but it was also a symbol of war. He believed someone informed on them, because the submarine disappeared before they could destroy it and later turned up in the Israeli navy.

Chris liked to listen to Dizsi. He was Hungarian and spoke through his gray beard with an accent that was perfect for telling about anarchist plots. Dizsi had escaped the Russians, traded Budapest for Detroit, taught fine art at Wayne State and supported student demonstrations until he was fired. Now he lived in a loft studio in Greektown where he painted wall-size canvases and was waited on by his mistress, Amelia.

"You remember Robin Abbott?"

"Yes, of course, and I'll tell you why."

Chris liked to watch him eat, too. Dizsi could make things Chris wouldn't dare even to smell look good. Today, having his lunch in the studio when Chris walked in, he was eating marinated squid and hummus, wiping Greek bread in the colorless paste. A bottle of Greek wine stood on the table where tubes of paint had been pushed aside. Chris didn't especially like retsina, either, but had some when Amelia appeared in a long white shirtdress and filled Dizsi's glass, Dizsi saying, "We tried to get Robin to join the Socialist Labor Party. Or it was the Young Socialist Alliance." Chris watching Amelia, her face clean and pale as a nun's within the soft curve of her dark hair parted in the middle, eyes cast down; Dizsi saying, "It was a fantastic opportunity, here in a blue-collar city, for a mass orientation program. . . ." Chris watching Amelia's eyes raise and lower again, Amelia leaving them now, Chris wondering what a mistress did all day, Dizsi saying, "But Robin was only words, pretentious rhetoric, writing about the proletariat without even knowing one person who worked on the line." He pushed the plate of hummus toward Chris.

"Please, help yourself."

"Mashed-up chickpeas doesn't make it with me."

"Then why do I think you want some?"

"Go ahead and eat," Chris said. He took an olive. "You know what organizations she belonged to? Was she in the Weathermen?"

"Yes, but in and out," Dizsi said. "She was in the White Panthers at one time helping the Black ones. I know that because I went to a cocktail party for them to raise bail money. There were so many different groups. The Yippies, the Revolutionary Youth Movement, the Action Faction, the Crazies, the Progressive Labor Party, strict Maoists. The Black Panthers were known here as the National Committee to Combat Fascism, and the White Panthers became the Rainbow People's Party. I was younger then, I knew what I believed. I ask these people, what's the matter with the friendly Socialist Labor Party, uh? I don't know, I think it was because we didn't drop acid and practice kundalini yoga. It turned them off."

"Was Robin involved in that submarine thing?"

"Oh, no, that was in 'sixty-seven, before her time."

"But she did set a few bombs."

"I don't know if Robin actually did or if it was her friend Skip."

"Who's Skip?"

"You don't know that name? Skip Gibbs?"

"I've heard of Emerson Gibbs."

"Yes, that's Skip. He came out of prison and went to Hollywood, someone told me, to work in the movies. In Special Effects."

"You're kidding."

"Sure, he knows how to blow up things."

"They were making a movie here," Chris said, "blowing up things." His gaze moved to the painting Dizsi was working on: a giant canvas that was solid black except for a diagonal streak of white that had some yellow in it, near the base of the painting. He said, "You don't suppose Skip was here, working on that movie." The streak of white could be headlights, the way it started narrow and widened out. "If he was . . ."

Dizsi said, "And if Robin knew he was here or happened to see him, and if they're still friends . . . and if I sell that painting I want twenty thousand for it. No, make it twenty-five."

Chris studied the painting, about seven feet high and fifteen feet wide. A door opened at the far end of the loft and Amelia appeared, daylight showing her body in the white dress. She stood there.

He looked at the painting again. "What is it?"

"Tell me what you see," Dizsi said.

"Car headlights coming out of woods at night."

"You're absolutely right. It means you can buy it."

"I don't have a wall for it," Chris said. "I don't even have a house." He watched Amelia close the door.

Dizsi was staring at his painting. "Those two could live in there, in the woods, Robin and Skip. They were lone wolves. I think half by choice and half of it because people didn't like to associate with them."

"Why not?"

"They were unpredictable, they scared the hell out of people."

"Did you know Woody and Mark Ricks?"

Dizsi grinned, eating his squid. "Ah, now we're getting to it. I didn't want to be rude, ask you what's this about. I met them, yes, and their mother. They're the ones had the party for the Black Panthers. I don't know what I was doing there, I left. But I did see the mother another time, when I was subpoenaed and had to go to the Federal Building."

"For what?"

"They were always inviting me to sit down and discuss subversive activities with them. Listen, I'll show you something. I have complete records of FBI and CIA investigations that concerned me directly or even where my name appeared. Like investigations of some of my friends or associates. All of this I got through the Freedom of Information Act, three entire file drawers full of stuff."

"Were Woody and Mark ever arrested?"

"Mark was picked up once," Dizsi said. "You know when those students at Kent State were shot and killed? After that, there was a demonstration in Kennedy Square. May ninth, 1970. I know, I was there. Mark was one of those taken in and then released, no charge filed."

"That's why his mother was at the Federal Building?"

"Oh, no," Dizsi said. "No, what I started to tell you I

have in my records? It shows that Mrs. Ricks, following the Black Panther fund-raising party, became an FBI informant. Told them things she learned right in her house."

"She snitched on her own kids?"

Dizsi was shaking his head. "To save her kids. She gave information about the Black Panthers, nothing important. No, but her biggest coup, she told the FBI where to find Robin and Skip."

"Jesus Christ," Chris said.

Now Dizsi was smiling a little. "Why does that make you happy?"

The notebook with the red cover marked MAY–AUGUST '70 was on Wendell Robinson's desk, the metal desk in the far corner of the squad room by the window with the air-conditioning unit that didn't work. Wendell, sitting behind the desk in a neat gray suit and rose-tinted necktie, watched Chris taking his time: looking around as if he'd never been here before, appraising the office full of old desks and file cabinets that made Barney Miller's TV squad room look swank. Mankowski taking his time 'cause he'd seen the notebook lying there and knew a search had been done. Wendell picked up his coffee mug with a "7" on it and took a sip. There—Chris finally turning this way, about to get to it.

"Where is everybody?"

"Out on the street, where they supposed to be."

"That's a good-looking suit. You don't seem to go with the decor around here."

"I have to say you do," Wendell said. "Is that what you're trying to tell me, you want a job?"

"You're gonna want to give me one."

"Why's that?"

"First, tell me what you know."

"I don't know shit. We didn't find nothing."

"You got the notebook."

"I still don't know shit. It's full of how smart she is and how dumb everybody else is."

"You talked to her. . . ."

"Yeah, *I* talked. That girl knows how to act with police. Kept her mouth closed tight."

"Gave you dirty looks?"

"Gave me *nothing.*"

"You want a motive?"

Wendell didn't answer, looking at this old-timey young cop comes in here in his worn-out sportcoat and some kind of angle, with that instinct of an old-timey cop, too.

"Mark and Woody's mom, now deceased, turned her in," Chris said. "Told the shoes where to find Robin and her buddy Skip Gibbs. They picked them up in Los Angeles and brought them back for trial."

Wendell got comfortable in his chair, sat back with his coffee, raised his tasseled loafers to the desk, next to the notebook.

"So the mama's dead, Robin takes it out on the two boys?"

"Why not?"

"I'm not arguing with you, I like it. I'll take anything given to me free. But how good is it?"

"It's good," Chris said. "It could even get better." He picked up Wendell's phone and dialed four numbers.

"Jerry? . . . Fine, I'm in the building, up at Seven. . . . No, I'm not talking to anybody higher than lieutenant," Chris said and looked at Wendell. "I want to ask you something. When you were with that movie crew and they blew up the cars, you met all the special-effects guys,

didn't you? . . . Was there a guy named Skip Gibbs?"
Chris listened for a moment. "Well, it must be. How
many Skips are there? . . . Can you check? . . . Call up the
company and ask them. . . . Out in Hollywood, the one
that made the movie. Would you do that? I'm sure it's the
guy, but let's nail it down. . . . No, it only sounds like I'm
working. Jerry, I'll talk to you. Thanks." Chris hung up
and looked at Wendell again.

"Skip was here with the movie crew."

"Some Skip was."

"It's the guy. He's a dynamite man."

"Say he was here. We don't know he still is."

"*I* could find that out," Chris said, "and I'm not even
an ace homicide dick."

"But you like to be one, huh? Win my respect," Wendell said, "and have me beg to get you. It could be done,
Mankowski, you ever move back to town. But this motive
now you telling me, is it good? Or you giving me some
more theorizing shit like with the peanuts?"

"It's solid," Chris said. "You want to know where to
look it up quick, without going to the feds? Save you valuable time, you can sit around drinking coffee?"

"Here comes the deal."

"I'll trade you the source for a Xerox of the notebook."

"There's nothing in it. Take it, long as you bring it
back."

"And Donnell Lewis's file, just for fun. Something to
read in bed."

Wendell said, "Now we coming to something. Slip that
in about Donnell. You been talking to him?"

"Once. Yesterday."

"How come he called here? Wants to know how to get
in touch with you?"

"Donnell?"

"Was just before Maureen called me, about eleven thirty. He wouldn't tell me what he wanted. And you're acting surprised as hell, like you not gonna be any help."

"You give him my number?"

"How could I do that? I don't even know it."

Wendell watched Chris look up at the dirty window, getting a thoughtful squint in the afternoon glare.

"He know you're suspended?"

"He was the witness for the lawyer's complaint, I roughed up his boss."

"Maybe he wants to tell you he's sorry."

"The only thing I can think of, what it might be," Chris said, "Donnell has an idea I've been on the take now and then. Maybe he knows cops that were, back during his life of crime, and he thinks I can be had."

"Couldn't be you let him think it," Wendell said, "driving around in your maroon Cadillac."

"You never know what somebody might tell you," Chris said, "when they think you're somebody else."

"You're having fun being suspended, aren't you?"

"Except for the pay."

"Do one thing for me," Wendell said, "don't impersonate a cop. Make that two things, and don't tell me what you're doing."

"Unless I get something good."

"Well, that goes without saying."

20

Woody said, "I guess the place to start, put down I want to cross out Mark's name and anything in it that has to do with him. Say, 'As he is no longer a successor co-trustee of the estate.' I'm pretty sure that's what he was. Put that down under his name, successor co-trustee. But you know someting? It must say in there what happens if he dies. I mean before I do."

Donnell, sitting at the library desk with the green lamp on, said, "Cross out Mark," as he wrote it on a legal pad, underlined it and stopped there.

"I got it, Mr. Woody. You understand the lawyer knows who comes out of the will. What we have to tell him is whoyou want to go *in*. Hmmm, let's think about that."

The man was pacing in his bathrobe, way over on the

other side of the room now, looking at the TV set like he wanted to turn it on. He'd been on his way to the swimming pool for his late-afternoon dog-paddle when Donnell caught him in the sunroom, told him not to go in there. The man asked why not. Donnell said to him, Mr. Woody, *the bomb.* The man said, Oh yeah, he forgot. He looked in at the pool like a kid looking out the window at rain. What was he going to do now? Didn't know whether to cry or have a drink. So Donnell had lit his face up and said, Hey, I got an idea. . . .

"You thinking, Mr. Woody?"

"The lawyer's also a co-trustee. But that doesn't mean he gets anything. I don't think he does."

"You have to watch those people, Mr. Woody. Who you want in there wasn't in there before?"

"Mark was my only brother."

"Doesn't have to be kin."

"Did I tell you? I decided I'm not gonna take singing lessons."

"I wouldn't."

"You notice I never sing in the morning? I like to sing in the pool, your voice carries. But I never sing in the morning."

"I notice that."

"You know what I used to think?"

"No, sir."

"That red things were best for hangovers, in the morning. A really bad one, I'd drink a bottle of ketchup."

Man was cuckoo.

"You know what I think I might do?"

"What's that?"

"Get married."

"You have to be in love, Mr. Woody. It's the law."

"I mean it. Not right away but pretty soon. There's one I like, too. The redhead."

"You mean the one say you raped her, wants to take you to court and have you thrown in jail?"

"The one that was here—when was it?"

"You had all kind of ladies here, Mr. Woody."

Donnell'd had some, too. Some of the man's, brought here by Mark, and some of his own. Ladies who'd stop by for a late supper and Donnell would take off Ezio Pinza for his own kind of enchanted evening: put on the Whodinis, put on Run-DMC, put on some oldies like the Funkadelics, like the Last Poets, the original rappers rapping to "Wake-up Niggers" and get some live sound in the house. The ladies would be gone in the early morning, before the man had his drinks on the silver tray.

"The redhead, with the red bush."

"Has, huh? You don't tell me."

"Ginger," the man said.

The man remembered her name. "She the one, huh?"

"I'm in love with her."

"Before you get married, how 'bout we get this new will done?"

"I could put her in it."

"You could. Let's see you have anybody closer to you."

"I can't think of any."

"Go through the alphabet. *A* . . . *B* . . . *C* . . . *D*. Anybody you like start with *D*, Mr. Woody?"

"Did you know I was suppose to wear glasses?"

"We thinking of *D*s, Mr. Woody. Come on, let's think of somebody." Donnell waited. If the man was any dumber you'd have to water him twice a week.

"What do I need glasses for, I can see all right. That's why I'm not gonna take singing lessons."

Man had chicken lo mein for brains. The trouble was, Donnell hadn't slipped him a 'lude at lunchtime, hoping to keep him more awake and get this fucking will taken care of. But the man was *too* awake, talking with his head wandering all over the place.

"I've been thinking of writing a book. I could dictate it, like we're doing now."

Donnell got up from the desk, went over to the man and eased him into his TV chair, staying over him, Donnell placing his hands on the fat arms of the chair. He was going to get it done and would sit on the motherfucker if he had to.

"I thought of somebody, Mr. Woody."

"Who?"

"Myself. I'd be proud to be in your will."

Donnell had to grin then to get the man to grin, but kept looking at the man's wet eyes to show he meant it.

"Well, yeah, you're gonna be in it."

"I said, who's name start with D? You didn't say nothing."

"I was waiting for you to get to L." The man still grinning.

"*Damn.* You way ahead of me, huh?" Donnell grinned with the man, wishing to Jesus he could make himself cry at this moment like movie stars. He rubbed one of his eyes anyway, put his hand back on the chair arm and said, "Mr. Woody, how much you have in mind to leave me when you go?"

The man tried to look away to think, but Donnell stayed over him.

"I don't know. . . ."

"About. Gimme a round number."

"How long have you been with me?"

Oh, man. . . . "Mr. Woody, how *long* doesn't have nothing to do with it. All by myself, who takes care of you? Feeds you, cleans your mess, keeps people from running games on you?" Keep going, the man was nodding. "Who protects your life from people that send you bombs?"

"You do."

"What is a man does all that worth to you after you gone and you don't need the money anyway?"

"I don't know."

"Or have anybody else to give it to."

"Twenty-five thousand?"

Shit.

"Mr. Woody, you giving that to a woman you don't even know."

"A hundred thousand?"

"Your lawyer gets that for taking you to lunch and you pay for it, at your club." Donnell paused but stayed over him. "Think a minute. Would you pay this woman two million dollars so she won't send you a bomb, blow you up?"

"If I have to."

"Then wouldn't you want to give the same amount, at *least*, to the person that's gonna keep it from happening? You understand what I'm saying, the person being me?"

Look at the man's glassy wet eyes, all the busted blood vessels in his nose, his face; the man was a mess. Yeah, but he was nodding, agreeing.

"I guess that's fair."

Donnell hurried back to the desk and sat down.

"Okay, I'm putting in—how's this? You being of sound

mind . . ."—pausing to write—"you want to leave Donnell Lewis . . . at least two million dollars . . . if and when . . . you ever die." Donnell finished, read it over—man, look at it—was about to say, Ready for you to sign, Mr. Woody.

The doorbell rang.

And what he said was, "Shit."

Got up and went out to the front hall hoping it was the paperboy come to collect, Donnell in a mood to kick the kid's ass across the street. He peeked through the peephole as he always did, cautious, and the dark cloud parted and the sun came out to shine on—lookit who's here—Sergeant Mankowski and the redhead name Ginger.

Chris said, "I hope we're not interrupting anything. If Mr. Woody's floating in the pool we'll come back."

"No, he's not floating today. Come in, come in."

"Miss Wyatt would like to have a word with him."

"Yeah, that's fine. He be glad to see you." Donnell full of life in his silky yellow shirt and pants, smiling white teeth at them, saying hi, Ginger, saying to Chris he'd been trying to get hold of him but nobody seemed to have his number; was he hiding or what? Giving them all this chatter crossing the hall to the library, saying yeah, this was nice they dropped by, saying, "Mr. Woody, look who come to see you. Ginger, Mr. Woody, and her friend." All talk and motion all at once.

Greta was giving Chris a look. He shrugged, no help. Donnell was going over to the desk, Woody was pulling himself out of his chair, straightening his bathrobe, making himself presentable, Donnell shoving papers into a desk drawer and opening another one. Now he was holding what looked like a leather-bound commercial checkbook. Greta's voice, kept low, said, "What's going on?" Chris said, "Beats me." Woody was creeping toward Greta on his swollen legs, arms bent but outstretched. "Boy-oh-boy . . . Ginger, is that you? Sit down and we'll have a drink. Donnell?" Chris watched Donnell move close to the man to say something to him and the man said, "Oh, yeah, that's right." Donnell came over with the checkbook and said to Chris, "Mr. Woody will fix Ginger up. He's got the bar there has a fridge in it"—looking at Greta—"if you like some wine. Or he'll make you a nice drink."

Chris said, "You have any peanuts?"

"Yeah, those peanuts, we fresh out. Listen, she be fine with Mr. Woody. Can watch some TV."

Chris liked the way Greta said, "I wasn't fine with Mr. Woody the last time I was here." Turned to the man creeping up in his bathrobe and said, "Are you gonna behave yourself?"

"Boy-oh-boy," Woody said.

Donnell touched the man's shoulder. "Yeah, that means he's mellow, feeling good. He'll be nice. Huh, Mr. Woody? Sure." Donnell looked at Chris again. "Come with me, I'll show you something will interest you."

Greta motioned to Chris, Go on, and that took care of that.

Once they were in the hall Donnell stopped and opened the checkbook. "See?" There were three green-tinted checks to the sheet, issued by Manufacturers National Bank, each imprinted with *Ricks Enterprises, Inc.* and bearing Woody's signature at the bottom.

"I have him sign three at a time when he's able to," Donnell said, "for whatever needs might come up. You being a need. You understand? This is opportunity looking at you." He closed the checkbook. They walked down the hall and through the sunroom to the shallow end of the swimming pool. "Go look on the bottom by the diving board."

Chris saw the black athletic bag floating in the clear water. He walked along the edge to the deep end, looked down and studied the dark shapes on the bottom, Donnell's voice filling the room now, telling him from a distance how he'd found the bag, brought it in here and thrown it, and the bag must've hit the board and those things came out of it.

Chris looked at his watch. "What time was that?"

"Was about quarter of eleven."

"You thought if you dropped dynamite in water it wouldn't go off?"

"I was hoping."

"You were wrong."

"Then why didn't it?"

"It still might. Or it could've shorted when it hit the water, blown you through the window. Why don't you come here, so I don't have to yell."

"I been as close to it as I want."

Chris walked back to the shallow end. "We don't know what time it's set for, do we? If it was put there early this morning, within the past twelve hours. . . ." He reached Donnell and said, "You know you could be arrested, withholding evidence of a crime."

"Man, I didn't make the bomb."

"Doesn't matter. Why didn't you call Nine-eleven?"

"Have the police come, the fire trucks? Pretty soon we have the TV news. Mr. Woody don't want none of that. Man likes his privacy and is willing to pay for it." Donnell brought a ballpoint pen out of his pants pocket and opened the checkbook. "Tell me what your shakedown price is these days."

Chris said, "Anything I want?"

"Long as it seems to be right."

"I say ten thousand?"

"I write it in."

"What if I say twenty?"

"I write it in. But now twenty you getting up there. I'd have to sell that figure to the man, convince him."

"He's already signed the check."

"Yeah, but that don't mean the money's in the bank. See, he keeps only so much in there. It gets low, the man calls a certain number and they transfer money from his trust account to his regular business account. I think I could talk the man into paying twenty, but I'd have to have a cut, like ten percent. Two grand for the service, understand?"

"I don't know," Chris said, looking out at the pool. "I'd have to take my clothes off, dive in there . . . the bomb could go off any time. I'm fooling with a fast high explosive under water, can barely see what I'm doing—"

"You cut the wire," Donnell said.

"Is that all?" Chris brought out the Spyder-Co knife that was always in his right-hand coat pocket. "Here, you do it."

"The shakedown pro. I should've known," Donnell said. "Drive up in your Cadillac, twenty don't meet your greed. Gonna go for what you can get."

"The way I have to look at it," Chris said, "I make a mistake, I'm floating face down in a fucking swimming pool, something I never thought of before." He paused. "You'd have to look in the Yellow Pages, see if you can find another bomb disposal man."

"For what, if the bomb's gone?"

"The next one. They'd have to try again."

Donnell stared at him. "You think so, huh?"

"You don't seem to understand what this is about. It's a payback," Chris said, "get even for getting snitched on and doing time. Mark and Woody's mom told the feds where to find Robin and her boyfriend, Skip. The mom's dead, so they go after the boys, thinking, Well, they probably told the mom anyway."

Donnell said, "Robin, huh?" and started to smile. "First time we met I said you must be dumb as shit, didn't I? I'll tell you something now that we talked again. You still dumb as shit. You live in your little get-even bomb world, down there bent over taking wires apart. See, that's why people like you get *hired* by people like me. I write down 'Mr. Mankowski' and 'twenty-oh-oh-oh' on one of these checks, man, you'll dive in with your clothes on. It don't matter who's doing what or why and don't tell me different. 'Cause once you on the take, man, you *on* it, for good."

Chris said, "Let's go sit down."

He walked off, going to the lounge area halfway up the length of the pool—the arrangement of chairs and low tables by the bar and stereo system—and poured himself a scotch. There was water in the ice bucket. A buzzing sound came from the phone sitting on the bar and a light went on. Chris took his drink to a table and sat down.

Donnell said, from the shallow end of the pool, "That's Mr. Woody. Wait half a minute, he'll forget what he wants."

Chris sipped his whiskey. The phone buzzed a few more times. Donnell was staring at the clear water.

"Say that thing could still go off?"

"You never know," Chris said. The phone had stopped buzzing. "Come on, sit down. Tell me what Robin said when she called."

That got his attention. Donnell looked over but didn't say anything.

"I'm dumb as shit," Chris said, "you have to straighten me out. So it's not a payback, it's a pay *up* or get blown up. The anarchist turned capitalist. It used to be political, now it's for money." He thought about it a moment, nodding. "It makes sense. Get out of that dump she's living in. Or she's bored, uh? Tired of writing those books. . . ." Chris sipped his drink.

Donnell was still watching him.

"So why didn't you call Nine-eleven? You find a bomb, you call the police, fire, anybody you can get. The only reason I can see why you didn't," Chris said, "you must be in on it. You're working it with her."

Donnell came away from the shallow end now. "I let somebody send me a bomb? Am I crazy? Then get you to get rid of the motherfucker? Explain that to me."

Chris said, "Maybe you got involved *after* the bomb was delivered . . . when she called. It was Robin, wasn't it?"

Donnell didn't answer that one but kept coming, not taking his eyes off Chris.

"I think what happened," Chris said, "she thinks the bomb's already gone off, outside. That's the warning shot. Now she tells you on the phone how much she wants and you're thinking, Man, why don't I get in on this? Or you don't think she's asking enough, so you tell her you'll be her agent, get her a better deal. Extortion, though, I imagine you'd want more than ten percent."

"What I want," Donnell said, laying the checkbook on the table, "is to know how much *you* want. That's the only business we have, understand?"

Chris sipped his drink, in no hurry. "I'll tell you what

I have a problem with, and I'll bet you do too. The first bomb, the one that took out Mark. That wasn't a warning shot, was it? That one had Woody's name on it. Yours, too, if you open doors for him. But how do they make any money if Woody's dead?"

Donnell didn't move or say a word.

"Unless their original idea," Chris said, "was to get Woody out of the way and go after Mark. Only Mark went after the peanuts. That can happen, something unforeseen. But you get down and look at it, I don't think Robin knows what she's doing. It seems to me she and Skip are as fucked up as they ever were. Back when they were crazies. I think about it some more and it doesn't surprise me. You know why?"

Donnell kept looking at him, but didn't answer.

"Because people don't get into crime unless they're fucked up to begin with."

Donnell said, "The policeman talking now."

"You know what I'm saying. Think of all the guys you used to hang out with are in the joint. You've been trying to think of ways yourself to fuck up, haven't you?"

Chris reached over to open the leather-bound book on the table and look at the three checks signed by Woodrow Ricks, the name written big, all curves and circles.

"You could write 'Donnell Lewis' and some big numbers on one of these, you must've thought of that. But first you have to get him to transfer enough money into the account to make it worthwhile, huh? And you haven't figured out how to work that."

Donnell said, "How much you want?"

"Twenty-five," Chris said, "nothing for you, no commission on this one. And if Woody stops payment, I put the bomb back in the pool."

"Gonna take the man for all you can get."

"Why not? Everybody else is."

In that big dim library Greta was saying to Woody, "You're trying to be nice to me now, because of what you did." He was making her nervous.

Telling her, Sit here. No, sit there, it's more comfortable. What could he get her, another drink? Did she want to watch a movie? Did she like Busby Berkeley? Ever see his banana number? But he didn't know how to put on the video cassette, and when he tried calling Donnell on the phone there was no answer.

Greta said, "Would you sit still so I can talk to you? That other time you hardly moved. Would you wipe your mouth, please? Doesn't that bother you? Look at your robe, it's a mess." He seemed to be listening now, but it was hard to tell. His face was like a road map, all the red and blue lines in it. If that liver spot on his cheek was Little Rock, there was U.S. 40 going over to West Memphis. The Mississippi came down his nose full of tributaries and drainage canals, curved around O.K. Bend at his mouth and went on down to the Louisiana line. Did he like being the way he was?

"Remember at the *Seesaw* audition, right after I tried out Mark had me sit with him? You were in the row behind us. I felt you touch my hair a couple times. I should've realized what the deal was, but I was busy listening to Mark talking to the director, being smart. That girl with the little plastic derby finished her number, she did 'Little Things' and the director goes, 'She must get a lot of love at home to have the confidence to come here.' That was okay; the girl really wasn't very good. But Mark said nasty things like 'She ought to have her vocal cords removed,' and I remember you laughing, thinking it was funny. You and Mark had no feeling for the person, what it's like to get up there with your legs shaking, trying to remember the words. . . . That one girl did 'The Sweetest Sounds I've Ever Heard' and Mark goes, 'Throwing up'd be a sweeter sound than that.' Trying to be funny, but everything he said was mean. I stayed and listened 'cause I wanted to play Gittel so bad, not knowing the deal was I'd have to play with *you.* Nobody asked me, okay, if I did, if I agreed to be humiliated, how much would I charge? See, you just went ahead, like buying something without asking the price. Well, now I'm gonna tell you what it is."

Chris went in the pool in his white briefs, dove straight down to the bottom, saw only one wire connected to the clock and made sure of it, a wire that ran to the dry-cell battery. He went up for a breath, dove again, removed the blasting cap from the dynamite and this time pushed off the bottom with the five sticks taped together, holding them over his head as he surfaced. Donnell was no help. He stayed at the shallow end, inside the doorway to the sunroom. On his third dive, Chris brought up the clock and the battery and placed them next to the dynamite on the tiled edge of the pool. Donnell approached as Chris swam over with the black athletic bag, swung it at him and let go, and Donnell jumped back as he caught the bag and dropped it, quick.

"Man, you get me all wet."

Chris pulled himself out of the pool. He picked up the bag, held it open in the light from the windows and got a surprise. Inside were a pair of pliers, a short coil of copper wire and several clothespins. Maybe left by mistake—the guy forgot the stuff was in there. Or it was a hurry-up job. Maybe the guy had to work in the dark. It was all evidence and Chris knew he should take it with him. Or put it in a safe place—he liked that better—and tell Donnell to keep his hands off, don't go near it. Scare him. He looked around the pool house. Maybe in the library; there were a lot of cabinets in there. And pick it up later on, if he had to.

Donnell said, "It's mean-looking shit, that dynamite." He put his hands on his knees for a closer study. "The clock, hey, only got one hand on it."

"The hour hand," Chris said. "You see the hole punched right next to the 'eleven'? There was a screw in there. Here, it's on the end of the wire that goes to the blasting cap. This wire connects the clock to the battery, and this other one goes from the battery to the blasting cap. You see how it works? The hour hand comes around, touches the screw set for eleven o'clock, the circuit is closed and the dynamite blows. Only the screw came out 'cause somebody did a half-assed job putting it together. It's simpler if you use the old-fashioned kind of alarm clock with the bell on top, you don't need the screw. You run your wires, one from the bell, the other from the hammer, the dinger, set the alarm and when it rings, that's it. You're probably lucky they didn't use that kind. The screw wasn't set in tight enough. You threw the bag, it hit the diving board and that's when it probably came out." Chris picked up the taped sticks of dynamite and placed them in the bag. "Let me have a towel, okay? I'll get dressed and we'll put this somewhere."

Donnell, hands on his knees, began to straighten with a thoughtful kind of frown, his mind working.

"Man, you knew it, didn't you? You look at this shit

laying on the bottom, you knew it wasn't gonna go off. You run the price up on me with nothing to worry about."

Chris said, "That's why people like me like to get hired by people like you."

Chris kept glancing at her, waiting, until finally he said, "Well? What happened?"

Greta said, "Have you ever noticed, the corners of his mouth are always sticky? He opens his mouth and you can see, it's like old saliva stuck there. I kept thinking about that time he kissed me."

"Not the other?"

"Well, both, but I was looking at his mouth. He never wipes it. Anyway, I told him I wanted a hundred thousand."

"You did?"

"What's the difference? Whatever I ask for, I'd just be picking it out of the air."

"What'd he say?"

"You won't believe this. He asked me to marry him."

Chris looked at her and the Cadillac jumped lanes and he had to get straightened out before he said, "Come on."

"I'm not kidding. I said, 'Look, let's just settle this and I'll leave. There's no way in the world I'd ever marry you.'"

"Yeah?"

"And then he tells me how he's worth a hundred million dollars and we'd share it, a hundred *million.*"

"Jesus Christ."

"I said, No, I wouldn't. He said, Think about it."

"Yeah?"

"That's all."

"What do you mean, that's all? Are you thinking about it?"

"Of course not. He said we should get to know each other before I decide."

"Jesus Christ."

"And if I'd rather have a hundred thousand than a hundred million he'd give it to me."

"He said that?"

"Well, not in so many words. It took him a while."

Chris turned east on Eight Mile and for several moments had to concentrate on the traffic. Greta was silent.

"What're you doing, thinking about it?"

"No, I'm not thinking about it."

"What're you doing?"

"I'm not doing anything, I'm sitting here."

"What about the settlement?"

"I go back, tell him I've thought about it . . . I guess, and then he gives it to me."

"You mean you're gonna think about it?"

"No, but I have to tell him I did."

"Why? Just tell him you want the hundred thousand."

"I feel sorry for him."

"What does that mean?"

"Why're you so picky? Can't I feel sorry for him?"

"I guess if you want to," Chris said, reaching into his inside coat pocket. "I didn't get a proposal of marriage, but I didn't do too bad." He brought out Woody's check and handed it to Greta. "Twenty-five grand, for cleaning out his swimming pool."

"Hi, it's me," Robin's voice said.

Donnell said, "It is, huh?"

He stood at the desk in the library. Mr. Woody, over watching Arnold Schwarzenegger killing dudes with his big two-hand sword, hadn't even looked up when the phone rang.

"Are you all right?"

"Just fine."

"I waited for the six o'clock news before I called. You want to tell me what happened?"

"I'll tell you *some*thing," Donnell said, "but not on the telephone."

"Great, I was hoping you'd say that," Robin's voice said. "Can we meet?"

"You want to take the chance, we can."

"What does that mean?"

"Girl, I don't have nice things to say to you."

"I'll bet you a million dollars," Robin's voice said, "you change your mind."

21

Chris and Greta were in his dad's king-size bed with both the gooseneck lamps, mounted above the headboard, turned on: Chris reading Robin Abbott's May–August 1970 journal, Greta reading photocopied material from various Donnell Lewis case files. She told Chris her first husband never read in bed, he watched TV. Then corrected that. "I mean the only husband I ever had." Chris said, "Uh-huh." He had on a pair of his dad's reading glasses, and she felt she was seeing another side of him. Greta looked over one time and said, "Excuse me, do I know you?" About eleven thirty he went out to the kitchen and brought back two cans of beer. Greta looked at him in his underwear and said, "You have scars on your legs," sounding surprised. "What in the world happened to you?" He got back in bed and told her about the old Vietnamese guy standing on the hand grenade, Greta sitting up chewing on her thumbnail, not saying a word. He finished and she kissed him, her eyes moist. They kissed some more and Greta asked Chris who did he think he was, Woody Allen? Woody was always making out in bed with Diane Keaton or somebody with his glasses on. In movies, anyway. They let it happen and made love, trying to take their time but then hurrying to get there. While they were drinking their beer Greta said, "Whenever you feel like showing me your scars, you can." Then after a few minutes she said, "Here your glasses, Dad," and they got back to reading, feeling at home with each other propped up on their pillows.

They would tell each other about parts they were reading.

Greta said Donnell Lewis had been arrested fourteen times but only went to prison once. She asked Chris, "You ever hear of being charged with creating an improper diversion? Violation of ordinance N.H. 613.404." He was selling Black Panther newspapers in downtown Detroit when he spotted a couple of undercover detectives watching him. So he pointed to them and told everybody that came by to look out for the pigs. He also called them fascist buffoon fools. The detectives said they were watching for pickpockets and when Donnell revealed their identity, that was the improper diversion. Three other times, while he was selling Black Panther papers, he was arrested for resisting and obstructing. Once he had to go to Detroit General to get ten stitches in the top of his head. The arresting officer said Donnell ran into a wall trying to avoid arrest. He was in a store collecting money for their kids' breakfast program and was arrested for attempting to commit extortion. The charge was reduced to soliciting for a charitable organization without a license. He was arrested another time for malicious destruction of property, painting *Free Huey Newton* on the side of the Penobscot Building. "Who's Huey Newton?"

"The guy that started the Black Panthers."

"How's the journal?"

Chris said, "I'm up to the rock concert at Goose Lake, two hundred thousand people. Robin says, 'Fifteen-dollar admission a bummer. Should be a free concert. The promoter, a smart-ass youth-culture rip-off artist, asks if we give our newspapers away free. . . . Dope scene unreal. Trash bags of Jamaican carried by strolling vendors. Organically grown mescaline. Blotter acid goes for a buck. Medics report bad trips, but not many. Strychnine poisoning. What else is new?' "

"Did you take dope?"

"I smoked pot and ate marshmallows for a few years. Listen, Robin says, 'It's private property, no pigs allowed. But they infiltrate. Beware of guys with short hair wearing dime-store beads, Bermuda shorts and tennies. I kid you not. Everything but a sign that says HI, I'M A NARC.' Here's Woody. This is good. 'Woody's case of champagne lasts a half day. He has booze in the limo and is completely smashed at all times. Woody's pissed. Went to the lake and couldn't get any chicks to take off their bathing suits. Even offered them money.' Listen to this. 'Hope I don't end up balling Woody out of the kindness of my heart.' "

He looked over at Greta looking at him.

"You think she did?"

"It doesn't say."

"She must be almost forty now."

"Yeah?"

"It just seems weird."

"Here's what she thinks of Mark," Chris said. " 'Nice bod, but spoiled, can be quite bitchy with others but will lick my hand to get me to look at him. Susceptible to bull-shit I haven't used since junior high.' Here's the good part. Robin says, 'We put up a sign on the limo, TOTAL FREEDOM NOW! that brings TV guy with camera crew. Smart-ass TV guy asks, Freedom from what? I give him stock response. Freedom from everything, man. Freedom from govern-ment, freedom from misery, from hunger, etc. etc. through anarchy. Smart-ass TV guy calls me a Marxist. I tell him, No way. He says, But you're preaching Marxism, aren't you? Zap answer: If Marx says he wasn't a Marxist, why should I call myself one? You want labels, man, we want change. Chairman Mao said to seek truth from facts and it will bring on perpetual revolution. Can you dig it? It's here, man, and it won't go away.' "

Greta was still looking at him.

"Did everybody talk like that?"

"I think she was putting the guy on," Chris said. "You'd hear students yelling 'Smash the state,' and some of them were serious, not just turned on by the excitement. I was in Washington, there must have been a half million people in the streets, all protesting the war and you could feel it. We knew we were right, we *had* to be—so many people together. . . . I mean you could really feel it."

"But you went to war," Greta said.

"I was against it," Chris said, "because it didn't make sense. But I still wanted to know what war was like."

He was aware of sights and sounds from that other time, strange ones, glimpses of Khiem Hanh and the smell of wood smoke, glimpses of Woodstock too, beads and headbands and dirty jeans, the smell of grass, the rain, faces with glazed smiles. . . .

"I try to remember the way it was," Chris said, "and I get it mixed up with the way it was shown in movies, with the hippies so much wiser and laid back than the straights. Except in the Woodstock movie where the young guy says, 'People who are nowhere come here because they think they're gonna be with people who are somewhere.' And the guy's dopey girlfriend doesn't get it. She says, 'Yeah, well, like there's plenty of freedom. We ball and everything. . . .' She was being used and didn't know it. You saw so much of that. All kinds of dumb kids taken advantage of by guys pretending to be gurus or Jesus, they had the hair, the beard. Or some asshole who called himself the Pussycat Prince and wore flowers in his hair and played a flute. All of them with that smug, stoned grin, like they knew something you didn't."

"Where are they now?" Greta said.

Robin and Donnell were at the Gnome on Woodward Avenue, a new-wave Middle Eastern restaurant that featured jazz, the McKinney brothers on piano and bass. Robin suggested it, her apartment was only a few blocks away. Donnell knew the place from bringing Mr. Woody here now and again; the man not caring too much for the lamb dishes, but ate up the way the brothers performed on show tunes. Donnell arrived a half hour late, picked up a scotch and Perrier at the bar, waved to the McKinneys and joined Robin, waiting in a booth with a glass of red wine, playing with her braid. He let her tell him, with three cigarette butts in the ashtray and another one going, she just got here; then felt her looking him over as he sipped his drink and settled in, letting his gaze wander over to the sound of mellow jazz.

She said, "I hope you have more to say than the last time we were together. Remember, in the bathroom? You watched yourself in the mirror . . . I suppose to see what a good time you were having." She said, "When I called today, the first time, did you have any idea who it was?"

"Yeah, I knew."

"You did not."

Donnell said, "Girl, I'm being nice to you. How long I can manage it is something else. I do remember us being in the bathroom. Only I ought to tell you, that wasn't the last time I had any pussy, understand? I've had some since then. Now we have that out of the way, you tell me what we come here for. See, I have to get back home soon, case Mr. Woody wakes up in the dark and don't know where he's at."

Robin said, "Yeah, but have you done it in a bathroom since then?"

Donnell said, "Shit," and had to grin at her. He took a sip of his drink. "Let's get to it. Tell me you setting the bombs or somebody else?"

"You remember Skip?"

"Which one was he?"

"Kind of a biker type with a ponytail."

"Look like a bum. Huey P. Newton's lawyer had a ponytail and that man was wealthy. Yeah, I remember Skip. He's the one done the bombs, huh?"

Robin gave him a nod. "What happened to the one today?"

"We'll get to that. First I want to know about Skippy. Where's he at, hiding someplace?"

"We'll have to get to that, too," Robin said. "After I called this morning, did you present my demands to Woody?"

Donnell smiled a little. "Yeah, I presented your demands. I'm trying to think of what Mr. Woody said. I think he said, 'Oh, really?' Something like that."

He watched Robin draw on her cigarette and blow the smoke out hard and then flick ash.

She said, "Well, obviously the bomb didn't go off."

Donnell didn't say anything.

"If it did it would've been on the news." She drew on her cigarette again. "We have to trust each other. Look, I know you're cool, okay? So don't overdo it."

"Girl, you the one called the meeting."

"I want to hear you say something, that's all. I want to be sure."

Donnell said, "Wait now. You blow up the man's car knowing I could've been in it, but not caring shit whether I was or not."

She was shaking her head saying, "No, uh-unh," even before he finished. "I never thought that for a minute."

"You didn't have to think it, you knew it. You send me a bag of dynamite, leave it by the door, and you want to know can you trust me. I have to think on that one, see if it makes any sense."

He listened to Robin say his name, "Donnell?" with a nice tone, slowing up and looking him in the eye, like to let him know this was from her soul. "We haven't seen each other in sixteen years. That's a long time, isn't it?"

Donnell said, "Let me get the McKinneys to play something bluesy."

That jerked her line.

"Don't *do* that. Don't fuck with me, okay? I'm saying it's been a long time, I wasn't thinking of you one way or the other. I wasn't even sure you worked for him. I saw you only once and thought, Is that Donnell? But when I was talking to you on the phone, this morning, I *knew*. I felt some awfully nice vibes. I wanted to call you right back, really, and say, Hey, let's do this together."

"Except there was a bomb gonna explode. You said to me I'd hear it in about two minutes. Oh, you were *angry*, I could hear that too."

Robin waited a moment, staring at him. "It didn't go off, did it?"

"Let me tell you what I feel about this, kind of vibes *I* get," Donnell said. "A person that sends bombs, they into heavy shit. What I see you doing, you're thinking how you can use me, being on the inside. See, I understand that. You're not thinking to favor me none 'less it helps you."

"We both make out," Robin said. "You've been with Woody how long, three years? And you're still driving him around. What else—cleaning up after him? You need somebody on the *out*side."

"I'm looking at that," Donnell said, "as it happens to fit into my plan. But do I need somebody outside known for making bombs? That's the question I ask myself. What happens the police want to talk to you?"

"They already have. It was all show, nothing to it."

The woman wanting him to think it was nothing. Donnell eased back against the cushion, watching her smoke her cigarette like she was enjoying it.

"They got on you quick, didn't they?"

She said to him, "They use computers now, Donnell."

He didn't care for that shitty tone of voice.

"They feed in names and if you know either one of the Ricks brothers and you happen to have a sheet, there it is. The cops talked to you, didn't they? What's the difference?"

"Man, we cool, huh?"

She said, "I'm not worried. Are you?"

Donnell put his arms on the table again. "They talk to Skippy?"

"Skippy's well hidden."

"Bet you thought you were, too, but they come knocking at your door." Donnell leaned on his arms, getting closer to her. "I'm gonna tell you something. There's a dude knows what you're doing. The dude even guessed close to what *I'm* doing. I mean it was barely in my head what I'm doing and the dude knew it."

She wasn't cool now, unh-unh, staring at him.

"You hear what I'm saying? This dude is *on* us."

"Who is he?"

"Name Mankowski."

That poked her.

She said, "I *know* him—he's a *cop.*" And stubbed her cigarette out, hard.

"Used to be. They suspended his ass, threw him out. But he keeps coming around like this." Donnell reached across the table, laying the palm of his hand in front of her. "You know what I'm saying? Comes by with his hand out. The dude's looking to score."

She was still on the edge of her seat.

"But I met him. He was one of the cops."

"He show you I.D.?"

"I don't remember."

" 'Cause he don't have none."

Confusing the poor woman.

"Then what's he up to?"

"What I'm telling you, girl, the dude's Mr. Shakedown. Was on their rape squad when they threw him out. And before that, guess what he was?"

"You know, at first," Greta said, "he doesn't seem like a bad guy. I mean getting arrested for creating an improper diversion. . . . But here's something else." She turned her head on the pillow to look at Chris. "You awake?"

"Yeah, I'm reading."

"Anything good?"

"I think I've found it. The part Robin doesn't want anybody to read."

"Go ahead, I'll wait."

"No, tell me about Donnell."

"Well, he and some other Black Panthers . . ." Greta looked at the sheet resting against her raised knees. "Here it is . . . were arrested and charged with kidnapping and beating a fellow member of the party. Young guy, eighteen years old. He said they beat him with, quote, blunt instruments and then burned him with cigarette lighters and poured scalding water on him mixed with grease. The victim admitted himself to New Grace and the hospital called the police. Upon being questioned he told them the names of his assailants, including Donnell, saying they had accused him of breaking rule number eight of the Black Panther Party. But then in court, at the pretrial examination, he changed his mind. He said he couldn't identify his assailants and that the police coerced him into signing the complaint. So Donnell and his buddies were released. He was picked up right after that on a federal gun charge, convicted and sent to prison."

Chris said, "What's rule number eight?"

Greta looked at the sheet again.

"It's written out. 'No party member will commit any crimes against other party members or black people at all, and cannot steal or take from the people, not even a needle or a piece of thread.' "

They looked at each other, heads turned on their pillows.

"I learn interesting facts in bed with you," Greta said. "When I was little, Camille and Robert Taylor and I would get in bed with our dad and he'd read the Bobbsey Twins to us."

Chris said, "Now you get the Ricks brothers and other crazies." He pushed his glasses up on his nose and looked at Robin's journal. "Here's the part about Mark, her opinion of him. Robin says, 'Mark digs the sound, the cant, the beat of revolution. He wants to be part of it, but political-science-wise knows next to nothing, zilch. He asks if I believe in the Movement, if I'm a member of the Communist Party. Why sure, Mark. He's either dumb or naive, but, man, is he loaded! I tell him to come by my tent tonight and I'll lay it out for him. So to speak.' "

"Her tent?"

"This is when they were at Goose Lake. The Ricks boys slept in the limo they rented and Robin had her own tent. She says in case she met somebody interesting."

"Mark wasn't interesting enough?"

"She was using him. Listen." Chris looked at the journal. "She finishes with Mark by saying, 'This guy is so impressionable. He's dying to be a star. If you want him, take him.' Then she has written in capital letters, 'TAKE HIM FOR EVERYTHING HE'S GOT!' "

Chris imagined Robin looking through old journals, this one, reliving those days, coming to this page and the words reaching out to grab her. It was worthless as evidence, but it let you look into her head. Chris closed the journal. It was quiet, Greta not saying a word. He was thinking she'd fallen asleep as he turned his head on the pillow, expecting to see her eyes closed.

She was staring at him. She said, "Is that what I'm doing? With Woody?"

Robin had become the ice woman, blowing her smoke out slow, stroking her braid, a thoughtful act, strok-

ing in time to "Little Girl Blue" in the background, Robin
looking at Donnell with quiet eyes, saying, "Man, it's been
a long time coming."

"What has?"

"Getting on track and feeling good about it. Yeah,
now, finally I can see where we're going." Saying the words
with a slight nod of the head, moving with the mellow beat.

Donnell liked how she did that. The woman was in
time and looking good, for her age.

"I'm not saying we don't have a problem," Robin said.
"If this Polack, Mankowski, is acting officially, and that was
the impression I got, then it's a major problem. Not because he's especially bright—I don't think he is. The way
he tried to set me up, get me to talk, didn't show a lot of
finesse. But if he's got the whole fucking police force behind
him—"

"He was kicked *off* the police," Donnell said. "I've told
you that, and he don't like it one bit."

"You think he doesn't like it or you know it?"

"I *know* it. I talked to the dude."

"Well, if all he wants is money. . . ." She gave a little
shrug with the beat.

"He's working for himself, nobody else."

"He told you that?"

This woman could be irritating.

"It was he *didn't* tell me. He had, I might suspect him.
Look, the dude bumped me up to twenty-five thousand to
get your bomb out of the swimming pool. He's in it for
bread, nothing else, and he'll keep coming back. I know,
I've seen the kind." Donnell hunched over the table on his
arms. "Listen to me. The dude will come back and he'll
come back. He'll leave the police if he hasn't done it already. The man smells a score. But that's only the one
problem. I see another one. I see too many people."

"You mean Skip," Robin said.

"Exactly. Your friend Skippy. What do we need him for? See, he's the kind of problem you can tell goodbye and it's gone. Like you say to him you not interested in the deal no more, you give up on it, he leaves."

"I don't think it would be quite that easy," Robin said.

"Sit on it till he goes away. That's easy. What I'm saying to you, I don't see cutting it three ways when we don't need to. I'm looking now at the economics of it. This kind of deal come along, you do it one time, understand? You pick a number, the most of what you can get, and that's all."

"If that's what you're worried about," Robin said, "there's no problem. You get half of a two-way split."

"I'm thinking more than half, and your number depends on my number."

"Okay, what's your number?"

"One million. I like the sound of it, I like the idea of it. One million, a one and six oughts."

"Take off and spend it, huh?"

"Stay right where I am. It's none of your business what I do with it."

Donnell watched Robin get out another cigarette saying, "Okay, if you're satisfied with a mil let's go for two and Skip and I split the other one."

Donnell shook his head. "I get more than you."

"Why?"

"It's my idea."

"Gee, I thought it was mine," Robin said.

Giving him that shitty tone again.

"I mean since I'm the one who called in the first place."

"Yeah, and how'd you expect the man to pay you? Cash? He suppose to leave it some place you tell him?"

He watched her shrug, being cool.

"That's one way."

"You dumb as shit," Donnell said. "Can you see the man go in the bank for the money? Drunk as usual, everybody looking at him? Everybody knowing his business? What did I say to you on the phone? I said, 'That gonna be cash or you take a check?' And you got mad, commence to threaten me, saying, 'Oh, you want to play, huh?' Giving me all this shit on the phone. You remember? Was only this morning."

Still being cool. Look at her blow the smoke, sip the wine, getting her head straight, what she wanted to say. Smiling at him now, just a speck of smile showing.

"What I get from that," Robin said, "you were serious. We could actually get paid by check?"

"There's a way."

"He could stop payment."

"I said there's a way to do it."

"This is wild," Robin said. "Far out."

She turned her head to gaze off at the piano, listening but not moving, Donnell watching her, remembering the woman in the bathroom a long, long time ago. Pants on the floor, her sweater pushed up, seeing the back of her head in the mirror, all that long hair, seeing a nice dreamy smile in her eyes when he looked at her. . . . Her eyes came back to him from the piano.

"Skip killed a guy one time."

"You mean little Markie?"

"Before. He did it for money. What I'm saying is, you can count on him."

"I admire that kind," Donnell said, "but it don't mean we need him."

"I was thinking he could get rid of our problem, the guy with his hand out."

Donnell hesitated. The idea stopped him, hit him cold. He didn't want to think about it, but said, "He'd do that?"

"If I asked him to."

"That's all?"

"If you say he's in."

Donnell shrugged, not saying yes or no, maybe not minding the guy being in if you could count on him and take his word. There were things to work out in this deal. It wasn't entirely set in his mind. Though it seemed to be in Robin's, the way she was smiling for real now, letting it come. . . .

Robin saying, "The extortion corporation, we accept checks. Hey, but we write Woody's driver's license I.D. on the back, right? In case he tries to stiff us."

22

Chris played scenes, lying in bed in that early morning half-light.

He heard himself tell Jerry Baker, "I go in the guy's swimming pool, remove an explosive device and he gives me twenty-five grand." Jerry says, "You take the device with you?" He tells Jerry, "I left it there but told him not to touch it, and I know he won't." Jerry says, "You should've taken it with you." Jerry's right; he should've. Jerry says, "But you did take the check." "Of course I took the check, for Christ sake." Jerry, thinking of all that money, thinking fast, says, "Well, there's a gray area there." He hears himself say to Jerry, "What's gray about it? It's withholding evidence, isn't it?" Jerry, with his many years of experience on the police, says, "That's a matter of interpretation. There's withholding evidence and there's holding evidence. It may be needed in the investigation, it may not be." He hears himself say to Jerry, "You don't see it as a rip?" Jerry says, "Where's the rip? The guy agreed to the price and you did the job, performed a service." Chris says, "But in receiving the check for removing evidence, isn't *it* evidence too?" Jerry says, "Not necessarily. The explosive device, yeah, is evidence. But now the check, that's definitely a gray area."

Chris pictured doing the scene with Wendell. "Hey, Wendell? I'd like to ask you something?" The dude lieutenant looks up from his desk. "Yeah? What?" And that was as far as the scene got. Chris asked himself why he hadn't thought of these questions yesterday, last night. He wondered if it was to avoid even thinking about it. Finally he asked himself what he believed was a key question: *When does holding evidence become withholding evidence?*

The answer came unexpectedly, flooding him with a sense of relief: *Monday.* He had the weekend to think about it, study that gray area.

Chris got up on an elbow to flip his pillow over to the cool side and paused in the half-light as he heard Greta say, "Oh, my Lord." She was lying with her eyes open, staring at the ceiling.

"What's wrong?"

"I don't think my car was stolen."

Greta said it must have been her concussion of the brain that made her forget where she parked it. The thing was, twice before when she'd gone to the Playhouse Theater she'd parked in the same aisle on the ground floor of the building, almost in the same exact space both times.

But then last Tuesday, or whenever it was, the place was jammed. She ended up parking on the third level, ran out of there with a lot on her mind having been raped and all and wanting to have Woody arrested, and then so much happened right after, ending up in the hospital. . . . She felt really dumb.

Chris said, Yeah, all that going on. He said he'd drive her to get her car. But then didn't talk much while they were having breakfast. Greta said, "I think about my car and then I think about Woody. I don't know what to do." Drinking her coffee she said, "And you're no help." She said, "You think I'm a flake, don't you?" He told her it was no big deal, people forgot where they parked their cars all the time. She said, "But what should I do about Woody?" Chris told her it was a gray area; it depended on how you looked at it. Giving her that much understanding. . . .

While thinking about the weekend, the two days giving him hope, seeing time enough in there to believe the investigation could all of a sudden be closed when he wasn't looking and he wouldn't be withholding anything. Would he?

In the Cadillac driving downtown Greta said, "Oh, God, I have to tell that guy at the precinct my car wasn't stolen. I know exactly what he's gonna say."

It gave Chris an idea. Stop by 1300 to see Wendell. Only you forgot it's Saturday, he isn't there. But whoever's on duty verifies it later on. Yeah, Mankowski was here, he was looking for Wendell.

So he told Greta he'd stop at the precinct desk and tell them the car had been returned, that's all; it just showed up. They didn't have to know she forgot where she put it. Greta said, "Thanks," without much life in it.

On the third level of the parking structure they pulled up next to her blue Ford Escort; Saturday morning not another car near it. Greta said, "Thanks for a nice time."

Chris said, "I'll see you later."

Greta held the door open. "I'm going home."

"You're coming back, aren't you?"

"I'll have to think about it."

"What's wrong?"

Greta hesitated. "You're different."

Chris said, "Wait a minute," as she got out of the Cadillac and was closing the door. "What do you mean, I'm different?" She was standing by her car now, her back to him. He pushed a button to lower the window on the passenger side. "I'm not different." She didn't turn around; she was unlocking her car. "I don't feel different." Maybe he was different, but not in the way she thought he was. She was in the car now, starting it. Christ. He got out of the Cadillac and went around to her car; she didn't lower her window. He tapped on the glass with the tip of his finger. "Ginguh? I'm not different." She looked up at him. "Really, I'm not." She didn't seem convinced; she looked sad. Shit. "What's wrong? Tell me."

"You're different," Greta said.

"How am I different?"

"I don't know, but you are."

She drove off.

Chris locked his dad's car and walked the two blocks to 1300.

Squad Seven's door, Room 500, was straight across the hall from the elevators. Chris walked in, stopped and wanted to turn around and walk out. Saturday morning, and it looked like a convention going on, a gang of people, cops and suspects, or else witnesses. The head homicide cop himself, Inspector Raymond Cruz, was stroking his mustache as he stood talking to Wendell, seated at his desk. A detective by the name of Hunter was taking a Polaroid shot of a good-looking young black woman, stylish enough to be a Supreme, sitting half turned in a desk chair, her arm hanging behind it, long slender fingers heavy with rings. The squad's executive sergeant, Norb Bryl, stood by the Norelco coffeemaker with a young black dude in a cream-colored suit and sunglasses. Two uniformed evidence techs lounged against a desk with grocery-store sacks bearing red tags. All this activity. . . .

And now Wendell was looking this way and the stylish black woman was looking up past her shoulder at Raymond Cruz going by in his narrow navy suit, top cop and he looked it, his down-curved bandit mustache giving him a solemn expression. His eyes moved and he said, "Chris, how's it going?" Chris hesitated. By the time he said, "Not too bad," the inspector was out the door.

Now Wendell was coming. Chris didn't move, getting ready for him. Wendell stopped by the door to the interrogation room and said, "I can't talk to you now." Chris wanted to go over and hug him, but gave him an easy shrug instead and said, "No problem." He turned to leave and heard Wendell say, "Wait. Come here a minute." So he had to go over to Wendell standing with his hand on the door, Wendell in shirtsleeves but his paisley tie knotted up there tight. He said, "These are Booker's people," keeping his voice low. "His houseman over there with Bryl, his lady, Moselle, and we got his bodyguard in here, Juicy Mouth. You know him?"

"He wasn't around," Chris said.

"That's what he tells me. But if Juicy didn't put the bomb in the chair he knows who did."

Chris said, "This hasn't got anything to do with . . ."

Wendell was shaking his head. "Doesn't seem like the least connection."

"What about Skip?"

"Skip Gibbs, worked for the film company. You were right. All we got so far, he turned in his rental car. We left off checking with airlines for the moment and got back on Booker."

Chris felt he had to keep going. "Anybody watching Robin?"

"She's not that good a suspect yet. I don't have the people to sit around in cars."

"I read her notebook. In capital letters she says she's gonna take Mark Ricks for everything she can get."

"And you see the date on the book, seventeen years ago."

"I know, but it was on her desk and she didn't want us to see it. She had it out, not stuck away somewhere."

Wendell said, "I understand what you're saying. I like it, even if it isn't any kind of evidence would hold up. But I have to let Robin sit while I tend to this one."

Chris said in a hurry, because he had to say it right now, get it out, "There's something else I want to talk to you about."

He kept staring at Wendell, the lieutenant's hand on the doorknob, about to enter, but staring back at him now, a change in his expression, his eyes. Wendell said, "You're not working for me."

"I know that."

"You might, sometime, but you're not now."

Chris didn't say anything.

"I don't want to hear a question I don't have an answer to. Or I don't want to know anything I'd have trouble explaining where I found it out. You understand?"

Chris nodded.

"Think about it and we'll talk Monday. All right?"

Chris said, "Whatever you say," sounding a little

disappointed but dying to get out of there. He turned to go and Wendell touched his arm.

"Wait, take a minute. See if you think this guy knows anything about bombs."

Juicy Mouth sat hunched over, arms resting on thick knees, eyes raised to them coming in: a young black guy with a build, shoulders stretching his silky jacket. He seemed to fill half of this narrow pink room that was no bigger than a walk-in closet. Next to him was a small wooden table, a tin ashtray on it full of old cigarette butts. Wendell said, "Juicy, this is Sergeant Mankowski, the last person on this earth to see Booker alive."

Chris had a feeling Juicy didn't give a shit, the way he yawned and leaned back against the wall, the pink surface stained from heads resting against it. Chris didn't notice anything unusual about the guy's mouth.

"I've been telling Juicy," Wendell said, "if he didn't actually set the bomb maybe we could lighten up on him, take it down to accessory."

Juicy said, "You gonna have to let me out any minute now. That's light enough."

"Sergeant Mankowski," Wendell said, "was the bomb man there that time. Talked to Booker, heard his last words. . . ."

What were they? Chris seemed to recall Booker saying, "Where you motherfuckers going?" Something like that. And saw Juicy Mouth looking at him, his head still pressed to the wall, Juicy saying, "Is that right? If you the bomb man, how come you didn't take the bomb out from under him?"

Chris didn't see anything especially juicy about the guy's mouth, even when he spoke.

"The question was how to get to it," Chris said. "Ten sticks of—what was it, sixty percent? Rigged to some kind of electronic pressure sensor. Where would you learn to put something like that together?"

No reaction. He wasn't sure Juicy was even listening. But then the guy said, "You right there with him, with Booker? Looking to see what you had?"

"I cut into the seat cushion," Chris said, "but couldn't get to the works from the front."

"You right there, but you didn't get blown to shit like Booker did?"

"I stepped outside for a minute."

"You did, huh? I stepped out to get some pizza," Juicy said. "What'd you step out for?"

"We told him don't move, we'll be right back," Chris said, and felt dumb, this big street kid turning it around on him. The kid wearing five hundred dollars worth of clothes, a Rolex watch. . . .

"Step outside and let the man get blown up by hisself," Juicy said. "Yeah, well, if it don't mean shit to you and it don't mean shit to me, why we even talking about it?"

"I still have to sit on you," Wendell said. "Anybody it says on their sheet kills people, been known to, that makes him a suspect."

"Look on the sheet again, man. No convictions."

"You did people for Booker, didn't you? Shot 'em in the back of the head, left 'em out at Metro?"

"Man, this is a bomb," Juicy said. "You know I didn't fool with no bomb."

"Yeah, but you next to whatever one of the Italians put it there. Once I find out which one, then I can let 'em know it was you told me. See, then I won't have to worry about you no more, you'll be *gone*."

Juicy said, "Shit. Can't trust nobody, can you?"

Wendell said, "It's nothing personal. It don't mean I think you're an asshole, anything like that, you understand? Hey, show Sergeant Mankowski why they call you Juicy Mouth. Go on."

Juicy looked up. He said, "Check it out," and Chris thought the sole of a shoe was coming out of the guy's mouth, a big gray tongue that filled his lips from corner to corner, Chris looking at it wondering how the tongue could even fit in the guy's mouth.

"Put it back," Wendell said.

Chris stared, Juicy grinning at him now, until Wendell touched Chris's arm and they left the room, Wendell closing the door after them.

"Can you see him on the playground when he was little," Wendell said, "showing that ugly thing to the other kids?"

"He's proud of it," Chris said.

"It's what I'm saying. He's like a little kid and we playing with him, take him in there and shoot the shit. We know he helped do Booker, there's no other way it could've been done." They stood by the door to the pink interrogation room, the stylish girl at Hunter's desk watching them over her shoulder, her hand with the rings swinging idly behind her chair. "All these ones here," Wendell said, "they got their game going, living on the edge. Booker's houseman, his bodyguard, his lady, the one got him to sit in the chair. . . . We get a feel for that kind of action, huh? Know when to step outside, so to speak, let them do their own kind of freaky deaky. You remember that sexy dance? Was about ten years ago. Man, we had people shooting each other over it—two homicides I know of come to mind. You freaky deak with somebody else's woman you could get seriously hurt."

"Or you could get lucky," Chris said.

Wendell smiled. He said, "All in how you look at it, huh?" and put his hand on Chris's shoulder. "The inspector likes your style, babe. You ever move back to the city. . . . Anyway, I'll see you Monday."

Chris waited less than a minute for an elevator, took the stairs to seven and hurried down the hall to Sex Crimes. The squad room was dim, lights off, no one here. He found Greta's Preliminary Complaint Report in the desk with the blue flowers, picked up the phone and dialed her number. He'd filled out her PCR only four days ago; it seemed more like four weeks. After five rings Greta's voice came on: "Hi, you've reached Ginger Jones, but she isn't here right now, doggone it." Chris thinking, Jesus Christ. "If you want, you can leave a message right after you hear the beep. 'Bye now." Chris waited for the beep and when he heard it he still waited. Finally he said, "Greta? I haven't changed one bit," and hung up. That was all he could say to a machine. He'd try her again later. But now he didn't know what to do. He sat down to think about it, looking at the blue flowers, a case file, a stack of PCR forms, a worn three-ring binder with DOWNEY written on it, and realized this was Maureen's desk. Well, he'd only been here two days officially, in and out. He looked at notes written neatly on a yellow legal pad, saw the name ROBIN ABBOTT and her phone number, her address on Canfield, and another phone number and address with MOTHER written after it, then a dash and the name MARILYN. Below this Maureen had written B.H. POLICE and a number. B.H. for Bloomfield Hills, where Maureen had said the mother lived.

Chris got up and went over to his own desk piled with case folders, looked at the typed list of Sex Crimes squad members beneath the plastic cover of the desk pad and phoned Maureen. They said hi and Chris asked her if she'd ever got hold of Robin's mother.

"I tried all day yesterday."

"How come, Maureen?"

"Remember Robin saying she kept all those books and newspapers at her mom's? I wondered if she kept any other stuff there, since Wendell didn't find anything."

"But you haven't talked to her, the mom."

"I got a busy signal for about ten minutes, then no answer after that," Maureen said, "so I called the Bloomfield Hills police. They said the mother was away on a trip."

"But somebody was on the phone."

"I told them that. They said it was probably the maid, or maybe painters, rug cleaners, you know."

"Are they gonna check?"

"They said they'd look into it. Why, what're you up to?"

"Not a thing. You tell Wendell you called and got a busy signal?"

"Yeah, but he didn't seem too excited."

"That's all you can do, Maureen."

"Have you talked to him?"

"He's busy. There a lot of people killing each other." She said, "Where are you?"

"I'm not sure," Chris said, "but if I find out I'll let you know."

He went back to Maureen's desk, dialed Robin's number and listened to four rings before she answered: her voice softer than Maureen's, sounding bored as she said hello.

"Robin? It's Skip."

There was a silence.

Chris said, "What's the matter?"

Now a long pause before she said, "Who is this?"

"I just told you, it's Skip."

She hung up.

Chris waited about twenty seconds and dialed Robin's number again. The line was busy. He looked at Maureen's notes, dialed Robin's mother's number, got a busy signal and continued to listen to it, telling himself it didn't mean it was Skip. Telling himself the hell it didn't. It was, it was Skip. During the next couple of minutes he dialed Robin's number five times before it finally rang and she answered.

"Hi. This is Chris Mankowski."

He waited. See if she remembered him. Picturing her in that dingy room with the zingy red design painted on the wall, Robin trying to think fast, get it together, wanting to sound cool when she came on.

She said, "You just called, didn't you?" With the bored tone.

"And you hung up on me," Chris said. "I tried to call you back, but I guess you were talking to Skip."

There was a silence.

"Hang up and call Donnell this time. If he hasn't already told you about me, ask him. Mankowski?"

She said, "I know who you are, but that's about it. You're either a cop or a two-bit hustler and I don't know why I'm even talking to you."

"I'll drop around and tell you," Chris said, "in about an hour."

"I won't be here. I have to see a lawyer."

"That's not a bad idea."

There was a pause before Robin said, "Well, if you're going to be downtown later. . . ."

"How about Galligan's?"

She said, "No, I'll meet you at Hart Plaza about six," and hung up.

Chris waited, dialed her number and got a busy signal. He copied phone numbers and addresses, Greta's, Robin's and her mother's, on a sheet of notepaper and put it in his coat pocket. When he dialed Robin's number again the line was still busy.

He couldn't think of why she wanted to meet him outside and not in a bar. There was not much doubt Skip would be with her. He didn't know Skip, if Skip was mean and nasty or what. He believed Skip was the type—judging from the way he put a bomb together—who didn't give a shit and would let you know it. Skip and Juicy Mouth.

Chris left Sex Crimes and went down to six, to Firearms and Explosives, his old hangout. He had turned in his police .38 along with his shield and I.D. The gun his dad had given him, the Glock 17 auto, was still here in a locked cabinet. He filled the magazine with 9-millimeter rounds, remembering the St. Antoine Clinic doctor trying to make something out of it, asking him if he liked guns and getting into all that shit about spiders. Spiders, Jesus, who worried about spiders.

23

Skip couldn't stand it for long down in the basement rec room, being underground. It seemed nice at first. The bar had a pinkish mirror back of it that made you look tan and healthy while you sat there getting smashed, all by yourself. He had to stay clear of the first floor, other than slipping into the kitchen now and then; somebody could look in a window and see him. So he hung out upstairs in Robin's mom's bedroom. It had a bed with a canopy over it, a fireplace and living room furniture, it was so big, and a bathroom full of different kinds of bubble bath, lotions, skin creams and shit and really smelled good in there.

Saturday afternoon lying on the couch he watched a movie on TV called *Straight Time* that had one of his all-time favorite actors in it, Harry Dean Stanton. Jesus, but the guy made it look so real, the nervous state you were in pulling a stickup. Then to have your partner turn geek on you and you can't get him out of the fucking jewelry store—Skip could imagine that feeling. He was starting to get it with Robin as she turned from fun-loving to being a female hard-on. Harry Dean Stanton had died in that picture only because he made a bad decision and agreed to associate with geeks. Had to run when their driver spooked and got shot off a fence by the cops.

It was weird. This morning Skip had caught the tail end of *The Sack of Rome* on cable TV and watched himself get killed as one of Attila the Hun's guys. He felt he looked like a biker in drag. On location near Almería he was run over by chariots and hacked to death with those short Roman swords. Then had to lie in the sun among the dead and wounded talking Spanish to each other while the director and his star sat in an air-conditioned trailer drinking German beer and shooting the shit. After a couple of months they moved up to Madrid to a five-million-dollar set of the Roman forum. Here, Skip was killed several more times in close shots wearing different wigs and fake animal skins, having been spotted as a good dier. Twice in Almería the star himself, Steve Walton playing the Centurion, Fidelus, had killed him. But when they picked Skip to die at his hands on the forum set, part of the big finish, Walton looked Skip up and down and said, "He's too short." Ray Heidtke, the director, said, "We're in Spain, Steve. He's the biggest one we have." Skip, almost six foot, sized up Walton as he and the director argued, Walton was maybe six three but knock-kneed and had hips like a girl. Ray Heidtke said, "You sense this Hun coming at you from behind, but you wait. Time it just right. You turn, nothing to it, and stick him as he's about to take your nuts off."

Fourteen times Skip, hiding behind a statue, jumped

down from the pedestal about eight feet off the ground, landed in his Hun shoes, Christ, that were like bedroom slippers, and fell the first couple of times. "Cut!" After that Skip had his moves down, but then Walton was never ready, the guy screaming, "He's coming too soon!" Ray Heidtke said to Skip, "Pause after you land. Give it a three count. A thousand and one, a thousand and two. . . ." Walton said, "You tell me it makes sense, I have to stand here while you teach this asshole his timing?" That was when Skip decided to kill the star. Stick him in the throat with the wooden sword and push him down the temple steps. Ray Heidtke said, "Here we go." Skip got up on the statue and when the A.D. yelled for action he jumped, paused, but only for a second instead of a three-count, ran at Steve Walton, raising the wooden sword to ram it into him, and the knock-kneed son of a bitch turned too fast, stumbled, lunged trying to stay on his feet and drove *his* wooden sword into Skip, into that tender area where the leg meets the groin. The puncture wound wasn't serious; it was the infection that kept Skip in the hospital ten days. After, he tried to go back to work, but they wouldn't let him on the set.

That's what could happen to you associating with geeks. You could get hurt and fired or, in Harry Dean Stanton's case, get shot off a fence in Beverly Hills.

Right after Harry Dean's geek partner drove off at the end of the picture, going down a highway on his way to hell, Skip heard somebody downstairs. A minute later Robin was in the room. She came over to Skip on the couch, kissed him on the head and he thought to himself, Look out.

"You're moving," Robin said, stepping over to the TV to turn it off. "Let's get your clothes and your dynamite."

He asked her how come.

On the phone a couple of times she'd mentioned this

guy Mankowski, the suspended cop, and Skip didn't like the sound of him. What she told now, about Mankowski knowing he was here, he liked even less, saying to Robin, "I might just go back to L.A. You and Donnell could be cutting me out as it is, once I do the heavy work for you. I've an idea what you want, too. Find out where this Mankowski parks his car and wire it up."

"You'd do it, wouldn't you?" Robin said.

She hooked a leg over the flowery arm of the couch, started fooling with his ponytail, and once again Skip told himself to look out.

"We haven't been able to talk much," Robin said.

Skip knew that. He waited.

"Donnell wants to cut you out."

Skip knew that too. It stood to reason.

"He thinks he's calling the shots, so I play along. You're going to be proud of me, the way I've worked it out."

Skip let her play with his ponytail.

"I have to call Donnell before we leave," Robin said. "See if he'll do us a favor."

Skip kept quiet. Let her talk.

"We *do* need him. At least till Monday morning when the bank opens. Donnell wants one million even, he likes all those oughts, as he says. But our take has to be less than his because he's the brains. You believe it? I said fine, we'll go in for seven hundred thousand."

"That's a familiar number," Skip said.

"Our original idea. But if you have no objections let's go for the whole thing."

"Cut Donnell out."

"It wouldn't be hard, the way I see it work."

Skip began to relax, feeling a little better about his one-time old lady.

"Sweetheart, tell me how we get paid."

"Woody gives us a check."

Skip grinned at her. "You're cuckoo, you know it?"

Robin was shaking her head and stroking her braid at the same time. "Monday morning, as soon as the bank opens, Woody calls the Trust Department and has a million seven transferred to his commercial account. We see him do it, so we know the check's good."

"We're holding a gun on him, or what?"

Robin shook her head, giving him that faint smile, and Skip closed one eye, looking up at her, trying to see if there was a hole in her idea. This was kind of fun.

He said, "Well, shit, Woody can stop payment any time right after."

Robin said, "Not if he's dead, he can't."

Skip said, "Uh-huh, and if you don't see giving Donnell his share . . . I suppose there's a big explosion of some kind and the two of them are found underneath the rubble."

Robin said, "Hey, there's an idea."

Skip looked down the road, thinking about it. "The cops find out we took a check off him for a million seven. . . . It has to be made out to one of us and we put it in a bank. You don't just cash a million seven. They're gonna find it out."

Why was she grinning at him?

"The check isn't made out to either of us," Robin said. "It's pay to the order of—you ready? Nicole Robinette."

It took Skip a moment. "That's *you,* huh? Your book name."

"Woody doesn't know it yet," Robin said, "but he's buying theatrical rights to all four of my novels, herein referred to as the 'Fire Series.' *Diamond Fire, Emerald Fire*—"

"Jesus Christ," Skip said.

"Gold Fire and *Silver Fire.* I'm meeting a lawyer," Robin said, looking at her watch, "guy I used to know. He's coming to his office on Saturday as a special favor. I typed up a Purchase Agreement and Assignment of Rights, pretty much boilerplate, from standard contracts I picked up when I worked in New York. He'll look them over, make sure they're okay."

Skip said, "This guy owe you one?"

"I'm going to pay him," Robin said, "if he asks. Maybe he will, I don't know."

"I bet you make sure he doesn't."

"Anyway, we get Woody's signature on the contracts, so it looks legit, for after. Okay, we deposit his check in Nicole Robinette's account and then—listen to this—I write checks payable to you and me in our own names, *and* a couple of the names we used when we were underground. Like good old Scott Wolf will get a check. What do you think?"

"I liked being Scotty Wolf," Skip said, "he was a nice guy. That other one I used—the hell was it? Derrick Powell—when I was living in New Mexico. But, shit, those I.D.s're old, they've expired."

"For a million seven," Robin said, "I'll bet we can think of ways to get them renewed, or make up new ones. I'll have to reactivate Diane Young and Betsy Bender."

Skip said, "Man, I remember Betsy Bender, with her 'fro. That motel in L.A. off Sunset. I wouldn't mind bending her again right now." He softened his eyes at Robin, waiting to give her a nice grin.

But she wasn't looking. Robin got up from the arm of the couch sounding like she was thinking out loud, telling him she was going to have to make up contracts between the fake names and Nicole Robinette. For different services the fake names provided. Otherwise the bank would report the deposit to the IRS and Nicole would owe . . . Christ, at least five hundred thousand dollars. Or she'd make up invoices or some goddamn thing, from the fake names to Nicole.

Skip watched her turn and head for the phone now, by her mom's canopied bed.

"I almost forgot. I have to call Donnell."

Skip said, "How do you like it?"

Robin dialed before she looked over. "How do I like what?"

"Being in the straight world."

Mr. Woody, seeming almost of sound mind but wet-eyed drunk, hooked onto the word "codicil" from somewhere in his past life, telling Donnell that's what it was, a codicil, like an addendum. You didn't scribble a codicil, it was a legal document and ought to be typewritten.

So they had to look through the cabinets in the library for the typewriter: found a favorite flashlight the man had misplaced; found tapes of monster movies, from when he was on that kick; came across the black athletic bag that had been put there by Mankowski, Mr. Woody wanting to know what was in it and Donnell telling him it was just stuff in there, nothing important. He put the typewriter on the desk and started copying what he'd written yesterday in longhand—about the man leaving him at least two million if and when he ever died—taking forever, looking for each letter as he poked the keys. So the man said to let him type it. He sat down and fussed, abused the typewriter, reading with his wet eyes as he typed, but damn if he didn't get it done. Finished, pulled the sheet out of the typewriter and signed it. There it was, scrawled right at the bottom in big loops, *Woodrow Ricks.*

Donnell picked up the sheet of paper and kissed it, the man not looking, stumbling away from the desk, starting to take his clothes off for his afternoon swim.

The phone rang.

Donnell slipped that lovely codicil into a desk drawer, picked up the phone and heard Robin's voice say, "Hi, it's me. How you doing?" He told her he couldn't talk now. But she was in a hurry and said she needed a favor, asking him if he could get somebody to do a job. He told her just a minute and put his hand over the phone.

"Mr. Woody, you take off your clothes at the swimming pool. Go on now. I be right there."

The man shuffled out and Donnell kept his hand on the phone a while longer thinking, Shit, the man could fall in the pool and drown and it would be too soon. The lawyer had to get the codicil first and put it in the will. *Then* the man could fall in the pool and drown or drink himself to death or hit his head on the toilet. . . .

So he hurried talking to Robin and agreed, okay, to get somebody, yeah, uh-huh, saying he understood when Robin said, "We want to take him out, but not all the way," and let her tell him why it wouldn't be good to have Skip do the job, risk his getting busted. Not at this point, blow the deal. Donnell had questions he didn't ask. He told her he'd see. Robin said he had to do more than *see,* he had to get somebody. She said this was crucial and Donnell said all *right,* he'd do it, but right now had to do something else. Hung up and ran down the hall to the swimming pool.

The man was already in the water, a scene of peace and contentment, floating naked on the rubber raft, fat little hands flapping at the water, barely moving him. . . . See? Everything was fine. Beautiful.

The man's voice raised to call. "Donnell?"

"I'm right here."

"I want Arthur Prysock instead of Ezio Pinza."

"I don't blame you."

"For a change."

"Yes sir, you got it."

" 'On the Street Where You Live.' "

"One of my favorites too, Mr. Woody."

What was wrong with *this* street where he lived, *this* house? Sit and wait for the man one day to take his last drink, throw up and die. What was the hurry to have a lot of money if he wasn't going anywhere? He believed he could trust Robin to give him his million out of the check, scare her ass not to think otherwise. This Skippy he'd have to see about. Best now to keep it moving, get it over with and done. Million seven, all the different kind of money accounts and shit the man had, he wouldn't even miss it. . . .

Sleeping on his rubber boat, Arthur Prysock running his voice up and down the street, belting the shit out of that old tune. Donnell brought the phone from the bar to the table and dialed a number.

He said, "Juicy, tell me what you been doing," and listened to this young dude growl and breathe animal sounds into the phone, in a bad mood after visiting the pink room up in Homicide, sitting hours in that closet while they asked him the same shit.

Donnell said, "You out of work, you out of finances. I have a man for you needs to be vamped on. Tell me what you charge to bust his leg, put him in the hospital about a month."

Juicy said, "I'm tired."

Donnell said, "Take you two minutes from the time he gets out of his Cadillac. Polack name Mankowski, not near big as you."

Juicy said, "Mankowski, shit, I know that name, that-man's a cop."

Donnell straightened him out. The man was suspended, didn't have a badge or a gun no more, was out of business.

Juicy said, "They took his gun, huh? . . . He's the motherfucker let Booker blow hisself up."

Donnell said, "I thought was you and Moselle did that."

Juicy said, "I wasn't there. You understand? *He* was there, I wasn't. He let it happen to my man. Yeah, I'll bust his legs good."

"Just one."

"I'll give you a deal for the same price. I'll put him away."

"Juicy?"

"I'll take him out someplace and lose his ass. Nobody ever see him again."

"Juicy? How much just for the one leg?"

24

Saturday afternoon Chris had time to kill, so he walked the few blocks from 1300 to the Renaissance Center and went to the show. He saw *Lethal Weapon* and watched how Mel Gibson took care of the bad guys; Chris thinking, So that's what you do, you shoot 'em. Mel Gibson played a burnout and supposedly didn't care if he got killed or not, which was harder for Chris to believe than how good Mel was with his fifteen-shot Beretta. Chris's pistol, the Glock auto, began to dig into his groin as he sat there, so he slipped it into his coat pocket in the dark of the theater watching Mel Gibson. Pretty cool for a burnout. Though he couldn't imagine a homicide cop being allowed to dress that scruffy, even in L.A. Homicide cops were dudes.

Eleven years ago, when Chris was working out of the

Twelfth Precinct in a radio car, there were a couple of guys known as the pizza bandits, white guys who specialized in the armed robbery of private homes. One of them would ring the bell standing there with a pizza box; the resident would open the door to say he didn't order a pizza and the second guy would come out of the bushes wearing a ski mask. They'd punch out the man of the house, make the wife, if she wasn't too old, take her clothes off and fool around with her and then haul away the TVs, silverware, jewelry and so on. They were working through a home not far from where Woody Ricks now lived when the maid got a chance to call 911. It was given to Chris and his partner, robbery in progress, and when they arrived Chris went around to cover the rear while his partner called for backup. Two cars came to assist, the second one wailing, its flashers on, and the pizza bandits dropped what they were doing and ran out the back door. Chris saw guns in their hands and came a hair away from firing. But he didn't, he put his .38 on them and said, "Right there. Don't move," thinking of other things he could've said. Freeze. Drop the guns. They stopped dead, both guys. Chris raised his voice a notch. "Don't *move.*" One of the guys spoke up fast. "It's cool," in an urgent tone of voice. "Nobody's moving." Chris raised his voice another notch. "Don't fucking move a muscle!" The first guy screamed back at him, "I'm not *moving,* man! Look at me!" As the second guy screamed, "I'm *not* fucking moving!" That was the way it happened, three guys in a backyard at night holding revolvers, all of them scared to death one of the guns was going to go off. Two nights later Chris answered a call, disturbance in a working-class neighborhood, a family argument. He and his partner walked into a house and here was a guy in his undershirt drunk out of his mind holding a gun on his wife, a woman in hair curlers and a ratty pink housecoat, crying, her nose running. . . . That time Chris kept his voice down, saying to the guy, "You don't want to shoot your wife. Give me the gun." Didn't want to shoot his wife—the guy was dying to shoot her and he did, shot her twice before Chris grabbed the gun away from him, twisting it out of his hand. The woman suffered superficial wounds, went into Emergency that Saturday night and was out of the hospital Monday morning. The guy suffered broken fingers and a shoulder injury where his arm was yanked out of its socket and it kept him in therapy a year. When he had to quit his job at Detroit Forge and Axle he sued the city, the police and retired to Deltona, Florida, on the settlement. Chris's precinct commander said, "Why didn't you shoot the son of a bitch?"

That's what Mel Gibson would've done, shot the drunk spot welder dead. Then you see Mel having to live with it and the next time he has to pull his gun he chokes when he should be squeezing off rounds and because of it he either gets shot or his partner does, the partner dies and so on.

Before leaving the theater Chris switched the Glock auto from his coat pocket back to his waist, the big grip against his belly. It was five thirty. He had a half hour, time to go across the street and have a couple. Get ready for his meeting.

Late Saturday afternoon, hardly anybody in the place, you could see what Galligan's looked like; you could see the booths, the posters and photographs on the walls, the brass rail separating the tables from the bar. Chris got a bourbon mist. A guy with a convention badge and a New York accent told him he was attending the dry cleaners show at Cobo Hall. He said he thought Detroit only had shot-and-a-beer joints, this place could be on Third Avenue, Upper East Side. Chris told the guy Detroit had everything: at least one of each. The guy said yeah, was that right? Chris excused himself; he had to make a phone call.

When he was living with Phyllis and they used to meet here after work she'd say, "Hi, guy," or "Hi, love," or once in a while, "Hi, tiger," and he'd feel like an asshole in that five o'clock press of young execs and secretaries turning to see who the tiger was. Phyllis wasn't trying to be funny, she was serious. It was her idea, after spending all day in the Trust Department of Manufacturers National Bank, of being hip. Phyllis knew who Sigourney Weaver was, but not Doodles.

When she answered the phone and he said hi, Phyllis said, "Hi, guy. I've been wondering when you'd call."

He could see her in a silky negligee holding the phone in the crook of her neck, hair up, foot on a chair, cotton balls wedged between her toes.

"I want to ask you something," Chris said.

"If you had called yesterday—no, Thursday," Phyllis said, "I might've given in, asked you to come home. I was feeling sort of down, to tell you the truth. Chris? We did have some laughs, didn't we?"

He tried to think.

Living with Phyllis, most of the time it meant watching her get ready: Phyllis bathing, painting her nails, anointing her big-girl body with lotions, putting on flimsy, see-through undergarments that showed dark places. . . . He gave her a pair of musical panties one time; you pressed the rose and it played the theme from *Love Story*—"Where do I begin, da *da* da da da da *da* . . ."—which got a laugh, but not much of one. Undergarments were her vestments. But then she'd "dress for power," as she called it, cover that soft white body in a business suit, and go off to the bank.

He began to say, "Phyllis . . . ?" but she beat him.

"I met a guy yesterday, Chris."

Then paused, and it intrigued him just enough that he said, "Yeah?"

"A neat guy. Bob owns quite a large plant in Fort Wayne, Indiana. They manufacture dry-cleaning solvents, dyes, spot removers. . . ."

Chris said, "I guess somebody has to."

Phyllis said in her grave tone, "That isn't fair, Chris."

"What isn't?"

"Taking how you feel out on Bob. Listen, I'm really sorry it didn't work. I tried, I'm sure you did too. It's just one of those things."

"Just one of those crazy flings," Chris said.

There was another pause.

A trip to the moon on some kind of wings. Gossamer.

"I think I detect a certain tone," Phyllis said. "I know you, Chris. I know when you're upset. Your friend Jerry told me what happened and I thought, Oh, the poor guy. On top of everything else."

"What did he tell you?"

"About your suspension."

"Phyllis, I just want to ask you something."

She said, "If you want my opinion, I think it's the best thing that could happen to you. Now you've got a chance to realize your potential and go for it. Get into marketing, that's where the action is, Chris, where it's happening."

"In marketing." It amazed him she could talk like that in the kind of underwear she wore.

"In a business that's on the move. You're a bright guy, Chris, and you're not afraid to take risks. Think of how many years you could've lost your hands, or even your life. We don't have to go into that, do we? The point I want to make: What did you stand to gain in return? Nothing. No bonus, no profit participation. . . . Chris, my friend Bob that I mentioned? He started out on the road selling days. He worked his way up to sales manager, director of marketing, and when his dad retired he was made president and executive chairman of the board."

"Phyllis?"

"Yes, Chris."

"I was wondering, if a guy transfers money from a trust account to a business account and writes you a check, is it good right away, or you have to wait for something to happen?"

There was a silence this time.

Chris waited. He thought of something else and said, "Is this Bob by any chance married?"

Skip strolled through Hart Plaza from Jefferson Avenue down to the embankment close to the river. He took a moment to look at Canada, then strolled back across the sweep of pavement, past a tubular arch of sheet metal, the Noguchi fountain, a mist of water shining on it. A block from here there was a metal sculpture of Joe Louis's fist and forearm, artwork for a workingman's town. Skip's gaze wandered, ready to settle on any guy in his late thirties who could be a cop: a guy with a certain amount of heft standing in one place, waiting, eyes moving. He spotted a few black guys who could go either way, pushers or narcs, but no one who met his idea of what Mankowski would look like. So he went across Jefferson to Galligan's, walked in at ten to six, and there was the guy, Mankowski, sitting at the bar.

Skip was pretty sure. The guy didn't have the heft Skip thought he would, but he was the right age and had enough of a cop look: like an ex-ballplayer who'd spent most of his years in the minors. There was one other guy down the bar and couples wearing convention badges in two of the booths and that was it. Skip took a stool on Mankowski's left, leaving a stool between them, and asked the bartender for a scotch and water. After taking a good sip, he leaned on the bar, turned his head and looked past his shoulder at Mankowski.

Chris had asked the bartender how the Tigers did today and Tommy told him they were playing tonight, Cleveland was in town. Saying there were only about five day games on Saturday this year. Saying all the beer drinkers'd be in about ten thirty. Chris had watched the guy in the black satin jacket come in and caught a glimpse of the movie name on the back, in red, as the guy looked around. After Tommy stepped over and poured the guy a scotch, Chris heard him say:

"You ever been to Perry's in San Francisco? It's on Union Street. I swear this place looks just like it."

"It looks like some place to everybody," Chris said. "Maybe that's the idea."

"Well, it's handy. You stay at any of the hotels, it's right here."

Chris said, "Yeah, it's right here." He took a quarter turn on the stool to face the guy and said, "But where's Robin? Didn't she come with you?"

The guy stayed low, looking past his shoulder. He turned his head to take a drink and then looked this way again. "We ever met, you and I?"

"No, this's the first time."

"Well, I'm gonna have to ask, how'd you make me?"

Chris said, "I know you're not in the dry-cleaning business, Skip. Maybe it's the ponytail, or the way you talk to your shoulder, like you're in the chow hall at Milan, I don't know. Or it's just you look dirty. You know what I mean?"

Chris watched the guy straighten and do a little number, a head shake as though he'd been hit. Skip said, "Hey, I don't want any part of you, man. Take it easy, okay?"

Chris touched the stool between them. "Sit here. I want to tell you something I won't have to raise my voice."

Skip shrugged and then slid over, bringing his drink with him, saying, "I know who you are, man. You're still playing the dick with me. Once a dick—am I right? I bet when you guys had some poor asshole in the chair, asking him questions, I bet you played the hardass, didn't you? Show 'em no fucking mercy."

Chris said, "No, I was always the nice guy. I'd stick up for the assholes and pretty soon they're dying to tell me anything I want to know. Like I say to you, Can I buy you a drink? Or I say, I understand you shoot dynamite like a pro. Rub your ego, see. Then I ask you where Robin is and you tell me. That's how it works."

"She'll meet you after," Skip said. "Shit, you got me to talk."

"Why didn't she come with you?"

"Says she doesn't know you well enough. See, we got conflicting opinions as to what the fuck you're up to. If you're not a cop anymore, what are you? Things like that."

"I'm on *you* now," Chris said.

"Jesus, I *know* that, but what else? All I have, you understand, is hearsay. I'm suppose to find out what your game is, before you talk to Robin. If I don't like what I hear then you don't talk to her. It's like that."

"All you have to know," Chris said, "I don't want to see anything happen to Woody."

"You don't work for him. Or do you?"

"I don't want to see him get hurt. I don't want to even see him nervous or upset. If I do, I'll pull the chain on you and you're gone."

Skip leaned closer, sliding his elbow along the bar. "You're telling me what you personally don't want to see happen. Am I right?"

"That's what I said."

"What I mean is, you're not playing the dick with me now. This's *you* talking. And what you don't want is anything could mess up the shakedown you got working." He said, "Am I right?" Grinning at Chris now. "You get all ready to make your move and somebody steps in front of you. Have to line up, huh, to get a piece of the guy. So you're saying if anything happens to blow your deal, you'll turn hardass dick and we'll be sorry. Well, I can't fault you for thinking like that. Shit, I would too."

"Where's Robin?"

Skip hesitated, easing back, picking up his drink. "You want to tell her yourself, huh?"

Chris said, "I want to make sure she understands."

"I can tell her, if that's all you're worried about."

"Where is she?"

Skip hesitated again. "It's up to you. She's over in a parking lot behind St. Andrews Hall. Couple blocks from here."

"I know where it is."

"Sitting in a red VW."

"I want to see her alone," Chris said. "You wait here."

Skip pushed up the sleeve of his jacket to glance at his

watch. He looked at Chris then with a mild expression and said it again. "It's up to you."

Last November there were rock fans in the alley behind St. Andrews Hall, new-wavers in studded leather, spiked hair in Easter colors; normal-looking fans went unnoticed. Inside this auditorium without seats they pressed in a mass against the stage and rocked to Iggy Pop and his Brits turned loose: Iggy nonstop trying to twist himself in the air to levitate over his reaching fans while Chris, in the low balcony, watched and wondered what it was like to have that energy, to feel that response rising from outstretched hands and lighters flaming and all those eyes never letting go.

Today there were young black guys in the alley by the back door to the hall, waiting there, watching Chris coming toward them. Three guys with wide shoulders and skinny pants, wearing Pony sneakers. Their attitude was familiar to Chris but not their faces. A fourth guy, with bigger shoulders stretching his silky green jacket and holding a baseball bat, came out of the row of cars facing the alley. This one was very familiar. He didn't have to stick out his tongue to be identified.

Chris took a quick look toward the parking lot full of cars. He didn't notice a red VW.

Juicy Mouth was saying, "This the man let Booker blow hisself up." Announcing it to the three young guys, who were too cool to do more than appear half asleep.

It gave Chris time to look for a connection and think of Wendell saying there wasn't one, not between Booker's bomb and Woody's. But look at this, there was some kind of connection. Robin and Juicy? That didn't sound right. Donnell and Juicy?

"Make it easy on you," Juicy was saying to him now. "No fuss, stick your leg out, your foot on the bumper of that car, we be done and gone."

"You want to break my leg?"

Juicy held up the bat. "Check it out. What have I got here?"

"For what?"

"Listen, I told the person I do more. They say no, don't put him away, put him in the hospital a while. That be fine, that do it."

"What person you talking about?"

"Can't tell you that, man. Same as like a lawyer won't tell you shit how he knows something. Check it out, it's the same thing what I'm saying."

"Was it Donnell Lewis?"

"Man, I just told you what I ain't gonna tell you."

Chris saw Juicy look up and move slowly toward the back of the old building. Chris stepped to the parking lot side and a car crept past them, going up the alley. Juicy came away from the building watching Chris, about twenty feet between them, but said to the young guys, "You get it open?"

One of them said, "I need a tire iron. Something to pop it."

Chris said, "You think I'm going in there with you?"

He unbuttoned his coat, his hand brushing the big grip of the automatic stuck in his waist, and held the coat open for Juicy. "You see it?" He half turned to the three guys by the door, still holding open the coat. "You see it?" Then said to Juicy again, "Was it Donnell?"

Juicy said, "You not suppose to have that, man. What is that, some kind of gun?"

Chris pulled the Glock from his waist and looked at the three well-built young guys as he palmed the slide, racked it and the gun was ready to fire. He said to them, "What you do now, you run, fast as you can. I don't want to ever see you again."

Juicy, taking his time, was coming toward him now, saying, "Man, is that thing real? That's a strange-looking piece, man. It shoot bullets or what?"

Chris said to the three young guys, "I'm gonna count to two."

The three guys stood posed at rest, dull-eyed, slack, hips cocked at studied angles.

Chris said, "One," raised the Glock and fired at the metal door behind them, past the nearest guy's head, and they were running as that hard sound filled the alley and Chris said, "Two."

He saw Juicy duck into the parking lot and went after him down a line of cars, catching glimpses of a moving figure, silky green, came to the exit drive, on the street, and there was no sign of him. An older black guy, the parking attendant, stood in the door of the shack, his office. He kept staring at the gun in Chris's hand till finally he pointed a direction and stepped back inside. Chris moved along the front of the cars facing the street, past the grill of a Rolls, another car, heard door locks snap closed and saw Juicy behind the wheel of a white Cadillac sedan, Juicy staring straight ahead. Chris approached on the passenger side and tapped the barrel of the Glock against the window.

"Hey, Juice? Who is it wants my leg busted?"

The guy refused to speak or turn his head, hands locked on the steering wheel.

"You can tell me, it's okay. Just don't stick out your tongue. Man, that thing is scary, like it's something alive, you know what I mean? Living in your mouth. . . . Who was it, Donnell?"

Juicy didn't answer or move or twitch or anything.

Chris said, "You think I don't see you? Okay, that's how you want it." Chris put the muzzle of the gun flat against the glass and said, "Juice? Look."

But the guy still wouldn't move.

Chris said, "You know what Mel Gibson would do?" and was anxious to show him as he thought of Mel blazing away with his Beretta. Shit, the Glock held more rounds.

First, though, Juicy had to be looking at him. And second, he had to be careful, not shoot through the car and hit something else, or somebody on the street a block away. So Chris walked around to the front of the Cadillac. He raised the Glock in one hand and stood sideways—not the way Mel Gibson did it, two-handed—Juicy looking right at him now, aimed at the fat top part of the seat next to the guy and began squeezing off shots—loud, Jesus, they'd hear it at 1300—counting "four" as the shatterproof windshield came apart, counted from five through ten and stopped. Where was Juicy? There, his head showing as he came up, very cautious, behind the steering wheel. Chris fired five more quick rounds into the car before Juicy could move, continued to hold the gun aimed in the silence and said, "Was it Donnell?"

Juicy nodded, up and down.

"Say it."

"It was him."

"You feel better now?"

"I don't owe him nothing. He busted off my tooth one time, was in a Men's."

"You could've told me it was Donnell before and saved your car getting wrecked."

Juicy said, "What, this? This ain't my car."

Robin used to roll joints Skip said were the next thing to being factory made. She had rolled him one hard and tight he was smoking now, sitting low in her fake-leather chair. Robin had a hip on the edge of her desk, red sunburst still on the wall behind her, watching him as she fooled with her braid.

"Are you afraid of him?"

"All I'm trying to tell you," Skip said, "I think he's the kind of fella we could've cut a deal with. Stays out of our way long as we don't make a lot of noise." Skip drew on the cigarette and his voice changed, tightened. "I didn'teven want to do it to him, send him over there to be crippled."

"I guess he could've picked up a gun," Robin said. "But to start shooting—"

"Listen," Skip said. "I was across the street. These guys come by me like they're out to set a new four-forty record. He goes after the other guy, finds him and I swear fires twenty shots into that car before he's through. You see him as some broke dick with his hand out. I saw him holding a gun in it that never stops firing."

"What did he do then?"

"I told you, I took off. He might've gone back to the bar. He *knows* who set him up."

"You're saying he might come here."

"I was him I'd already be here. That's why we have to clear out. What I've been trying to tell you."

"You have a gun, don't you?"

Skip said, "You want *me* to do it? You keep changing

the plan, come up with different ideas, shit, now you want me to clean up your mess. He comes in, shoot him right here in your apartment. That what you want?" He inhaled and reached out, offering her the joint.

Robin shook her head; she straightened. Skip watched her step away from the desk but not going anywhere. Inside her head now, still stroking her braid.

Skip said, "I think we better move out to your mom's for the night."

"He knows you were there."

"Then let's go to a motel."

She stopped pacing and turned to him and he liked the schemy smile coming into her eyes.

"I've got a better idea," Robin said.

25

The part Greta played in the movie they shot in Detroit was GIRL IN BAR, filmed in an actual bar, Jacoby's, on Brush Street. The camera follows an actor playing a detective as he enters and comes over to the bar where she's standing with another actor. (Both of them had familiar faces, but she didn't know their names.) The one at the bar says to the one that comes in, "She's trying to figure out what I do for a living." GIRL IN BAR: "Don't tell me, okay?" The guy is wearing a tie with a plaid wool shirt and a suitcoat that doesn't match the pants. GIRL IN BAR: "You teach shop at a high school, right?" Then there's the sound of a beeper going off. As the one that comes in takes the beeper from his belt, she sees his holstered gun. GIRL IN

BAR: "You're *cops*. That's the next thing I was gonna say."

When she told Chris about the scene he said, "Yeah, then what happens?"

Nothing. That was all she did in the movie, the one scene. Every once in a while she'd imagine being in Jacoby's and wonder what might happen next if it were real life. If for some reason she's there alone and the guy with the wool shirt and tie comes up to her and starts talking. . . . It still wouldn't go anywhere, because she wasn't GIRL IN BAR. Played by Ginger Jones. She wasn't either of them.

She was Greta Wyatt, resting on her elbows at the kitchen table, the only place in the empty house to sit down, outside of her bed, and she didn't want to go upstairs yet. The idea of being alone was to have time to look at her situation: see where she was in relation to her goal in life, if she had one, and figure out why she was confused—if it took all night.

As it turned out, she had a revelation in less than half an hour.

Dance Fever appeared on the black-and-white TV her folks had left for her on the kitchen counter. *Dance Fever* was a talent contest judged by semi-well-known names from the entertainment world. Greta watched couples come out and perform acrobatic dances in sequined costumes that would catch the studio lights and flash on the black-and-white screen. She watched the girls especially, studied each one and thought, Oh my God, she's a Ginger Jones. Four part-time Ginger Joneses, one after another, with their huge thighs and show-biz smiles locked in place, throwing themselves into their routines and trusting their muscular little partners to catch them. She had even said to Chris the other night, "You know how many Ginger

Joneses there are just in Detroit?" Talking about if she had talent or not. And he said, "There's only one Greta Wyatt that I know of."

She realized now a revelation could be right smack in front of you all the time, but so simple you miss it.

Why use a fake name that makes you think of yourself as a third-rate performer?

The movie director had told her she was really good, a natural, as GIRL IN BAR. Greta Wyatt acting, playing a part that wasn't anything like her. Why give Ginger Jones the credit? Someone she didn't respect. She'd call up the movie company in Hollywood and tell them she'd like her credit changed to read: GIRL IN BAR, dot dot dot, Greta Wyatt. How many Gretas were there in Hollywood these days?

Next. See Woody and relieve her mind of that part.

Settle with him fairly; accept his original offer. Even if he did rape her, or try to, it didn't mean she should take advantage of him. Twenty-five thousand was plenty. She didn't need a car anymore. Or need to get mixed up in what could become a mess, his brother already dead, and find herself caught in the middle. End up being one of those girls that gets her hair done, then opens her door for the news people, the TV cameras, and acts innocent, holding a hanky to her nose. . . . Or open the door wearing sunglasses and act mysterious, escorted through the crowd to a big car, and the next thing you know Farrah Fawcett wants to play you in the movie.

New rules to live by. One, be yourself. No more Ginger. Two, see Woody and get that over with. Three . . .

Three was still up in the air but seemed okay. What to do about Chris Mankowski. His voice on the message recorder said, "Greta, I haven't changed one bit," and it made her feel good, the way seeing him walking around in his underwear made her feel good. She was herself with him, or she could play around acting cute with him and he loved it. Now she missed him and wanted him to hurry up and call. But then thought of the scene in Jacoby's again and wondered what she would look like on the screen.

She thought of Woody and saw him handing her a check.

Thought of Chris in bed wearing his dad's glasses.

Thought of the director, the way he looked at her when she finished the scene, the way he put his hand on her arm.

She saw Woody, he was making her take a check for a hundred thousand, insisting, and saw herself coming out of his house putting on sunglasses.

Greta smiled.

She thought of Chris, his body, the scars on his legs.

And now she was in a dark movie theater, watching titles appear on the screen, waiting for her name . . .

It was after seven by the time Chris got hold of the building manager, back from somewhere with his toolbox, and told him Miss Abbott didn't answer when he buzzed her apartment. The manager, grim as ever, said when that happened it meant the person wasn't home. Not trying to be funny. Chris came close to grabbing him by the throat. He held on and said in a fairly nice tone, What he was about to ask, would it be too much trouble to look in her apartment and make sure? The manager said he was already late sitting down to his supper. Standing in that dingy hall by the manager's apartment Chris said, "I better inform you, you could be charged here with creating an improper diversion, in violation of ordinance 613.404. Carries, I think, up to a year."

The manager, frowning, thinking about it, said, "Creating a what?"

Chris hunched in close to the guy's flashing bifocals and said, "Get the goddamn pass key."

Robin wasn't home.

He got back in his dad's car and drove out to Bloomfield Hills. Northbound traffic was light on the freeway and he was able to go seventy or better, feeling an urgent need to get Robin and Skip nailed down, located, under some kind of surveillance. He knew where to find Donnell.

No more fooling around in the gray area, the first one. There was a second gray area now: a white '87 Cadillac sedan, license number JVS 681. He was thinking about asking Jerry Baker if he'd check with the First Precinct, see if the owner had reported a blown-out windshield and fifteen 9-millimeter rounds in the backrest of his front seat. Or through and through, into the back seat. There might even be a couple in the trunk. At this point Jerry Baker, the gray area expert, might ask, "What's gray about it?"

It was something to think about driving up the freeway, eight o'clock and still light. Chris imagined a conversation as sort of a rehearsal for conversations to come, a chance to get a few answers straight in his mind, starting with Jerry asking what's gray about the guy getting his car shot up.

CHRIS: Let's say it happened in the line of duty. The city pays for the damage, right?

JERRY: But it didn't.

CHRIS: Looking at it retroactively, it could turn out that it was in the line of duty. That's the gray area.

Jerry doesn't understand that. No one would.

CHRIS: Look at it this way. While holding evidence until Monday, I've put myself in a position to observe the perpetrators, aware of the possibility they could, *A,* show their hand, *B,* fuck up, or *C,* as it happens sometimes with these people, they have a disagreement and go after each other instead of the intended victim, Woody.

JERRY: Or they could go after you.

CHRIS: That's right. You could get a leg broken. But when the attempt fails and a Cadillac sedan, JVS 681, is damaged in the process, there are two ways to look at it. One, it was a matter of a private citizen defending his life.

JERRY: Who's the private citizen?

CHRIS: Me. Or, another way to look at it, the car was damaged by a police officer in the performance of his duty.

JERRY: But you're not a police officer.

CHRIS: I am if they'll reinstate me retroactively, in consideration of the undercover work I've been doing, lining up the perpetrators. All right, that's done. Or it will be. Then Monday, Homicide throws a full investigation at them. Get them with dynamite in their possession. Then I bring out the evidence I've been holding over the weekend, five sticks of Austin Powder. We match it to their dynamite, same lot number and all, and we're on our way. Maybe Homicide'll want to go about it a little different, but here's hard evidence that could lead to a conviction. Get 'em for one homicide, one attempted.

JERRY: You produce the five sticks of dynamite—that's all? Not the check for twenty-five grand?

CHRIS: I don't know. That's still in the gray area all its own, isn't it?

Jerry doesn't answer. The gray area expert doesn't know either. Or won't say. . . .

In the next hour and a half Chris arrived at Robin's mother's house, off Lone Pine Road, pressed close to the windows in all three garage doors and saw a Lincoln and two clean, empty spaces; no red VW. He pressed close to windows along the back of the house, came to a door and rang the bell. If he had I.D. he'd get the Bloomfield Hills cops to go in. Just checking. But he didn't have I.D., so he poked his elbow through a pane of glass, reached in and opened the door. Right next to it on the wall was the panel of buttons you punched as soon as you entered, to turn off the silent alarm system. Shit. So he got in his dad's car and drove back to Robin's:

Buzzed her apartment and got no answer. Buzzed the manager. . . .

From 9:30 till 3:00 A.M. Chris sat in the car parked across the street from 515 Canfield, in the dark. He pictured Robin and Skip in a bar, two ex-cons talking past their shoulders, scheming, grinning at each other as they had fun getting smashed. Seeing them in a bar because he would love a drink. Go somewhere to have a few and get something to eat. He hadn't had anything since breakfast. A box of popcorn in the show. He should've called Greta. He caught a glimpse of Phyllis, the cotton between her toes. . . .

Then saw Greta in her T-shirt now, bending over the stove.

E L M O R E · L E O N A R D

Saw her sitting at the desk in the squad room. Saw her walking, her thighs moving in the skirt. Saw her in his dad's car, in profile.

And saw Mel Gibson playing the burnout and saw Juicy in the Cadillac, the Glock going off, Jesus, and saw Juicy's gray tongue in the pink interrogation room.

Greta was alone in that empty house, the phone and message recorder on the bare floor. He should've called.

He wasn't different.

He saw Donnell in the library, that dismal room, it seemed dusty, a gray area of figurine lamps and leather chairs, Donnell getting the checkbook out of the desk, holding it close to him.

Greta, he liked her name. He liked her red hair against the pillow, her mouth. . . .

He saw Donnell and Skip and Robin standing slack, not moving a muscle. They better not. He was covering them with the Glock auto. But where would it happen?

Donnell kept waiting for the man to fall asleep so he could go downstairs a while, have some time to himself. The house would be quiet and Donnell in his room listening would think, Finally. Then would hear the man's voice from down the hall.

"Donnell?"

And he'd move through the dark to the master bedroom, light showing inside. Three times now, walk out of the room dim, the night light on in the bathroom, come back to it lit up.

"I'm right here, Mr. Woody."

"I can't sleep."

"You keep turning the light on, how can you?"

"But I can't *see.*"

"That's the idea. You close your eyes and you have sweet dreams. Think of like you lying in a hammock and this lovely woman, has a flower in her black hair, is holding a banana rum daiquiri, big, big one, kind you love, and you sipping it through a straw." Give the man some kind of shit his wet mind would recognize and accept. Patient with the man, kindly, that new page for the will downstairs in the desk drawer.

"Put the light on in the bathroom."

"The night light's on in there. You see it?"

"I want the *light* on."

"You got it."

Donnell stepped over to the bathroom. As he came back the man, the mound under the covers, big curly head against the pillow, said, "I thought I heard you go out."

"Ain't I right here?"

"You went out last night. I woke up, I didn't know where you were."

What the man meant, he didn't know where *he* was.

"I told you I had to go out, Mr. Woody. My mother had a dream I died and I had to show her I was fine. Then I had to look in the Dream Book for her, see what number it meant to play."

That quieted the man. Either give him some shit his mind would accept or, the other way, confuse him, shut him up. "You be fine now," Donnell said and reached down to touch the man's toes under the covers, about to tell him good night. What he said to him instead was, "Mr. Woody, you forget to take your shoes off, didn't you?"

Picking the knots out of the man's shoelaces woke him up some more. One thirty in the morning he believed maybe a drink would help him go to sleep. Donnell said, "Yeah, that's what you need"—on top the fifth or more of scotch, the fifth of gin, the half dozen cans of beer the man'd had today—"a nightcap. Why don't I bring it to your bed?"

And if that didn't do it, hit him over the head with something.

Donnell went downstairs wishing he had a baby bottle. Fill it with booze and let the man fall asleep sucking on it. There was scotch at the bar in the library, but no ice left from the man's evening entertainment; the refilled trays in the fridge underneath the bar weren't half frozen. He'd have to get a couple of cubes from the kitchen. Always something, catering to or picking up after. He turned off the light in the library, walked through the front hall to the dining room turning lights on, pushed through the swing door to the butler's pantry and was in darkness again edging into the kitchen, running his hand along the wall. There it was. Donnell flicked the light on, turned and said, "Jesus!" loud, feeling his insides jump.

A man and a woman were sitting at the kitchen table.

He said, "Jesus Christ Almighty," sounding out of breath.

They were grinning at him now.

"How'd you get in here?"

Robin said, "It wasn't hard," and looked at Skip. "Was it?"

Skip let Robin handle it. When Donnell wanted to know what they thought they were doing, Robin told him they were here because he'd fucked up. Donnell said, "Wait now, I have to hear this." But first had to run upstairs, get the man settled with his nightcap. He left and Robin said to Skip, "Bring our stuff in."

"All of it?"

She said, "We're going to use it, aren't we?"

Skip went out through a back hall where there were two doors: one that went into the garage and the one he'd jimmied open with a screwdriver, nothing to it. (Coming in, Robin said, "No alarm system?" He told her maybe Donnell was afraid a burglar alarm might catch one of his buddies. Skip bet, though, the ex-Panther had a gun in the house.) He went out through the busted door to the VW parked in the drive by the garage. First he brought their bags in. Robin, still alone in the kitchen, was looking in the refrigerator.

When he came in the next time, lugging the wooden case of Austin Powder, *Used in 1833 and Ever Since,* Donnell was at the kitchen table talking to Robin.

He looked up, appeared to become rigid, and said, "You ain't bringing that in here."

In this moment Skip decided he wasn't going to have any trouble with Donnell. If the man was ever an ass-kicking Black Panther he must've forgotten what it was like. Skip put the case on the end of the table away from them and Donnell stood right up. Look at that. Made him nervous. Skip could tell Robin saw it, too.

She said to Donnell, "It won't hurt you," with a tone meant to soothe him. "All we want to do is stash it someplace. By Monday morning I promise it'll be gone."

Skip liked that. It would be gone, all right, along with whoever was standing nearby. He wanted to wink at her, but she wasn't through with Donnell yet, saying to him now, "You must have a gun in the house."

Skip could tell Donnell didn't want to say.

"I believe there might be one."

"I'd find it if I were you," Robin said. "You know why?" Talking down to him, making the guy ask, No, why?

Skip didn't care for her tone now, going from soothing
to bored and superior. Or the way she said, " 'Cause your
buddy the cop's going to come looking for you. The kids
you sent to do a job on him blew it."

That wasn't right. She wasn't there, she didn't know
what she was talking about. It seemed to antagonize the
man, from his expression, more than it scared him.

Skip stepped in and said to the ex-Panther man to man,
leaving the snotty woman out of it, "Actually it wasn't they
blew it so much as they misread him, thought it was gonna
be easy and it wasn't. What she's trying to say, Donnell, we
don't want to make the same mistake."

Donnell said, "Mankowski is coming here?"

Skip said, "I 'magine he will. See, but *I'm* the one set
him up with the brothers. He comes here with a wild hair
up his ass—man, I'd like to have something to hold him off
with. You dig?" Skip shook his head as though imagining
that situation and then said to Donnell, "A long time ago
I tried to buy a gun offa you. You didn't know who I was,
you told me to take a hike. Well, I wouldn't mind borrowing
one now, for my own peace of mind. What do you say?
Or—I don't like to think about it, but if it does get
down to the nitty-gritty and one of us has to take him out,
well . . ."

Donnell went upstairs to find the gun, and now Skip
had his chance to wink at Robin, giving him a cold look.

"Hon, that's how you do it with niggers that used to
be Black Panthers. You don't talk down to 'em or you don't
arm-wrestle 'em, either. You act like we're all created equal,
got bussed to their school and loved it."

26

Okay, here was the plan, the one Chris went to sleep on in his dad's bed about 4:00 A.M.:

Call Greta first thing in the morning. Ask her if he could move in with her for a few days. She'll say there isn't any furniture. He'll tell her that's all right; what he needs more than a place to sit down is a Detroit residence address. And would she pick him up this afternoon? Move his things over. She'll say fine, but the people who bought the house could be moving in soon. He'll say, Well, since we're both looking for a place to live—and she'd say something in her cute way. . . . So, call Greta about nine. At ten, drive over to Woody's and put the gun in Donnell's face. "Where are they?" Robin and Skip. Or throw him in the swimming pool and hold the gun on him. Fire a couple into the

water close to him. "Where are they?" Haul Donnell's ter-
rified ass out of the pool and get him to make a statement.
Maybe to use later, maybe not. See what happens. . . . Go
over there about ten. He wouldn't have to wear a coat and
tie. But would never wear that raunchy-looking outfit Mel
Gibson had on. Something casual. . . .

The phone next to the bed woke him up at twenty after
eleven Sunday morning, his dad calling from Toronto.

"How about meeting us at the airport?"

Chris said, "Yeah, I guess I could," feeling his plan
coming apart before he'd even spoken to Greta. "What
time you get in?"

"We're standby on a flight that arrives around three
thirty. We don't make it, then we'll be on one that gets in—I
have it written down somewhere. Here it is, five forty."

"How'll I know which one you'll be on?"

"The way you work that," his dad said, "you go out to
the airport and stand at the gate. If you don't see us come
off the plane at three thirty, it means we're on the other
one."

"That's . . . over two hours later."

His dad said, "Yeah?" and waited.

Chris said, "I bet it takes longer to drive from here out
to Metro than it does to fly from Toronto to Detroit."
Thinking, And then drive back here. It could be seven
thirty, the earliest, before he'd be able to get away.

His dad said, "We can take a cab. It only costs about
fifty bucks, with the tip."

"It does? That much?"

"I don't want to inconvenience you . . ."

"No, that's all right."

"I thought since you been using my car . . ."

"No, I'll be glad to pick you up."

"And it's Sunday and you're not working anyway. . . . They put you back on yet?"

"I'm hoping this week."

"You find a place to live?"

"I think so."

"What about—is your friend still there?"

"Who, Greta? No, she went home."

His dad said, "Uh-huh." He said, "Well, listen, we'll see you later."

"I'll be there." Chris could hear Esther's voice then and his dad speaking away from the phone, saying, "What? . . . Yeah, we could." His dad talking to a woman in a hotel room in Toronto. Chris said, "You having fun on your trip?"

His dad said, "Yeah, it's a nice town, lotta things to do. Listen, Esther says British Airways comes through here to Detroit. We'll see what they have. Don't go anywhere the next hour or so. We get a different flight I'll call you back."

Chris tried Greta's number. The line was busy.

He went into the kitchen and began revising his plan as he put the coffee on and got three eggs out of the refrigerator. He should talk to Greta first. Tried her again, but the line was still busy. At least she was home. Fixing his breakfast he realized how hungry he was. The idea of having scrambled eggs became a cheese and onion omelet. He looked for a can of tomato sauce in the cupboard, give it a Spanish touch, brought out a can of chili instead and kept swallowing as he watched it bubble in a saucepan, poured the chili over the eggs and ate it, Jesus, it was good, wiping his plate with bread, ate every bite before he thought of Greta again.

This time when he called her phone-answering voice came on, though not the cute Ginger one saying she wasn't home, doggone it. The voice said, "Hi, this is Greta Wyatt. If you'll leave your name and number, please, after you hear the beep, I'll get back to you." Chris waited for the beep and said, "Greta? It's Chris. I'm home—"

Then heard her real voice come on saying, "Hi. I was listening, hoping it was you."

"You have a different way of answering."

"Yeah, I changed it. It's a long story. Well, actually it isn't so long, but it's hard to explain."

"I called before, your line was busy."

"It's Mother's Day, I was talking to my mom and dad. Also, the real estate guy called first thing this morning. The people buying the house have to get out of theirs—I think they've been putting it off—and now they want to move in Tuesday."

"That soon?"

"I told the real estate guy, Swell, now I have to hurry up and find a place. I've been reading the classifieds, but I don't know where any of the streets are and the two I called up both sounded colored."

Chris said, "I have to do that too. Find a place."

There was a silence on the line. Now that he was facing it he wasn't sure what to say. Moving in with a young lady and going apartment-hunting with her were two different things. He was glad Greta didn't say anything cute.

"My dad's coming home this afternoon. I have to meet them at the airport."

"I have to wait for the real estate guy to call me back," Greta said. "He thinks maybe he can find me something, but if he doesn't. . . . I don't know, I'll call a few more."

Giving him his cue again. Chris said, "Well, listen, after I get back from the airport, how about if we go out, get something to eat?"

"Sounds good."

There was another silence.

"I'd help you look for a place, but I have to wait for my dad to call."

"That's okay."

"See if they get an earlier flight. Then I'll be over soon as I can."

"Fine, but you better call first."

"Okay."

"If I have to go out I'll leave a message on the answering thing, when I'll be back, okay?"

He didn't want to hang up.

"I couldn't call you last night. I got into something. . . . Well, I'll tell you about it. What did you do?"

"Nothing. Watched television and went to bed." She said, "Chris, I miss you."

"I miss you too. I wish you were here."

"I'm gonna have to hire a mover, for my stuff."

"I can get a truck. Don't worry about it."

She said, "What would I do without you?"

They said goodbye right after that and hung up, and he wondered if she was being sarcastic. Except she'd said she missed him. He thought maybe she sounded different. Yesterday she thought *he* was different. They weren't yet in touch with what slight change meant in each other. He shouldn't assume anything, outside of she was a little more serious, her mind taken up with finding a place to live, and he hadn't been any help to her at all. He should call her back and tell her there was nothing to worry about, they'd find a place.

Or tell her at least that he'd *help* her find a place.

Or talk about something else. Tell her about Juicy.

She might not think living together was such a good idea anyway. This soon.

If his dad and Esther got on the flight that arrived at

E L M O R E · L E O N A R D

three thirty, they'd be at the Toronto airport by two-some-
thing. Leave the hotel an hour before that. . . . He'd have
to leave here by two, drive all the way to Metro, find a place
to park. . . . He'd have time if he left right now to stop off
and see Donnell first. Except it wasn't a stop-off kind of job.
Holding the gun on the guy, say, "We'll have to finish this
later. I have to go pick up my dad." Shit, he'd have to stop
off at 1300 and reload the Glock or else pick up a box of
nines somewhere. Find a gun shop open on Sunday. He *had*
to see Donnell today. Locate Robin and Skip. Be ready for
Monday morning. He should've told his dad he was working or made something up. There was nothing worse than
waiting for a phone to ring when you knew it might not.

And it didn't.

Two P.M. he was ready to leave, wearing a blue button-
down shirt and khakis, and didn't feel right. For six years
he'd never left wherever he was living without his Spyder-
Co knife, his Mini-Mag flashlight and a gun, things you
needed pockets for. So he put on his beige sportcoat. Then
put on a faded red tie and felt better. He left the apartment
a little after two and made one stop, at 1300, went up to
Firearms and Explosives and reloaded the Glock auto. He
considered taking along a box of 9-millimeters but decided
against it. If he couldn't scare the shit out of Donnell with
seventeen rounds he had no business trying.

His dad came off the plane with a dazed look, shaking
his head, his raincoat and Esther's mink over one arm. He
put the other arm around Chris and they gave each other
a kiss on the cheek. Chris went to Esther, flashing her
blue-shadowed, sixty-four-year-old eyes at him, hunched
over and gave her a kiss while his dad told them they

shouldn't make up a schedule if it don't mean anything. Look at what time it was, seven thirty, for Christ sake. Standing there talking about it. Moving finally, creeping along, Esther telling about Toronto, asking him to guess who they saw, staying at the Sutton Place. Touching his arm and stopping in the crowded aisle of the terminal to tell him: Tom Selleck. And the one who was in "Cheers," Ted Danson. His dad saying, And that broad, what's her name, the blonde. Esther saying, Kathleen Turner, staying at the same hotel, they saw her in the lobby, twice. . . . Chris trying to move them through the crowd, get them out of there.

It was after nine by the time they'd crossed Detroit and reached St. Clair Shores. Chris had to help Esther up with her luggage and then stand in the doorway while she told him what a fine man his dad was, Chris nodding—till he opened his sportcoat and put his hands on his hips, let her notice the automatic stuck in his pants. Esther cut it short and said good night.

His dad wanted him to have a drink. Chris said, Just a short one, calling to him in the kitchen as he went down the hall to his dad's bedroom. He sat on the bed and dialed Greta's number.

Her phone-message voice said, "Chris? Hi. I'm going to see Woody and get that over with. Tell him I'm not going to marry him." There was a pause. "That's a joke. You're supposed to laugh. Anyway, I should be back around five." There was another pause before her voice said, "See you later. I hope."

Chris waited, heard the beep and kept waiting for her real voice to come on. . . .

27

All afternoon Skip kept trying to place a call to Bedford, Indiana, to wish his mom a Happy Mother's Day. He'd dial the number and then the operator would come on to tell him the circuits were still busy—everybody in the entire country calling their moms. He'd hang up the phone and there would be Robin waiting for him, practically tapping her toe with impatience.

"Have you found a place yet?" Meaning to wire a charge that would go off after they left Monday morning.

He'd tell her he was still looking.

"Oh, on the phone?" Using that pissy tone. At one point she said to him, "I'm doing all the goddamn work," and he told her it was about time she did *some*thing. It was fun to get her pulling on her braid, like she was going to

305

tear it off. Then, out of bitchiness wouldn't let him have any blotter when a craving for acid took hold of him, telling him in that pissy tone, "Not till you do your work." Still anxious for him to wire the charge that would kill two people and leave him and her rich. So he promoted some weed off Donnell and started calling her Mom. "Okay, Mom. . . . Anything you say, Mom." He believed if he squinted hard enough he'd see smoke coming out of her fucking ears. It was a weird situation.

Last night, Donnell had returned to the kitchen and laid a .38 revolver on the table, like the one Skip had stuck in his pants. Donnell waited for Robin to go upstairs, find a guest room, before he said, "That's the gun, but ain't nothing in it. Look at me. You think I just come off a cotton field? I'm gonna tell you how it is. Only first, you put that dynamite out in the garage." They had some scotch and Skip decided a white man and a colored man could have more in common than a white man and woman—easy, if the woman was Robin. A whiz at thinking up dirty tricks and getting you to do things her way, but otherwise a pain in the ass.

What Robin meant by "doing all the work" was having to act sweet and girlish with Woody.

The man didn't come downstairs till afternoon and was already half in the bag. Skip would never have recognized him on the street after all these years. Woody blinked, startled by this woman giving him a hug and a kiss and then acting hurt, curling her lower lip, saying, "You don't remember me?" Woody said, "Gimme a hint." Robin gave him more than that. She unbuttoned her shirt and his eyes opened to a picture from his past, though now hanging a bit lower. "Robin!" Woody said. "How much you need?"

He remembered that, how she used to get him to loan

her money. And he remembered her being here last Saturday, now he did, but didn't recall agreeing to buy her books to turn into a musical. So Robin pouted again and seemed about to cry—Skip wondering if she ever actually had, at some time in her life. Robin said, "But we did, we talked about it," and showed Woody the contract, all the legal bullshit—"herein referred to as the Fire Series"—without mentioning the amount out loud, the $425,000 for each of the four books.

Donnell stepped over to say to Skip, "The man ain't buzzed enough. I could slip him a 'lude."

For that matter, Skip was thinking, he could put an arm lock on the man till he signed. The contracts were something to show the police, after, proof they'd made a deal with Woody before a mysterious explosion took his life. (And the life of his chauffeur.) Skip couldn't tell Donnell that, so he said, "Robin'll handle him."

And she did, by convincing Woody they'd lined up Gordon Macrae to star. "Don't you remember talking about Gordon Macrae?" Sure he did. Woody said, "Boy-oh-boy," taking the pen Robin offered. Skip made a face, watching the man sign the contracts: it seemed the next thing to robbing the dead.

Yet here was the man happy as could be, saying, Let's celebrate, have a party, telling Donnell to go pick up some Chinese for when they got hungry.

Robin said she'd go with him.

Skip had to wonder about that. He followed them out to the kitchen, where Robin was saying she wanted to see Woody's signed check. Anxious. Donnell said, "The checkbook is in the desk and it stays there. Nobody touches it till I write in this name and the numbers and hand it to you as you leave. After the man has called the bank. Understand? Be cool, girl. You know how to be cool? Try."

Donnell took car keys off a hook by the door. Skip saw Robin getting her killer look and held on to her arm, letting Donnell walk out, down the back hall to the garage.

Close to her Skip said, "He's showing us who's boss, that's all. It doesn't hurt any. You took something away from him last night and now he's got it back."

Robin turned to look Skip in the face. After a moment she said, a little surprised, "What'd I take?"

"His manhood. Don't you know anything? You put him down, I have to pick him up." Skip stepped to the window as he saw a gray Mercedes appear in the back drive, out of the garage. He saw Donnell, behind the wheel, raise a remote control switch to close the garage door. The car moved off, past Robin's VW and around the corner of the house. Skip stared out at the backyard now.

Robin said, "We don't need Don-*nell.*"

"Then what'd you bring him in for?"

Standing with his back to her he heard Robin say, "I don't know, it seemed like a good idea."

He heard the *flick* of her lighter.

"You know yet where you'll put the dynamite?"

Skip turned from the window and had to grin at her. Funny she should ask. He said, "Once you have the idea, it's easy. Later on, after Donnell gets back, take him in the bathroom or someplace. Huh? You do what you're good at and I'll do what I'm good at, maybe we'll get lucky and pull this off."

Robin said, "Luck has nothing to do with it." She blew smoke at Skip and walked out of the kitchen.

He turned to the window again and looked at Robin's red VW thinking, Five sticks under the hood, wired to the ignition. *Go on get the car started, I'll be right with you.* Tell her you forgot something and watch from a window. It made more sense than placing the charge where he had in mind.

Skip was still in the kitchen when Donnell returned with three sacks of Chinese cartons. They shared a joint while Donnell placed the cartons inside the big restaurant-size oven, Skip thinking that disrespecting a man and killing him were two entirely different things.

Full of thoughts today.

He said, "Robin rolls a joint."

Donnell said, "She good for something, huh?"

"She's dying to get you in the bathroom."

"What you telling me that for?"

"It's the only time she's pleasant."

Skip drew on the joint, handed it to Donnell and said in his constricted dope voice, "I gotta go call my mother."

Donnell said, "Hey, shit, I have to do that too."

Donnell knew the one to keep an eye on was Robin. Skip was a man went headfirst right to it. Robin, you had to watch your back with her, she'd circle on you. Said she'd like to see the signed check; shit, she like to slip one out of the book, put her name on it later on. When she gave him eyes, letting him know she wanted her needs met, that was all right. Skip had said this situation excited her and she was hot. Fine, but it wouldn't be in no bathroom this time, not with all the beds in the house. It made it easy to keep an eye on her, lying underneath him, straining her head against the pillow going *"Ouuuu . . . ouuuu."* There was a woman Donnell had in this same bed *screamed* when she was peaking, cute woman that came in to clean the house and loved to sing but would get the words all fucked up. Like the Christmas song about chestnuts roasting in an open fire, then the next part, instead of Jack Frost, she'd say "Jack Paar nippin' at your nose." But, man, she *moved* underneath you, and even screaming was better than Robin with that *ouuu, ouuu*. When they were done, getting dressed, Robin gave him this cool look over the shoulder like she was prize pussy. Donnell said to her, "Robin?" serious, giving her a look back. When she said what, he said, "I think you getting better."

Skip walked into the pool house and said, "Jesus Christ," at the sight of Woody floating on his rubber raft, flapping his hands in the water. Robin came out with Sunday papers under her arm and Skip said, "Catch this."

"Beautiful," Robin said.

Skip watched her walk over to the table and sit down, barely glancing at the mound of flesh out there.

He said to her, "I been a good boy, Mommy. I did what you told me while you were upstairs getting laid. Can I have my candy now?"

"Where'd you put it?" Still curious about the dynamite, but not enough to look up from the paper.

"You're gonna love how it works," Skip said, and had to let it go at that. Donnell was coming out of the sunroom and around the shallow end. Look at the dude, a regular breath of spring in a yellow outfit now, like he was going to a party, Donnell's gaze holding on that sight out in the water. Skip said to him, "The man's bare naked."

"Yeah, I think he must've forgot he has company. You leave him here alone?"

"Few minutes. I had to go the bathroom."

"Yeah, he thought it was time for his swim. Man will take a shower and come out rubbing his hands together, means it's the cocktail hour."

"Shit, he won't miss that money, will he?"

"Won't even remember it's gone."

Skip turned his back to Robin sitting at the table. "You ever drop acid?"

"I have, but it don't agree with me."

"If you want to try again . . ."

"I like the bad habits I have."

"Well, I think I'll trip, if you'll watch the store."

All three of them heard the doorbell, Robin looking up from the paper. Donnell said, "Everybody be cool now."

Skip watched him walk out through the sunroom and come back a few minutes later with a good-looking red-head, escorting her the way a cop will hold you by the arm.

As soon as she saw Woody, Greta said, "Oh, my Lord," and looked away. What was going *on* here? People watching a naked man. . . . She recognized Robin, dressed this time, wearing jeans and a light sweater, the woman staring at her; but didn't know the guy with the beard and ponytail, scruffy looking, grinning at her. Donnell seemed friendly, holding onto her arm, saying, "This is Mr. Woody's friend Ginger."

The bearded guy said, "Hey, Ginger, how you doing?" But not Robin, she didn't say a word or look very happy about this interruption.

"I'm sorry to barge in like this. . . ."

Donnell said, "Well, you here now."

"I just wanted to talk to Woody a minute."

"He's right there—go ahead."

Greta said, "Yeah, I noticed," raising her eyebrows in fun. "I better come back some other time."

Donnell said, "No, it's all right. Talk loud, he hear you. Watch." Donnell brought her around by the arm to face the pool. "Mr. Woody, look who come to see you. Over this way, Mr. Woody. Look, it's Ginger."

"I should've called, I'm sorry."

"Hey, he's waving to you." Donnell raised his voice. "Better get out, Mr. Woody. You gonna be all wrinkled like a prune."

"I can come back tomorrow."

Donnell said it again, "You here now," turning her from the pool to the table. "You sit down. Mr. Woody's about done with his swim. Make yourself at home, I'll get you something to drink." Sounding friendly, but he wasn't, his hand tightening around her arm as she made a move to pull it away.

"I really can't stay. I thought I might have just a minute, you know, to talk to him, but I'll come back some other time. I'm supposed to meet somebody anyway."

The next moment it became scary.

Robin said, "For God's sake, will you sit down."

The bearded guy came over and pulled a canvas chair out for her, saying, "You may as well enjoy yourself. What would you like, sweetheart, a drink?" He had spooky eyes, pale, pale blue.

Sitting down, at least she was able to free her arm of Donnell. She looked up at the bearded guy and shook her head. "I don't care for anything, thanks."

He was looking at Robin with his pale eyes, just barely grinning as he said, "I bet I know what she'd like."

Greta saw Robin look up through her rose-tinted glasses and pause before she said, "Yeah . . ." dragging the word out in a thoughtful sound.

"I really don't care for anything." None of them paid any attention to her. "Really."

Robin got up and left without saying a word. Donnell and the bearded guy went over toward the bar, behind where Greta was sitting. She turned her head to one side, alert, wanting to hear if they said anything, and all of a sudden rock music came blaring out, filling the whole room. What was going *on?* None of them acted drunk or stoned. They sounded friendly, except for Robin. Then why was she scared? They couldn't *hold* her here if she didn't want to stay. They weren't going to tie her up. Greta felt herself getting mad. Damn right. . . . Turned her head and said, "Oh, my God!"

Woody was out of the swimming pool, coming toward her bare naked, shaking his head back and forth, saying, "No no no no no, that isn't what I want to hear. Donnell!"

They did seem friendlier. Even Robin was sort of smiling as she kept watching her. When the bearded guy handed her the vodka-and-tonic Greta said, All right, just one, then she was leaving. And the bearded guy said, "One's all you'll need, Ginger." She told him not to call her that. The bearded guy said, "You're a cute girl, you know it? How you feeling?" He kept asking her how she felt and Robin kept watching her. She felt fine. Woody sat next to her saying boy-oh-boy in a terrycloth robe. She felt a little funny, but generally fine, thinking maybe she could get Woody aside for a minute, and said, "About your offer. I think I'll take it." Woody said, something like, "Yeah? Okay. What offer?" And she realized it was going to take longer than a minute. She could smell marijuana. Now the bearded guy and Woody were singing "On the Street Where You Live" along with the deep, syncopating voice on the stereo, trying to do it with the same timing and inflections as the voice. They were awful but thought they were good. Donnell handed her a joint, saying, "Here, girl, ease yourself off," and she thought, What the heck, and took it. Robin was saying, "Jesus Christ, will you play something else?" They kept playing it over and over. Now Donnell was saying, "Five o'clock, munchie-wunchie time," and she thought, It couldn't be, and tried to remember what time she got here. About three? Now Donnell and the bearded guy were putting take-out cartons and paper plates on the table, pouring wine, dishing out something that seemed alive. They *were* alive—little white worms crawling over each other on the plates and these people were eating them. Woody had worms all over his chin. The funny part was, the worms didn't look too bad. They seemed pure. Heck, everybody was digging in, so Greta said, "Here goes nothing," and took a big bite. Mmmmm. But when she felt how slimy they were crawling around in her mouth and down her throat, she gagged and all of a sudden jumped up from the table, knocking over wineglasses, wanting so bad to clean out her insides, ran straight to the swimming pool and threw herself at the water.

28

The light above the door showed Donnell in his yellow outfit, his expression almost a grin, getting ready to or thinking if he should or not, the look becoming a relaxed pose. Maybe a little vague, stoned. He was holding a brown plastic trash bag, folded flat.

"I've been standing here five minutes," Chris said, "ringing the bell."

"Couldn't hear it with the music. Having a jivey kind of evening out by the swimming pool. I happen to go in the kitchen for something. . . ." He showed Chris the trash bag. "Man, you might not believe it, but I'm glad to see you stop by. Get some things straightened out here."

"Where's Greta?"

"Mean Ginger? She's out there."

"What's going on?"

"Man's having a party, entertaining his guests, what he does. Come on in, it's fine."

Donnell started to turn, hand on the door, then waited as Chris looked out at the street, at his dad's Cadillac parked behind Greta's blue Escort.

"The other people," Donnell said, "their car's around the back."

"Friends of Woody's?"

"Old ones. They been doing a little business, now they having some fun. Man, this is the most could happen, you showing up here. I expect you looking for Ginger. She mention she suppose to meet somebody, I figured was you."

"I was coming anyway," Chris said.

Donnell squinted to show pain and moved his shoulders, looking out at the night. "That business with Juicy, huh? That wasn't suppose to been like that." His gaze came back to Chris, calm now, serious. "The Juice, what I meant for him was to talk to you was all. You understand? Ask you kindly would you mind stepping away from something wasn't any of your business."

Chris said, "Or get my other leg broken."

"*No*"—Donnell again showing pain—"nothing like that was to happen."

"You and the Juice may have to pay for a windshield and new seats," Chris said, "but that's something else. What I want you to tell me right now's where I can find Robin. We'll see how you do with that and then we'll go on from there."

Donnell's face turned deadpan.

"Like to speak with Robin, huh? How 'bout the Skipper? Like to speak with him too?"

Chris took a moment, looking at Donnell trying hard

not to show any expression, the man playing with him, putting him on. Chris said, "You gonna bring them out or what?"

Donnell said, "Shit," and let his stoned grin come. "How'd you know?"

"You'd better lead the way."

"We been waiting on you, man. What you been doing all day, sleeping?"

Once they reached the hall Chris could hear the stereo and recognized U2, the Irish rockers. He said, "That doesn't sound like Woody."

"It's Robin's tape," Donnell said. "Robin's had enough of Mr. Woody's shit."

Coming out of the sunroom Chris saw the pool illuminated pale green in semidarkness and saw figures in soft lamplight, in the lounge area by the bar and stereo. Three seated, one standing. The beat and Bono's voice filled the room. Moving ahead of him, opening the trash bag, Donnell said, "Look at who I found, everybody. It's Officer Mankowski come looking to see what he can score."

He heard a voice, Robin's, say, "He's too late."

"We got leftovers here, officer." Donnell was at the table now, dumping the dinner remains into the trash bag. "Help yourself."

Chris moved past him. He saw Greta get up from the sofa, her hair strange-looking, pasted to her head. She was wearing an oversized sweatshirt, white with a black band around the middle, that reached to her mid-thighs: legs and feet bare in the sweatshirt minidress.

Robin, smoking, sat at the end of the sofa. Skip, next to her, was in a director's chair tilted back against the wall.

On the cocktail table in front of them were their drinks and sets of typewritten sheets of paper. Woody, in a bathrobe, stood at the bar pouring a scotch.

Greta stood waiting. She gave Chris a weak smile.

"What's the matter?"

She shrugged, raised her hands and pushed up the sleeves of the sweatshirt. Her face was drawn, without makeup.

"What'd they give you?"

Behind him, Donnell: "She fell in the pool."

"She tripped," Skip said. He reached out, waited, and Robin handed him the joint.

Donnell's voice, behind Chris, said, "Yeah, shit, that's what she did, she tripped."

Chris looked at Robin. "You gave her acid?"

"I didn't give her anything," Robin said. "Skip did."

Skip said, "Hey, what's wrong with you? You don't tell him something like that. He could go fucking crazy on us." He said to Chris, "It was just a half a one. She wanted it. Ask her."

"You tell her what could happen?"

"Hell, she's okay. Don't sweat it."

Chris stepped toward him and swiped the leg of the chair with his foot, taking it out from under him, Skip yelling, "Hey!" banging his head on the wall as he hit the floor. Chris stood over him.

"You tell her what could happen?"

"Man, look at her. She's fine."

"You slipped it to her, didn't you?"

"Ask her, go on, how she feels."

Chris said, "Don't move."

As he turned to Greta, Robin said to Skip, "Are you going to take that from him?"

Skip said, "Will you stay out of this, for Christ sake?"

Chris put his hands on Greta's shoulders. She looked up at him, her face pale. "How do you feel?"

"Just kinda tired, that's all."

"He tell you what he was giving you?"

"I don't know, I had a drink and he said . . . I don't know what he said."

"Sit down, okay? Just for a little while; we'll be going soon." Chris eased her into the sofa. He turned to Robin and saw her sly look in those pink glasses, almost a grin.

Tell this one to Wendell. They come to threaten money out of the guy, the same ones that killed his brother, and end up they have a party and everybody gets ripped. Wendell says, Is that right? And you were there, huh? What did you do? You hang around, you leave, what?

"What time'd she take it?"

Robin shrugged. "I didn't notice." She offered the joint, extending it toward him.

"You must've been one of the crazies, way back."

"No, I was political. I had a crush on Che Guevara."

"What'd you do, blow up a ladies' room in the General Motors Building?"

"That was somebody else."

"Do police cars? Stick of dynamite underneath?"

"Not me. Skip might've."

"I *never,*" Skip said. "Jesus Christ." Down on the floor shaking his head.

"It's cool," Donnell said, coming over with the trash bag. "Was like seven eight hours ago, we into mellow now. Ain't nothing can get us upset or turned sideways—even you picking on poor Skippy. Come on, you need to have that edge taken off. You want weed, you want booze? How 'bout both? You see how it is, you gonna need *some*thing, believe me."

"When I see how what is?" Chris said.

Donnell had turned and was saying, "Mr. Woody, look at who's here. That nice police officer, come around collecting again."

"Well, I'll be," Woody said from the bar. "I know that guy, that's—he has a Polack name like Kaka. . . . It's Kakakowski, isn't it?"

Donnell said, "You close, Mr. Woody. That's what they call him, Kaka, on account of he don't know shit."

Now all four of them were grinning, including Woody, having fun at the party, Chris looking at them, thinking, You gotta get out of here. But then took a few moments, time nothing to them, and looked at Donnell.

"I'm missing something, aren't I?"

Donnell's grin got bigger. "Not just something, man, everything. Sit down there next to your Ginger. Skip'll pour you a drink and Robin, she's gonna read you something, sitting right there on the table, will show you how fulla shit you are in judging people." Donnell lifted the brown plastic bag by the neck. "While I go throw this in the trash."

Donnell walked through the main hall liking himself and the sound of his voice, replaying it in his head, Mr. Woody saying Kaka, not knowing shit what he was saying, then taking it from the man and running with it. He was back on top. The only part that had bothered him was having to trust Robin to give him his million out of the check later on; which had bothered him more with her being disrespectful last night, but he'd got that settled. Said to her, "Convince me I should trust you. You don't give me a good answer the deal's off." She'd said, "You know why you're going to? Because this is so easy we can do it again next year. But if I try to fake you out of your share, I'm through. Right?" He liked that. Seeing as there were two kinds of greed, take-it-and-get greed and long-term greed. Since she had spent time to write all those books to pull the stunt, then she must operate on long-term greed and that was good. Donnell hadn't thought about doing it again next year.

From the kitchen he went down the back hall and opened the door to the garage thinking, Yeah, but wait a minute. How was she gonna write four more books in a year?

Then his mind was taken off that as he flipped on the light switch and nothing happened. Shit, the light was burnt out. He went back to the kitchen, opened drawers till he found one of Mr. Woody's many flashlights. Tried it, it worked fine.

Now he followed the flashlight beam into the three-car garage, swept clean, just the Mercedes in there now; followed the beam to a row of plastic garbage cans and got rid of the trash bag. The light beam turned with Donnell, moved over the plaster wall past bamboo rakes, gardening tools . . . stopped and came back, lower along the wall by the floor, stopped again and held near the lighted doorway, where Skip had set down the case of dynamite last night. Where Donnell had *watched* him set down the case of dynamite. Right there. Only it wasn't there now.

It wasn't anywhere. Donnell swept the garage with the flashlight, got down and looked underneath the Mercedes. That wooden case wasn't anywhere in sight. He ran through the back hall to the kitchen and looked around. Ran through the front hall to the library before he told himself to slow down, be cool. He laid the flashlight on the bar, poured himself an ounce of scotch and drank it.

Now then. Look at it.

Donnell looked and thought, Get the signed will out of the desk and leave the motherfucking house, *now*.

He took another little shot of the scotch. Looked again and thought, Ask Skip what he did with it.

Thought, You crazy? He sneaky, scheming something or he would've told you. Him and Robin.

Thought, He could've put it back in her car. . . .

And ran from the library back to the garage, reached inside and pressed the button on the wall that would raise the garage door. Nothing happened. Pressed it some more. Nothing happened. He moved through the dark to the Mercedes—use the remote control box in the car.

The car was locked. He had come back from the Chinaman's and had not locked it, but now it was. He wanted to see in the car. But he'd left the flashlight in the library.

Donnell said it to himself again, Be cool.

They talked about the man to his face and he didn't seem to realize it, sitting in his bathrobe with his drink, Robin standing next to his chair in a kind of protective pose. She had turned off the stereo. It was quiet, talk running down. What else was there to say? Chris looked at Greta, eyes closed, head nodding. He looked at Skip, making a drink at the bar, and then at Robin again.

"You make it sound like you're defending him."

"He knew what he was doing," Robin said. She put her hand on Woody's shoulder. "Didn't you?" Woody didn't move. "You weren't drunk when you signed the contracts."

"The man's alcoholic, he's always drunk," Chris said. "His lawyer knows that. You're conspiring to extort money.

The only difference, you're using paper now instead of a bomb."

Robin said, "All right, what's the problem? If you think it'll be contested, let's wait and see."

Chris looked at Woody. "Are you listening to any of this?"

"He's asleep," Robin said.

"I almost feel asleep myself," Skip said, "the way you're beating it to death. It's done, let's get the party going."

Chris watched Donnell come out of the sunroom and cross to the bar, taking his time; watched him pour a scotch, not saying a word. Skip nudged him. "Go put a tape on. We got to pick this up before it dies." Chris watched Donnell give Skip a look, deadpan, that Skip missed as he walked away from the bar with a drink. He came over to Chris.

"Hold this for me."

Chris looked up at him.

"Just hold it a second, it won't hurt you."

"Put it on the table."

"Take it, or I'll pour the goddamn thing on you."

Chris held out his hand and Skip put the drink in it.

"You got a good grip on it?"

Skip reached behind his back, beneath his jacket and came out with his .38 Special.

"Now show me that goddamn gun you have, whatever it is, with just two fingers of your one hand. Take the magazine out and hand it to me and chuck the gun in the swimming pool. Can you remember all that, or you want me to go through it again?"

Robin came over. She said, "Break his nose."

Skip said, "Just take it from him—Jesus."

Chris brought the automatic out with his left hand and Skip stepped back, arms rigid aiming the .38.

"Let me have it," Robin said.

Chris said, "Don't tempt me."

She reached down and snatched the pistol out of his hand and said, "Weird," looking at it.

Skip said to Chris, "You're spending the night here so we won't have to worry about you. Tomorrow morning, fine, you can leave. But not before we say."

Robin extended the Glock in both hands, aiming at Chris's face and closing one stoned eye.

"Is this how you do it?"

They brought Chris and Greta to the library. Chris watched Robin, still holding the Glock, waving it idly as she looked around. She said, "You're sure?" Skip pulled aside a panel of the heavy damask draperies to show grillwork covering the inside of the window. "Been on there forever, but he'd need a wrecking bar, at least." Chris watched Robin move to the desk. She was opening a drawer when Donnell came in with Woody. Donnell gave her a look and she gave him a shrug, closing the drawer. Now she raised the Glock in two hands, sighted on Donnell guiding Woody to his TV chair and said, "Pow." Donnell looked over, stared a moment before helping Woody into the chair, Woody saying, "What's the movie?" Donnell didn't answer. Chris said to Greta, "We're gonna be here a while." She didn't seem to mind. She looked so small in the sweatshirt. He put her in the chair next to Woody. Donnell looked at him. Chris waited. He heard Robin say, "Donnell? Bring the phone when you come." Donnell said, "It ain't the kind you move." Robin opened the drawer again, brought out a pair of scissors and snipped the line close to the phone. She said, "Never mind." She walked away from the desk with the Glock auto and the scissors. Donnell turned the set on. Woody asked him again, "What's the movie?" Donnell said, "Whatever comes on," his voice flat. "This's surprise night." Chris waited. Donnell looked across Greta at him. "You have to go to the bathroom you tell me and I tell him."

Chris said, "The Skipper?"

Donnell stared at him deadpan. He walked away, following Robin and Skip out of the library. The door closed. Chris turned to the TV screen. He didn't recognize the movie or any of the actors; they were all teenagers. He looked at his watch. It was 12:10.

At 2:20 the library door opened. Donnell entered. He took time to close the door quietly. Chris, seated at the desk, watched him come through the lamplight showing in dull green shades, a dark figure now. Donnell had changed his clothes. Chris followed his gaze as Donnell glanced at the TV screen, at a young woman in an empty house at night, backing away from a door, scared to death.

Chris said, "When they do that, not look where they're going, you know some disfigured asshole is waiting for them."

"They come here," Donnell said, planting his hands on the desk, getting right to it, "they have a box of dynamite I make him put in the garage. I go out there, it's gone and the car's locked and there's no way to open the garage up. The 'lectric thing you push don't work. And the light's out."

"You ask Skip about it?"

"What? Ask him how he's gonna blow me up? I *know* he's set it someplace."

"Stay out of the garage, you'll probably be all right."

"How would he work it?"

"You look around the house?"

"Enough. Box of dynamite ain't that easy to hide."

"Where's Robin and Skip?"

"In the kitchen mostly."

"Let's say he put the dynamite in the car," Chris said. "A gray Mercedes, right? I remember it from when the limo blew up, with his brother."

"How would he *do* it?"

"When you drive in and out you use a garage door opener?"

"Little thing with a button on it you push, yeah."

"It sounds like he put the charge in the Mercedes and wired it to the door opener, the motor. They put us in the garage and go out the other way. Drive off in the VW, Robin presses the button—bang. No witnesses. By the time the investigation gets to a canceled check with her name on it . . . I don't know, I guess she's got that worked out. But why're they staying all night? Now's the time to do it."

"The man has to transfer the money, call up the bank at nine A.M. They want to see him, make sure the check don't bounce."

Chris said, "Yeah, that's right, from his trust account. Has he paid them yet? Given 'em the check?"

"After he phones. Then I fill out the name and the amount. Shit, and get put in the garage, huh?" Donnell looked at the TV screen and back to Chris. "I'm the one has to make the move. I ain't gonna let Mr. Woody get killed."

"I'm glad to hear you say that."

"Not this soon. I had a gun. . . . Man, they fucked my head good."

"What was your cut?"

"I'm not in this deal."

"You mean now you're not." Chris said, "We don't have a gun . . . but you know what we do have—if you haven't thrown it out."

"What do we have?"

"Five sticks of Austin Powder, in a black bag. In this room, the last time I saw it."

Donnell stared at him. He took a moment to say, "It still is." Another moment to say, "But what good is it to us?"

"There's wire in the bag," Chris said, "and a battery. The battery's probably shot, but I notice there's a flashlight on the bar. Another one by the TV."

"Has 'em all over the house," Donnell said, "the man's afraid of the dark."

Getting up from the desk Chris said, "Bless his heart."

29

Woody saw naked mole rats coming at him, no hair or eyes, a sack of bones with teeth so big they couldn't close their mouth. Creatures that never saw light, never supposed to come out of the ground, but they were on his bed, on *him*, naked mole rats crawling up his body and he couldn't *move*. All he could do was raise his head and scream, "Yaaaah!"

And the naked mole rats disappeared.

Woody didn't want to open his eyes. He thought now he was in the hospital and had wet the bed during the night. It must be where he was, the bed was cranked up against his back and under his legs, holding him wedged in. Now he believed he could feel tubes in his nose, his arms and his peter and if he opened his robe would see the incision across his tummy and pink stuff seeping out from the infection. It was where they had cut him open looking for an ulcer and found he had acute gastritis, the lining of his tummy raw. He told the doctor he'd cut down on the rich food. The doctor told him he should go easier on the cocktails, too, saying one before dinner wouldn't hurt him. As if there was such a thing as one drink. He began to realize that was six years ago, it wasn't now and there wasn't a tube down his throat—he coughed—it felt like that from not swallowing all night. He could hear that noise in his ears, that *zing zing zing*, and the feeling his head was filled with hot exhaust smoke, in his head and his mouth, so wherever he was it must be morning. He wanted to open his eyes a little and reach for the drink on the silver tray, have that first one and feel the relief, oh, Jesus, that would go through him leaving some pain, nausea, but worth it as the feeling got up into his head and began to cool that hot exhaust. He wanted to hear Donnell telling him to rise and shine, open his eyes a little and see the silver tray, the drink in the morning light. He did hear a voice, but it wasn't Donnell's. It was a girl's voice, close to him, saying, "I think he's awake." Then another voice, not as close. Then the girl's voice saying, "Boy, did I sleep." He heard her again, but not so close now, tell the other person, "Don't. My breath must be awful." The other person was a man. Woody could hear their voices but not what they were saying. Until the girl's voice rose as she said, "But why?" The man said something and she said, "I don't believe this." The man spoke to her without raising his voice and Woody didn't hear the girl's voice after that. He must have slept again. . . . Now the voice he heard was Donnell's.

"Time to get up."

It was Donnell, but it didn't sound like him. Woody opened his eyes to a dim room. "Where am I?"

"You home."

Donnell moved closer and Woody saw the drink he was holding, the crystal dull; there was no morning light shining on it, but that was all right. Woody took the drink in his hands, secure now, able to spare a moment. He said to Donnell, "I saw the mole rats again."

"Is that all, just the rats?" Donnell said. "Gonna put your other drink in your coffee. Come on to the bathroom now and throw up. They waiting on you."

Greta, seated, watched Donnell follow Woody out of the library and close the door. "That poor guy . . . I'm glad I changed my mind." She pulled herself out of the chair and raised her arms, stretching, looked around to see Chris standing behind Woody's desk, staring at it.

"I wouldn't mind a cup of coffee," Greta said. "Is it okay if I ask?"

Earlier this morning Chris had told her they were watching the commission of a crime and there was nothing they could do about it or be able to prove later. That Robin and Skip were going to walk off with a lot of money and would be on edge; they had guns, so don't say anything to make them mad. That was all he told her and answered questions after that saying he didn't know.

Chris said, "Let's see if we can get a cup," coming around from behind the desk.

"I'd like to talk to Woody too," Greta said, "if it's okay. I'm gonna accept his original offer of twenty-five thousand.

If he still wants to give it to me, fine. If he doesn't—well, the hell with it."

Chris stopped close to Greta. He put his arms around her and kissed her and said, "You're fun, you know it?"

Greta said, "I wish I felt like it."

Skip brought Chris and Greta into the kitchen at gunpoint, seated them on a bench with their backs to a wall of cupboards, then with Robin's help shoved the table up against them, tight. Chris watched Skip slip the .38 into his waist, behind him and beneath the black *Speedball* jacket. Robin carried the Glock in front, shoved into her jeans. She stood at the sink with a cup of coffee and a cigarette.

Chris said to her, "You're having fun, aren't you?"

Robin said, "Not as much as I'm going to have."

Skip brought cups to the table and poured coffee. Now Donnell, a bottle of cognac in his hand, brought Woody in and got him seated at the end of the table.

Robin said, "Bring the phone over."

Donnell looked at her and said, "You want the phone, you bring it over." He poured cognac into Woody's coffee.

Chris watched Robin, the pistol grip tight against her white sweater, wishing to God he hadn't brought it. She kept staring at Donnell. After a few moments Robin brought the phone from a counter to the table, placing it in front of Woody. He looked at it, then up at Donnell.

"What about Beaver?"

Chris could smell him; the man looked sick, in a daze.

"You early this morning," Donnell said. "The Beaver come on after while, when I give you your Alpha-Bits."

Skip said, "Is that what he eats? Does he want some eggs? I'll fix him some."

Donnell shook his head. "We out of eggs."

"I can fix 'em any way you want," Skip said. "I was a short-order cook one time in L.A., when I was looking for movie work."

"*That's* where I saw you," Greta said, "I've been trying to think. It was while they were making that movie, week before last. You were talking to people on the set."

"You watch some of that?"

"I was *in* it."

Skip said, "Well, I didn't know you were a movie star."

"I was only in one scene, but I had lines. The director said, well, that I did okay."

"He's a good one," Skip said, "Ray Heidtke. I worked for him before. If he likes you he'll use you again."

"You think so?"

Chris, listening, wanted to ask Greta something, but he was watching Robin with her fidgety little moves: the way she smoked the cigarette, looked at the clock, sucked on that cigarette again looking at Skip—not liking what was going on, left out—and mashed the cigarette in the sink. She said, "All right, let's do it."

Donnell looked at the clock. "It's only five till."

"Humor me," Robin said.

And Chris thought, Please.

Donnell picked up the phone and said to the man, "You ready? We gonna transfer the money now." The man looked up at him through the blood in his eyes not knowing shit what it was all about, lost in his head, but nodding, saying oh, yeah, sure he was ready. Donnell dialed and said into the phone, "Doris, how you doing? . . . Don't have time to chat this morning, here's Mr. Ricks." The man took the phone from him, said, "Hi, Dorie, how are you? . . . Yeah, I guess we are." He said, "Heeeeere's Donnell," doing his routine, and handed the phone back grinning. Donnell, not feeling any grins inside him, told Doris straight Mr. Ricks was moving a million seven from his trust account to the commercial one, gave her the account numbers by heart and listened to her repeat the whole thing. "That's it. Okay, here's Mr. Ricks back." Donnell passed the phone to the man. The man said, "What?" Probably forgot who he was talking to. Said, "Oh. Yeah, one . . . uh-huh, yeah, seven, that's right. Thanks a million, Dorie." Donnell took the phone back from the man's shaky hand and hung it up.

Robin said, "She didn't ask any questions?"

"It's the man's money," Donnell said to her. "He can do what he wants with it."

Skip came over saying, "Give me a hand," and they pulled the table away from Chris and Greta wedged in there. Skip said to them, "You don't mind, you're going in the garage till we leave. Get you out of our hair." Then looked this way at Donnell and said, "You take Mr. Woody, all right?"

Man with a gun stuck in his pants being so polite.

Donnell wondered for a second if he should say, Wait now, he was supposed to fill in the checks. But he didn't. Best just to go in there. It was happening the way Chris Mankowski had said last night he thought it would. They'd get put in the garage. Then Skip and Robin would go in the library to get the check. He'd said to Chris, "What about the bomb in the garage?" Chris said, "Don't worry about it. I'll find the wire and cut it." He'd said to Chris, "But what if they come back from the library?" And Chris said, "They won't." Without having time to say how it would work. What he said was to let it happen and don't get Skip or Robin mad.

That's why Donnell couldn't believe it when Robin started out of the kitchen and Chris said, "Robin?"

She stopped and looked at him.

"Put the gun on the table and lay on the floor."

It was like Robin couldn't believe it either, the way she was looking at him, going, "What?"

He was saying to Skip, "You too. Gun on the table, lay face down on the floor."

Skip said, "I like your spunk, man. Heavy."

Robin said, "You believe it?"

Skip said, "That's from the dick handbook, how you're suppose to do it."

Donnell, a step off from Skip and behind him, tried shaking his head at Chris, but the man wouldn't look at him. Doing what he said not to, causing a mean, bitchy look to come over Robin's face. Then making it worse.

Chris saying, "I have to give you a chance. You don't take it, it's up to you."

Sure enough, Robin pulled the gun out of her jeans and stiff-armed it in Chris's face. She said, "I'll give you a chance to get in the fucking garage, man. How's that? Or die here."

Skip made a face in his beard, telling her, "Hey, let's stick to the goddamn script, okay? You get the check, I'll put them in the garage."

Donnell thinking, That's it, let it happen. But no.

The hard-on cop had to say to her now, in his quiet way, "Robin? You're not gonna make it."

Why was he telling her? Donnell kept shaking his head, saying inside it, Look at me, look at me. But the man wouldn't.

Skip told her, "Go, will you."

Robin did, but stepped up to Chris first to touch the gun to his head and tell him, "I'll be right back."

He didn't say anything to her, kept still as she walked into the butler's pantry, finally leaving. Didn't say a word till Skip, staring at him, said:

"What's gonna stop her?"

Asking it like that—Chris still didn't have to say one word, let it happen, but he did.

He said, "Five sticks of Austin Powder."

Skip's hand moved slow-motion over his beard. He said, "Five sticks . . ."

"In a black bag," Chris said.

And Skip said, "Oh, shit."

"In the desk now," Chris said. "In the drawer with the checkbook."

Skip paused. He said, "You're trying to fake me out, aren't you? How would you know how to wire a charge?"

Right there—too good to resist. "I guess nobody told you," Donnell said, having to say it, "my friend here was on the Bomb Squad."

Skip banged open the swing door yelling "Robin!" running through the dining room, knowing in his mind he should never have got into this, yelling "Robin!" in the front hall, the woman working it, changing it, messing it up and never telling him a goddamn thing. He was too old for this—got to the library door to see her across the room at the desk, had time to breathe and yell at her, "Don't touch it!"

It was quiet in the kitchen. Chris looked at Greta, her face raised, listening. Donnell stood across the table. He put his hand on the man's shoulder, and Woody opened his eyes and blinked a few times at Greta. He said, "Hey, I know you."

Greta said, "Well, that's good."

Donnell said, "He got to her by now," and said to Chris, "You had to tell him, huh? Say to me don't say nothing, you had to tell him."

Chris said, "You want Skip with us or with Robin?"

Donnell had to think about that.

Greta said, "Maybe we should just leave."

Donnell jumped on that. "Before they come back in here, with their guns."

Chris said, "Wait."

Donnell said, "I like to know what they doing."

"She's close to it," Chris said. "It's right there."

Donnell said, "Wait now. Man, wait just a minute. Mr. Woody's new will I spent my fucking life getting him to sign is in that same place, man, in the *desk.*" Donnell was moving toward the pantry. "He *can't* let the woman open that drawer."

Chris said, "Five bucks she does."

They might not have heard him. At that moment dynamite exploded a few rooms away, not as loud as imagined waiting for it to happen; but the sound of it, so hard and sudden, did fill the room and the impact rattled the windows and the table and made the coffee cups jump.

30

"The tricky part," Chris said, "you have to figure out how much wire to use. You run an exposed wire from the dynamite and hook it to the underside of the desktop in a loop. Then you run your insulated wire to the inside of the front of the drawer, staple it there and run it back through the loop, with about three inches of insulation at the end of the wire peeled off. See, then when you open the drawer it pulls the wire through till the exposed end touches the loop and completes the circuit."

Donnell said, "You understand that, Mr. Woody?"

Woody, eating his cereal with the TV on but the sound off, said, "What?"

It was the following Sunday morning. Chris had stopped by to ask Donnell a question.

He was saying now, "There's a little more to it. With the drawer open you lay a sheet of paper between the two wires, 'cause in that position the exposed parts would be touching. Then, it's like this," Chris said, demonstrating. "You pull the sheet out as you push the drawer closed. You want, I can draw you a picture how it works."

"No, that's all right," Donnell said. He poured coffee for Chris and refilled Woody's cup, saying, "We be in the other room, Mr. Woody. Call, you need anything."

Chris followed Donnell through the butler's pantry.

"He has Jimmy Swaggart on but no sound."

"Mr. Woody don't like to hear Jimmy preach, it scares the shit out of him. But, see, 'The Lone Ranger' come on right after. Next hour or so he'll call me Tonto. I said to him, 'Mr. Woody, remember that new will me and you made up?' Looks at me, says, 'What new will?'"

They walked through the front hall to the library and stood in the doorway to look at the shattered interior, the ceiling scorched, books ripped from the shelves.

"You haven't done anything," Chris said.

"I'm getting bids on the work. Don't have one yet that pleases me."

Chris said, "I'll bet there's still some of Robin in there."

"Man, she was all over the library, huh? Didn't Skippy say something to you?"

"He opened his eyes. I think he said, 'Oh, shit,' but I could barely hear him."

Donnell said, "Yeah, well. . . ." Sipped his coffee and said, "How you doing with Ginger?"

"You mean Greta. She went out to L.A., try and get in the movies. She makes it, I can say I helped finance her career. In a way, I mean. I gave her the check Woody gave me."

"Get out."

"I wasn't gonna keep it and Woody didn't have any more checks, so . . . what's the difference?"

"The difference between being smart and dumb as shit," Donnell said, "is what the difference is. Man, I don't believe it. You out of work, you give money away."

"There's a good chance I'm going back, get in Homicide . . . after this hearing tomorrow. They want to ask me a few questions."

"I bet they do."

"There's one area where I might have a problem. See, I've talked to them already during the investigation—you know how they go after all the little details. They want to know where I got the dynamite; I said it was in the house. They say, Okay, but why did you go there? I tell them, To pick up Greta. They say, Oh? With a gun? And I just said, without thinking, What gun?"

"Not saying you didn't have one."

"Unh-unh, I said, What gun?"

"I 'magine they mean the one I found blown clear out in the yard and give to a policeman. That funny gun."

"That's what I was afraid might've happened."

"So you have to explain why a laid-off cop is walking around with a piece, huh? Like what was your intent?"

"I kept it at work, but I never used it on duty."

"Tell 'em you were taking it home."

"And just happened to have it," Chris said and thought about it a moment. "That's not bad."

Turn the page for
a special bonus chapter of

KILLSHOT

by

Elmore Leonard

**Coming April 1989
from
Arbor House/William Morrow**

ONE

THE Blackbird told himself he was drinking too much because he lived in this hotel and the Silver Dollar was close by, right downstairs. Try to walk out the door past it. Try to come along Spadina Avenue, see that goddamn Silver Dollar sign, hundreds of lightbulbs in your face, and not be drawn in there. Have a few drinks before coming up to this room with a ceiling that looked like a road map, all the cracks in it. Or it was the people in the Silver Dollar talking about the Blue Jays all the time that made him drink too much. He didn't give a shit about the Blue Jays. He believed it was time to get away from here, leave Toronto and the Waverley Hotel for good and he wouldn't drink so much and be sick in the morning. Follow one of those cracks in the ceiling.

The phone rang. He listened to several rings before picking up the receiver, wanting it to be a sign. He liked signs. The Blackbird said, "Yes?" and a voice he recognized asked would he like to go to Detroit. See a man at a hotel Friday morning. It would take him maybe two minutes.

In the moment the voice on the phone said "Detroit," the Blackbird thought of his grandmother, who lived near there, and began to see himself and his brothers with her when they were young boys and thought, This could be a sign. The voice on the phone said, "What do you say, Chief?"

"How much?"

"Out of town, I'll go fifteen."

The Blackbird lay in his bed staring at the ceiling, at

the cracks making highways and rivers. The stains were lakes, big ones.

"I can't hear you, Chief."

"I'm thinking you're low."

"All right, gimme a number."

"I like twenty thousand."

"You're drunk. I'll call you back."

"I'm thinking this guy staying at a hotel, he's from here, no?"

"What difference is it where he's from?"

"You mean what difference is it to *me*. I think it's somebody you don't want to look in the face."

The voice on the phone said, "Hey, Chief? Fuck you. I'll get somebody else."

This guy was a punk, he had to talk like that. It was okay. The Blackbird knew what this guy and his people thought of him. Half-breed tough guy one time from Montreal, maybe a little crazy, they gave the dirty jobs to. If you took the jobs, you took the way they spoke to you. You spoke back if you could get away with it, if they needed you. It wasn't social, it was business.

He said, "You don't have no somebody else. You call me when your people won't do it. I'm thinking that tells me the guy in the hotel—I wonder if it's the old guy you line up to kiss his hand. Guy past his time, he don't like how you do things."

There was a silence on the line before the voice said, "Forget it. We never had this conversation."

See? He was a punk. The Blackbird said, "I never kiss his hand or any part of him. What do I care?"

"So, you want it?"

"I'm thinking," the Blackbird said, staring at the ceiling, "you have a Cadillac, that blue one." It was the same vivid light-blue color as his grandmother's cottage on Walpole Island. "What is it, about a year old?"

"About that."

So it was two years old, or three. That was okay, it looked good and it was the right color.

"All right, you give me that car, we have a deal."

"Plus the twenty?"

"Keep it. Just the car."

This guy would be telling his people, see, he's crazy. You can give him trading beads, a Mickey Mouse watch. But said over the phone, "If that's what you want, Chief." The voice gave him the name of the hotel in Detroit and the room number, a suite on the sixty-fourth floor, and told him it would have to be done the day after tomorrow, Friday around nine-thirty, give or take a few minutes. The old man would be getting dressed or reading the sports, he was in town for the ball game, Jays and the Tigers. Walk in and walk out.

"I know how to walk out. How do I get in?"

"He has a girl with him, the one he sees when he's there. It's arranged for her to let you in."

"Yeah? What do I do with her?"

The voice on the phone said, "Whatever your custom allows, Chief." Confident now; listen to him. "What else can I tell you?"

The Blackbird hung up the phone and stared at the ceiling again, picking out a crack that could be the Detroit River among stains he narrowed his eyes to see as the Great Lakes. Ontario, Erie, Lake Huron . . .

His name was Armand Degas, born in Montreal. His mother was Ojibway, his father he didn't remember, French-Canadian. Both were dead. Until eight years ago he had lived and worked with his two brothers. The younger one

3

was dead and the older one was in prison forever. Armand Degas was fifty years old. He had lived in Toronto most of his life, but didn't know if he should stay here. He could go downstairs to the Silver Dollar and after a while feel pretty good. There was a bunch of Ojibway that hung out there. Maybe he looked like some of them with his thick body and his thick black hair lacquered back hard with hair spray. They'd talk, but he could tell they were afraid of him. Also there were more punks coming in there, crazy ones who colored their hair pink and green; he didn't like the way they called him the Blackbird, the way they said it. The Italians, most of the time, called him Chief. It was like they could call him anything they wanted, the guineas posing in their expensive clothes, talking with their hands. Even if they said he could be a made guy, one of them, he wouldn't ever belong to them. When the phone rang he had been trying to figure out why he drank so much. He was thinking now, as he began to picture a young girl in the hotel room in Detroit, he drank because he needed to drink.

The girl would be young and very pretty. It was the kind they found for the old man. She'd be scared. Even if they told her, you open the door, that's all you have to do, and gave her some money, she'd be scared to death. He wondered if the old man would notice it. You didn't become old in his business missing signs. He wondered if he should wear his suit to go in that hotel. It was tight on him when he buttoned the coat. He'd drive to Detroit in the Cadillac . . . and began to think about his grandmother, trying to picture her now, older than the old man he was going to see. They called him Papa, a guy who'd had his way a long time, but no more. The Blackbird saw himself drive up to the blue cottage in the matching Cadillac and saw his grandmother come out . . . Then saw a young girl in a hotel room again, scared to death.

But when the girl opened the door she didn't seem scared at all. She was about eighteen maybe, wearing a robe, with long blond hair down over her shoulders like a little girl. Except her expression wasn't a little girl's. She looked him over and walked away and was going into the bedroom as he entered the suite and saw the room-service table and what was left of breakfast. The bedroom door was open. He could hear her voice saying something—that nice-looking young girl, not the kind he expected. The Blackbird glanced at the bedroom but didn't see either of them. He walked past the room-service table to the room's wide expanse of windows filled with an overcast sky. Now he was looking at Canada from six hundred feet in the air, Windsor, Ontario, across the river, Toronto two hundred fifty miles beyond. Not straight across but more east, that way, where the Detroit River turned into Lake St. Clair. Keep going and you come to Walpole Island. Staring in that direction he squinted into the distance. A sound behind him made him turn.

The old man they called Papa, head bent, showing the straight part in his white hair combed flat, was pouring himself a cup of coffee. He stood at the room-service table with a bath towel wrapped high around his waist, white against tan skin, almost to his chest: this man who always dressed in style, a gold pin fixed to his shirt collar, always with a tan. But look how frail he was, dried up, aged in the sun. A bird could perch on his shoulder blades, hop to his collarbone.

Now a shower was turned on. In there beyond the open bedroom door. The girl giving him privacy.

"Papa?"

The old man looked up. Surprised and then frowning with the windows in his eyes: the same way he had looked when a government commission, the one investigating organized crime in Canada, asked him what he did for a living and the old man said he was in the pepperoni business, he sold it to places they made pizza.

He said with his heavy accent and a note of hope, "You got something for me?"

"From your son-in-law."

The old man's hope left him as he said, "Oh, Christ," sounding tired. He looked down at the room-service table but seemed to have forgotten what he wanted. He stared for several moments before looking up. "I told my daughter don't marry that guy, he's a punk. She don't listen. I'll give him six months, they gonna be another funeral."

The Blackbird said, "You want him done sooner than that, tell me." He saw the old man staring at him, frowning again, and he said, "You don't know who I am?"

"I can't see you," the old man said, coming around the table, one hand gripping the towel, the fingers of his other hand touching the edge of the table. He seemed so small, his bones showing, his eyes, as they looked up, tired and moist. He said, "Yes, of course," and seemed to shrug as he moved close to the window.

The Blackbird watched the old man staring at the beginning of Ontario reaching out beyond the city and across open land to the sky.

"You know Walpole Island, Papa?" The Blackbird pointed upriver. "It's that way past the lake, on the Canadian side of the channel. The big ships go by there, up the St. Clair River to Lake Huron and around through Lake Superior, go to places over there, and back again till the ice comes. Walpole Island, it's an Indian reserve where my grandmother lives.''

The old man took his time to look up at him, patient, not going anywhere, making these moments last.

''She's Ojibway, same as me. You know what else? She's a medicine woman. She was going to turn me into an owl one time, I said to her, 'I don't want to be no owl, I want to be a blackbird,' and that's how I got this name. From my brothers, when we were boys and we visited there.''

The old man was staring out again and seemed off in his mind.

''You remember us, the Degas brothers? One dead working for you, shot dead by the police. One in Kingston doing life for you. Papa, you listening to me? And I'm here.''

''Can she do that,'' the old man said, ''turn you into an owl?''

''If she wants to. Listen, when we went there in the summer when we were boys, we had a twenty-two rifle, a single-shot we used, go in the marsh and hunt for muskrats. See, but we hardly ever found any, so on the way home to her house we'd shoot at dogs, you know, cats, birds. Man, it got people mad, but they wouldn't say nothing. You know why? They were afraid the grandmother would do something to them.''

The old man was listening. He said, ''Turn them into something they don't want. How does she do that?''

''She has a drum she beats on and sings in Ojibway, so I don't know what she's saying,'' the Blackbird said. ''Imagine a day you don't even see the trees move. She beats on the drum and sings and a wind comes in under the door and stirs the fire in the fireplace. She wants to, she can burn a house down. Or like if you do something to her and she gets mad? She can get a bird to shit on your car. She does it best with seagulls. A seagull flies over, she beats on the drum, points to the car. That one. The seagull shits on the hood, on the windshield. Or she can get a whole flock of them to do it, all over the car. I'm going to go see her. Drive up there, you take the ferry over from Algonac, a half mile across the St. Clair River from the U.S. side to Walpole Island."

The old man's head was nodding as he thought of something and said, "I could use a woman like that. Have her turn me into a blue jay." He smiled, showing his perfect dentures. "Those fucking Jays, they gonna do it this year, go all the way to the World Series. I'll give you five to three, I don't care who they play. We going tonight, see them beat the Tigers." The old man paused. He turned and looked up with his tired eyes. "No, I'm gonna go in there, put on my robe . . ." He paused again. "No, I think I like to be dressed. Is that okay with you?"

"Whatever you want."

The old man walked toward the bedroom saying, "That fucking son-in-law, I never liked that guy."

The Blackbird gave him time. He stepped to the room-service table and poured a cup of coffee. It was barely warm. He ate a croissant with it and two strips of cold bacon he believed the girl had ordered and didn't eat. What did she care, she wasn't paying for it. She had taken one bite out of each half piece of toast. He could hear the shower running. There was a Coca-Cola bottle on the table and a glass half full she had left, wasting it, not caring.

It was warm in here and he was uncomfortable in his wool suit, a black one, double-breasted, he wore with a white shirt and green-blue tie that had little green fish on it. A Browning three-eighty automatic, stuck in his waist at the small of his back, dug into his spine. It was a relief to pull it out. The Blackbird worked the slide to rack a cartridge into the chamber. The pistol was ready to fire and he believed he was ready. But now his pants felt loose and he had to adjust them and stick his shirt in good and straighten his tie and button his coat before going into the bedroom. He had to feel presentable. It was something he did for himself; no one else would think about how he looked, notice the suit was too tight for him and needed to be pressed. The old man wouldn't care.

The old man wouldn't even see him. He was lying on the unmade bed in a starched white shirt and tan trousers, brown shoes and socks, hands folded on his chest, his eyes closed.

The shower was running in the bathroom, the door open a few inches.

The Blackbird brought the sheet up over the old man's body all the way, covering his face. Now he was looking at the outline of the face and saw the sheet move as the old man breathed in, sucking the white cloth flat against his mouth. That was where the Blackbird placed the muzzle of the Browning and shot him. He fired once. The sound filled the room and maybe it was heard on the other side of the wall in another room, or maybe not. It was sudden; if anyone heard it and said what was that and stopped to listen, there was nothing else to hear.

Only the shower running in the bathroom.

When he pulled the shower curtain aside the girl with long blond hair, the hair darker now, her face and body glistening wet, looked at him and said, "Are you through?"

The Blackbird said, "Not yet," raising the pistol, and watched the girl's expression finally change.

The last time he came to Walpole Island was nine years

ago, with his two brothers. They had finished some business in Sarnia for the Italians and drove down through Wallaceburg and across the bridge. That way, it wasn't like coming to an island.

This time he came from Algonac, Michigan, on the U.S. side, drove over the metal plates from the nine-car ferry to the dock, and pulled up in the Cadillac to tell the customs guy he used to live here when he was a boy and had come back. He followed the road south along the ship channel where he and his brothers used to throw stones at the freighters going by. They had seemed so close in the channel, those ore carriers sliding past forever without a sound. This was when their mother would send them here from Toronto, in the summer. Once they swam the channel to Harsen's Island on the U.S. side, maybe a quarter of a mile, and his brother now in Kingston for life had almost drowned.

Then he and his brothers didn't come again till they were grown men: came to visit because they were nearby, that time in Sarnia, and stayed to repaint the blue cottage and fix some leaks in the roof. The cottage was damp and smelled, full of mice the Degas brothers caught in glue traps they got at the A&P in Algonac. The traps held the mice by their feet in a sticky substance; or sometimes the mouse's face would be stuck in it. The brothers would carry the traps outside, the mice still alive, and shoot them with their high-caliber pistols. *Bam*, that mouse would be gone, disappear, and the Degas brothers would look at each other and grin like they were young boys again shooting at dogs and cats. The grandmother, getting old, had watched them but didn't say much or work any kind of medicine.

This time, when he came to the cottage, it seemed deeper in the trees, its blue paint faded and peeling, its plywood storm shutters down covering the windows, the yard overgrown with weeds.

The woman at Island Variety, across the road from the ferry dock, said yes, the grandmother was in the cemetery, buried last winter. The woman said the Band office didn't know what to do about the house or the furniture, all the grandmother's things. Armand Degas told her he'd take care of it and turned away, not wanting to talk to this woman in the noise of kids playing video games, Breakout and Zaxxon. There were other people too. Some duck hunters in the store were buying candy bars and potato chips, talking loud to each other. Their cars with Michigan plates were parked outside where Walpole guides waited smoking cigarettes. They had stopped talking as Armand walked by them, coming in. They knew who he was.

Pretty soon the duck hunters in their camouflage outfits and two-tone rubber boots, still talking loud and taking forever, moved out the door and Armand saw a guy he recognized, toward the back of the store.

Lionel something. Coming away from the cooler with two cans of Pepsi. Sure, Lionel, walking with that limp. He was a kid when the Degas brothers came here as kids. They beat him up the first time they met; Lionel came after them with a live snake and they got to be friends. Then nine years ago they saw him in the bar at San Souci on Harsen's Island where the Indians went to get drunk and he was using a cane to walk. They had some beers and he told them how he fell off a building, "into the hole" as he called it, and broke his legs pretty good. He was an ironworker then. Lionel Adam, that was his name. He was still limping, swinging one leg way around, but didn't have the cane—taking the Pepsis over to a guy leaning against the craft counter, where they sold hand-made Indian stuff.

The guy was taller than Lionel, maybe younger, with light-colored hair. He wasn't Indian. He was thin but looked strong. Now he straightened up, turning away from the counter as Lionel handed him a Pepsi, and Armand saw something written on the back of the guy's blue jacket. In white letters it said IRONWORKERS, and under it, smaller, BUILD AMERICA. So he was another one of them, probably an old buddy of Lionel's.

Armand went to the cooler and got himself a Pepsi. He popped it open edging closer to Lionel and the ironworker, looking at a poster that announced BINGO TONIGHT at the Sports Center. VISIT THE CANTEEN FOR ALL YOUR REFRESH-MENT NEEDS! Lionel didn't seem to notice him. They were talking about hunting whitetail.

It sounded strange, the ironworker telling the Indian he was going to make sure Lionel got a buck to hang on his meat pole. Saying he bought a salt lick to put out in the woods. Lionel was saying they should take a sweat bath and not eat any meat for a week. A whitetail could smell it if you had a hamburger and tell if you had mustard or ketchup on it. The ironworker said you had to take time beforehand to read the deer, think like them and you'd get your shot.

"Pretend you're a buck," Lionel said, "with a big rack."

"Sixteen points," the ironworker said.

"You see a doe, her tail standing up in the air waving at you," Lionel said, "you won't know whether to shoot it or hump it."

"Or both, and then eat it," the ironworker said. "I fill the freezer every November and it's gone by May."

They walked toward the door, Lionel telling the iron-worker he could make it tomorrow afternoon about four o'clock. Armand came to the front of the store with his

Pepsi. Through the window he saw them standing by a tan Dodge pickup. When the ironworker backed around and drove off toward the ferry dock, Armand saw a toolbox in the pickup bed and a Michigan license plate. He waited for Lionel to come back in the store, but saw him walking away, limping past the window. Armand had to go after him.

"Hey, where's your cane?"

Lionel stopped and half-turned to look back, standing behind Armand's blue Cadillac. He said, "I thought maybe it was you," sounding different from when he was talking to the ironworker, not much life in his voice now. "You go by the Band office?"

"For what?"

"About your grandmother. We been trying to get hold of somebody, a relative, find out what to do with her house."

"I don't know," Armand said, "I been thinking, I could fix the place up." His gaze moved to the trees along the road, then over to the tip of Russell Island, where the freighter channel joined the St. Clair River. He saw gulls out there, specks against the afternoon sky. Lionel was telling him he could sell the house the way it was. Why spend money on it?

"No, I mean fix it up and live there," Armand said, turning enough to look down the river road. You couldn't see any houses, only trees changing color. This island was all woods and marsh, and some cornfields. He couldn't imagine staying here for more than a few weeks. Still, he wanted Lionel to say sure, that's a good idea, live here, become part of it.

But Lionel said, "What would you do? You know, a guy used to living in the city. That place, all it has is a wood stove."

13

Armand's gaze returned to Lionel in his wool shirt and jeans, rubber hunting boots, Lionel still half-turned like he wanted this to be over and walk away.

"What are you, a guide for those big-shot duck hunters come here from the States? I could do that, be a guide," Armand said. "I know how to shoot. In the winter trap muskrats." He wanted Lionel to say sure, why not?

"We do it in the spring," Lionel said, "burn off the marsh. You get all dirty out there, filthy. You wear a nice suit of clothes. . . . You wouldn't like it."

Armand watched Lionel shift his weight from one leg to the other and for a moment seemed in pain.

"How long were you an ironworker?"

Lionel shrugged. "Ten years."

"Now you work for those big-shot hunters come here, think everything's funny. You live here but have to go across the river to get drunk in a bar. Or you stay here and play bingo, visit the canteen for all your refreshment needs. But I can't live here, 'ey? That what you telling me?"

Lionel stared back at him like he was getting up courage to answer and Armand looked away, giving him time, Armand's gaze following the ferry on its way to Algonac, Michigan, another world over there. He heard Lionel say:

"There's no life for you here. There's nothing for you."

Armand wanted to ask him, Then tell me where there is. But when he looked at Lionel again he said, "You ever ride in a Cadillac? Come on, we'll drive over there, have some drinks."

"You have some," Lionel said. "I'm going home."

He walked over to his pickup truck swinging one leg, leaving Armand standing there in his suit of clothes by his blue Cadillac.

Bestselling author

ELMORE LEONARD

"...is a pro."
—*Los Angeles Times*

__*Bandits*__ (B30-130, $4.95, U.S.A.) (B30-132, $5.95, Canada)

"Enthralling...vintage Leonard."—*USA Today*

"May well be his best."—*Philadelphia Inquirer*

"BANDITS should fill the land with the sound of turning pages!—*Time*

"Leonard grabs his readers by the lapels on the first page and never lets go."—*Chicago Sun-Times*

"Leonard has produced another winner."—*People*

__*Glitz*__ (A34-343, $4.95, U.S.A.) (A34-344-7, $5.95, Canada)

"Intense."—*New York Times*

"Each scene sparkles."—*USA Today*

"Hottest thriller in the U.S."—*Time*

 **Warner Books P.O. Box 690
New York, NY 10019**

Please send me the books I have checked. I enclose a check or money order (not cash), plus 95¢ per order and 95¢ per copy to cover postage and handling.* (Allow 4-6 weeks for delivery.)

___Please send me your free mail order catalog. (If ordering only the catalog, include a large self-addressed, stamped envelope.)

Name _____

Address _____

City _____ State _____ Zip _____

*New York and California residents add applicable sales tax.